By GEORGE SEATON

One Pulse (Dreamspinner Anthology)
Shane Thorpe Knew Jesus and Rode Bulls
Whispers of Old Winds

Published by DREAMSPINNER PRESS
www.dreamspinnerpress.com

Whispers of Old Winds

GEORGE SEATON

DREAMSPINNER PRESS

Published by

DREAMSPINNER PRESS

5032 Capital Circle SW, Suite 2, PMB# 279, Tallahassee, FL 32305-7886 USA
www.dreamspinnerpress.com

Whispers of Old Winds
© 2016 George Seaton.

Cover Art
© 2016 Anne Cain.
annecain.art@gmail.com
Cover content is for illustrative purposes only and any person depicted on the cover is a model.

ISBN: 978-1-63533-119-6
Digital ISBN: 978-1-63533-120-2
Library of Congress Control Number: 2016916827
Published December 2016
v. 2.0
First Edition published by Dreamspinner Press, 2015.

Printed in the United States of America
(∞)
This paper meets the requirements of
ANSI/NISO Z39.48-1992 (Permanence of Paper).

For David

CHAPTER ONE

I ONCE told Michael about the Navajo kid in my unit who believed the lore of his ancestors was true and irrefutable. The kid's name was Joe Hill, and his eyes would sparkle, and his arms and hands would speak a language of their own when he'd sit with me and retell the stories he'd been told as a child by his grandparents and the elders of his tribe. There was the Sun God, who rode from east to west each day on one of his five horses, carrying the sun with him. And Spider Woman, who sat upon Spider Rock and taught the Navajo how to weave on a loom, using the sky and the earth as materials, with lightning and sun halos to perfect the strength, vibrancy, and beauty of the weave. There was the First Woman, who married the Sun God and gave birth to the Sun God's child, and then, after resting under a cliff and being sprinkled with stream water, she gave birth to the Water God's child. Yes, and there were the stories of creatures who were once human but became shape-shifters through witchcraft when they desired to change or when the situation called for it. Joe called these creatures skinwalkers, who could take the form of the animals of the forest, desert, and plains.

"Did you believe the story about the skinwalkers?" Michael asked, his head resting on his arms as he lay on the rug of many colors in front of the rock-lined fireplace. The fire reflected in his brown eyes and also the crystal glass into which I'd just poured more red wine. His hair too shone with the rise and fall of the flames.

"I think *he* believed it. He was a good kid—a good soldier. He was from northwestern New Mexico."

The deadly quiet mountain night was upon us, the only illumination in the cabin coming from the fire. The rug provided its own heat, the Puebloan weavers surely having infused it with their own ancestral lore. I sat cross-legged in front of Michael and concluded that any happiness I'd ever sought in this world was at hand. I knew this simple moment would reside forever in that place in my mind where such precious things are stored for later retrieval, for the times when they're needed the most.

"Were there skinwalkers in Iraq? Afghanistan?" Michael asked.

"Several incidences. Or so Joe said."

"But you believed him?"

"To a point." I paused to sip wine.

Michael sat up, faced me, and crossed his legs like mine. "Tell me," he said, with the expression on his face that had come to explain so much about the man that fate or dumb luck or heaven above had brought into my life when I needed him the most. It expressed Michael's insatiable hunger for truths that were hidden behind opaque surfaces. He yearned to get to the bottom of things.

"One time," I said, smiling, knowing what I told him was ambrosia, a sweetly fulfilling gift that fed his passion for knowing the unknowable. "One time," I repeated, "we were on night patrol near a village of mud houses. There was no moon or electric lights. Some of the villagers had generators for electricity, but they'd all been turned off. It was very quiet. Joe sat down beside me. He was a small man but tightly muscled. Had the sweetest smile and the whitest teeth I'd ever seen. He'd just been promoted to PFC and was proud of that. Anyway, we had stopped on a small rise that overlooked a village we believed had been infiltrated by the Taliban. I told my men to spread out. Joe and I were looking through our NODs—night vision goggles—at the village below us when Joe said, 'I saw an owl.'

"'Cool,' I said, thinking that seeing an owl was pretty special for Joe given…. Well, given that he was an Indian.

"Then Joe put his hand on my shoulder. 'No. Not so cool,' he said. 'I think it's a skinwalker. An owl. Somebody is gonna die.'

"I flipped my goggles up and looked at Joe. 'What do you mean?' I asked.

"'Maybe they're already dead,' Joe said. 'Look! There!' He pointed.

"I flipped my NODs back down and looked at where Joe was pointing. I saw a vividly white blur, as if a bird were flapping its wings and alighting on the ground. When the flapping stopped, the white blur became the shadow of a man."

"A skinwalker?" Michael asked.

"Maybe. The next thing I knew, I heard another one of my unit say, 'Oh! Christ!' I looked to my right, about twenty yards away, and saw two or three of my men hovering over something on the ground. We rushed over there. A staff sergeant named McGill was lying on the ground, his throat cut ear to ear."

"Damn." Michael's eyes were wide, a concerned look on his face.

"Yeah. No one had seen or heard anything—except Joe."

"But you.... You saw it too," Michael said.

"Yeah. I saw something."

"Wow. What about the other times? You said there were several?"

I sipped some more wine, then reached out and drew my fingers through Michael's hair. "Dear heart, I don't really want to remember those things. There was nothing good about them."

"Okay." He nodded. "But you believe? Skinwalkers?"

"Ah," I sighed. "I believe there are some things that are unknowable, mysteries that we can never untangle."

He smiled then and nodded as he picked up his glass and sipped.

I don't know why, but I felt that maybe he knew more than I did about such things.

CHAPTER TWO

I GLANCE out the window, and there's a figure approaching the door, a fur-lined hood over the head, the head bent down against the sideways-blowing snow. The door opens, and I see it's Digger as he pulls the hood off and slams the door behind him.

"Whew!" he says, taking off his gloves and vigorously rubbing his hands against each other. "Cold as a witch's tit."

Digger—Dick Snead—is one of my three deputies, who—and I've made this conclusion several times—is about as useful as, yes, tits on a boar. But he's a good-looking kid, with dark blond hair, blue eyes, and a nice ass. He's got the potential for becoming a good deputy. He volunteered for the Army directly out of high school and applied for the deputy job with credentials spanning three years of military police experience. Worked in noncombat duty stations in Germany, Japan, and Virginia. But like I said, after his four months on the job here, I've concluded he's a slow starter. He was my first and so far only hire, and I don't regret bringing him on the job. I thought when I did it that he'd be a breath of fresh air for the department, a place that desperately needed oxygen-rich ideas and new blood. I just wish he'd hurry up and get with the program.

And we didn't give him his nickname. He showed up with it at our front door.

"Got a report of a body up the mountain." He pulls off his coat, hangs it on a hook next to the door, and steps to the small table where Mary keeps the coffeepot full and hot. She's also put a little Christmas tree on the table, with lights, little ornaments, and tinsel.

I lean my shoulder on my office doorframe, admire Digger's ass for a moment as he prepares his coffee, and then ask the pertinent question: "This body alive or dead?"

"Oh," he says, turning toward me, cup in his hand. "Hank flagged me down on the road. Said he'd been up near Elk Creek cutting Christmas trees and saw a body lying spread-eagle, facedown in the bowl about a hundred yards from him. He didn't want to go down there 'cause…. Well, you know how that bowl is when there's snowpack."

I nod. Any urgency I'd felt about heading up the mountain to check this report pales at the mention of that name. Hank is Henry Tall Horse, a Ute Indian who has been up here for probably the last ninety years, though nobody knows for sure how old he is. He's a sly old man who has probably made the same conclusion about Digger that I have. Hank seems to enjoy toying with him by sending him on wild-goose chases that have just enough credibility to engage Digger's curiosity. Digger has yet to catch on to Hank's wiliness.

And every time I run into Hank, he gives me a wink and says, "Helluva deputy you got, Chief."

"You gonna check it out?" I ask, glancing at Mary, who is trying to stifle a laugh as she works on the department's budget for next year, her adding machine clicking away. She too knows what Hank is up to.

"Gotta put some gas in the Ski-Doo," Digger says.

"That bowl'll eat the Ski-Doo in a quick minute."

"Besides that," Jim Harris, my number-one deputy, says, "if he saw the body a while ago, it ain't visible now. You see how much snow we got over the past hour?"

"I'll go up there with you in a bit, Digger," I say. "Go get the snowshoes from the storage shed." I do wish, though, that my number-two deputy, Don Hoag, had not started his vacation two days ago. He took his wife and kids to Disney World in Orlando. Not that I don't think Digger will have my back if anything happens up there, but Don's got more experience with these mountains. Hell, *he's* got a nice ass too.

"Yes, sir," Digger says, setting his coffee cup down and grabbing his coat.

I sit behind my desk, look at the mess on top of it, and wonder why I thought being the sheriff of a sparsely populated county in Colorado would be one exciting thing after another. The paperwork and supervisory responsibilities make short shrift of whatever excitement I had anticipated when I got the bug up my ass to run for office.

SHORTLY AFTER my thirtieth birthday, I decided to run for Sheriff of Pine County, and I won by seventeen votes. My opponent was the incumbent,

Howard Slaughter, who'd been sheriff up here for the past twenty-seven years. He'd been a good sheriff, tough as nails and dedicated to an unshakeable philosophy that all things in life are either black or white. Gray areas just didn't exist, except as conspiratorial endeavors by God-hating, limp-wristed, left-wing sonsabitches who were out to destroy the essential fabric of America. I suspect those seventeen winning votes came from that same cadre of evildoers Sheriff Slaughter believed populated the gray areas of life in Pine County. And besides that, Michael and I made a point to knock on every door we could find—and believe me, some doors up here, much less the cabins they're attached to, are not that easy to locate. Most folks we met were impressed with my background, and some even thought it was time for new blood in the sheriff's office. Others weren't as receptive, but only a few were outright rude, with one of them reaching for his Mauser 98 bolt-action rifle as he told us to get the hell off his property.

Two years before my election, Michael and I moved up here to make the best of our new life together, away from the fast lane in Denver and the increasing dissatisfaction we both felt with city life in general. I met Michael in a Denver bar, not a week after I returned from two tours in Iraq and Afghanistan, and if you want to call it love at first sight, then go ahead. The senseless passion that initially put us in bed together soon developed into something as precious as life itself. He was only twenty-two, Italian, lithe, bright, and beautiful. I was twenty-six, Irish, and hardened by the things I'd seen and done in that faraway place where hell was a reality for the living as well as a destination for the dead.

Michael had the ability to calm the inner demons that followed me home from the war, sometimes with only a smile, but most of the time with his words, his voice a salve as soothing as a springtime morning in these mountains. We married in Taos a year after we'd decided to move in together. We then moved to Pine County a year after that. And in two years, we finished rebuilding—with help from Michael's father's construction outfit—what had been a dilapidated shack on our seventeen acres of forest and meadow into a two-bedroom log home—a paradise that was our dream destination and is now our everyday reality.

The county seat of Pine County is Gunderson Junction, a small town named after a Methodist minister who came this way in the 1850s to bestow the Christian message to the red-skinned savages who lived here for probably more than a thousand years. The savages, according to

Gunderson, mistakenly believed that Mother Earth and Father Sky were responsible for life's blessings rather than a Semite who died on a cross. It wasn't a pretty subjugation. But the Manifest Destiny of the white man had prevailed in Colorado as it had everywhere else. And now those few Indians who remain here are much like old Henry Tall Horse, still quietly attuned to their ancestral beliefs and gracious enough to give a wink and a smile to tourist mommies and daddies who point Hank out to their children, saying, "Look there. An Indian. A real live Indian."

It didn't take long for Michael and me to get to know the locals, and we never obfuscated our relationship to anyone. We were accepted by most because that's the rule up here: live and let live. There were a few who looked on us with the same eyes I suspect Gunderson looked upon those savages. Religious fervor will do that to any person who believes rules for living a good life come from a book and not from the heart.

We were surprised to find that there were two other couples— James and Carl and Denice and Audra—who lived nearby, a relative term up here, and with whom we've spent some quality time. The plan is that all six of us are going to have Christmas Eve dinner and drinks tonight at our cabin.

Michael invested some of his inheritance from a doting uncle in the opening and operation of a small storefront in the Junction. He sells his own acrylic paintings, photographs of the countryside and critters, and other fare manufactured in Third World enclaves that is the kind of crap tourists buy as remembrances of the places they've been. He will close his shop early this afternoon to start preparations for the Christmas Eve shindig. Not that he gets a whole lot of customers this time of year. I think he keeps his shop open year-round just to see if I ever do more with Digger's ass than look at it. His shop is just down and across the street from the sheriff's office—the building shared with a meeting room for the county commissioners, the county attorney, a judge, and a one-person DMV—and his view is pretty good if he's looking for any indiscretions that might occur across the street. Michael appreciates a fine ass as much as I do, and though we've never discussed it, I think Michael believes I'm open to temptation. I'm not, and I suppose if the subject ever comes up, I'll convince him otherwise… two or three times in one night. Besides that, neither one of us has ever been interested in investigating the possibilities of being intimate with a straight man. There's something wrong about that. At least for Michael and me there is.

Something about Michael that I'm not yet sure I understand is what he told me in Taos the night before we got married. We had a nice dinner, then returned to our B&B, probably drank too much wine, made love, and then lay in bed, talking and watching the fire in the kiva gradually burn itself out. I hadn't yet met Michael's family, except for the doting uncle, who, although Michael denied it, was as gay as could be. It was no mystery why Michael had become his favorite nephew. We talked a bit about that uncle, who had recently died, and then I asked him about the rest of his family. He hadn't told me much of anything about them, and I was curious.

"We're one hundred percent Sicilian," Michael said. "Our name, Bellomo, means 'handsome man.'"

"Of course it does."

"Anyway.... My father is in the, um, family business, and my mother is a full-time seeker of martyrdom."

"What's the family business?"

"You don't want to know."

"Okay. And your mother? Martyrdom?"

Michael reached over to the nightstand and grabbed the two glasses of wine we put there earlier. He handed me one and then sipped from his. I waited for him to continue, and when he did, it was tentative, as if this was a story he didn't want to tell.

"My mother, my grandmother, and who knows how many generations back this goes.... They believed in, oh, I guess the mysticism of the Catholic Church—the stigmata, the suffering, the guilt. They fed on everything about Catholicism that is... dark."

I waited for him to go on, and when he didn't, I said, "And you were... around this growing up?"

"Yes. How could I not be? But see, the thing was... I was born with a caul—behind the veil is what they call it."

"I've heard of that. It means something."

"It does. And I think, ever since I was born with that thing around my head, my mother has tried to pray herself out of it."

"Pray herself out of it?"

"She thinks it was her fault. Even though a caul is supposed to be a good thing, an omen that the child is... special, her darkness—

the darkness she took from all those generations of women—turned it around and made it a bad thing. Like it was... I don't know. Like it was witchcraft or something."

I was reminded then of the times I'd noticed Michael's own darkness—passing moments when I thought he was somewhere inside himself, trying to deal with some damned thing he couldn't share with me. He'd always come out of his transitory funks with a smile, and I'd never thought there was anything to them except Michael being Michael.

"But let's not even think about all that right now. Okay?" Michael said, taking hold of my hand. "We're getting fucking married tomorrow! Can you believe that!"

I did believe that. And we did get married the next morning in the great room of the B&B, with the owners of the place as witnesses and a district court judge presiding. It was a good day. But since then, whenever I notice Michael with that faraway look in his eyes, I do wonder... about a lot of things.

CHAPTER THREE

DIGGER WALKS into my office with two pairs of snowshoes, holds them up, and says, "Okay. Ready to go."

"Yeah. Well…. You hang on for a bit. Something I need to do first." I stand and grab my coat from the back of my chair and my hat from the top of the filing cabinet. "I'll be back in an hour," I say as I squeeze by him.

"You out?" Mary asks as I walk past her desk.

"Just for a bit. I've got my phone."

She grabs a handheld radio from the credenza behind her desk and holds it out to me. "You'll take this too. Your phone will crap out up there."

I take the handheld and go out into the snow apocalypse that began in the earliest hours of this morning. I walk to Brunhilda, the ten-year-old Suburban with a gold star on both front doors, get in, and start up the behemoth. The lamentation she provides is a little like "You've got to be kidding," but she does crank herself up to her usual burpy purr. I back out of the space and head for Hank's place, halfway up the mountain.

The climb isn't that difficult, as I had Jim put on the chains earlier. He didn't fuss with me at all about completing that directive. Jim's like that: duty, honor, all those things he learned in the Corps while doing his own duty in Nam a thousand years ago. He's now sixty-five with no thoughts about retiring. His war experience allows him to see the worth of digging in for the duration, whether it be a firefight in the sticky mire of a jungle or a snow event, like today, that requires equipment to be ready for any unforeseen disaster or emergency. I would have told Digger to do it but figured Jim would've had to show him how.

After fifteen minutes climbing, the landscape evens out a bit. Hank's cabin is up ahead, and I notice the flash-spark of embers coming out of the chimney. I've told him more times than I can remember that he needs to repair the wire mesh on the top of that metal pipe, and each time I do, he says, "Okay, I'll do that." He's never done it, and right now it doesn't matter. I look at the juniper berries Hank attaches to strings and hangs around the frames of his windows and door, the fruit now black with age. He'll replace them in the spring with fresh ones. I've asked him about that too, and he always smiles and says, "I think it is pretty."

As I stop Brunhilda about twenty yards in front of his house, the door opens and Hank steps onto his porch, his long gray hair billowing with the force of the wind. He waves, and I quickly get out and run up to the cabin.

I sit in one of the two recliners he's got in his small parlor, see he's got his own epic event going on within his woodstove—it's got to be a hundred degrees in here—and I unbutton my coat and pull the flaps off my chest.

"It's snowin' pretty good," he says, taking the other chair.

"You get your trees cut before it got bad?"

"A few. Took them down to Michael's store. He gave me fifty bucks for them. Maybe he can sell them. Maybe he can't."

"Good." I nod. "Wanted to ask you about what you told Digger. A body down in the bowl by Elk Creek? That the truth, or you just playing with him again?"

Hank raises his arms, spreads them out, then raises his legs and spreads them out too. "Just like that. Like he was making a snow angel down there in the bowl."

"You're not kidding?"

"No. I hollered at him and he fell down. Thought about going down there, but Charlie held me back."

At the mention of that name, Hank's massive but half-crippled malamute pads into the parlor from wherever he's been. He sniffs my pants, glances at Hank, and then returns to wherever he'd hidden himself from the conflagration in the parlor.

"Besides," Hank says, "that bowl is like quicksand when it snows like this."

"So, the guy didn't move? Just lay there?"

"Yup. Told your helluva deputy when I took the trees down to Michael's, and that was that."

"Couldn't have been something else?"

"Yes, it could have."

When he doesn't say anything else, I slap my hands on my thighs and stand. "I guess we'll have to go check it out."

"Guess you will." Hank stands and walks me to the door. Before I step outside, he adds, "Wear snowshoes."

I button my coat, flip my collar up, and nod. "Thanks for your help, Hank." I stop after opening the door, turn back to him, and ask, "When are you going to get a phone?"

"I'll do that," he says, his smile as sly as the fox's Michael and I have seen three mornings in a row outside our bedroom window.

I head back down the mountain, get Digger and the snowshoes, and then turn Brunhilda around and head back the way I came.

As we pass Hank's cabin, Digger says, "He better fix his chimney."

"Why? What's wrong with it?"

"Well... I just thought that with all those sparks.... It.... Never mind."

Yeah, I play with Digger too. I shouldn't, but I do.

ELK CREEK is fed by the high mountains that lose their snowpack well after the end of May. It meanders through the forest for miles and eventually spills into the South Platte River. The dirt road that takes us near its headwaters is about a six-mile gentle climb from Hank's cabin. Once you get there, the road ends, providing a view fashioned by the combined efforts of Mother Earth and Father Sky. There are two fourteeners to the northwest, a massive valley to the south, and on clear days, a sky as broad and blue as the Caribbean.

Just west of where the road ends, though, is what is called the bowl—a circular depression in the landscape that is about three hundred yards wide and probably fifty yards deep at the center. In the late spring and summer, it appears as a meadow where wildflowers and grasses abound, and at its center is a small lake that is probably five or six feet deep. In the winter, after the accumulation of one snowfall upon another, the bowl becomes a beautiful but deadly hazard. Only the most robust deer, elk, and other critters who venture into it will make it out alive. What appears as just the latest layer of snow is really multiple layers, hard packed on the downslopes but gradually and deceptively fragile the nearer you get to the center.

Just before we get to the end of the road, the clouds overtake us—we're at about 9500 feet—and the nearly total whiteout is as eerie as the darkest room in a house believed to be haunted. Luckily the bowl has not yet been enveloped by the clouds, and we can see it off to our left.

"Wow," Digger says.

"Yeah. You follow me. Walk where I walk, and keep your voice to a whisper. We don't want our own personal avalanche down there."

"Yes, sir."

We get out of Brunhilda, walk to the back, open the hatch, and grab the snowshoes. They're nothing fancy, and we both take off our gloves to tighten the leather straps around the front of our boots.

Once we do that, we put our gloves back on, and I turn and face Digger. "You remember what I just told you?"

He nods. "Follow you. Walk where you walk and whisper."

"You'll remember that?"

"Sure."

"Okay. Now, reach in there and get those ski poles." I learned a long time ago that Brunhilda can't go everywhere and installed a rack inside the SUV to hold a pair of skis and poles.

Digger leans over into the back and grabs the poles, hands me one, and keeps the other.

"Get that rope in there too."

He snatches the rope, and I close the hatch.

"Tie one end of the rope around your waist." I take the other end of the rope and tie it around mine.

After we've done that, I'll be damned if Digger doesn't start walking toward the edge of the bowl.

"What did we just talk about?"

He stops and looks at me. His smile could momentarily tame a lion. "Sorry."

I walk to where he stands, shake my head, and then look at the spread of the bowl below. "Hank said the guy was about a hundred yards out. Right? You see anything down there?"

"No. Not a thing."

I walk farther and stop at the edge. "Slow and easy," I say, carefully taking the first gently descending step.

"Right behind you."

The snowpack feels solid, and I continue down, noticing the farther I go that there's an odd vortex or something created by the bowl that's sending what up above was sideways-blowing snow into a swirl coming at us from every side. I look up and see the clouds are still hovering near the rim of the bowl. I mentally kick myself for not thinking to bring goggles with us.

"Hard to see now," Digger says.

"Yeah, it is." I plant my ski pole in front of me before I take another step. Still solid. After we've gone about a hundred yards, I stop and turn to Digger. "You okay?"

"Yes. You?"

"I'm fine." I turn back and try to pinpoint where the middle of the bowl is and think I see it, and I see something else, just a speck of something not white this side of where I've determined the middle is. "You see that?" I say, pointing.

"It's...," Digger says and pauses. "Yes, it's something black. Maybe blue."

I plant my pole in front of me again, and there's a little give as it sinks down about a foot. "Okay. You stay where you are. Dig in your snowshoes and stick your pole as far as you can get it in the ground. Be ready to hang on to the rope if I start to... disappear. Okay?"

"Yeah. I'm ready."

Very carefully, I take a step, and my snowshoe sinks down in the softer snow. My next step affirms even more that what everybody up here knows about the bowl is absolutely true. After about ten more steps, I'm wading through snow nearly up to my waist, and the dark-colored anomaly has formed itself into what is clearly an arm. If it's human, this was one hairy son of a bitch, or he's got an animal-hide coat. If it's not human.... Well, maybe it's a bear.

"Another twenty-five, thirty feet," I say, turning my head slightly toward Digger. "Keep the rope taut."

"Yes, sir," he says.

With each additional step I take, I feel like I'm walking on a bottomless layer of cotton. The snow is now up to my waist, and there, right in front of me, is that arm. I slowly hunker down on my haunches, reach out, and grab it.

Frozen stiff would be an understatement.

"How much more rope you got?" I say.

"What?"

I turn my head and say it again.

"About five feet."

"Okay. I'm going to untie myself and retie it on the body. Let me have a little slack."

"A dead body?"

I don't answer as I feel myself sinking another foot. I wait a moment, and when I don't feel any more movement, I untie the rope from my waist and wrap it around the body's arm and tie it securely. I slowly stand and turn my head to the side.

"Okay. You brace yourself. Keep the rope tight and start pulling as soon as I turn around."

"Okay."

Very carefully I maneuver myself around as best I can. The awkwardness of the snowshoes doesn't make that easy, but I manage and start pulling on the rope as I head back up. The path I made coming down is nearly gone, as the snow has collapsed in from the sides.

"Start pulling," I say, and he does. The proverbial deadweight behind me begins to move, and as it does, what sounds like a clogged drain opening up follows. The whoosh sound is immediate, as is the collapse of the fragile terra firma beneath me. I hang on to the rope, but it too is collapsing, and something large and heavy smacks me on the head, and I am falling, falling....

Michael stands naked above me, his smile foretelling some mischief he's about to make. I raise my head, and he gently pushes it back down with his toes. "Slip off your shorts," he says.

I look at him, at the spread of him going upward. His legs are open like a V turned on its top. His dick is hard, pointing slightly up, and the black tuft of hair at the base of it is like short strands of silk from some exotic Moroccan bazaar. I see the flatness of his belly, and his chest has two distinct layers of muscle. His nipples are red-brown dots, erect nubs that beg for the touch of my tongue. His chin, mouth, nose. His eyes show that naughty smile in them. His hair. His black hair is feathered at his forehead.

"All right," I say, tugging at my shorts and slipping them down to my thighs.

He spits on his hand and then moves his hand to his ass. Silently, he eases himself down, grabbing my dick as he does, and he....

But, damn, Michael, I've got this bitch of a headache that....

When I open my eyes, I see darkness. I try to raise my right hand to wipe my eyes and find resistance. My head throbs with pain. I tug with more force and am able to pull my arm from whatever is holding it down. I wipe my eyes, and still I see darkness. Across my chin, I feel warmth. I move my hand and touch what's against my chin, and yes, it's Digger's mouth, his breaths rapid and full. I dig out the snow that is packed around our faces and find there is a hollow space, a void above our heads as if something is bracing the snow above us.

"Digger," I say, and there is no response. I struggle to move my arm to my side, and then I feel what I know is a ski pole. I grab it. *Which way is up?* I work up some spit and huff it out of my mouth. I feel it drool down my chin to my neck. *Good. Up is up.* I feel the ski pole, determine that it is, luckily, perpendicular to me, and I thrust it upward. There is resistance, but I keep working at it, and finally it moves freely. I see a pinprick of light above. The pole is about four feet long. *Okay, not that much snow covering us.* I struggle to enlarge the pinprick above, and succeed at that. A slight downdraft of air reaches my face. The vortex, I think, or whatever it was that was swirling within the bowl is funneling air down to us.

I can now see that Digger is lying slightly off to my side, his head bent toward my own, his mouth over my chin. "Digger," I say again. The only response is his breath, now slightly slower than when I first sensed it. *What to do?*

"Keep the hole open, you idiot," I answer myself. "You want to breathe, you keep the fucking hole open." *But what else?* I try to move my legs and feel only an enormous weight on them. Darkness again descends, and I wiggle the pole. As I see the light again, I know our way out is only three, three and a half feet above. "Digger!"

Still, no response.

I close my eyes and again feel the ache in my head. Whether I black out for a moment or not, I don't know, but....

I see you, Michael, sitting in your shop—the tourists enjoy watching you work—your face as serious as it ever gets, and your brown eyes stare at the canvas on the easel before you. You are painting a black bear reaching for wild berries. You started the painting only days ago, and now as I see the bare outline of your subject, I glance at the photograph from which you are working.

"I remember when you took that," I say. "It was our first month up here."

"The beginning of our second month." You smile as you turn to look at me. "You remember everything about that pic?"

"Of course." And I do.

We hiked up the mountain, took the trail that bottomed out at a meadow that showed an extravagant display of wildflowers and grasses. We walked to the middle of it, sat, and you pulled a bottle of red wine from your pack.

After we both took a few swigs straight from the bottle, you lay down on your stomach, your elbows to the ground, your head propped on your palms. "Do you know what I like best about this place?" you asked.

"No," I said, sitting by your side, seeing the lovely pooch of your ass against your hiking shorts, your brown hair against your neck, the spread of you as lovely as the meadow itself.

"I like the gift of it. Like out of nowhere, unexpectedly, it's Christmas, my birthday, the Fourth of July, New Year's Eve... all in one," you said.

"Yes," I said as I lay next to you. I ran my palm down your back and over your ass, then fingered the spread of hair along your neck.

"Awwrgggg." Digger's vocalization snaps me out of my reverie.

"Digger," I say, and not wanting to let go of the ski pole, I nudge my face against his. "Digger!"

"Ah," he says, and I feel him attempt to move.

"We're okay. Stay still."

"What... happened?"

"The bowl ate us," I say.

"Wow."

"Yeah."

"The dead guy?"

"Him too."

"Wow," he says, and I feel him again attempt to shift his weight.

"Try to stay still. We've got to take this slowly."

"Okay."

I see that the light from above is again fading and turn my attention back to swirling the ski pole. I move my head back to Digger. "Digger?" There is no response, but I feel his breath again against my chin. "Digger!" When he doesn't answer, it occurs to me that he's coming in and going out of consciousness. *What happened during his fall?* I feel the throb in my head and remember something hitting it hard and assume that something was Digger's head. *Great! Now what?*

I hear myself sigh and again close my eyes.

I was fucking you, Michael, that day in the meadow when you suddenly reached back with your hand and stopped me.

"Look," you whispered, moving your hand and pointing to a copse of wild berries not far in front of us.

I looked, and there was a black bear settling himself before the wild fruit.

"Get my camera," you whispered.

I grabbed the camera from where you'd sat it beside us.

You gently pulled the lens cover off, focused, and snapped four pictures as the bear reached for the berries. You set the camera down, wiggled your ass, and said, "Come inside me."

I want to smile with that image, but I can't. I feel the lump in my throat. *God, oh, how I love him. I'm here, Michael. Digger and I, we've got a little situation here that I'm not sure I can get us out of. I'm just not sure....*

"No," I say. "We're going to survive this."

"Wha...?" I hear Digger's whisper.

"Digger, wake up. Stay awake."

"So... sleepy."

I raise my head as much as I can, grab a bit of his cheek in my mouth, and bite him. Not hard, but just enough that it gets a reaction.

"Ow!"

"I said, stay awake."

"Trying...."

I again move the ski pole. My head is hurting like a son of a bitch, I can't feel my feet, and my fingers are starting to tingle. *Shit! Shit! Shit!*

I turn my head away from Digger, and there is Michael. *We can do this, Sam. You and I. Together. We can beat this thing.*

That was only our second night together, and I told him those three words—I love you—and he repeated them to me. We slept then, but I awoke from the nightmares, the persistent, horrible baggage that I came back with from the war. The images, the sounds, the odors of that damnable place, where the difference between life and death was too often just a mere instant. An enormous boom, a cloud of dust, soldiers and Marines dead and dying, children screaming under the broken bodies of their mothers, who tried to protect them, knowing well before the soldiers did that once again the hellish devastation signaled by the cry, Allahu Akbar, *was at hand.*

I crawled out of the bed, left him there, his breaths deep, his head turned away from me. I'd gone into the living room, backed up against the wall, and let my body slide down. As I sat on the floor, I put my hands to my face. When I took them away, Michael was sitting opposite me, as naked as I was. His eyes... oh, his eyes staring into mine, a question on his face.

"I can't do this," I told him. "I can't bring you into my life right now. I've got.... Oh man... I can't do this to you." I lowered my eyes from his stare.

"The war?" he asked.

"Yes."

He pressed his fingers against the bottom of my chin. I raised my head then and again looked into his eyes. And he said those words: "We can do this, Sam. You and I. Together. We can beat this thing."

I feel the new wetness on my face and realize it's Digger's drool or snot seeping from him as he's managed to rest his head on mine. "Digger," I say.

"Yeah?"

"You staying awake?"

"Trying."

"Okay." *Me too, Digger.* "Can you move your arms?"

"Haven't tried."

"Try it. Slowly."

He grunts with the effort. "Yeah, just a little."

"How about your legs?"

I feel a slight movement against my own legs. "Good."

"Don't think I can stand up, though."

"No. Don't try it."

"What are we gonna do, Sheriff?"

"I'm working on it."

"It's getting cold."

"Ah, it's not that bad," I say. *It is cold, Digger. And it's only going to get worse.*

"Really sleepy."

I think I hear him say *creepy* as I again turn my head away from him and close my eyes.

You're smiling, Michael. You have something behind your back, and you move this way and that and won't let me see what you have. Finally, I pin you against the wall, reach around, and grab your hands, which are clutched behind you.

"I made it," you say.

I manage to pull your arms out from behind you, pry your hands apart, and I see a small figurine of something crafted from wood. "What is it?"

"It's a badger."

"Okay."

"It's for you."

I pick it out of your hand and hold it up. I tell you that you've done a good job. It's so lifelike, and you'd stained and lacquered it. "Beautiful."

"It's an Indian symbol, a charm," you say. "You squeeze that and you can do anything you put your mind to."

"Does it work?"

"You'll just have to find out."

I open my eyes, and I'm afraid to let go of the ski pole, but I need to do something right now. I very carefully open my hand and find the pole is secure, staying where it is. I move my hand to my face, then shove my hand down along my body, finally to my waist. I dig out the snow from alongside my leg, stick my hand in my pocket, and squeeze the badger.

"Do your stuff, buddy," I say.

"What?" Digger says.

I slide my hand out of my pocket and reach for the ski pole. "Nothing," I say as I swirl the pole.

"I'm really getting cold." I feel Digger's lips mouthing those words on the side of my face.

"I want you to try something."

"Okay."

"Move your arms, your hands. Can you do that?" I feel him try.

"Yeah. A little."

"Try to unbutton your coat."

"No. I'm cold."

"Digger, if we can open up our coats, maybe our shirts too, we can… share our heat."

"Oh," he says. "My right arm is stuck. My left arm…."

I feel his left arm move, and he manages to get his hand under him. He then tries to raise himself slightly, and he does. Again, I sense there's something solid above us, between us and the snowpack.

"Yeah," he says. "I can do this."

"Get me unzipped too," I say, feeling the movement of his hand slowly working his own zipper down. "I've got to hang on to the ski pole."

"Why?"

"Keeping the air coming in. It's in my right hand. I can't let go. Unbutton your shirt too. Then mine."

"Gotta rest a minute," he says, and I feel him slump back down, his mouth now against my cheek.

"Okay. Try to stay awake."

When he doesn't answer, I again wiggle the pole. The throb in my head seems to explode for a moment, and I close my eyes. I wonder what Michael would say if he could see us. I wonder….

Dear heart, what are you doing right now? Oh yes, you're there, aren't you? You're closing your shop, and you take one last look at the loving space you've created—your paintings, the wood carvings, the photographs. I see you smile now as you look at the junk you've had to display because that's what the tourists seem to want. The tom-toms, the dream catchers, the moccasins, all the stuff that has lately come from Pakistan and China. I see you lock the door behind you, walk to the old pickup we bought from Denice and Audra, get in, and head out of town.

Oh, Michael, don't go to the cabin. Come here. Come up the mountain to the bowl. Digger and I are…. We've got ourselves into a fix here, Michael, that I don't think we're going to…. No, I won't say it. We, you and I, have another Christmas to share.

Our Christmases have always been… special. Not a month had passed since we met when we decorated our first tree. Do you remember? I didn't want to, but you… oh, you insisted because you said…. You said it was the least we could do for the tree that was dying and would soon be dead. You did it for the tree.

Then we, you and I, sat on the floor in front of the tree and traded gifts. I gave you my dog tags, placing the chain over your head and around your neck. You pressed the metal to your chest, saying that now I must tell you where the tags had been and why they seemed to pulse with sadness. I said I would, but I haven't yet really told you anything except about that night when Joe Hill pointed and said, "Look! There." You gave me a small painting on porcelain of a brown-eyed boy with a sprig of hyacinth in his hair. You said it was a self-portrait done in the springtime, finished on the equinox, and.... And I....

I feel something digging on my chest, open my eyes, and know that Digger is still working to get my shirt open.

"That's about all I can get," Digger says.

"Okay. Good," I say, actually feeling the exposed warmth from his body. I swirl the ski pole, now almost an automatic movement not requiring any thought or intent—it just happens. *We need to breathe.*

"I feel like I'm cramping up," Digger says as he manages to slightly move his legs.

"Yeah, me too." I try to move my legs, and I can't. I can't feel my toes. My legs, yes, but I can't feel my toes.

"When will they get here?" Digger says.

"Who?"

"Jim. The others."

"Oh...." I don't really know how long we've been here. I know Jim Harris will wonder where we are. But when? How long will it take him or Mary to think something might have happened to us? "I don't know. They'll be coming, though. Soon." Do I believe this? Of course I do. I have to.

"You and Michael?" Digger says.

"Yes?"

"You're good together. I mean... I don't have anyone. Yet. And I just thought that it would be nice to have someone... care right now."

"Oh, Digger, we all care. Everybody thinks you're...." What do I say? *You're a sweet kid, a kind soul who's got a lovely ass, and yes, you're not the brightest bulb—maybe just naive, not dumb—and we all....* "You're a good man, Digger. We all care."

"Yeah, but...."

This is bullshit! We've got to get out of here! I won't have this conversation with Digger. What the hell are we doing? Commiserating about our feelings? Wishing things were different because well, by golly, we're going to die here, and a little "Kumbaya" is just the thing to send us off into....

"Digger!" I say a little too forcefully. "I want you to really concentrate on trying to move yourself. I can't because you're right on top of me. Move your legs, your arms."

"Oh, Sheriff—"

"I mean it. You've got to try."

"Okay."

"Try to move to your left, my right. There's space to my right that seems to be a void or something where the snow isn't packed as hard. I think you can push yourself up too. Something up above is... shielding us from the snowpack."

Digger's movements are agonizingly slow, but I feel him make progress. His left arm or hand actually moves the ski pole.

"Good," I say. "Keep moving."

"Trying to," he says. "Hard work."

"I know. But, we need to do something."

He continues to inch himself to my right. His mouth is now directly over mine, his breaths coming fast and warm. "Gotta rest," he huffs.

"Okay."

He turns his head and rests the side of his face on mine, his ear now on my mouth.

I turn my head to the left while again moving the ski pole with my right hand. I hear….

"I don't know if—"

"Be quiet. I think I hear something."

And I do hear something. Someone is yelling, and there's the unmistakable sound of a diesel engine clanking in the distance.

"You hear that?"

"Yeah," Digger says. "A truck."

I adjust my hold on the ski pole, moving my hand as far down on it as I can. I then shove it up as far as I can and twirl it, and I keep twirling it. I hear more shouting, and the diesel revs. There's a metal-on-metal sound too.

"Someone is here, Digger. Reach out with your left arm and grab the ski pole."

He grunts with the effort to stretch his arm out. "Where is it?"

"I think you're too far up. Bring your arm back a little toward your feet."

He grunts some more, and I almost lose my grip on the pole when he finally grabs it. "I got it," he says.

"Okay. You've got to raise it up. Get a good hold of it and raise it up. Twirl it around." I can't see the hole above anymore as his head is over mine. I feel his movement, though, and more light seeps into the space around me. "Good deal, Digger."

"Yeah. You hear that?"

The sound of the diesel is now a constant rev. The shouting continues. "Yes, I do," I say, seeing only Michael's smile as if he's here, right now, right here.

CHAPTER FOUR

MICHAEL IS here. He's not crying, but I think he's close to it. "I saw you," he says, his eyes meeting mine, his expression so sad.

I'm lying on a stretcher, and someone tells Michael they've got to go. I'm lifted into a boxy ambulance, and the last thing I see is Michael standing there, his hand to his chest, where he clutches my dog tags.

"I'll follow you down the mountain," he says. It appears as though he wants to say something more, but someone closes the ambulance door.

Merle Hogan, a volunteer fireman with the Pine County Fire District, sits beside me as Bob somebody—I can't remember his last name—stretches my arm out and says, "You'll feel a small prick." He carefully inserts the IV needle, and I think, well, small pricks are okay if they're sleepers.

I sense the ambulance begin to move. "How's Digger?" I ask, turning to Merle.

"He's as good as you. They took him in the other ambulance."

"Good. That was Skip's tow truck. Right?"

"Sure was," Merle says. "Deputy Jim came up with the idea, and it was a good one."

"I know they pulled me up with his cable, but how'd somebody get down to us without causing a slide?"

"Deputy Jim again. He got those two twenty-foot ladders Old Man Landon paints with and just kept sliding one in front of the other as he made his way down to you guys. One of you kept waving that pole around, and he zeroed in on that."

"Digger okay?"

"You already asked that, Sheriff, and yeah, he's doing good. I'm going to get your boots off."

"Okay."

"You hurting anywhere?"

"Just my head."

"Yeah. You and Digger both got some ugly on your foreheads. What happened?"

"I think we hit each other when we fell."

"You feeling woozy?"

"A little."

"Look at my light," Bob says, and he shines his tiny flashlight into my eyes. "Might have a concussion."

"Great," I say. "Do you know who finally decided that Digger and I might be in trouble?"

"Oh yeah. Mary said Michael came into the station a while ago and said something was wrong. Then Henry Tall Horse came in almost right behind Michael and said the same thing. He told Mary exactly where you were. Deputy Jim got the ladders and pulled Skip outta the bar and told him to get his ass up here."

Michael. "Michael, you say?"

"Yup. Don't know how he knew, but he was right."

"There was something on top of us. A frozen body maybe?"

"Strangest thing I ever saw. It was a black bear, but it wasn't. It had long legs and arms. Spread-eagle. Frozen stiff. Had mostly a bear's face and all, but there was more bare flesh on it than a bear usually has, and those arms and legs... I think Deputy Jim is gonna have the forest service take a look at it."

I feel as though my eyelids have become too heavy to stay open. And they don't. My mind too becomes heavy. Dark and heavy.

I AWAKE. I don't know where I'm at. I see the tube in my arm and then turn my head and see Michael is curled up on a chair to my right. He is asleep, using his coat as a cover. It is dark except for the dim lighting I see through the glass pane in the door. Yes, I'm in the small hospital thirty miles from Gunderson Junction.

"How you feeling?"

The voice is old, ancient. I turn my head to the left and see Henry Tall Horse, his face bathed in shadows. "Hank," I say.

"Yes."

I try to remember. It all started with Hank. I went to see him. Then I went back with Digger. And then.... "It was a bear."

"No, that was John Spotted Elk. He was a skinwalker. He lived over the mountain a ways. But he was a skinwalker."

I see PFC Joe Hill pointing at the blurry specter of an owl that became the shadow of a man. "That's…. No, that was…." I shake my head.

"Yeah," Hank says. "He came up to my cabin lots of times. Wanted to come in. Skinwalkers don't like juniper berries, so I kept him out by putting them around my door and windows. I saw a black bear when I was cutting Christmas trees. It was on the other side of the bowl. But it was walking funny, like it didn't really know how to walk like a bear. Then I knew it was John Spotted Elk. He was skinwalking."

"You said you hollered at it," I say, remembering what he told me in his parlor.

"Yeah. Only way to kill a skinwalker. I yelled, 'John Spotted Elk, you are a skinwalker!' and he spread out his arms and legs and fell dead into the bowl."

"You told Digger you saw a body."

"Yeah. I was having some fun with your helluva deputy."

"Jesus, Hank."

"Yeah. I watched you and your helluva deputy go up the mountain. Went up there myself a little later. Heard you call out to Michael…."

I hear rustling to my right. I turn my head, and Michael is standing there.

He grabs my hand. "Sam," he says, "you're awake. Are you okay?"

I see his eyes, his beautiful face. "I'm fine. Head hurts, but I'm fine."

"You were talking," Michael says.

"Yeah." As I turn my head to the left, I say, "Hank was telling me…."

And Hank isn't there. I look around the room. No Hank.

"Yes," Michael says when I turn back to him.

"No…. Guess I'm just… dreaming."

"Doctor said you have a mild concussion."

"That would explain a lot."

"He said you could go home tomorr—"

"Michael, you said you saw me. When they were putting me in the ambulance, you said you saw me."

"I did."

"When?"

He squeezes my hand and shakes his head. "I'd closed up the shop and was backing out of my parking space, and I saw you. Heard you first.

You told me not to go to the cabin. You told me to come up the mountain to the bowl. Then I saw you. Just a flash, but I saw you in a cold, dark place. I knew something was wrong, so I went to the sheriff's office. Told them where you were, that you were in trouble."

"And Hank showed up too?"

"Yes. He came in right behind me."

"Wow." I'm not sure what to think at this point, but I imagine the unknowable multitude of magic on this earth is born in places that defy any understanding of it. "Wow," I say again, knowing I had just spoken to Hank. *He was right here, for Christ's sake!*

"We're saving the party for when you get out of here," Michael says.

"Oh. The party... I'm sorry, I...."

"It was a skinwalker, wasn't it?"

"What?"

"I saw it, Sam. It wasn't a normal bear."

"Oh, I don't know. I...."

"You're here now," Michael says, and I see his eyes begin to well up. "That's all that matters."

"I spoke to you," I say. "I kept remembering... us."

"I know."

"Every moment I was there, you were there with me."

"I know."

My own eyes are blurry with wetness, and I draw my fingers across them.

CHAPTER FIVE

I INVITED Digger to our delayed Christmas party because—and I told Michael this—Digger and I had been as intimate as two men can be with each other without having sex. Besides that, I knew Digger was alone up here, his family somewhere in Kansas, and he lived by himself in the little trailer park just outside the Junction. It was a dismal place to live because it had been constructed on cheap land with a view of the highway and little else. So it was three couples—James and Carl, Denice and Audra, Michael and me—and Digger.

Digger and I came out of the hospital within forty-eight hours, both with ugly bruises on the left side of our foreheads. Two fingers on Digger's right hand were watched closely for frostbite. The color came back in those fingers, and except for the trauma of the experience itself, he and I were fine, though we both continued to have headaches of decreasing intensity.

I think Digger was somewhat intimidated at first by the casualness with which we all interacted with one another.

I don't know if he'd ever experienced same-sex couples just being themselves, but he soon eased into the situation, even telling us about his frustrated sex life, admitting, "You know, a trailer park is not the best place to meet women."

We had a nice time. Michael made gifts, all wood-sculpted figures, each different—a bear, elk, mule deer, owl. He'd not had time to make one for Digger and instead gave him an acrylic painting on tile of a naked boy riding a horse.

"Wow," Digger said when he saw it.

Michael then told me my gift would come later.

I STOKE the fire with Douglas fir logs cut from our property and now dried for two seasons. It burns well, bright and hot.

Michael brings two glasses and a bottle of wine from the kitchen and sits on the rug as I pull the screen across the fire and join him.

"It was a nice party," Michael says as he pours the wine. "Digger was fun. He's so... naive I guess is the right word."

I take the glass Michael holds out to me. "Yes, he is. And it was a great party. Your gifts were perfect. I've never seen the painting you gave Digger."

"I did it last year."

"Any symbolism to it?"

He smiles. "Oh, innocence, I guess."

I nod. "Naive, innocent.... That's Digger for sure."

Michael smiles, then sips his wine. "Do you want your present?"

I shake my head. "Not necessary. I've got all the gifts I need. Right here. Right now."

"I know. But," he says, standing, "it means something. What I made means something."

I watch his face as he says this, and I see in his expression sadness, or maybe confusion. "Sure," I say as he turns and walks to the bedroom.

He returns with what is clearly a painting, larger than the ones he usually creates. He keeps the back of it turned toward me as he sits, resting the bottom of the painting on the rug. He sighs and turns the front of the painting toward me.

It depicts two men from a viewpoint below them. One man lies on his back, his head turned to the right. The other man lies facedown atop the first, his head turned to his right. Above the men is what looks like a black cross hovering over them, but it is not a cross, as it is thicker, more rounded on the edges. At the top left, there is a small figure standing a distance from the men, looking directly at them. His hair is long and gray and is obviously being blown by a fierce wind.

I look closer at the faces of the two prone men. "That's...." I glance at Michael, then back at the painting. "That's Digger and me. The way we were. And Hank is there," I say, pointing at the figure in the distance. I again look at Michael. "How did you have time to paint this? It's only been three days and...."

"I finished it a month ago," he says.

I stare at Michael for another moment and then look at the painting again. "How could you have known?"

"I don't know. I wanted to paint something special for this Christmas, something different than what I usually do and…. The scene just got stuck in my mind. You know I usually paint from pictures, but this…. This was the picture in my mind that I couldn't shake. I had to finish it."

"Man oh man." I take the picture from him and place it against the wall. "Come here," I say.

Michael scoots next to me.

I grab his glass from the floor and hand it to him. We both sit silently, staring at the painting. One of the logs hisses and snaps, and a momentary burst of bright flame illuminates us and the painting.

"I don't know what to think about this," I say. "It's beautiful." I put my arm around his shoulders. "It tells a story…. No, it tells *the* story. But how did you know?"

"When Hank was talking to you in the hospital, I—"

"You saw him? You heard him?"

Michael hesitates before answering. "Yes, I did."

"Wow…."

"But…." He hesitates again. "He wasn't really there, Sam. I mean, his body wasn't really there. I wanted to tell you then that… I guess I've always wanted to tell you that I see things, hear things that I… shouldn't. Or maybe I should. The caul thing, I guess. All the time I was growing up, I experienced it. I…. When you gave me your dog tags, I told you I felt the pulse of sadness in them. Do you remember?"

"Yes. Of course."

"I can't wear them anymore. I can't touch them anymore. When I do, I see…." He sets his wineglass down and wraps his arms around me. He begins to sob into my shoulder.

I also set my glass down and hold him tightly to me. So tightly. It is as if I must shelter him from the torrent of my own demons.

CHAPTER SIX

DON HOAG came back from Orlando suntanned and determined never to make that trip again. Said he didn't mind his own children's whining but had enough of everybody else's kids making life miserable for everyone else the second day he was there.

Jim Harris told me today the VA finally diagnosed the mysterious symptoms he'd brought back with him from Nam, that were until now thought to be part of his PTSD. They told him it is cerebral malaria. He'd had malaria in Nam, which had put him down for about two weeks, and he'd thought that had been the end of that. But it hadn't, and now he says he's got to retire and move closer to Denver, where he can get the treatment he needs. Don't know what I'll do without him.

Digger is.... Well... Digger is Digger. We've not talked much about our experience in the bowl. I think we both know it was a kind of enforced intimacy that is best left shoved to the corner and out of sight or mind. I know we'll never forget it. I do admit to myself that I missed the opportunity to cop a feel of his lovely ass as we lay there with the body of... a freakish bear hovering above us. Yeah, it would have been nice to run my hand over those sweet cheeks, but I still get pleasure just looking at them. What healthy, virile man wouldn't? Oh, I know a lot of men who, if it ever came up in conversation, would say they're repulsed by even thinking about looking at the beauty of another man's ass. I suspect those men are not comfortable with their own sexuality, and they're too caught up in what their parents, church, and society prescribed for them when they were children. I'm sending him to Denver next month to get some training in forensics. I don't think he'll ever be a very good patrol officer. He's just too, oh, nice is probably the right word. And not that we have much need for a good forensics officer up here, but hell, the smile he gave me when I told him about it was worth the hit our budget is going to take.

Right now I'm heading up the mountain to Hank's place. Brunhilda is spitting and coughing her discontent, and I know she needs some TLC at Skip's Garage. I'll drop her off there later.

I pull onto Hank's property and again notice the deficiency of his chimney and those black dried berries that surround his door and windows. It's not that cold today, and it hasn't snowed for two days, but damned if it isn't obvious he's still burning wood to beat the band in there.

The door opens when I turn off the engine, and he steps out on the porch, his gray hair in a ponytail. Old Charlie sticks his head out from behind Hank for a moment and then goes back into the house.

When I get to his door, he's already sitting in his parlor, his feet resting on a hassock made from the skin of some damned thing and probably stuffed with juniper berries. I close the door, unbutton my coat, and take a seat in the other recliner.

"You normal now?" Hank asks.

"Oh, I'll never be normal, Hank. How are you?"

"Feel good. Staying warm. How's your helluva deputy?"

"More normal than I am."

"You want a beer?" he asks, leaning forward and looking at me.

"No, thanks. Wanted to ask you about a couple things."

"Okay." He sits back in his chair.

"Got a call from the forest service. The guy said he came up here to take a look at the bear that died."

"John Spotted Elk?"

"Well, yeah. Or so you said. But they left the body—the bear's body—up here at the rim of the bowl the day of the incident, and the guy said when he got here, it was gone. He talk to you?"

"No. He didn't come and see me."

"You know what happened to the body?"

"Yes. I put it in my shed. Dragged it here with my ATV. Covered it with cedar ash."

"Cedar ash?"

"Yes. Didn't have no more juniper berries. I cut down that cedar tree last year, burned the wood all night and all day after you and your helluva deputy fell into the bowl. Got the body in my shed and dumped the cedar ash on it."

"Why?"

"So he doesn't get up. Works kinda like the berries."

"He's not dead?"

"Prob'ly is, but can't take a chance."

I sit for a moment, considering what Hank has just said. I decide not to pursue it. Rather, I ask him my second question. "Did you know Michael saw you in the hospital that night?"

"Sure. I was in your head. Michael sees things. You didn't know?"

"I do now. But you weren't really there."

"Maybe I wasn't."

"Listen, Hank." I quickly slide to the edge of the chair and turn toward him. I hear a deep-throated growl from behind me and then see Charlie limping into the parlor, his teeth bared.

"C'mere, Charlie," Hank says, and the huge animal keeps his eyes pointed at me and slowly hobbles to Hank's side. "It's okay," Hank says, gently stroking the dog's head.

"Sorry. Guess I moved too quickly."

"It's okay."

"What I wanted to say…. Michael told me some things and…. What's going on, Hank?" I hear in my voice a plea I didn't intend but realize that's exactly what I'm doing—pleading with Hank to make some sense out of all this.

Charlie lies down beside Hank's chair.

Hank looks into the stove, where the fire burns bright yellow with ridges of blue and orange as he continues to pet the dog. "I went into Michael's store just after he first opened it," he says. "I was the only one there, and he had his back turned to me, putting stuff on a shelf. He knew I was there, but he didn't turn around. I told him he had a nice store. I saw his shoulders drop a bit, and he slowly turned toward me. I knew then that he was… special."

"He—"

Hank raises his hand and stops me. "We looked at each other. In the eyes. We spoke without speaking. I hadn't seen magic like that since I was a little boy. He can speak with the spirits."

"You too?"

"Oh. Sure. But not like him. He is special."

Hank turns his eyes away from the fire and looks at me.

I stare back, and not knowing what to say, I nod.

"He is a good man to have as a lover," Hank says. "He will protect you from witches. From skinwalkers."

"From demons," I say.

It's Hank's turn to nod.

"But how do I…?" I pause, knowing what I'm about to say and afraid of the answer. "How do I protect him?"

Hank smiles. "He is an old soul caught in the whispers of old winds. I think the way you do that is to love him."

The only sound in the small parlor is the creaking of Hank's stove. We sit a moment, not speaking. Charlie has closed his eyes… *the whispers of old winds….*

"Thanks," I say as I stand and pull up my coat's zipper.

Hank remains in his chair, his hand resting on Charlie's head.

I show myself out and walk to Brunhilda, stoically waiting for me under a sky that has once again opened up. I stop, spread my arms out, and turn my palms upward. The snow is falling slowly, softly, the flakes large and wet, a slight breeze carrying with it a whisper. *Love him*, it says, as gently and fragile as the flakes that find the palms of my hand. *Just love him….*

Yes, of course, I think. *That will be easy. So easy.*

CHAPTER SEVEN

I'M ABOUT to get into Brunhilda when I look back toward Hank's cabin. He's got a shed that sits about twenty yards away from the cabin, and I know what I've got to do. I walk up there, head for the shed, and wonder if I should ask Hank if I can take a look at…. Well, whatever it is he's got in there. I don't think he'd mind, and I suspect that he knows I'm going to do it anyway. He's put a peg-shaped piece of wood through the hasp loop. I pull that out and open the door. I look at the faintly lit shelves that hold Hank's tools and other items I can't identify. Toward the far wall, the dirt floor is outlined with 2x4s nailed together to form a rectangle, and within it is what I saw in Michael's painting—a cross-shaped black figure on its back that could be a bear, frozen with its arms spread as if beseeching something that never arrived. Stepping closer, I lower to my haunches. The cedar ash covers it, appearing as though Hank might have rubbed it in some. The face of this thing is oddly shaped, not a bear, but not a man either. If it's a bear, it's lost the hair on its cheeks and snout. I reach my hand out to touch it.

"John Spotted Elk."

Hank's voice comes from behind me, and I jerk my hand back, stand up, and turn toward him.

"Doesn't look like a man, Hank."

"John was an ugly human being. Looked better as a bear."

"What're you going to do with it?"

"Gonna prob'ly burn it come spring when it thaws out."

"I think the forest service ought to take a look at it."

"Nah, I don't think so."

I glance at the macabre thing, then turn back to Hank. "So, you want me to keep this a secret?"

"If you don't, all kinds of people will come up here and want to take a look around. See if they can find another one. Don't think I'd like that."

I envision exactly what Hank has just said. The tinfoil would probably call it a Colorado yeti, a Rocky Mountain abominable snowman. Hank's life would become a nightmare, and mine probably would too with all the yahoos with guns and alcohol who'd want to come up here to find their fifteen minutes.

"Okay." I nod. "We'll keep it our secret."

"You'll tell everybody who saw it to keep it a secret?"

I walk over to Hank. "If I tell everybody it's a secret, it won't stay a secret for long," I say, placing my hand on his shoulder, then giving him a pat on his back. I step out of the shed. "Those who saw it will tell their kids and grandchildren about it, and it'll probably go no further than that. Oh, here." I hand him the wooden peg.

He takes the peg, closes the door, and secures the hasp. "Tell you one thing," he says turning toward me, "you might want to put up juniper berries on your house."

"Why's that?"

"Insurance."

He said that word with one of his sly smiles, but I get the feeling he's serious. "I...." I think better of what I was going to say and don't pursue it. "Talk to you later."

I walk back to Brunhilda, knowing I'll resist the temptation I've got right now to gather up my own berries come spring—God knows Michael and I have more than enough of those nasty, prickly wild shrubs on our property—and string them over our doors and windows. I sit behind the wheel and start her up. As I turn around and head down the road, I decide not to tell Michael about my visit to Hank and what I saw in his shed. Michael would just want to check it out and ask questions that I'm sure Hank would answer by enhancing it with a retelling of the spiritual lore of his people. Michael's got enough *spiritual* going on for himself right now, thank you very much, and I'm not sure I want to deal with adding fuel to that fire.

I promised Brunhilda that I'd drop her off at Skip's Garage, and once I've gotten off the mountain, instead of heading back to town, I take the fork on the road toward the highway.

The garage is a little less than a mile out and sits just before the road/highway junction. It's a good location because Skip is often called to tow some nitwit's vehicle off the side of the highway to his place for repairs that should have been done before that nitwit decided to drive to the high country. Skip also gets calls from the CSP—Colorado State Patrol—to tow vehicles to his place after accidents occur on the highway, or for temporary storage of vehicles whose drivers have been arrested for one thing or another—usually DUI offenses, but sometimes something more sinister.

As I turn into Skip's lot, I see he's got four other cars parked outside and one on the lift inside. I pull Brunhilda next to one of the cars waiting for Skip's attentions.

As I turn off the engine, I hear her sigh of relief. "Finally," she says.

Entering Skip's little office is like walking into a shrine for men with small dicks. You know the ones, the kind of men who deal with that deficiency by adorning their walls with the bodiless heads of innocent critters whose only mistake was that they were at the wrong place at the wrong time. Skip is a hunter who has never seen a deer, elk, bear, moose, mountain goat, rabbit, and other critters he didn't want to kill and decapitate, hanging the resulting glassy-eyed evidence of his sporting prowess on his walls. His wife, a large woman who enjoys soap operas, Marlboros, and beer, won't let him hang them in their house, and thus the gruesome menagerie adorns the walls of the garage's office. I avoid looking at them as I walk over to the doorway to his single-bay garage. He's standing underneath an SUV raised six feet off the ground.

"Skip," I holler above the sound of his compressor.

He glances over at me, smiles, and sets the impact wrench on the floor. "Hey, Sheriff. Things all back to normal for you," he says, wiping his hands on a red rag he pulls from his rear pocket. He walks toward me. "What can I do you for?"

I notice again that he's a handsome man. Too skinny for me, but handsome. He's one of those small men who usually hooks up with large women. Don't know why that is.

I nod toward Brunhilda. "Yeah, I'm fine. The old gal needs a tune-up."

He looks out his bay door, then turns back to me. "Change fluids, radiator check, alignment?"

"Yeah," I say. "The works."

"Got a couple in front of you."

"S'okay." I pull out my cell, scroll to the department's main number, and press it.

"How's tomorrow sound?" Skip says.

I nod as I hear Mary answer. "Mary, I need somebody to give me a ride back to town."

She tells me that Digger is out on a call, Jim called in sick, and Don isn't scheduled to come in until 3:00 p.m.

"Okay. I'll just walk. Be back in a while." I end the call and put my cell in my pocket.

"I can take you into town," Skip says.

"No need. I think I can still walk a mile." I take the car key off my ring and hand it to him. "Tomorrow morning?"

"No. Try sometime after lunch. I'll call you if she's not ready."

"Good deal." I turn around and look up at all those sad eyes staring down at me. "Skip." I turn back to him. "You ever seen a bear that doesn't really look like a bear? The arms and legs too long and more bare skin on the head than hair?"

"No. Can't say that I have unless you're talkin' about what you and Digger were sleepin' with up on the mountain."

"That would be what I'm talking about."

"Odd-lookin' critter for sure."

I nod, then take another look at all those disembodied heads. "You ever think about taking up golf or skiing or some other sport that doesn't involve decapitation?"

Skip looks confused for a moment and then nods and laughs. "Hah! You betcha."

When he doesn't say anything else, I realize he didn't get it. I nod and walk out into the storm that seems to have picked up a bit since I left Hank's cabin.

I PULL up my coat collar, put on my gloves, and walk to the road, staying in the depressions in the snow Brunhilda made when I drove her out here. A little breeze has kicked up, coming from my right side. It's not that cold yet, but breezes up here generally turn into winds that may or may not turn into gales whipping through the treetops sounding like massive rivers on steroids. I figure I better get back to town before that happens. If it happens.

I tug on my black hat—a Resistol Michael gave me the day I pinned on my badge—and lower my head a bit. I've thought about buying one of those floppy-eared skull hats lined with fur, but for all my thinking about it, I've yet to do it. Maybe it has something to do with preserving my image. You know, the hat, Wrangler jeans, leather in all the right places. My weapon, though, does not rely on a revolving cylinder, rather it's a 1911 Remington .45 caliber semiautomatic given to me by my father. But right now I'm thinking to hell with my image as I cover my ears with my hands and wish I'd let Skip give me that ride back to town.

As I approach a curve, there's a single elk bull standing in the middle of the road staring at me. He's a mature boy, about five feet tall, and I would guess he's seven or eight feet from head to butt and weighs probably seven hundred pounds. His antlers are massive, and his stare is intense, but not as intense as if I were standing closer. Nearer to this big boy, I'd see in his eyes what is best described as defiance. I've seen those close-up intimidating stares often, both from bulls and cows alike. Best advice in a situation like this is just to stop, don't stare back, and give him, and the herd that is likely still hidden within the trees, a wide berth. He alerts, snaps his head toward the portion of the road I can't see, and immediately leaps into a lope. Now the herd emerges from the tree line; cows, some younger bulls, and calves too stampede across the road. The sound is like muffled thunder. I stop counting at forty and watch probably another forty cross the road and disappear into the tree line on the other side. I hear the snap of limbs as they make their way to wherever they're going. Now there is only silence. Complete silence. It is as if they were phantoms, a magical thing that must be experienced to be believed. The only evidence that they were actually here are the droppings strewn across the road.

I start walking again and reach the curve where I can barely see the road beyond, to the place where the bull looked before he'd leapt into the trees. My eyes water from the wind, and the blowing snow obscures what's up ahead. A critter, black against the snow, is standing on two legs, and it's staring at me. *Christ! Not again!* It stands there for a moment, and then it too heads for the tree line and is gone.

WHEN I reach town, I pass by Michael's store and glance at the sign above the door. He asked me what I thought he ought to name the store, and I told him I didn't know but that the name ought to reflect what he had inside of it.

"Okay," he said.

Two days before he opened the store, he dragged me from the office, and we walked across the street. "What do you think?" he said, pulling off the paper covering from the sign he'd put above the door.

"Oh, Michael.... Needful Things? You really think...?" I'd then looked at his face and saw his smile and nodded. "Okay. Kind of a gimmick?"

"No." He'd shaken his head. "Yeah, I borrowed it from Stephen King, but.... That's what I have in there, Sam—needful things. They're... necessary things. Better than Michael's Curios. Or better yet, Pretty Things by Michael."

"Oh, I like that one—Pretty Things...."

NOW, AS I pass Michael's store, I notice the Closed sign on the door. He hasn't returned to work since the incident up the mountain. It's been a week, but he's been so quiet, so creepily quiet since then that I've avoided discussing it with him. The night of our party, after everyone left and we went bed, he lay with his back to me, my arms around his chest. We spoke about what was on his mind, namely the picture he'd painted that presaged what had happened to Digger and me at the bowl.

"It scares me, Sam," he said, and I felt his body jerk slightly when he said it. "I mean.... What if the other paintings I do that come from my imagination and not from a photo have some...? What if they're just representations of things that are actually going to happen sometime in the future?"

"No, no," I whispered, kissing his neck. "It was all just coincidence. It was—"

"It was more than that. And I think you know it."

I thought about what he said for a moment and couldn't find an adequate response. Of course it was more than just coincidence. The picture had been too right, too accurate to be just some fluke.

"I guess I do know that."

"What if I sell a painting to somebody and something bad happens to them just like what happened to you and Digger? What if—"

"Michael, how many paintings have you done that show something bad happening?"

"A few I guess."

"But even the one you did of Digger and me could be interpreted a number of ways. The painting itself, unless someone knows exactly what it depicts, could be seen as just two guys being intimate."

"No," he said, shaking his head. "That's not what I painted. That's... I've got to think about all this. I'm not going to open the shop for a while."

"Okay," I said. "No tourists hanging around anyway. Take your time."

"I need time, Sam."

"I know it."

We didn't make love that night. I thought it would have been wrong to even suggest it.

I SHAKE the snow off my hat, brush it off my shoulders, and walk into the office. Mary raises her eyes from whatever she's got spread out on her desk and smiles. "Rick is in your office," she says.

Rick Williams is the local forest service guy who's got property not far from Michael and me. He's good at what he does but sometimes thinks his priorities trump anything my department might have going on. I take my coat off as I walk to my office, hang it on the tree, and put my hat on the filing cabinet.

"Quite a storm out there," I say as I walk behind my desk. "What's going on, Rick?"

"Yeah, this might be the big one, Sam. What I'm here for, though, is... I told you that I went up to take a look at whatever it was they found up at the bowl, but I couldn't find it. Not a sign of it."

"Yeah, you told me. Didn't get buried by the snow?"

"No. It was just gone. You think Hank might've done something with it?"

Mary steps in and places a cup of coffee on my desk. "Thought you might want this," she says. "Rick, can I get you a cup?"

"No thanks, Mary."

"Since when did you start serving coffee, beside making it?" I ask her.

"Don't get used to it, Sheriff." She gives me a wink and steps out.

I take a sip of the coffee and then caress the cup with my palms. "I don't know of any reason Hank would want the thing," I say, looking at Rick. "He's not a collector or anything like that."

"Well, Deputy Jim asked me to take a look at it, and Merle Hogan—the volunteer fireman?"

"Yeah, I know Merle. He rode back in the ambulance with me."

"He told me it was about the strangest thing he'd ever seen. Did you get a good look at it? Anybody take pictures that you know of?"

I hate lying, but that's just the way it is. "No," I say. "I was kind of out of it, Rick. Didn't get a good look at it. As far as I know, no one took pictures. Thank God it ended up where it did. It gave Digger and me some breathing room with all that snow on top of us."

Rick stands up. "Okay. Guess it'll just go down as a strange-looking black bear. You take it easy, Sam."

"Will do," I say, as Rick leaves my office. I take another sip of coffee and again regret the lies. I see that Mary has put next year's completed budget on my desk with a little note: *I need a raise. Otherwise, you can all make your own damned coffee.*

I don't blame her. Mary is our rock. She's appreciated more than she knows, but somehow we seldom tell her about that. She came to the department about ten years ago when her husband of thirty years died of a heart attack while pulling the edible meat from a bull elk kill up a mountain. He'd had no interest in caping the thing but dressed the critter in the field and ended up with a canvas-covered bundle of meat that weighed about two hundred pounds. He'd had his and Mary's grandson, Phillip, with him, but the kid was only thirteen and could only shoulder so much of the pulling, and, well…. When he died, Mary needed a job, and Sheriff Slaughter hired her. For all Slaughter's faults, he did right by the department and Mary in turning over the mundane administrative duties to her. And that grandson of hers grew into a handsome young man who got a degree in fine arts. When he comes up for a visit, it's hard to separate him and Michael for longer than two minutes. They're kindred spirits. In fact, we have no doubt that Phillip is more kindred to Michael and me than I believe Mary realizes. Maybe she does. Mothers and grandmothers, too, have a way of knowing about those kinds of things. We've never discussed it, though. But if we were to discuss it, I think she'd be fine with it.

I sit back in my chair and think about something that should have occurred to me long before this. The black bear, if it were a black bear, that contributed to Digger's and my continued existence on this earth should have been curled up in a den somewhere, sleeping the winter through rather than traipsing around the mountain. And it surprises me that no one else has brought it up. I'm surprised too that nobody has come in with a picture of it. Of course, if it wasn't a black bear at all but John Spotted Elk.... Skinwalkers? Hell, I don't know. Yeah, I did tell Michael that I believe some things are unknowable, mysteries that we can never untangle. And right now I'm not inclined to attempt any untangling at all. I think about what Hank said about Michael being an old soul caught in the whispers of old winds. That haunts me. It really does. And what exactly does that mean?

I turn around and look out the window that faces the street. Michael's truck is there, in front of his shop. It wasn't there when I came into the office. I look at my watch and see it's almost lunchtime. I stand up, grab my hat and coat, and walk into the outer office.

"Digger has a problem," Mary says as I pull on my coat.

"What?"

"If you'd ever turn up your radio, you'd know."

I reach for my waist where I clip on the handheld radio, and it's not there. "Sorry. Damned thing just spouts static most of the time."

"He's over at Joe Parsons's place. Somebody or something killed Joe's dog."

"Okay." I nod. It's a sad truth, but dogs up here often find themselves on the wrong end of a mountain lion's or bobcat's ire. Bears usually just run away from a dog, but felines are more inclined to stand their ground, as are moose.

"He says Joe thinks it was a demonic sacrifice."

I nod again and see that Mary isn't smiling. "How so?"

"Took out the heart, sliced off the pads on his paws, and took some bone from the back of the skull."

"And?"

"And Digger says Joe is demanding you do something about it."

"Tell Digger I'll be out to see Joe in about an hour."

"Can Digger come back?"

"Sure." I button my coat and walk to the door. Before opening it, I turn to Mary. "Also, tell him to tell Joe not to bury the dog until I see it."

I walk across the street and peek in Michael's window. He's sitting behind the display counter staring into something I cannot see. I immediately think of those old winds and shake off the thought as quick as it comes. As I step into the shop, he looks at me and smiles.

"Hi," he says.

"Hi, yourself. Good to see your shop open."

"Sorry I wasn't up when you left this morning."

I walk over to the counter, fold my hands on top of it, and look into his eyes. "That's okay. I watched you sleep for a minute. You had a smile on your face."

"Guess I was dreaming," he says.

"What about?"

"You, probably. Don't remember exactly."

"Want to go to lunch with me? Doesn't look like you've got a glut of customers right now."

Michael shakes his head. "Nope. The last one, before I closed up the shop a week ago, was some guy who needed directions. Before he left, he bought the painting I did of the fox with the mangled snout we see every once in a while."

"Excellent. What'd you get for it?"

"Twenty bucks."

"Could have gotten more."

"I know. But who wants a picture of a fox who probably got his nose caught in some idiot's trap? I was glad he liked it enough to buy it."

"Come on. Let's go eat," I say, taking a step toward the door.

"Let me get my coat."

He stands from the stool and walks into the little office he's got in the back of the shop. When he comes out, he's got on his thin jean jacket. I bought him a fur-insulated jean jacket in the fall, but he's yet to wear it.

"Where's your warm coat?"

"At home," he says, looking at me like I'm an idiot.

"Well, yeah…. But…."

"I like the cold. I get too warm and I…. You want to go over to Cathy's?"

I nod. "Sure," I say. Not that there's anywhere else to eat lunch in the Junction, but Michael knows that as well as I do, and there's no sense in me bringing it up.

Cathy's Café is a homey place with pine log walls and a wooden floor that saw its better days probably fifty years ago. Cathy is Cathy Miles, a fortysomething unmarried woman who has yet to declare her sexuality except for the unspoken evidence of it. Her blond-gray hair is shorter than mine, she wears cargo shorts and hiking boots year-round,

T-shirts in the spring and summer, and red-and-black patterned flannel shirts in the fall and winter. Not that that means anything, but to my practiced eye, it does give a hint. Her T-shirts always shout one thing or another in bold letters and vivid pictures. The one with the snarling wolf on it reads *Of Wolves and Women*. The one with the angry bull's head staring at you says *Bodaciousness*. I know. So what? The one she wears today reads *If I Wanted Your Attitude, I'd Ask For it!*

"Well," Cathy says as she approaches us, drying her hands on a towel. She stops about a foot away.

"Hi, Cathy," Michael says.

She looks at me with a slight tilt of her head, then smiles at Michael. "This asshole treating you okay?"

"So far," Michael says.

I ask her who's she calling an asshole, and she says, "Who do you think? C'mon." She motions with her hand and turns. "You can sit where I can keep an eye on the silverware."

"Walmart tinware is more like it," I say as she leads us to a table near the streetside window.

"Something an asshole would say." She stops at the table and pulls a chair out for Michael. "And you," she says, staring at me with a half smile on her face, "can seat yourself."

I give her a wink and sit down.

The first time Cathy and I met, we both saw something in each other we liked. We're both pretty hard on the outside, but underneath we're about as dangerous as Winnie the Pooh. I don't know how we figured this out, except that we connected almost immediately after our first short conversation. Yeah, we trade barbs every time we see each other, and we smile at the reactions of others who think we might be serious about it. We're not. But neither of us will admit that to anybody else. Cathy and I are as tight as two people can be who don't sleep together.

Michael's got his head turned toward the window. He's staring at his store, and I'm staring at his profile. There's something about concentrating on the side view of the person you love that, at least for me, sends little shivers down my neck. Looking at your lover in the eyes is one thing, but catching the profile is like seeing another sublime dimension of the whole. I savor it for a moment until Melissa, called Missie, arrives to take our order.

"You two ready yet?" she asks.

I look up and see she's got the blue side of her hair tied in a bun today. The black side just hangs free. As usual, she'd dressed in black. She's even got black eyeliner that appears to have been applied with a paintbrush. She's a sweet young woman, maybe eighteen or nineteen, who Cathy hired because Missie showed up one morning about four months ago on the café's porch. She slept there after her two male companions left her high and dry in the middle of the night. She hitched a ride with the boys in Denver, with the promise they'd get her to where she told them she wanted to go—Las Vegas. As far as I know, Missie has never revealed the details of why the boys just left her in the Junction, or if she got out of that car willingly or not. I suspect she and Cathy did have a heart-to-heart that morning when Cathy found her huddled against the cold on the porch. But she's stayed on, working at the café and living with Cathy, though sleeping in separate bedrooms. Or so Cathy tells me. Not that Cathy needed extra help, but there's that Winnie the Pooh thing coming through.

"Hey, Missie," I say. "I'll have the burger with cheese. No fries. And, I guess a Coke will do."

"You want the salad, Michael?" she says. That's what Michael usually orders. He's not a fan of red meat.

"Yes, please. And just water."

Missie walks back to the kitchen to give our order to Cathy while I look at Michael's eyes.

"So...," I say, gladly being drowned within the inescapable depths of his stare. "You decided to come to town? Open up the shop?"

He closes his eyes for a moment. When he opens them, he gazes at the tabletop. "Don't know if I'm actually opening the place again. Just thought it was time...." He looks at me and shakes his head. "I need to get on with things."

I nod. "Yes, you do. It's somewhere to go every day, and if you don't feel like painting, you don't have to. Not that you're going to see many customers this time of year, but who knows? Maybe you'll get a few who'll want something, oh, more substantial than a cheesy dream catcher that falls apart when you try to hang it up."

"Yeah. I was getting a little tired of staying at home. But...." He raises his head for a moment and then looks back down at the table where he's folded his hands. "I can't get rid of this vision or idea that's in my head."

"Here you go," Missie says as she brings us our drinks. "Food will be up in a minute."

As she turns from us, I say, "What's the vision?"

"Well...." He smiles, then takes a sip of water. "There's this dog. He's a big guy with pointy ears. Looks kind of like a wolf, but he isn't. Just a dog."

"Like Hank's dog? Charlie?"

"Sort of. Yes." He nods. "Anyway, this dog is standing in the middle of a circle made of rocks, and he glows as if he's giving off heat. And coming off the dog are wisps of smoke or mist. His head is raised, and he's looking at another circle of haze coming off him that congeals into human forms, heads mostly. I think the forms are Indians, or at least their faces are reminiscent of Native Americans."

"Okay. And?"

"I don't know. There's some kind of communication going on, but it's... it's like I'm too far away to hear what they're saying."

"The dog is speaking?"

"It's not speaking, really. It's more.... Oh, I guess it's just mental communication. Something I know is happening but—"

"Good enough to eat." Missie sets our plates on the table. "Anything else I can get you?"

"No thank you," I say. "Looks like we're good for a while."

I grab the mustard and think about what Michael has just said. He's sensing those *whispers* Hank said he's caught up in, and that bothers me. "Well," I say, lifting the bun and squirting yellow stuff under it, "that would make a pretty picture. Nothing frightening or potentially harmful to anybody with what you've described."

"Maybe," he says.

I look at him, and he's sitting there not touching his salad but looking over my shoulder at something I'm sure no one else can see. "You going to eat?"

"Oh.... Yeah." He looks down at the plate, picks up his fork, and stabs one of the purple leaves. "Is Digger doing okay?"

"He is." I take my first bite. Cathy does make a good burger, and she knows better than to put any purple leaves on top of the meat, trying to pass it off as lettuce.

"Good. Has he said anything about being... sandwiched in with you at the bowl?"

I put my burger on the plate and wipe my mouth. "Why, Michael Bellomo, I do think you've aroused my fantasy."

"What?"

"A sandwich. You, me, and Digger."

"Nooooo," he says, smiling.

"But—"

"Nope." He cuts me off at that pass without hesitation.

I watch him take a few more bites of the salad, a smile still on his face.

"When it's fifteen below outside, it'd be kinda nice to have the extra warmth."

He rolls his eyes and continues eating.

I pick up my burger and take my second bite.

"I didn't see Brunhilda outside," he says.

"Yeah, she's spending some time with Skip. I'll get her back tomorrow."

We both eat in silence for a few moments. Then Michael says, "The Hopi believe that weaving doesn't involve creating something new—the patterns, the colors."

I look at him. He's put his fork down and has put his elbows up on the table, and he rests his chin on his intertwined fingers.

"All right," I say.

"They believe," he says, "that weaving only brings out something that was already there."

I nod. *Old winds just keep blowin'.* "Interesting."

"What if...?" He stops himself, lowers his arms from the table, and leans back a bit in his chair. "What if what happened to you and Digger at the bowl was foreordained? And when I painted it, I was just putting to canvas something that was already there, something that was... predetermined to happen."

I grab the napkin and wipe my mouth. "Well, that's deep."

He smiles that smile of his that over time I've identified as his *not kidding about this* smile, and he says, "Just a thought."

He picks up his fork and digs into his salad again. I look down at my cheeseburger. If this moment were scripted or, as Michael said, foreordained—me staring at my burger, him eating that purple stuff— who would write such mundanities? Who would care? Who? Or what? I can't help but shake my head and give a second thought to what Michael has just told me and what must be going through his mind about now. I know he's just touched the bare edge of what he's thinking about.

I WATCH Michael cross the street, now thankful that he's worn the light jean jacket that doesn't cover his ass. He still wears the Levi's he wore in college, now gray with age. He seldom wears underwear, and well....

I head back to the office, stick my head in the door, and tell Mary I'm going up to Joe Parsons's to take a look at his dog. "Throw me your keys," I say to Digger, who is sitting at his desk.

"You want me to come with you?" Digger asks as he pulls his keys from his pocket and tosses them across the room to me.

"No. I think I can handle this one by myself."

He gets a hurt look on his face. I don't know what that's about and don't ask him. I step back out of the office and walk to the Cherokee—one of two SUVs we've got, besides Brunhilda—and get in. It starts up without any moaning, and I give a thought to how Brunhilda is doing about now. I do miss her. She's like a cantankerous old friend you put up with because, rain or shine, they're dependable and true. Before I back onto the street, it occurs to me that Digger's pouty expression may have had something to do with what happened at the bowl, that he may think it was his fault and I'm now wary of having him at my side. I give a moment's thought to taking him with me. But I don't. He'll get over it.

Joe Parsons has a place about three miles west of the Junction. It's about thirty acres of trees and rocks. There's a reason somebody named these mountains Rocky. They are, and the soil is just as hard. Every time I pass by or head into his place, his four German shepherds raise intense hell, running up and down the roadside, barking with froth-filled exuberance. When you drive up Joe's road, the dogs—each of them is 100 pounds or more—accompany you, two on either side of your vehicle, spewing slime onto the doors and windows.

Now only three dogs accompany me up Joe's road. I stop about twenty yards from the cabin and wait for him or his wife to call off the dogs before I get out. Lucy does come out of the cabin, yells a single word, and the dogs immediately respond, scampering off to the side of the cabin where there's a chain-link-enclosed dog run with four doghouses inside. Lucy waves, and I get out of the Cherokee. She then points to the small bluff about sixty yards to the side of the house. I start walking toward the bluff, and Joe appears at the top of it. He motions for me to come on up, and I head that way.

"He's down there," Joe says, pointing to an aspen grove beyond. "Breaks my heart."

I glance at Joe, and he's pulling his hand across his eyes. "So you think it was some kind of ritual?"

"The way it was done, yes. Clean cuts. Mountain lion or a pack of coyotes wouldn't be that precise. Besides that, they left the insides, except for the heart."

We reach the other side of the bluff, and Joe leads me to the grove of aspens, now bare of their leaves, their light-gray limbs stretching out as if beseeching something the sky cannot give them. Joe stands to the side of where his dog lies, the carcass now frozen, the snowpack around it tinged with crimson, Joe's, and I assume Digger's, footprints circling it. We both study the scene.

"This is Thor?" I ask.

"No. That's Apollo," Joe says.

I get to my haunches and take a closer look. "Yeah, no wounds you'd see from a bear or lion attack. How long was he down here before you found him?"

"Probably overnight."

"Any thoughts on why critters didn't get to him after he'd been taken down?"

"Thought about it, and I can't answer that." He lowers himself down next to me. "He wasn't disturbed other than the slice on his chest, the back of his head, and look at his paws."

I do look, and see that the dog's pads have been sliced off. "Wow."

"I believe it's a ritual killing, Sam. Satanists or something."

I stand up and look at the surroundings. The bluff we came down hides the area from the house, and the aspens border a small meadow that extends to the base of hills that rise to the north and east. To the south is the road that fronts Joe's property. "Couple things, Joe. I suspect you didn't hear anything, or you would've been out here in a minute. The carcass wasn't chewed on or dragged, as far as I can tell, and the things they or it did to the body.... Well, what they or it did is unusual. You agree?"

"Sure. Of course." Joe stands up and shakes his head. "Goddammit, Sam, I'm torn up about this. It's gotta be a ritual of some kind. And why didn't the other dogs raise holy goddamned hell while it was happening?"

"Don't know."

"Satanists," Joe says as if that's the last word on the subject.

"That might be a good explanation, Joe, if we had some practicing witches around here, but we don't that I know of."

"Hell, they coulda come up from Denver."

He obviously didn't detect the wink in my eye when I mentioned witches. "Yeah. They could have, but I think we ought to get Rick to come out and take a look at this before you bury this guy. He's dealt with these kind of kills before, and he might see something we don't."

"I hate to leave him out here any longer, Sam. You say Rick has seen this kind of mutilation before?"

"No, no. Just that he's seen dogs killed by bears, lions. That sort of thing." I pull my cell out and try to get a signal and realize that's not going to happen. I reach to my side and then remember I'd forgotten to take a handheld with me when I left. "Let me get back to the car, and I'll radio in and see if Rick can come out today. Hell, I just talked to him a while ago."

"Okay. But if he can't, I'm not leaving Apollo out here overnight."

"I understand." I walk back toward the bluff, knowing that Joe's love for Apollo is probably clouding his good sense right now. If Rick can tell us anything about what happened here, especially if he can somehow rule out witches for Christ's sake, I'll feel better about the whole thing. Besides that, since I denied Rick a closer look at the freak bear, maybe I can redeem my conscience a bit by making sure he sees Joe's dog before it's buried.

I sit down in the Cherokee, start the engine, grab the mike, and speak into it. When Mary says she hears me, I ask her to get in touch with Rick and have him come out to the Parsons's place to take a look at the dead dog.

"You want him to come out now?" she asks, her voice bathed in static.

"Yes, ma'am."

"Will do. You stay by the radio."

"Yes, ma'am."

I watch Joe walk toward the Cherokee. When he reaches it, he rests his arms on the top of the door and looks in at me.

"He coming?"

"Hope so. Mary's going to track him down. How exactly did you find Apollo?"

"The other three found him. I opened up the gate to their run this morning and noticed there were only the three that ran out. I always let them run first thing in the morning. They all made a beeline for the bluff and ran down the other side. When I got to the aspen grove, I saw them sitting, just sitting there as if they'd been commanded to do it. Then I saw Apollo."

"They didn't raise hell or whine? They didn't act disturbed by it?"

"No, they didn't. Like I said, they were just sitting there."

"Sheriff! You there?" Mary's voice cracks from the radio.

"I'm here."

"Rick is on his way. Over."

"Thank you." I hook the mike on the dash. "Odd behavior for dogs, don't you think? Especially since it was one of their pack?"

"Nothin' normal about this, Sheriff," Joe says, stepping back from the door and digging in his chest pocket for his cigarettes.

I get out of the Cherokee and watch Joe light up. "We'll see what Rick has to say and go from there. One other thing. You said the gate to the dog run was latched when you came out this morning?"

"Yes, it was. And I have no idea how Apollo got out."

Joe huffs smoke out. The slight breeze grabs it and sends it off to invisibility. I give a thought to Michael's story about the Hopi weavers and wonder if the scene that just played out would have been depicted in the weave at the moment Joe's smoke was visible or after it dispersed. I don't know why this has crossed my mind again, but I see Michael's *not kidding about this* smile from earlier today as we'd eaten lunch. As Joe inhales again, I know with certainty Rick is going to be as baffled about this as I am.

DIGGER GIVES me a ride to the cabin. It's already dark outside, it's cold, and it's starting to snow again. I walk in the front door and smell the aroma of burning pine. I take off my coat and hang my hat on the hook in the small foyer just inside the door. I unsnap my holster from my belt and hang it and the weapon within it on the hook next to my hat. We call it the mudroom, and it is. It's the only space in the cabin with a ceramic tile floor. The dirt, mud, moisture, pine needles, and other substances we bring into the cabin from outside usually stay in this room, the tiles easily cleaned when we get around to doing that. I step into the parlor and see the fire Michael has going in the rock-lined fireplace.

"Sorry I didn't wait for you in town," Michael says, coming from the kitchen.

"No problem. Digger brought me home."

We embrace, as we always do when one of us comes home after the other, kiss, and my hand just naturally finds his ass. He's still in those faded Levi's, and what I'd earlier adored with my eyes, my hand now caresses. His hand sneaks down to the front of my jeans, and we stand there for a while just enjoying the moment.

"This could lead to something," he says, gently backing away. "But dinner's almost ready." He turns and walks into the kitchen, leaving me to quickly stick my hand down my pants to adjust myself.

I follow him and take a look at what's on the stove. There's nothing there, and I see that the oven knob is turned on. "Another casserole?"

"Yes." He grabs a sack of grated cheese from the refrigerator and sets it on the counter. He opens the oven door and then pulls out the bubbling dish. "Tuna with lots of vegetables," he says, flipping up the foil that covers the concoction. He sprinkles the cheese over the top of it and then shoves it back in the oven. "It'll just be a few more minutes."

"I can hardly wait," I say, knowing that he knows I'm not a big fan of casseroles. The alternative, of course, would be salads every time it's his turn to prepare a meal, most of the time sprinkled with some kind of nuts, and pieces of fruit on top. There is something inherently wrong about putting nuts and fruit in salads, especially if you're fond of salad dressing. A piece of apple slathered in oil and vinegar just doesn't cut it.

I grab a beer from the refrigerator and take it to our dining table, situated between the parlor and the kitchen. Michael has already set out the plates and silverware, and he's placed two hot pad holders in the middle of the table. I sit down, turn my head, and watch him lean on the kitchen counter, his ass pooched out a little as he waits for the cheese to melt. I'm about to suggest we just delay dinner for a while and head to the bedroom, when he turns the knob on the oven, puts on his insulated mitten, opens the oven door, and pulls out the goods. He carries it to the table, takes off his mitten, and sits down.

"Enjoy," he says, smiling.

"I'll try." I pull the cork from the bottle of chardonnay he's set out for himself and fill his glass. "Love me a good casserole." I spoon some onto my plate and watch the steam rise from the glop. "Might be able to eat this tomorrow after it cools down."

Michael dishes up a helping, then takes a sip of his wine and looks at me with his head cocked slightly to the side. "You remember the T-shirt Cathy had on today? The one that said *If I Wanted Your Attitude, I'd Ask For it!?*"

"Yes, I do. Thing is, though," I say, as I stir the little mountain of stuff on my plate, "I can take Cathy with a grain of salt. You, on the other hand…. Well, let's just say I love you with all my heart, honey."

"I know you do." He smiles and takes his first taste. "Mmm, that's good. Best casserole yet."

I take his hint. I shovel some onto my fork, put it in my mouth, and swivel it around a bit to try to get it cool enough to swallow. After I swallow, I shake my head. "I do believe that's by far your best, honey. Why, I don't believe I've ever tasted anything—"

"Okay. All right." He cuts me off. "It's filling and easy to cook. It's your turn tomorrow night. If you can come up with something without trans fats or carbs, I'll… I'll eat it… joyously. Agreed?"

"Agreed. No fat, no carbs."

We each take another bite, and I give a few seconds' thought to tomorrow's menu.

"How'd your day go?" he says.

"Oh, pretty good. After lunch, I went out to the Parsons's place. Joe thinks a witch killed one of his dogs."

"No. Really? One of those beautiful shepherds?"

"Yeah. It, whatever, got Apollo."

"Why does he think a witch did it?"

"He thinks it was a ritualistic killing. Satanists from Denver or some damned thing. Rick from the forest service came out and took a look at the body. He'd never seen anything like it."

I realize what I've just done. Dammit to hell and back. I should have told him the rest of my day was uneventful and left it at that.

"How was the dog killed?"

I look at him. He's put his fork down, and he's staring at me with a seriousness covering his face that I've seen before and wished never to see again. "Oh, just an unusual kind of.... It wasn't something a bear or mountain lion would do."

"What?"

"Michael, they were just odd wounds. I really don't want to talk about it over supper."

We sit staring at each other for a minute, and he finally nods once, picks up his glass, and sips his wine. I know I can't let this silence last, and we desperately need a change of subject right now.

"How was your day? You stay at the shop awhile?"

"Just cleaned some, dusted, rearranged things. Did Joe say if he saw anything peculiar?"

Yeah, he's not going to stop until he hears the whole story. I mentally kick myself in the ass for not thinking before I told him anything about my visit to the Parsons's. "No, he didn't."

"He didn't say, or he didn't see anything?"

"He didn't see anything, other than...." *Shit, I did it again.* "Michael, let's just finish our supper, and I'll give you the details later."

We again stare at each other for a moment. "Okay," he says.

"Good." I shovel in some more tuna, vegetables, cheese, and whatever else is swimming around in the glob on my plate and wonder how the hell I'm going to play this with him. I won't, no, I *can't* lie to him. I've never done that, and I'm not going to start now. But, goddammit.

When the phone rings, we both turn our head toward the landline on the table beside the entrance to the kitchen. It's ring is one of those electronic bells that is grating as hell.

Michael stands up, grabs the receiver, and says, "Hello.... Hi. Yeah, he's here." He holds it out to me. "It's Cathy."

I stand up and grab the phone. Cathy tells me that Missie isn't home. She gives me some more details, and I put the receiver back on the base. "I've got to go over to Cathy's," I tell Michael, who is still standing there.

"What's wrong?"

"Missie never came home. Cathy left early and told Missie to close up for her. And she never came home."

"What...?" Michael begins, then stops himself. I imagine he's going to ask me what happened to her and realizes that's the question at hand.

I give Michael a hug and tell him I'll give him a call when I know something.

"You've got your cell?"

I pat my shirt pocket. "Yeah," I say as I walk into the mudroom. I grab my holster and snap it back onto my belt, then take my coat off the hook and put it on. I put on my hat and snatch the keys to Michael's truck from one of the little brass hooks on the small wooden plaque that hangs on the wall. Michael made the plaque specifically for keys. I tend to lose mine, and early on in our relationship, he figured that out.

I stop before opening the door and then walk into the parlor. "You okay?"

"Yes." He nods. "I'm fine. Go to the café first."

I wait a moment before answering. "Okay. I'll see you in a bit."

CATHY'S PLACE is about two miles from us, not counting the half-mile access road that leads to the house. Halfway there, I decide to turn around, drive into town, and take a look at the café. Even if Michael hadn't suggested it, I tell myself, I would have done it anyway. I'm trying not to read anything into Michael's suggestion, though, but try as I might, I do. What has he seen? Cathy told me on the phone that she'd already driven down to the café to see if something was amiss there. Then she'd driven back home to call me, just on the off chance that Missie had finally returned. She hadn't.

I pull in front of the café, grab my flashlight, get out, and step to the side of the stairs leading to the front door. Cathy told me months ago that she put a spare key under a mica-covered rock just in case of emergencies. I turn on the flashlight and there's the rock, which appears to be about three hundred pounds.

Thank God the rock is round. I give it a shove, and yes, there's a little green metal box underneath it that I snatch up. I open it, and there's the key inside, along with a folded note that reads: *Put the key back where you found it. The Management.*

I walk up the steps to the front door. The porch light is on, and there's nothing on the porch that interests me. I do remember this is where Cathy first found Missie, and I imagine her lying in the corner, huddled against the cold and snow. After putting the key in the lock, I open the door, and the only light that's on is in the kitchen. I shine my flashlight around the dining room, then on the walls near me where the main panel for the rest of the lights should be. I don't see it. Walking a few more steps, I turn the flashlight on the hallway leading to the two bathrooms, and there's the main switch. I flip up all four of the switches, and the lights pop on, illuminating the entire café as it usually is when it's open.

After slowly walking through the dining room, then taking a look in both of the bathrooms, I step into the kitchen. Everything looks okay. The door is unlocked, and I step outside onto the back porch. *There's got to be a light out here.* I lean inside, see the switch, and turn it on. As I take a step farther outside, there's a flash of something to my left moving quickly from the side of the building and hightailing it to the tree line twenty yards beyond. The sound of whatever's or whoever's escape is just a shuffling, and then I hear the rustle of low-hanging branches as it goes deeper into the trees. Quickly raising my flashlight, I focus it toward the trees and sweep it back and forth. Nothing.

"Who's out there!" I shout. "Make yourself known!"

I step off the porch and walk to where I believe it, whatever, was when I first turned on the outside light. Nothing. I walk toward the tree line, sweeping my flashlight over the ground. Still nothing. Just as I'm about to turn toward the building, my light passes over something on the ground a few feet into the trees. I walk over there and lower to my haunches. It's a small black bag of something with loose ties looped through holes on the top of it. I open it up and shine my flashlight inside. It looks like sand. Gray sand. I pick it up and pull the top closed with the ties. I study the tracks in the snow. Other than my own, I see the impressions of boots, the sole pattern a bunch of Xs. I bend down, pull my cell out, and take a picture of the boot pattern.

When I get inside, I open the bag and take a better look. It's not sand but something finer, like talc. I have no idea what I'm looking at. I close it up, take one last look inside the café, turn off the lights, and go out the front door. I put the key back in the box, put the box where I found it, and push the rock over it.

As I drive to Cathy's place, I wish Michael would have told me his windshield wipers are just about useless and his heater doesn't work at all. Hell, he probably never turns on the heater. *Cold-blooded* is my thought right now, and I immediately take that back. Yeah, there's something cold inside Michael that I've yet to understand and probably don't want to. But that's not who Michael is. No, he's not that. He's.... Hell, he's my life, my love. Nothing cold about that.

Chapter Eight

I MET Michael for the first time in a bar in downtown Denver. I'd just come back from my second deployment to the Middle East and was about to get discharged from the Army.

I'd spent some time with my parents, sleeping one night in the bedroom they kept for me at the house I'd grown up in. I'd had an apartment in the Capitol Hill neighborhood ever since graduating from college, but my parents had insisted I stay with them for a while, and I did that for two days and one night. They'd already decided to move to Florida once I came home safe and sound, and I found boxes all over the house. They'd kept my room pristine—a child's room full of memories. But now that I'd seen the reality of warfare, my childhood room had become too fragile, too ephemeral to believe that it had once centered my life. Yes, it was where I'd grown up, but when I stepped into it that night, it became surreal, a place of barely remembered fantasies where innocence had once resided.

There's something about coming home from war that sets you apart from the rest of humanity, except of course for your brothers in arms, who also find themselves strangers in a place they once knew but are now estranged from. It is a child's place you left behind so long ago, where your mother's love had been absolute, and your father's pride in your imminent journey to defend the flag, freedom, and apple pie had been effusive, something he'd boasted about to neighbors over the backyard fence, a broad smile on his face. Oh, returning to that is not an easy thing to do. Especially if the place from where you've returned was without a doubt, yes, no doubt at all the nine circles of hell, where death and destruction became so commonplace that at times you found yourself not really caring anymore. A place where even the innocent became faceless, soulless, and your brother, the man next to you became your only reason for going on, to live another day. No, your mother's meatloaf, green beans, and mashed potatoes and your father's scotch and big cigars were no comfort against the razor's edge of the memories you'd brought back with you from the place where you'd been close enough to the devil to see a sly smile glisten from his eyes.

I stayed the night with my parents and left the next evening after we'd had dinner. I went back to my apartment and slept for almost two days. I woke up starving, and though I'd promised myself after I'd graduated college never to do it again, I went to McDonald's, ordered a Big Mac, a vanilla shake, and fries. Goddamn, that was a delicious meal. Decided too that I needed to get out, be around people for a while who had no idea where I'd been—physically or emotionally. I cleaned myself up and walked the several blocks to the bar I'd felt comfortable in years before.

The bar wasn't at all glitzy or a showplace for pretty young men who'd yet to figure out that there was more to being gay than 24/7 party time. Not that I didn't appreciate younger men. In fact, they've always been my preference. What can I say? I was only twenty-six, and a younger man for me was someone at least old enough to vote. And I'd spent some time at clubs when I was in college where triple-digit decibels shook the walls and shirts were the first thing cast away, and then good sense, and finally the trick you took home the night before. No, this bar was favored by older and less pretty men. There were pine benches and tables along the walls, pinball machines and pool tables in the back, and a sound system that didn't deny conversation. Most of the men who favored this bar were as down-to-earth as flannel shirts and jeans that didn't sag at the ass.

I ordered a beer and found a relatively quiet corner with a view of the front door. As much as I'd told myself I needed to be around people, I still wanted my own space. I was happy to leave the clumps of happy men to themselves, their animated chatter not grating but something I wasn't ready to do myself. I didn't return smiles directed my way. Nothing new, as I'd always avoided that kind of interaction with strangers except for the moment *my type* flashed their dental work—*How do they get them so white!*—at me, which, of course, usually commenced the rites of the night, ending at my apartment the next morning with the realization that it really was a damned shame that youth was wasted on the young. A lithe, nubile, beautiful body was, I gradually came to understand, no substitute for a brain firing on all cylinders, capable of processing the nuances of one-night stands as opposed to happily ever afters.

Like I said, I'd placed myself where I could see the front door. I watched the comings and goings, seeing the friendly faces of men comfortable with their imperfections—their slight or substantial guts, teeth not *that* white, thinning hair, some features cut from dough rather than granite. It was a good crowd. A comfortable crowd.

I'd just resettled myself in my corner after getting another beer, when the front door opened and *my type* entered. He was young, beautiful, dark hair, and his eyes, even from where I sat, reflected intelligence and kindness. He wore old Levi's and a button-up shirt, the sleeves rolled to his biceps, the color and pattern artsy. He was obviously alone, smiling, and appeared as though he'd never been here before. He gazed around the room with the eyes of someone who seemed to be preserving what he saw for later transcription. He slowly walked to the serving station at the bar, leaned in to the bartender, and ordered what in a few moments I saw was a glass of white wine. He turned with glass in hand, once again surveyed his surroundings, and began walking through the crowd.

I'd not come to the bar with any expectation of meeting someone, much less taking someone home. I didn't know if I was ready for that. But the young man who had just walked in the front door, who'd ordered white wine—*white wine, for Christ's sakes!*—and was now heading my way—he'd already made eye contact with me—was unexpected and a little unnerving. Was I up for this?

He leaned against the wall next to me, took a sip of his wine, continued to look at the crowd, and said, "If I were to paint this scene, I'd probably put in a fireplace and a good old dog. Right there—" He motioned with his wine toward the center of the room. "—because that would complete the story."

"What story is that?"

"The one about this place. I'm Michael." He held his unoccupied hand out to me.

"Sam," I said, taking his hand, knowing this was the first young male flesh I'd touched in a very long time not coated in dust, blood, or sweat—the sweat reeking the offal of fear, the blood evoking panic if it spurted rhythmically, utter gloom if the wound didn't bleed at all.

"This is my first time here," Michael said.

"I thought that was the case."

"Oh?" He looked at my eyes for the first time since leaning against the wall.

"Yeah." His stare was so deep, so knowing, so starkly void of mendacity and anything but concern, intelligence, caring, that for a moment he must have thought I'd swallowed my tongue. I could not speak. I cleared my throat and said, "I guess I've had a lot of practice, uh, reading people."

He again turned and stared at the crowd. "Me too," he said. "I've read you, you know."

It was my turn to say, "Oh?" Yeah, I know. This was kind of a creepy come-on—painting the scene, reading me. But you weren't there. It wasn't creepy at all. It was different but not creepy.

"Yes." Turning back to me, he smiled. "You're just back from a sad place or experience. You're, oh... I guess the right description would be that you're cooling off, trying to get yourself together." He lowered his eyes and looked at my boots, then followed my body with his eyes up my jeans, shirt, then back to my eyes. "You're trying to fit in again."

"Again? Like after that sad place or experience I've come from?"

He nodded. "Yes. That's it. Now, you read me some more."

I shifted myself and turned toward him. "You're just out of college, kind of an artsy-craftsy kind of guy—your shirt does give you away—and you're probably the spoiled child of a rich daddy, you insist that your hair is cut with a razor rather than scissors, and I'll bet those are the same Levi's you started college with."

"Good. Very good," he said. He smiled again, his teeth, yes, too white.

We stood there, both of us turning our gaze back to the crowd. I glanced at him a couple times, looking at his profile, wondering if I could just for a fucking moment set aside all the baggage I'd brought back home from the war and invite him to come over. But what would happen once I'd gotten him there? All that baggage wouldn't just decide to take a little sabbatical while I adored his eyes, his body, his mind, and after removing those Levi's, his ass. I'd learned from the war that courage isn't something you turn on and off. It's cocked and loaded by fear. And there, with Michael standing only inches from me, I acknowledged that I was one pitiful, scared dipshit who'd assumed my little trip to the neighborhood bar would somehow change anything about my life at that particular point of it.

"You don't have a boyfriend either," Michael said.

I looked again at his profile. "No." I shook my head. "I don't."

He looked at me. "Because that's important."

His eyes said he meant what he'd just said. "Of course it is." I wasn't sure if he was telling me that he didn't fuck with guys who had boyfriends or if just the concept of *boyfriend* was what was important.

"I'd invite you over," he said, "but I'm between apartments right now. I'm staying at my father's house, and.... You don't want to come over to my father's house."

"Okay." This boy, this reader of men, this beautiful kid who'd drunk maybe two sips of his wine while I was ready for my third beer, had somehow, some way, managed to pack all my baggage and send it away, telling it to go fuck itself. Courage? Shit, who needs courage to invite a beautiful boy to go home with you? At that moment, I didn't need any. And I did invite him home.

That was the evening we fell in love with each other. No, I take that back. I'd fallen in love with him when he first walked into that bar. That was the first time in a long time that the war had not come between me and life itself. Michael became my life that day. And if I regret anything about those first hours we got acquainted—body, mind, and soul—it is that I didn't take pictures. Yeah, that night and the following day will forever be preserved in my memory. But how many of us wish we'd taken a few pictures upon meeting the love of our lives for the first time? A lot of us, I bet. Oh, Michael would eventually paint that bar the way he'd found it on that night, adding, as he'd said he would, a fireplace and a good old dog. But still....

THE FACT that Michael was between apartments when we met proved to be fortuitous. Two weeks after we met, he moved into my apartment. He didn't have much furniture, but that which he did have was stuff I'd seen only in magazines and online ads devoted to the tastes of the wealthy. We hauled my junk out and gave it to the VFW. We moved his items in, and I can tell you that a king-sized bed with a mattress manufactured in heaven is about as close to nirvana as a person can get... along with the person you share that bed with. I'm not a Buddhist, but I understood then what they strive for the first time I tried out that bed with Michael in it.

Those first few weeks together, I told Michael about myself, described my childhood, family, education, and my military service. He told me very little about his family and his childhood, and when I pressed him about those things, he'd change the subject.

"You're my family now," he said, and I was content for the time being to leave it at that.

The third night we slept in that big bed, I woke up, and the nightmare I'd been having followed me to wakefulness. I scrambled out of bed, grabbed my .45 from the bedside drawer, and stood in the corner, my concentration intent on the djellaba-clad figures with no faces and red eyes that had followed me home.

"Sam." It was my name, coming from the most comforting voice I'd ever heard, as I jerked my weapon from one dark corner of the room to the other. "Sam," the voice said again. As the demons faded, the loveliest face I'd ever seen in my life appeared just a few feet in front of me. "Sam, it's Michael."

"Michael."

"Yes. There's no one else here. Just us, Sam."

I felt a gentle touch take the weapon out of my hand and another hand placed on my chest. I came back to the world then, seeing Michael in front of me, knowing what had happened, and I was ashamed of myself.

He was naked, and so was I. I pulled him to me, my hand on the back of his head, and we kissed. "I'm so sorry," I said.

"It's all right. You had a nightmare."

He backed up a bit, standing there in front of me, my weapon held at his side, his body exposed as I imagined an angel must appear to some. "Here," I said, reaching for my weapon. "Let's put that away before you shoot yourself in the foot or something."

"I'm not afraid of guns." He turned and put the .45 back in the drawer. "C'mon. Let's go back to bed."

We did go back to bed that night, and he was still holding me when we woke up in the morning. Before I crawled out of bed, I revisited what had happened the night before. His reaction had been too calm, too… knowing. I wanted to pursue that, but it would be a while before that happened.

CHAPTER NINE

I MANAGE to get Michael's truck up Cathy's unplowed drive, a half mile of nine inch or more deeply piled snow. The faint depressions in the snow made by her Jeep are still visible but fading fast. I make a mental note to talk to Michael about his four-wheel drive slipping on and off, besides the fucked-up heater and windshield wipers. Cathy's got her porch light on, and the falling snow reflects the light and appears as a gentle cascade. Otherwise her house is only a shadow surrounded by the pointed spires of Douglas fir trees that rise blackly to points sixty feet above the ground. The door opens the moment I get out of the truck, and Cathy is standing on the porch.

"You didn't find her?" Cathy says, her voice not raised but carrying easily over the immense quiet of the night.

"No, I didn't." I step onto her porch, she turns, and I follow her into the house.

It's a moderately sized cabin, loaded with pine furniture and Indian blankets of vivid colors hung on the walls and over the two love seats in her parlor. She's got a nice fire going in her woodstove on one side of the room. There's a large fireplace on the other side of the room, the firebox covered with a metal sheet. Cast-iron stoves are more efficient when it's this cold.

"You want something to drink?" Cathy asks as I sit down on one of the love seats.

"You got bourbon?"

"Does a cow shit?" She walks into the little side room off the parlor and shortly returns with two tumblers a third full. She hands me one and then sits on the other love seat.

"I stopped at the café. Everything looks fine."

"Yeah, like I told you, I checked it out too. Where could she be, Sam?"

"She's using that shitty Subaru you used to drive?"

"That Subaru will outlive you. Yes, I've let her use it since she moved in with me."

"You don't think she could have just slid off the road somewhere?"

"No, I don't." She takes a sip and looks out the tall windows behind the woodstove, the vista now draped by the blackness of the night. "When I was coming back from the café, I stopped at every spot on the road where that could have happened. Didn't see a thing."

I take my first sip and am happy she keeps the good stuff on hand. I feel the little fire in the bourbon slide itself down to my stomach. "Good stuff."

Cathy stands up and puts her hands on her hips. I hadn't noticed when I first came in, but she's actually wearing sweatpants. I believe it's the first time I've seen her in anything except shorts.

She takes a few steps toward the windows and turns to me. "She's a good girl, Sam. She wouldn't just take off without telling me."

"I know she is. Let me ask you something that's been on my mind, though. When she first came up here? You know, when she told you about those two guys who just up and left her in town? You ever get any more of that story?"

"Oh, bits and pieces." She drops her hands from her hips, sits back down, and takes another sip of her drink. "What I gather is that they were all going to go to Las Vegas. She met them somewhere in Denver, and.... She didn't realize they wanted more than just a traveling companion."

"She was that naive?"

"Apparently."

I think about what I'm going to ask, knowing how strange it's going to sound. Even I think it's ridiculous, but what the hell. "You ever get the feeling she's interested in the, uh, occult? Witchcraft, maybe?"

She looks at me with that stare I know so well. "You gotta be shittin' me."

"Just thought I'd ask."

We both take another sip of our drinks. Cathy again stands up, walks to the stove, grabs a poker from the rack, and then stirs up the fire. She leaves the firebox door open, steps to the pile of fir and aspen logs to the side of the stove, snatches one up, and throws it into the box.

"You going to tell me why you asked that stupid question?" she says, closing the firebox door. She walks back to the love seat.

"Someone or something killed one of Joe Parsons's dogs. He thinks it was a ritual killing, and I think it was.... Hell, I don't know what I think it was, but it was something I'd never seen before. Rick Williams took a look at it too, and he's as stumped as I am."

"What happened to the dog?"

"Clean cut up the chest. Took the heart out, scraped off the dog's pads. And the back of the head was opened up and some of the skull was taken. Other things about it are weird too. But it wasn't a typical kill you'd see with a lion, bear, or bobcat attack."

"Jesus. Okay." She nods and says, "I understand why somebody might think it was ritualistic, but why would you think Missie had anything to do with it?"

"I didn't say she did."

"C'mon, Sam. Why would you ask that question? Into the occult?"

"Just touching all the bases." I know my response isn't going to appease her. And it doesn't.

"No. There's something else. You think her blue hair is reflective of her inner hag? That she's a witch, for Christ's sake?"

"Sorry I brought it up."

She finishes her drink and sets it down on the coffee table in front her a little too forcefully. "So what are you going to do? Did you put out an APB or whatever the fuck it's called on the Subaru yet? You get a search party organized? You—"

"Cathy, it's only been—" I glance at my watch. "—what? Going on three hours? Hell, she might have just headed for some ski lodge where there are always horny kids looking for—"

"Goddammit, Sam. She's not like that. She'd tell me if she was going somewhere. She's got only one friend near town that I know of. I don't know who it is, and I haven't pressed her to tell me. And she's not horny. We're.... She and I are...." She stands up, rubs her hands together, and picks up her glass. "You want another one?"

I don't tell myself I told you so, but my suspicions about her and Missie's relationship have been confirmed, though she didn't come right out and say it. "No. Thanks, but I probably ought to go. Oh," I say, remembering the black bag I picked up at the café. "I've got something I want you to take a look at. I'll be right back."

I go outside, grab the bag, and come back in. She's sitting on the love seat again, and she's refilled her glass, this time about half full.

I set the bag on the coffee table in front of her. "Found this behind the café, just at the edge of the tree line."

"It's hers," Cathy says, reaching for it. "She kept her.... Oh, it's an antique watch she thinks came from her great-grandmother or something. She kept it in here. What the hell is this?" she says as she opens up the strings on top and looks inside.

"I don't know."

"And you found it outside the café?"

"I did."

She dips her thumb and forefinger inside and presses the powdery substance between them. She pulls her finger and thumb out and rubs them together. "It's powder. Is it cocaine or something?"

"Haven't tested it yet, but I don't think it is."

She pulls her hand against her sweats, wiping off the residue. "Jesus, Sam. The fucking watch was a cheap reproduction, but she loved it. Why...? Who...? Something's happened, Sam. Something bad." She stands up, quickly walks to where her coat hangs on the wall, and pulls it off the hook. "I've got to get back out there."

I've never seen this expression from Cathy, but I imagine it would be the look Pooh would show if Christopher Robin disappeared one day, leaving his left shoe behind.

I walk over to her and grab the coat. "We don't know that, Cathy. I'll keep working on it, and I'll pull somebody out of bed to help me. You don't need to go out there again. Hell, we'll be looking for two instead of one."

She lets me rehang her coat on the hook. "You'll notify the state patrol? If you find the car, you'll find her."

"Yes, I'll do that." I step back to the coffee table, bend down, and pick up the black bag. "I want to have this analyzed. I'll see if the CBI will do it. Probably send Digger down to Denver with it tomorrow." I secure the ends tight around the top, then put it in my coat pocket.

"CBI?"

"Colorado Bureau of Investigation."

"Damn." She shakes her head, and I swear I can see her eyes beginning to tear up.

"Okay," I say, feeling the urge to put my arm around her shoulders. I would do that, but she wouldn't like it. Sentimentality is something she doesn't do well. Or maybe she does. "I'll get on this. You call me if you hear from her."

"I will," she says as we walk to the front door together.

Just before I open the door, I remember the picture I took of the boot tracks outside the café. I pull out my cell and find the picture. "Do you recognize this boot pattern?"

She looks at the picture and shakes her head. "No. Why?"

"I found them in back of the café."

"Sorry. I'm not one to memorize boot patterns. Do you think it might be hers?"

"Don't know. She does have a pair of boots?"

"Of course she does. She wears them all the time."

"Okay. Just doing my job." When I open the door, the rush of frigid air against us speaks of an intensifying storm. She leans in and gives me a kiss on the cheek.

"Find her, Sam," she says.

I remember my mother's word, flabbergasted, and now know what that word means. Cathy kissed me. *I'll be damned.* All I can do is give her a nod and step off the porch.

I START Michael's truck, reach under my coat, and pull out my cell. I've got one bar, and I know that's good enough. I punch his number, and he answers immediately.

"Sam," he says. "Did you find her?"

"No, not yet. I'm at Cathy's, but I've got to go into the office for a while. You okay with that?"

"Yes, of course. Sam?"

"Yeah?"

"You found something," he says, and it's not a question.

I remember my earlier angst when I told him about Joe's dog. But I can't lie to him. "Yes, I did."

There's a moment of silence on the line, and then he says, "Okay. Just be careful. I love you."

"And I love you. Don't wait up."

"I might."

I end the call, then turn the truck around. I guess I'm no longer surprised with what Michael knows or sees that he shouldn't be able to. And as I navigate through the blowing snow down Cathy's drive, I desperately hope I won't find a picture he painted weeks ago of a young girl with blue hair, the scene a tragic one, or even able to be interpreted as tragic. No, I don't hope for that at all.

CHAPTER TEN

NOW, AS I drive to town, the left headlight on Michael's truck seems to have sagged a bit, shining worthlessly at a point right in front and slightly to the left of the front bumper. I'll add that to the list. Or maybe I'll just leave the truck at Skip's when I pick up Brunhilda tomorrow. I pull my cell out and scroll down my contacts and find Digger's number. It has to be Digger. Jim Harris has already put in his retirement papers, and Don Hoag has kids, a wife, and he lacks an appreciation for getting called out in the dead of night. I don't have any bars right now and put the cell back in my pocket.

A gust of wind shakes the truck, and the whiteout it creates in front of me is total. I gently apply the brakes, inching the truck along, and keep just to the left of the reflective poles the county commissioners had installed last winter—they'd approved it during one of the few enlightened moments of their incumbency—on the main road that connects to most of the properties up here. Besides that, with only the right headlight working properly, I know from experience only an idiot would drive this road in these conditions in an unworthy vehicle. I imagine telling Michael that his truck is not roadworthy, and I know what he'd say: *It's worthy enough for me.* Hell, that's probably why he loves this piece of crap. For him, imperfections are not imperfections at all. They're *unique attributes*. Those would be his words.

The county road becomes Main Street. Yes, like just about every other small town in America our main street is Main Street. I decide to go back to the café and take another look at the area where I found the bag. I pull alongside the café, turn off the engine, and once again take a look at my cell. Two bars. I dial Digger's number and wait for him to pick up. When he does, I tell him to come into work.

"Now?"

"No, next Thursday."

"Okay. But why are you telling me now? Oh," he says with an embarrassed laugh. "Okay, Sheriff. About a half hour. Will you be at the office?"

"Probably. If I'm not there, meet me at the café."

"What's going on?"

"Missie's missing."

"Shit. What happened?"

"If I knew that, she wouldn't be missing. Just get over here."

I put the cell back in my pocket, grab my flashlight, and get out of the truck. I start to head to the back of the café and then remember there's a light on the back porch, and I've got to go inside again to turn it on. I turn around and walk to the rock where I'd earlier found the key. The rock should be covered with snow, but it isn't, and it's recently been moved. The depression in the ground where the green box was is visible, and there's only a dusting of snow over it. I shine my flashlight over the area, and there's the green box, open and empty on the porch, and the front door too is halfway open. I unsnap the leather flap over the butt of my .45, then pull the weapon out and climb the stairs.

"This is the sheriff," I holler, staying behind the open door, with only my arm and part of my head exposed as I shine the flashlight into the interior and peek in. "Make yourself known!"

I hear nothing except the gusts of wind across treetops. A rush of cold air finds the open door and lightly blankets the floor inside with snow. I inch back from the doorway and kick the door fully open. Nothing. Not a sound. My caution is born from my experience in hell. Hearing nothing in an enclosed space proved more times than not to be the first warning that something was indeed there and that that something was intent on ending my life. I turn off my flashlight, wait a moment for my eyes to adjust, then back up to the inside wall. I inch toward the hallway to the right where I know the light switches are. I reach my hand over and flip up all the switches at once.

The first thing I notice is wetness on the floor, clearly from boots or shoes that not long ago stepped from the snow outside. I keep my weapon raised and pointed to my front as I check both the women's and men's bathrooms. I then walk slowly into the kitchen, prepared for whatever might appear before me. The wet footprints on the floor are here as well. At the far corner of the kitchen is a bookshelf kind of structure where Cathy's staff puts their personal belongings—purses, coats, whatever—

when they show up for work. There's some stuff on the floor in front of it that I don't remember seeing from when I was here earlier. I walk over to it, bend down, and there's a pair of knitted gloves, a candy bar, a Tampax, and some loose change spread out on the floor. Standing up, I look at the bookshelf, and there are masking tape labels here and there with employee names printed on them. The space that reads *Melissa* is empty. Sure, I conclude, the stuff on the floor belongs to Missie, and a brain surgeon would also conclude, as I have, that somebody was looking for something on that shelf, and they were in a hurry doing it.

I walk over to the back door, flip the porch light on, and go outside. I raise my .45 again, turn on my flashlight, then take the stairs carefully, one at a time, stopping each time I place both feet on a step.

"Sheriff's department," I holler at the black wall of the tree line. I shine my flashlight over there, and the recesses in the trees become eerie and, as someone might relate in a mystery novel, foreboding. The wind is howling through the tops of the trees, the snow is falling almost sideways, and the gusts of wind are creating little scenes of perceived movement within the recesses.

I reach the ground and walk to the tree line where I found the bag. The boot tracks I'd seen there earlier are gone. The snowpack is maybe an inch more than when I was here earlier. I walk the tree line, keeping my flashlight pointed to the ground. Nothing. I walk back to the stairs, and as I climb them, I put my weapon back in the holster. Back into the kitchen, I look around and find the place where Cathy keeps her food storage bags. I pull one out, then put everything I found on the floor inside it and seal it up. One last tour of the dining room and I turn off the lights.

As I go out the front door, I check to see if the key might be in the lock. It isn't. I press the door lock button on the inside and pull the door closed. Looking up the street, I see Digger's Cherokee outside the office. Good. I'll put his ass to work.

WHEN I step into the office, Digger is hovering over the little table where Mary keeps the coffeepot. He startles a bit when I come in and then gives me one of his sweet smiles.

"Hey, Sheriff. Trying to figure out this coffeepot. Thought I'd make some before I went up to the café. You find Missie?"

"Not yet. Fill the reservoir with water," I say as I walk to my office. "Put one of those little paper funnel things on that black thingy on top, and then put the grounds in the paper funnel."

"Yeah. I think I figured that out," he says. "Then what?"

I place the plastic bag I took from the café on my desk, then take off my coat and drape it over my chair. "Turn it on."

"Oh," I hear him say to himself.

He appears in the doorway as I ease down in my chair. "Have a seat. Gotta make a phone call." I dial our landline at the cabin. Michael again answers before the first ring is finished. "I'm at the office. You okay?"

He tells me he is, and I tell him I'll be another hour or two.

"No progress, then?" he asks.

"Well, nothing concrete. But Digger's here, and we're going to start a missing person protocol."

"She's not missing."

I'm not surprised that my stomach turns once when he says that, and I feel just an instantaneous rush of sadness. "What?"

"I mean she's nearby. I don't know where, but I feel…."

When he doesn't continue, I know the sadness I'd just felt is for him and not for her. Why the fuck can't he turn those whispers off! "I think she's nearby too, Michael. Please don't be obsessing about this. We'll find her."

There's silence on the line for a moment, and then he says, "All right. Just stay safe. Okay?"

"Sure I will. Got Digger here to keep me that way."

"Okay. I'll be waiting for you."

I decide not to argue with him. He should just go to bed, but I know he won't do that. "Just a couple more hours."

We say our good-byes, and I hang up the phone.

"Michael okay?" Digger says.

"Yes." I nod. "He's fine." I take a moment to push Michael to the side, putting him in that place in my mind and heart where demons have no power and his peculiarities settle into quietude. I look at Digger, see his pretty face, and hope the woman he eventually finds for himself will be as uncomplicated as he is.

"So what's going on?" he asks.

"Well," I say. I take him through what my night has consisted of for the past three hours. I tell him to call Cathy and get a complete description of Melissa—full name, birthdate, prior addresses, the whole nine yards of everything Cathy can tell us about her—nail down the license number of Cathy's Subaru, and then get on the computer with the CBI and have them issue an Amber Alert. "Oh, and tell Cathy to e-mail you a picture of Missie."

"Might need some help with the Amber thing," he says as he stands up.

"I'll be right here, Digger."

"Okay. You want some coffee?"

"Sure."

"Cream? Sugar?" he hollers.

"Black."

He comes back with a cup of coffee that I know by just looking at it is the result of probably twice as many grounds being dumped into that little paper funnel than ever should be. I thank him, and as he walks back to his desk, I pour a little of the coffee into my trash can and then grab the half-full bottle of water I'd left on my desk probably two days ago and pour some of that in the cup. I take a sip. It's still strong, but it hits the spot.

I hear Digger talking to Cathy on his landline. I wait for my computer to boot and then google *satanic ritual killings of dogs*. No, I'm not convinced that Joe Parsons knows what he's talking about, but I am curious, and Google is a good place to start. What pops up is a string of posts about two Nacogdoches Texas teenagers, a boy and a girl, who skinned an old dog and took out his heart. *Of course, it would be Texas.* They also killed a cat and some kittens. I delete the word *satanic* from the search and get a whole string of disgusting reports about suspected ritualistic killings of dogs. I scan a few of the stories and confirm what I already know: there are more than a few sick sonsabitches in this world who have lost their souls to the dark and bottomless abyss. I don't think what happened to Joe Parsons's dog had anything to do with some asshole's perception of what the so-called dark arts demanded of him or her. These subhuman sonsabitches are the ultimate of amateurs when it comes to.... Well, I'll say magic, and by that, I mean things we will never understand and can never untangle. I get out of Google and think a moment about Michael and all those whispers his old soul perceives. And as I think about that, I know if I'm ever able to get a handle on what happened to Joe's dog, I'll need Michael's help to do that. But at what cost to Michael? Hell, he probably already knows what happened.

"Whoa!" I hear Digger say, and the next instant he's standing in my doorway waving a piece of paper. "I know where her car is!"

"Where?"

"At the trailer park."

"Okay," I say, standing up. I walk from behind my desk. "Let's go."

CHAPTER ELEVEN

DURING OUR first year together, Michael and I settled into what would become a routine necessitated by the various aspects of domesticity. We had to pay the rent and utilities, buy food, clothing, and save enough to go out to dinner, see a movie every once in a while, and sometimes go to a club where, upon our return, we both understood the comfort of not having to perform alone in that milieu anymore.

Although Michael had insinuated during our first year with offhand remarks that his family had provided well for his future, I never pursued it and insisted we keep within our budget. He agreed, and we did just that. Besides, I had some money socked away from my military service, but I'd already identified what I wanted to spend that on and kept it in the bank.

I'd gotten a position with a security firm in Denver, my degree in criminal justice relevant only for resume purposes, and what I found myself doing for the firm bordered on clerical work. I'd thought about applying to the Denver Police Department but knew I wasn't looking for a career in Denver.

Michael, with his degree in art, found a job dressing store windows in the upscale Cherry Creek Shopping Mall. He was good at it and found it fulfilling. Me? No, I wasn't fulfilled. My job was just a stopgap until I was able to settle my emotional side down to what most folks thought was normal, a place where I could push the war away from me without anyone knowing I was doing that.

IT WAS Christmastime at the end of that first year when Michael said I ought to come and look at the windows he'd dressed, and I thought that was a good idea. We drove to Cherry Creek, parked in the cavernous three-tiered lot, and I followed him inside the mall.

Clumps of children stood before the display windows, most silently awed by what they were seeing, some with their little fingers pointing to one thing or another behind the glass. Michael pulled me closer to the displays, past the parents watching their children's reactions and into the crowd of little people who stared at what was before them as if the world had become magical.

"Right there," Michael said, leaning his head close to my ear, "is the train Santa uses to gather up all the toys his elves have worked so hard to create through the year."

And yes, it was a little red-and-green train with open boxcars piled high with tiny toys, yet to be wrapped, passing little houses where elves waved, their arms moving up and down.

"And there," he said, pointing, "is where the presents are wrapped and loaded into the sleigh."

From a Victorian house covered in gingerbread moldings, elves went in empty-handed and came out carrying wee boxes with bows, which they tipped into Santa's sleigh. Then on a track of some sort I couldn't see, the elves returned to the house and loaded up again. Reindeer lolled around the sleigh, and Santa stood atop it, dressed in red velvet, nodding his head up and down.

"How on earth did you do that?" I asked.

"Well," he said, gently pulling me with him away from the window. "I made all the figures and their clothes, but I enlisted some help from some friends."

"Who?"

"College friends. One is now in grad school, studying mechanical engineering. The other two were, *are* computer geeks."

"It must have cost a fortune."

"Not quite, but almost. The store wasn't willing to be that lavish, but I...."

"You what?"

He smiled. "I took care of it. C'mon, let me show you the other windows I did."

ON OUR way home from the mall, we passed a Christmas tree lot that had very few trees left. "Oh," Michael said. "Let's stop. We haven't gotten our tree yet."

He'd known since the first Christmas we'd been together that I wasn't really into Christmas trees and all the work it takes to adorn them and the eventual mess they create.

"Christmas isn't the happiest time for me," I'd told him and repeated that sentiment as we drove past the lot.

"But that was before me. And you enjoyed it last year."

"I guess I did to a point."

"So go around the block and let's pick one out."

We did go into that lot, saw the slim pickings, but Michael would not be dissuaded. "This is the perfect one," he said, standing before a pitiful spruce that was beginning to droop.

"Michael, it's almost dead, just like the one we had last year."

"Yes, it is. That's why we have to take it. It's dying, Sam," he said, turning his face to me.

"This sounds familiar." I looked at him, his eyes, and knew that what I'd come to know about him over the past year was who he was, a young man uncompromised by rational arguments when it came to what he believed was important. At that moment, that pitiful excuse for a Christmas tree, just like our first Christmas, had become his raison d'être, his sole purpose on earth for living at that particular moment, and I could not, no, I *would* not refuse him that.

"Okay," I said. "But I don't know where we put the ornaments."

"I know where they are, and we'll make some more if we don't have enough," he said as he picked up the tree.

AFTER WE'D decorated the tree, not putting the heavier ornaments on the limbs because the tree was so fatigued, sadly drooping, we exchanged gifts, sitting on the floor in front of the tree. I gave him a picture book of scenes from the Colorado mountains. He gave me a small box with a tiny replica of an adobe house inside.

"Thank you, dear," I said. "Did you make this?"

"Yes, I did. It means something too."

I waited for him to go on, but he didn't. "And what does it mean?"

"We're going to Taos next month to get married. That's what the B&B looks like where we're going to stay."

I wasn't expecting this, of course, and stared at him for a moment without saying anything. Well, I thought, yes, why not? "Okay."

He smiled. "I don't even have to ask you if you'll marry me?"

"You already know the answer."

"I do. And the book is lovely," he said, picking it up from the floor. He flipped through it, then closed it and rested it in his lap. "When are we going to move to the mountains?"

"When we find a place we like."

"Good plan."

"Best Christmas ever, Michael Bellomo."

"I agree, Sam Daly."

AT THE end of January, we drove to Taos, spent three days exploring the area, and on the fourth day, we married in the great room of a B&B not far from Arroyo Seco with the Sangre de Cristo Mountains framed in the great room's tall windows.

And it was there, the night before we married, that Michael told me something of his childhood and his family. It wasn't much, but it did explain a lot. That first year had been revelatory, not only exposing what was for me the essential epiphany of just how much one person can love another but also revealing that Michael was a soulful man caught in a spiritual darkness that at times defied any sense I could make of it. Defied too the amazing brightness of his presence in my life.

We spent many weekends of our second year together traveling the immense spread of the Colorado Rockies, stopping in small towns, exploring the valleys, hiking the trails, all of it done with the thought we'd know where we wanted to live when we saw it. And we did eventually see it on one Sunday morning in July. The countryside spread out from Gunderson Junction in Pine County beckoned us both as a loving mother, her arms spread, her smile effusive.

"Come," she said. "Come, and stay awhile," she whispered.

I would, though, later have occasion to pause and wonder if that loving mother had forsaken us, as if she'd put us to bed, turned off the light, and closed the door without ridding our closet of monsters.

CHAPTER TWELVE

"AS SOON as Cathy gave me a description of the car, I knew I'd seen it," Digger says, his excitement effusive. "I'd looked out my window at home earlier, and right there, right across the drive was a red Subaru that I'd never seen before."

He's got the Cherokee cranked, and I almost tell him to slow down as we approach the curve that will take us by Skip's Garage then to the highway. But I don't tell him that and instead ask him how he knows it's Melissa's car. I hold on to the door handle as he manages to take the curve without slowing as much as he should have, the rear end fishtailing a bit, but we're okay.

"I just know it is, Sheriff."

"When we get there, just stop at the entrance to the court. We'll walk in."

"Right. Don't want to spook anybody."

He slides to a stop at the stop sign, turns right onto the highway, and we're only about a half mile from the trailer park.

The entrance to the trailer park has a wrought-iron welcome arch over it that reads Vista View, and it's still strung with Christmas lights that are on, but half the string is burned out. They weren't working the day the management put them up, and they hadn't yet bothered to fix that. I suppose you could call the management of the park half-assed, and the park is too. Every time I pass it, I wish Digger could find somewhere else to live. And there's no vista to view at Vista View.

Digger slows the Cherokee and makes the turn into the park.

"Just pull over here," I tell him as we clear the welcome arch. He does that, turns off the lights, and then points to the red Subaru sitting outside a trailer about halfway down the road.

"See it?"

"Yeah. Is there access to the back of the trailer?"

"Yes. Along the tree line."

"You go ahead and start down that way, and I'll approach from the front. Don't do anything until I say. You got your flashlight?"

He reaches for the loop on his belt where his flashlight should be, and it's not there. "Guess I left without it."

I reach into my coat pocket and pull out my flashlight. It's only about six inches long, but it's got a helluva powerful beam. "Here, take this. There's enough light out front for me. We bought five of these. Didn't you get one?"

He takes the little flashlight and studies it for a moment. "I prefer the bigger one," he says. "Never know when you're going to have to knock somebody upside the head."

I try to see Digger, sweet Digger, actually knocking somebody upside the head with a flashlight, and the image just doesn't present itself. "Okay. Just get in there behind the trailer and wait until I tell you to do something."

"Will do," he says, opening up his door and stepping out of the Cherokee.

I step out too and wait a minute until he walks toward the tree line. Once he gets there, I start walking toward the Subaru.

After walking only about ten steps, I hear the creak of a door opening, and then a phlegmy male voice intones, "What the hell are you doing?"

There to my right, on the tiny porch of his trailer, is Merle Stacy, the manager of the park, and he's holding what I believe is a silver-plated .44 caliber revolver out from his body, his white hair spiked up, his terry cloth robe a light blue color but not tied around his bulging gut. I can see his white T-shirt and jockey shorts as a gust of wind catches the flaps of his robe.

"Merle, it's Sheriff Daly. Lower your weapon."

He pulls his glasses from the robe's pocket and puts them on. "That you, Sheriff?"

"I just told you it was. Now, lower your weapon."

"Oh. Sure," he says, doing what I'd told him to do. "What's goin' on?"

I walk toward him and stand just outside his little yard. "You know anything about that red Subaru over there?"

"No, I don't. Prob'ly one of Karen's friends come to visit."

"Karen who?"

"Hargrove. You know, Judge Corwin's clerk."

"Thought she lived with her husband out on Eagle Drive?"

"She did 'til she moved in here less than a week ago."

I look over at the trailer. Digger is back there, sending me Morse code or something, flashing his light on and off from the tree line. "Well, I'm just going to check it out. Might be a stolen car. You go on back inside."

"I could help, Sheriff." Merle takes a step off his porch.

"No, don't do that, Merle. Just go on back inside, and I'll let you know what we find out."

"I'll be watchin' out the window."

"Okay." I nod and watch him step back into his trailer and shut the door behind him. Then all the lights in his trailer go off, and I see him appear before his window. He gives me a wave, and I again walk toward the Subaru.

I know immediately that it is indeed Cathy's piece-of-shit-series but, as she says, *reliable* old car when I stand beside it. The porch lamp on Karen's trailer gives me enough light that I can see what's inside the car, and there doesn't appear to be anything interesting in there. I try the door handle. It's locked. I decide to see if Karen is in the trailer.

The waist-high fence outside of Karen's trailer has, probably long ago, fallen onto the ground, but there's still an upright gate there that I step around and then walk the few steps to the door on the side of the trailer.

Digger again flashes his light at me, and I raise my hand and flap it a couple of times, hopefully communicating to him that he should just hold on a minute.

I knock on the door. There's some shuffling behind it, and I knock again. "Sheriff's department," I say.

"Just a minute."

I hear a woman's voice from inside. I wait a minute, and then the door opens up just a few inches.

"Sheriff," Karen Hargrove says, peeking through the small opening. "What can I do for you?"

"Hi, Karen. This is Cathy's car parked out here, and Melissa was using it. You know why it's here?"

"Missie's inside, Sam."

As Karen opens the door wider, I reach for the aluminum screen door, tug on it, and from up above, a string pulls away from the frame, and I get a faceful of what I know are dried juniper berries. Karen sees this happen, leans out a little, and looks up at the doorframe.

"What's all that?" she says, as I pull the string away from my face.

"Juniper berries."

"What are they doing up there?"

"Long story," I say, motioning for Digger to come up here. I step into Karen's small parlor. Melissa is sitting on the couch across the room, and her eyes appear as though she's been crying. "Missie, we were worried about you."

Digger comes into the parlor and stands beside me. "Missie," he says, "we were looking for you."

"Sam, Digger," Karen says, pulling out two chairs from under the kitchen table, "why don't you sit down. Can I get you some coffee?"

"No, but thank you, Karen," I say as Digger and I sit down. "You should have called Cathy," I say to Melissa.

"I know, Sheriff," she says, and then she begins to bawl, her hands covering her face. I'm sure she's already had a good cry about something, and Digger, sweet Digger, stands up and walks over to her. He sits next to her and puts his arm around her shoulders.

Karen motions for me to step into the kitchen area. I go in there, and she lowers her voice almost to a whisper. "This has something to do with the guy who used to live here."

"Boyfriend?" I say, remembering Cathy's earlier cryptic admission about her relationship with Melissa.

"No. Maybe. I don't know, Sheriff." Karen shakes her head. "The guy had promised to do something for her, but I guess it didn't work out. And there's an old watch she kept mentioning. It's an heirloom or something. I haven't been able to make much sense of anything. She's really upset."

"Who's the guy?"

"I don't know. He used to live here, and Missie thought he still did. That's why she came here."

"Don't want to get personal, Karen, but why aren't you still out on Eagle Drive?"

She turns her head toward the cupboards and sighs. When she looks back at me, she shakes her head. "Ned and I are just taking some time off from each other. You know how that goes."

I nod, knowing that marriage vows are sometimes broken for good reasons, and besides that, Michael had told me some time ago that Karen was going to leave Ned. Ned was a son of a bitch who Michael described as an evil man.

"Sure I do, Karen. Sorry to hear that, and I hope you can work it out."

We both turn toward the parlor when Melissa again begins to softly wail.

"We'll get her and her car back to Cathy's. I might stop by and see if you can remember anything else about what she said to you. Gotta find out who the guy is too. Merle would know. Right?"

"Oh, sure. I think the guy was an Indian."

I think about the Native Americans who live up here, and I can't immediately place one who used to live in the trailer park. "Okay. That helps. I'll talk to Merle too."

"Missie," I say as I step back into the parlor, "you give Digger your keys. He can drive the car back to Cathy's, and you can ride with me. How's that sound?"

She mumbles something and pulls the keys from her coat pocket and hands them to Digger.

"Go ahead and get started, Digger. I'm going to call Cathy, and we'll follow you up there."

Digger stands up, hands me the keys to the Cherokee, and walks to the door. "You'll be okay, Missie. I guarantee it."

Melissa manages to thank him. He opens the door, but before he steps out, I ask him if he posted the Amber Alert.

"Didn't have time to, Sheriff."

"Okay. See you in a bit," I say and watch him open the door and step out.

"Can I use your phone, Karen?"

"Sure," she says. "It's right there on the end table."

"You feel up to talking to Cathy?" I say, walking to the landline and picking up the receiver.

"I guess," Melissa mumbles, wiping the back of her hand against her eyes, then stands up.

I hand the receiver to her. "You dial. I don't know the number by heart."

She dials the number and then turns her body away from Karen and me. I can't really hear what she's telling Cathy, but she starts to cry again and then hands the receiver to me.

"She wants to talk to you," she says, catching her breath in a sob.

I tell Cathy that Digger's driving the Subaru back and that I'll bring Missie back with me. She asks me what the hell happened, and I tell her I don't know.

I thank Karen, and so does Melissa. I follow Melissa outside and help her walk to where we left the Cherokee. As we pass Merle Stacy's trailer, he steps out onto his porch.

"Everything all right?" he says.

"Just fine, Merle." I stop and tell Melissa to go ahead and get in the car. I turn to Merle. "Who used to live in that trailer? Before Karen?"

"Stan Rivers," Merle says. "He worked for some tree company. You know, clearing dead stuff, chipping, that sort of thing."

"He an Indian?"

"Looked like one. Don't really know. Paid his rent on time and kept to himself."

"Thanks, Merle."

As I drive Melissa back to Cathy's, she says very little that would explain what has happened. Her tears have dried up, and she keeps her head turned slightly to the side window, looking out at the night with no moon. The snow has stopped falling, and I can see some stars, which means the low clouds have passed over us. It won't be the storm I was expecting, but it will be a very cold night.

Digger is waiting for me at Cathy's, and when Melissa gets out of the Cherokee, he gets in. I drive back to the trailer park, drop him off, and then head for home.

CHAPTER THIRTEEN

MICHAEL OPENS the door as I step onto the porch. "You're back," he says, standing aside as I walk into the cabin. He closes the door behind me. "Did you find her?"

"Yes, we did. She'd gone to the trailer park where Digger lives." I take off my coat and hat, hang them up, and then unsnap my holster and hang it on the hook. As I walk into the parlor, I notice that Michael isn't following me. I look back, and he is standing there in the mudroom looking at my coat. *Shit!* I'd had that black bag in my coat pocket ever since I'd left Cathy's place. "C'mere," I say, "I need a kiss."

He turns his attention from my coat and walks into the parlor smiling, his arms reaching out for me. "But why was she there? Why didn't she call Cathy?" he says, putting his arms around my waist.

"I don't know." I put my hands on the back of his head and lean in for a kiss. "But she's back home now." I raise my head and look into his eyes. "You're beautiful, Mister Bellomo."

"And you're probably hungry?" He drops his hands from my waist and walks toward the kitchen.

"Sure. What you got in mind?" I feel the heat coming from the nice fire he built. I take the few steps toward it, turn my back, and savor the warmth it gives off.

"I could fry some eggs, or we could have some cheese and crackers and wine."

"No, don't cook. The cheese and crackers are fine. I'd like some bourbon, though."

"You want ice?"

"No. Too cold for ice."

He comes back into the parlor with a small serving plate holding the round crackers I like and white and yellow cheese. He sets it down on the coffee table in front of our couch, then returns to the kitchen for the drinks.

I sit down and hope to hell what's in my coat pocket doesn't become the topic of our conversation. I don't know for sure, but I suspect he, oh, *sensed* its presence or something when I walked in the front door. *Sensed its presence. Jesus.* I shake my head as he comes back in with the drinks.

"What are you shaking your head for?" He sets the drinks on the coffee table, then sits next to me.

"Nothing other than that I love you about as much as...."

"Yes," he says when I don't finish my sentence, lifting his glass of red wine and holding it out to me.

I pick up my drink and lightly clink his glass. "I was trying to think of something I love as much as you, and I couldn't think of anything."

"Good save," he says, taking a sip.

I take a sip of my drink and know without really thinking about it that he's going to ask me about my night. And he does.

"When you called me from Cathy's, you said you'd found something."

I set my drink on the coffee table. "No, you told me that I'd found something, and I confirmed that."

"And you brought it home with you."

"Yes, I did." I don't hesitate to tell him this because I know he already knows the answer.

"Can I see it?"

"Michael, I don't want to.... I'm trying my best to understand this thing you've got. This extra set of eyes and ears that seem to transcend... reality—at least *my* reality—and I really, really don't want to—"

"Sam," he interrupts. "How long have we been together?"

I'm surprised by his question, but I answer him. "Well, we're going on five years."

"And in all those years, have we ever really discussed this extra set of eyes and ears, as you say, that I've been blessed with?"

"I might not say blessed, but yes, a couple times we have. You told me about the caul, and then when that freak bear fell on top of Digger and me, you made the painting and.... Yeah, we've talked about it."

He pulls his legs up on the couch and tucks them under him. "And when I told you I couldn't touch your dog tags anymore?"

"Yes. That too."

"Okay," he says, smiling. "But we've never discussed how I filter all of this... weirdness. How I, oh, put everything in its place so that I can function as a—God, how I hate the word—*normal* person."

The occasional funks I've seen him in over the past four years come to mind, but they've never lasted longer than a few days. It occurs to me that, yes, he has to have some way to filter the *weirdness* or I'd be living with a fucking zombie.

"No, we've never discussed that." I take another sip of bourbon as he slips off the couch and then places another log on the fire. He returns to the couch and, once again, pulls his legs under him.

"When I was a kid," he says, "the perceptions I received would sometimes scare me. They really would. But gradually I figured out how to deal with them. It's like I set up some file cabinets in my brain where I could put the scary stuff away. I gave all the drawers locks, and only I had a key. That worked for a while. I'd see something, or perceive something, and I'd quickly shove it into a drawer and lock it down. When I got over the initial fright of it, I'd usually unlock the drawer and take a second look. Those second looks were always more, um, insightful than when the perceptions first hit me. They'd come from nowhere, and I wasn't able to understand them until I locked them away for a while and then eventually pulled them out again."

"You still do that?"

He shakes his head. "No. I learned how to deal with them without locking them down. Now I just shove them way, way back in my mind where I can retrieve them whenever I want."

"What about when you painted that picture of Digger and me under that freak bear? You did that before it happened. What were you thinking when you painted that?"

"Oh, that's something else. That's... I guess it's precognition. Or if you have to call it something, that's what it would be. No, when I was painting that, I was just reflecting what was in my mind. I had no idea that what I had envisioned would actually come true. In real life."

As he leans over to grab his glass, I want to ask him, Why you? Why were you picked to carry what must be a burden no man should have to deal with? "I know you said it all has to do with the caul, but why...? Who? What's the reason for all this? Why?"

"Magic," he says with a smile on his face that makes me smile too.

"So you're not that bothered by it?"

"Of course I am. Especially if it's something you're involved with. But I can't change it, Sam. I've realized it's something I've just got to live with. There's no pill or, God forbid, therapy that's going to take it away. It just is."

I look at the expression in his eyes for a moment and know he's probably right. "So…. If I show you what I brought home…. If it's some weird shit, you're not going to shut down for a month like you did after the freak bear?"

"It wasn't a bear, and you know it. And besides, it wasn't a month. Just a week. I need to see what you brought home."

Yes, he's insistent, and I've learned over the years not to trifle with his insistences. Once he sets his mind to something, I have no power to dissuade him.

I shake my head, stand up, and as I walk toward the mudroom, I stop and look back at him. "Like I said, if this is some weird shit, you'd better not clam up and go into some… mystical reality or something."

"I won't," he says.

I don't believe him, but what the hell…. I walk into the mudroom and grab the bag from my coat pocket, walk back to the parlor, sit down on the couch, and set the bag down on the coffee table. Michael reaches for the bag, and I grab his hand.

"One last chance," I say.

"Sam. Please," he says, rolling his eyes.

I let go of his hand, and he gently picks up the bag, then scoots himself off the couch and sits on the floor between the couch and the coffee table. He sets the bag on the coffee table, undoes the tie strings, and pulls the top open.

"Wow," he says as he leans over and looks inside.

"I'm going to have the CBI analyze it," I say, in spite of my gut hunch that he's going to tell me exactly what it is in about two seconds.

He turns the bag on its side and carefully scooches it a little across the table, and some of what's inside filters out the top. "Wow," he says again.

Okay. I've had about enough of the wows. Just like Cathy did, he pinches some of the powder between his thumb and forefinger. "Please don't say wow again."

He doesn't answer me. He bows his head slightly, and I lean down and look at his face. He's got his eyes closed. "Michael," I say, fearing that he's off into some dark region of his mind.

"It's bones. Human bones," he says. He raises his head and looks at me. "It's ground-up parts of a human and maybe something else. Maybe another animal."

No way not to think about Joe's dog laid out with his pads cut off and the back of his head missing. "Not dog?"

"Maybe. Why would somebody...?"

To describe what I'm feeling right now as eerie would be an understatement. "Let's get that back in the bag."

Michael draws his fingers across the powder on the table and lightly brushes it back into the bag. "There's a meaning to this," he says, his voice flat as if he's talking to himself.

We both stand up and walk into the kitchen where I tear a piece of paper towel from the roll, wet it slightly under the tap, and as Michael washes his hands, I bring it back into the parlor. I wipe up the dust left on the coffee table. Michael kneels down and pulls tight the ties at the top of the bag. He leaves the bag on the coffee table and then stands up and sits back down on the couch.

"You okay?" I say, looking at his profile. He's staring at the windows where there's only blackness.

"Yeah," he says, nodding. He pulls his legs up under him again and turns toward me. "There is some meaning to what's in that bag."

"Well," I say, hoping to hell there is indeed some meaning to it. "Not that it would explain it any better, but maybe it's just the remains of somebody's cremated mother or something. And you don't know what that meaning might be?"

"Magic," he says.

That's the second time he's said that word. I shouldn't have expected less. Of course it's magic. And I'm sure the CBI lab in Denver would come up with the same conclusion: "Sheriff Daly, we're dealing with magic here." Yeah. Right.

CHAPTER FOURTEEN

WHEN MICHAEL and I started searching for available properties near Gunderson Junction, I was surprised at how much land was going for up there. I had my savings, the money I'd socked away for what I knew I'd eventually do—move to the mountains. But as we scoured the listings, my dream started to take on an ugly reality—I couldn't afford it. But as it turned out, Michael could.

We'd hooked up with a real estate broker who, for three weekends in a row, had shown us available properties in the area that for one reason or another either Michael or I didn't like that much. Then, after I'd about resigned myself to putting off my dream for another couple of years, she said there was one last property she wanted to show us. I asked her how much the owner wanted for it, and she gave us a number that was about four times what I figured I could spend.

I told her that was out of the question, but Michael said, "Hey. It won't hurt to just look at it."

We did look, and we both loved it. It was seventeen acres of meadow and forest, the meadow surrounded on three sides by tree lines of Douglas fir, blue spruce, and aspen that dressed the modest hills that rose up on the periphery of the property in a kind of unbroken, magnificent green drape. There was an old structure made of logs at the edge of the meadow that had clearly been abandoned for many years.

"This is it," Michael said.

As much as I loved the place, I couldn't stop thinking about how much they were asking for it and, besides that, the amount of money we'd have to spend rebuilding and adding on to the old cabin that was already there. Not to mention the probability we'd have to dig a new well and put in a new septic system.

"We can't do it, Michael," I told him in front of the broker, who just stood there with a stupid smile on her face. She was a very nice woman whom we'd never seen in anything other than what appeared to be designer outfits, her hair always nicely done, her Lexus always sparkling clean.

"We're just going to take a walk and talk about this," Michael told her when I said we couldn't do it. He grabbed the top of my arm and tugged me along with him.

"Take your time," she said, pulling her cell out of her purse.

"What are you thinking?" I asked him once we got about thirty yards away.

"I'm thinking," he said, "that we can do this. It's perfect."

"It may be perfect, Michael, but we can't afford it."

"Oh, yes we can."

I stopped walking and turned to him. "Michael, we can't afford it."

He smiled and put his hands on my shoulders. "Sam, we can. I've got more than enough to buy this place."

"No." I shook my head. "I've told you—"

"Stop it!" he said, the seriousness of his expression reversing our roles. He became at that moment the elder of us, every hardass commander I'd ever dealt with in Afghanistan, and he'd taken on my father's demeanor, who'd always been more Attila the Hun than Mister Rogers. "I'm going to do this whether you like it or not. This is where I want to live."

I looked at the determination in his eyes for a moment, his voice, also, communicating nothing but the imperative he'd just spoken, and I nodded. "Okay," I said.

"Okay." He smiled.

IT WAS then that I learned a lot more about his family than he'd ever mentioned before. In fact, he took me to meet them about a week before we put in our thirty-day notice to vacate my apartment.

When I'd previously asked Michael about what his father did for a living, he told me his father took care of the family business. He'd never explained exactly what the family business was, but as we drove through town toward his childhood home—this was the first time Michael had ever suggested we go over there—he opened up like a goddamned piñata, telling me that yes, the Bellomo family had been around for a long time, and yes, my vague recollection that the Bellomo name was connected to some past nefariousness was true but certainly skewed by news accounts of it.

"The family," he told me, "has probably lived kind of on the edge of the law for a long time, but all that is in the past, and now everything my father's involved with is legitimate and legal."

"God," I said. "I remember now. They were *the* crime family in Denver going all the way back to Prohibition days. There was gambling, and they were involved in dog and horse racing irregularities, and.... Jesus, Michael. I remember that there were even murders attributed to the Bellomo family."

"Well, yes," he said as we continued west out of the core city, "your memory is correct. But that's all in the past. My family is now into real estate and construction and some liquor distribution centers and.... The family has cleaned up its act, Sam."

I'd long ago decided my life's work would be law enforcement, and I'd fallen in love with a child of the Italian mob, for Christ's sake! I just stared at his profile as he continued to jabber about his ancestry, including the fact that his uncle—the one who'd set up a trust fund for Michael, part of which he'd used to open his storefront and who I'd pegged as queer as a three dollar bill—had never married but had served the family well with his accounting prowess, not to mention the trust fund his father had set up for him, money that he was using to buy the property near Gunderson Junction. All I could do was shake my head and wonder where the hell we were going.

"Westminster," Michael said. "The family moved out of North Denver before I was born. A lot of Italian families moved out here years ago."

Pretty soon he turned off the four-lane road and drove up a side street that rose to a hill topped with a cul-de-sac where a black iron gate stopped further progress. He reached for his sun visor and pressed a button that was clipped to it. The gate began to open.

"Nice security," I said.

"Well—" Michael glanced at me and smiled. "—you never know."

I envisioned rival gangs with tommy guns being momentarily foiled by the iron-gate impediment. "You never know what?"

"Oh," he said, accelerating up the drive to a house I couldn't yet see. "You know."

I shook my head a lot that day. Michael had told me we were going to have dinner with his mother and father, and as the red brick house came into view—three stories with white columns at the entrance—I wondered for a moment how many other secrets he had up his sleeve. Yes, this beautiful man who I'd fallen in love with the first time I'd seen him in that homey bar in Denver had secrets he'd never shared. And it would be a while before I understood to what extent those as-yet-unknown secrets would affect our lives.

CHAPTER FIFTEEN

MICHAEL AND I went to bed, leaving the black bag of powder on the coffee table. He'd gotten quiet after he told me what he thought it was. I tried to lighten the mood a bit, hoping like hell he wouldn't lapse into another weeklong funk. I even grabbed him when he stood up to go to bed, tickling his sides and running my tongue up his neck. But he told me to stop it, slapping at my hands, turning around and giving me a kiss.

"I'm tired," he said, smiling.

I let him go on to bed, hoping his smile was a good sign, that what he'd told me was magic would be explained in the morning as just the effect of the wine we'd had and the eerie presence of the crunched-up bones on the coffee table. But when I woke up, he'd already managed to dress and left the cabin without me hearing a sound.

I GET Mary on my cell and tell her I'll be in the office in about an hour.

"That would make you about an hour and a half late," she says.

"Sorry. I was up late last night."

"I know. Digger told me."

"Did he walk to work? I kept the Cherokee last night."

"Yes. He even made the coffee."

"How'd that go?"

"Don't ask. Where you going?"

"Want to stop at Hank's place for a minute. Did you notice if Michael is at his shop?"

"Just a minute. I'll take a look."

I turn onto Hank's road, and Mary comes back and tells me that Michael's truck isn't parked outside, and the shop looks like it's still closed.

"Okay. You see him around, give me a call."

She says she'll do that. I put my phone back in my pocket, and there's Michael's truck parked near Hank's cabin. It dawns on me that I hadn't checked the coffee table before I left to see if the black bag was still there. It probably wasn't, and I've got a good idea where it's at.

I'm used to Hank stepping out on his porch whenever I visit, but this time he doesn't. I get out of the Cherokee and walk up to the cabin, glancing at the shed where Hank put the freak bear, covered it in cedar ash, and I hope it remains dead.

I knock on the door and turn the handle at the same time. "Hank, it's me," I say, stepping into the cabin and closing the door behind me. And as always, it's hotter than hell in here.

"C'mon in," Hank says from his little parlor.

Hank's in his recliner, and Michael is sitting in the other recliner as Charlie rests his head on Michael's thigh. Charlie has never been what I would call an affectionate animal, at least with me he hasn't, and seeing him and Michael so obviously comfortable with each other strikes me as slightly odd. Charlie raises his head a moment and gives me one of his surly stares, and then again rests his head on Michael's leg.

"How'd you know I'd be here?" Michael says, turning toward me.

"I didn't. Wanted to talk to Hank."

"Get my kitchen chair and sit down with us," Hank says.

I unbutton my coat and take my hat off and lay it on the little round table that I assume is where Hank eats his meals. I grab the chair next to the table and carry it into the parlor. I place it facing Michael's chair, and as I'm about to sit down, Charlie raises his head again and bares his teeth.

"Whoa," I say, pulling the chair back a few inches.

"He's okay," Hank says. "Sit down."

I sit and notice the black bag on the rectangular table between Hank's and Michael's chairs.

"So." I look at Michael. "You brought the bag."

"Yes, I did. And like I said, it does mean something."

Hank and Michael just sit there, both staring at the woodstove, as Michael scratches Charlie's ears. When neither of them says anything more, I nod and say, "You want to share what it means?"

"Witches," Michael says.

I think a moment about that and wait for either one of them to expound a bit about what Michael has just said, and when they don't, I say, "Okay. Witches. Well, that explains everything." And of course I'm reminded that Joe Parsons thought Apollo was killed by Satanists or witches, and I told Michael about that. I kick myself for planting that seed.

Charlie rises to his feet, gives me a serious glance, hobbles around Hank, and leaves the parlor for cooler climes somewhere in the interior of the cabin.

"Maybe it's old," Hank says. "Maybe it isn't. If it isn't, I think we got a problem."

I assume he's talking about what's in the black bag. "Why's that, Hank?"

When Hank doesn't answer, Michael stands up. "I've got to go," he says as he steps around me and heads for the front door.

"Michael," I say.

He stops before he opens the door and turns back to me. "Hank will tell you, Sam. I've just got to go." He opens the door and leaves.

I look at Hank, who's still staring into the fire. "Hank?"

"Michael knew when he touched it," Hank says. "He didn't want to tell you, but he knew."

I've never liked cryptic meanderings from anybody, and though I've come to expect them from Hank, I'm a little pissed off right now with Michael's sudden exit into probably another trip into himself every time he hears those goddamned whispers.

"Dammit, Hank. What the hell is going on?"

Hank scoots up a little in his chair and turns toward me. "Skinwalkers," he says, "can be witches. They make magic sometimes from the bones of human beings. Animal bone too."

"All right. Yes, Michael told me that. But, Hank…. It could be somebody's, oh…. It could just be the remains of somebody's dearly departed. You know? A little keepsake from a cremation." Yes, I realize I've just offered a really creepy explanation for what's in that bag, and so too, I remember where it'd come from. Was Missie really keeping a bag full of bone dust just for the sentimental value of it? "I mean—"

"Nah," Hank says. "It's magic. A witch took some bones from somebody. Gonna curse somebody with them. Give them black tongue. Make them die, maybe."

Okay, then. Freak bears are one thing, but what Hank has just told me takes the cake. "You really believe this?"

"Hah," Hank says. "You better too." He looks back at the fire. "If somebody was carrying this around with them.... If they have some more of this, then somebody is gonna get sick or die, Sheriff."

I hear a slight noise to my left, and Charlie emerges from wherever it is he goes. He stands there looking at me as if emphasizing what Hank has just told me.

"How exactly is the curse... administered?"

"How does the witch do it?"

"Yeah."

"Oh, they just shake some of the powder on the skin or feed some of it to the one they want to kill. Maybe just a splinter shoved into the skin."

I nod. If there's any logic at all to what Hank has said, I suppose the next question has got to pin down whether all witches are skinwalkers or vice versa. "What comes first—the witch or the skinwalker?"

"One and the same," Hank says. "Or maybe not."

"But—" No, I'm not going to pursue this. What the hell kind of conversation are we having? Witches? Curses?

"Something tried to get in the shed," Hank says.

"Where the bear is?"

"John Spotted Elk. Only shed I got, Sheriff."

"How do you know that?"

"Saw scratch marks on the door a couple days ago. Dug in the ground in front of the door too. Probably a skinwalker. Tracks look like a wolf."

Yeah, all I can do is sigh. "Okay, Hank." I stand up and take the black bag. I put the chair back where I found it. I grab my hat and coat from the little round table and put them on. "Michael knows about all this?"

"As much as I do," Hank says. "Prob'ly more."

"Take care," I say as I show myself out, putting the bag in my coat pocket. I walk over to the shed and look for the scratches on the door and the evidence of digging Hank told me about. Yup, there it is.

And the tracks in the snow do look like a canine. A big canine. I follow them back to the tree line as far as I can go. The snow drifts, and the general accumulation gets deeper the higher I go, and then a felled tree stops my progress. Interesting that it appears the wolf or whatever it was came down this way and then went back the same way. There are identical tracks going in opposite directions. I don't know what that means, if anything. I do know that there haven't been wolves up here for a long time.

Hank is waiting for me when I come out of the tree line, and Charlie is sitting on the porch staring at me.

"Whatever it was came from up there." I nod toward the tree line.

"Yeah, I know," Hank says.

"Looks like the tracks of a big dog."

"Think it was a wolf."

"No wolves around here, Hank."

"No, there aren't."

I know what he's thinking. "Skinwalker?"

"Prob'ly."

We look at each other for a moment. I know he's waiting for me to voice my skepticism about the existence of skinwalkers, but I don't do that. Logic still precludes me from believing in such things, but now I'm wondering if logic is the best tool to get to the bottom of what's been going on. Maybe it isn't.

"Okay, Hank," I say as I walk to the Cherokee.

As I get in the SUV, I wonder where Michael went. Did he go home? His shop? Better yet, where has all this taken him in his mind? I guess I'll find out soon enough.

WHEN I get to the office, Digger is sitting at his desk doing nothing as far as I can see, and Mary is working on her computer. Jim Harris, who will retire next week, is also at his desk talking on the phone. They all look at me as I come in the door.

"Where's Don?" I ask Mary.

"He's on patrol duty."

I take my coat off as I walk across the room to my office. "Digger, I've got a job for you."

He follows me into my office and just stands there, watching me hang up my coat and then put my hat on top of the filing cabinet. I take the black bag from my coat's pocket and step behind my desk and sit down. I stare back at him, and he looks down at the floor.

"What's wrong?"

He raises his head and glances at Mary through the window between my office and the outer office. I look out there, and damned if Mary isn't staring at me too.

"What the hell is going on?"

"Ah, well…," he says, looking at me and then glancing at Mary again.

I motion for Mary to come into my office. She shakes her head and comes from behind her desk.

Now they're both standing here. "What is going on?"

"Michael came in a few minutes ago," Mary says.

"And?"

"He said to tell you he's leaving for a few days and that you shouldn't try to find him."

Shit! "Did he say where he's going?"

"No," Mary says.

They both stare at me as if they're waiting for me to either start bawling or go into a mindless rage. "You get that hiring notice done yet, Mary?"

"I'm working on it," she says.

I pick up the black bag. "Digger, I want you to drive into Denver and take this to the CBI for analysis. You get on the phone and tell them you're coming. Tell them it's high priority."

Digger takes a step toward my desk, leans over, and takes the bag from me. "Okay," he says a little meekly.

"Listen," I say, knowing they're both thinking something has happened between Michael and me, something personal that's sent Michael off to lick his wounds or something. "I made a mistake and told Michael what's going on with Missie and the Parsons's dog and…. He even went up to talk to Hank. We all know Michael is… sensitive to things and… I just made a mistake. I should have known better."

"He looked bad," Mary says. "Worried."

"Did you see which way he went?"

"West," Digger says.

There's nothing west except acres of private property and, yes, the mountains, where there's not much of anything except a lot of snow and opportunities to drive off the edge of a poorly marked road.

"Okay. You get going, Digger. Mary, get Don on the radio and tell him to look out for Michael's truck. I'm going to see if Skip's got Brunhilda ready." I stand up and grab my coat and hat as Mary and Digger step out of my office.

"Weather report is bad, Sheriff," Mary says as she steps behind her desk.

"How bad?"

"Two to three feet by tomorrow morning."

"Great." I open the door and button up my coat.

I WALK to Skip's because I want some alone time. I try Michael's number again on my cell and get his message.

I've dialed it three times since I left the office, and this time I do leave a message. "Michael, I need to know where you are. I won't ask you why you've gone wherever you're going, but wherever it is, you better come on back. A storm is due later this evening, and I don't want you in it. Call me. I love you."

The wind starts to kick up, and I pull my hat tighter on my head. There's a vehicle coming behind me, I turn, and it's Don Hoag in the other Cherokee. He pulls alongside me and stops.

"Want a ride?" he says, having opened the passenger window.

"Sure." I get in and raise the window. "Did Mary get ahold of you?"

"Yeah, she did. What's up with Michael?"

"He went to see Hank this morning. God knows what they talked about, but when I got there, the conversation was about witches."

"Witches?"

"Yeah. It's a long story, Don. Just drop me off at Skip's."

"Mary said you wanted me to look for Michael's truck."

"Yeah. He headed west out of town. Don't want him to get stuck out there."

"You two having issues?"

"No, we're not. It's just that.... He takes things too seriously. He's into all that spiritualism crap. And Hank doesn't help the situation."

Don pulls into Skip's lot. "What do you want me to tell Michael if I find him?"

To get his ass home. "Just tell him to give me a call."

"If he's going west, he won't have a signal."

I open the door and step out. "Tell him," I say, leaning into the vehicle, "there's a storm coming."

CHAPTER SIXTEEN

MICHAEL'S PARENTS were mostly gracious the day we had lunch with them, but it didn't end well. Their house was huge, kind of tacky in places where the decorating seemed to have been inspired by *The Godfather* rather than *Better Homes and Gardens*. Some of the furnishings were dark and heavy, including the dining room where the chairs were upholstered in blue velvet. We had spaghetti with meatballs. Best meatballs I've ever had in my life.

Mrs. Bellomo, Michael's mother, was somewhat aloof, appearing to me as someone who knows something you don't and isn't willing to share. She had a little smile on her face the entire time we were there. Maybe a little coquettish. She didn't say much, and when she did speak, she kept her words to a minimum. It was clear, though, where Michael got his looks—his mother was beautiful. A kind of dark beauty who oozed mystery and sensuousness.

His father, on the other hand, projected quiet strength that gave me the impression he was not one to be trifled with. Or maybe that was just me reading a little too much into him from the history I knew about the family. His features were purely Italian—swarthy with a hint of coiled energy, maybe even anger or violence.

"Dad already has a crew working on the cabin," Michael said after we'd sat in the living room, all of us sipping the grappa the heavyset maid or housekeeper or whatever the hell she was had served to us. I didn't even know that Michael had gotten his father involved in the rebuild of the existing structure on the property. I glanced at him with what I hoped was a WTF glare.

"We've got to have somewhere to sleep," Michael said.

"I thought we were going to sort of rough it for a while," I said, trying to smile, though I don't think I pulled it off very well.

"Gotta have a place to shit," his father said, pulling a fat cigar from a wooden box on the coffee table. "Gotta put in septic too. The boys told me there ain't one there," he said, grabbing a large silver lighter in the shape of a lion from the table. He flicked the tail, and a flame popped out of the lion's mouth. "You want a cigar, Sam?"

"Ah, no," I said, watching him exhale a stream of smoke toward the ceiling.

"Diggin' a well too," his father said as he took his second puff.

Yeah, I should have been grateful, but Michael and I had talked about this. We were going to camp out on the site, start the remodel ourselves, and as we went along, figure out what exactly we'd need to do as far as a new well and septic system was concerned.

"Your father said his crew thinks that property is beautiful," Mrs. Bellomo said after sipping from the little crystal glass and setting it back on the side table next to her chair.

"Oh, it is, Mother," Michael said. "You and Dad have to come up as soon as we get settled. I'd like Uncle Frank to come up too."

"Frank's heart is failing, dear," Mrs. Bellomo said. "You're in his will, you know?"

"He told me," Michael said.

"Yeah," Mr. Bellomo said. "He likes you, Michael. He served the family good over the years. I always thought you might take up where he left off. He can't do the numbers anymore, and I thought you might join the business and…. Well, workin' the numbers like Frank did."

"My degree is in fine arts, Dad. You know that."

"Ain't no problem gettin' a CPA. What? You don't want to join the business?"

"Dad," Michael said, looking up at the ceiling, then looking back at his father. "We've had this conversation before. If I do anything, I'll probably open up an art store in Gunderson Junction where I can sell my paintings. I don't want to be a CPA."

"Leave him alone, Paul," Mrs. Bellomo said. "He's an artist. He's… sensitive."

"Ahh," Mr. Bellomo said. "That. Again."

"Mother," Michael said, his voice dark.

"What, dear?" she said, picking up her glass and sipping.

I looked at Michael. His eyes were boring holes into his mother.

"I don't want to hear this," Mr. Bellomo said. "Sam"—he raised his voice—"what have you got in mind for a career?"

I'd been watching and listening to this conversation as though I were a bug on the wall. When Mr. Bellomo said my name, I flinched. "Sorry," I said. "What was that?"

"What are you going to do for a job up there?"

"Oh. Well, I'm thinking about some things. But—"

"You'll never let me forget it, will you?" Michael said.

"It's not me, Michael," his mother said. "It's your fate. The monsignor said you would be cursed by it and—"

"The monsignor is a crazy old man who drinks his own piss." Michael stood. "I think we better go. Thanks, Dad, for what you're doing for us. C'mon, Sam."

"Michael," his mother said as I was wondering what the hell had just happened. "Sam." She reached over and patted my thigh. "Just stay where you are."

"Shouldn't talk to your mother like that," Mr. Bellomo said. "Sit down."

Michael stood there, still staring at his mother. He then he sat back down.

"I'm sorry," his mother said. "I just worry about you. You know that. I pray every day that—"

"Mother. Please," Michael said. "I don't need your prayers. Maybe you need them, but I don't."

"Like his mother said," Mr. Bellomo said, "Michael's sensitive." He tapped the edge of a glass ashtray on the side table with the business end of his cigar. "All his life, he's been sensitive."

"Dad," Michael said, shaking his head.

"He knows things," Mrs. Bellomo said, holding her fragile glass up as the maid or housekeeper made the rounds with the grappa bottle.

We all waited until the maid or housekeeper went back to wherever she'd come from. And after a moment's silence, I thought I should try to ease the palpable tension in the room. I cleared my throat.

"The dinner was very nice, Mrs. Bellomo, and you've got a lovely house."

"Thank you, Sam."

"You like those meatballs?" Mr. Bellomo said, reaching for his glass.

"Yes. They were wonderful."

"Mother's cook, Christina, makes them with sausage and beef," Michael said. "She puts in her mystery spices, and…. That was Nana's recipe wasn't it, Mother?" Michael too was trying to ease the tension.

"Yes," Mrs. Bellomo said. "I taught Christina how to make them. Actually, it was your great-grandmother's recipe, Michael."

"Ah," Michael said. "The maternal lineage."

I had thought Michael had taken my cue to just let whatever sleeping dogs that had shadowed the earlier discussion lie for a while. But no. He downed his grappa and again shook his head.

"Did you know, Sam," Michael said, "that all the women in my mother's family—and my mother too—believed in stigmata? You know. That holy people could at a moment's notice bleed from the places where Jesus did when he was crucified? And did you know that all these fine women wore a cilice, a hair shirt, under their silk or cotton blouses because they were so sorry for their sins? And—"

"That's enough, Michael," Mrs. Bellomo said with what I gathered was a rare display of any kind of emotion in front of guests.

"And," Michael continued, "did you know that I'm kind of…? Oh, I guess you call it a punishment from God that my mother carries on her shoulders, because—"

"Stop it!" Michael's father said very firmly, rubbing his cigar in the ashtray. "We raised you better, Michael. You and your mother gotta stop this. I'm tired of it." He stood and reached for my hand. "Very nice to meet you, Sam. Take care of my boy." He then walked out of the room.

Mrs. Bellomo also stood, straightened her dress a little, and smiled. "It was very nice that you came over tonight, Sam. I'll pray that you and Michael remain safe and… sound. And Michael." She turned to him. "I love you dearly, with all my heart. None of us asked for the dark veil. It's no one's fault." She paused a moment, then left the room, taking the same route her husband had.

I looked at Michael and stood up. "Well, I guess that's it, then."

DRIVING BACK to the apartment, I didn't say a word, and Michael didn't either. The little he'd told me about his mother the night before we got married in Taos came back to me. As cryptic as he'd been that night, I now thought I understood a little more about the family dynamic—his mother was a fucking nutcase.

After we'd gone to bed, I held him, his back to me, my arms around his chest.

"I should have known how that would turn out," he said.

"It was okay," I said, not really meaning it, but I had to say something.

"The dark veil thing?"

"Yes."

"That's the caul. She sometimes calls it a dark cloud."

"You told me in Taos that she blames herself for—"

"She blames herself for a lot of things."

"She seemed to be blaming you, though."

"It's complicated."

I didn't know if I should bring it up, but it had been on my mind ever since his father had mentioned it. "Why is your father involved with the property? I thought we were going to do it ourselves?"

"He wanted to do it. He's got the resources, and we don't."

"But you never told me."

He turned over and faced me. "I knew you wouldn't agree."

"Michael, I—"

He put his finger to my lips. "All he's doing is the well and the septic and getting the cabin ready for us to live in. I know it's summer, but fall comes early up there, Sam. We can't camp out for six months."

"The house the mob built," I said with a smile, knowing too that I was sharing a bed with a mob kid. That thought immediately evoked an involuntary lustful reaction that had me turning Michael over onto his stomach. He, of course, reciprocated, pooching his ass up to meet my thrusts. I often think about that and haven't yet figured out why I reacted the way I did. Fucking the beautiful son of a mobster does, I guess, evoke a sense of danger, something that has always made me horny as hell. Except in Afghanistan. The danger there usually included the prospect of my own death.

CHAPTER SEVENTEEN

I WALK into Skip's little office and nod to the glum stares from all the critters hanging on the walls. He's got Brunhilda up on the lift. I walk into the bay, where he's fiddling with something on the front end.

"Hey, Skip."

He looks at me and wipes his hands on his red shop towel. "Sheriff. I was just finishing up."

"How's she look?"

"For an old gal, she looks pretty good. Tie rods are beginning to look a little worn, but they'll be okay for a while yet."

"So, she's ready to go?"

"Sure." He reaches back to the lift lever, flips it down, and Brunhilda slowly descends to the ground.

We both walk into the office, and Skip writes up the bill. "You want me to add this to the county tab?"

"Yeah, if you would."

He looks at me for a moment and then says, "You got a worried look. What's up?"

"Oh, a few things. Tell me something. You've lived up here all your life. Right?"

"Yeah. For all of it."

"Heading west on the county road from town? I know about most of the properties out there, but what else is up in the hills that maybe I don't know about?"

"What are you gettin' at, Sheriff?"

"You know. Old miners' cabins. Maybe some shacks up there where somebody might hide out in or that hunters might use during the season?"

Yes, I think Hank might have put a bug up Michael's ass about.... Well, I don't know exactly what it might be about but can't discount the specter of somebody in those remote spaces grinding up human bones to effect a curse and, yes, where old winds blow with impunity.

"Sure," Skip says. "There's little places all over the hills. Up high too. Even lots of stories about Indians who used to live up there. You're not gonna try to go up there, are you?"

"Prob'ly not. Wouldn't get very far with all the snow. So, she's ready to go?"

"Sure. Let me open the bay door for you."

I get in Brunhilda, and before closing the door, I've got one more question for Skip. "There was a guy living in the trailer park. Karen Hargrove is now in that trailer, but she said the guy who moved out of it might have been an Indian. Stan Rivers was his name. You know him?"

"Ran into him a couple times. Quiet guy. He's a tree cutter by trade. And yeah, he's an Indian."

"That's all you know about him?"

"That's it."

"Okay. Thanks."

BRUNHILDA PURRS a thank-you when I start her up. I back out of the bay knowing what I've got to do.

When I get to Cathy's Café, I pull into the space right in front, get out, and walk up the steps. As I open the door, Cathy meets me there.

"You find out anything?" she says.

"No, not really. Is Missie here?"

"I told her to stay home today."

"She tell you anything else about what happened?"

"She won't talk about it. I tried, but she asked me to just leave it alone, and I did. I took her car keys, though. She won't be going anywhere."

"Good. You think she'd talk to me?"

"Oh, Sam," she says, shaking her head. "I don't know. She was still in bed when I left. Are you going up there?"

"Maybe. She ever mention a guy by the name of Stan Rivers?"

"No. Who's that?"

"I think that's who she was trying to find last night."

"Why?"

"That's what I'd like to know. Okay," I say. "I'll let you know what I find out." I start to leave, and she grabs my arm.

"I love her, Sam."

Knowing Cathy as I do, I know what she's just told me wasn't an easy thing for her to do. I nod. "I know you do, Cathy." I turn and go back outside, walk down the steps, and get back in Brunhilda.

As I drive past the office, I grab the mike hooked to the dash. "Mary. You there?"

Static ensues for a moment; then I hear Mary's voice. "Right here, Sam."

"Going up to see Hank. You get me on the radio if you hear anything about Michael. You too, Don."

"Will do," Mary says. And then Don's voice makes it through another bout of static.

"Nothin' yet," he says. "I'll let you know."

I hang the mike back on the dash and head for Hank's cabin for the second time today.

As I walk toward Hank's cabin, I notice that the shed's door is ajar. I walk toward it and hear some mumbling, and then I see a thin stream of smoke coming from the barely open door. After another few steps, I'm able to see inside. Hank is sitting cross-legged on the ground, hunched near a small fire just to the left of the freak bear now covered with a blanket. I reach for the door and start to open it a little more, and there's Charlie, sitting just inside and staring at me. He's showing his canines, and as he commences a deep-throated growl, I lower my hand from the door.

"Knew you'd come back," Hank says. He tells Charlie to settle down, and he does.

"We need to talk, Hank."

"Yeah," he says. He tosses some dust from the ground onto the fire, stands up, and turns toward me. "I told Michael there was nothing he could do. But he said he wanted to try."

I step aside as Hank walks out of the shed with Charlie behind.

"Where'd he go?"

"Up there," he says, raising his arm toward the mountains, to the west.

I WAIT for Hank to feed his stove and then settle onto his recliner. Charlie has as usual sought out his unseen comfortable corner somewhere in the house. I open up my coat and sit down.

"What were you doing out there?"

"Talking to the spirits."

"The dead ones?"

"They never die, Sheriff."

I envision the freak bear suddenly sitting up and saying something like "Heeeere's Johnny." I would smile, but then I see Michael out there in his piece-of-shit truck doing whatever it is he decided to do when he and Hank last spoke.

"Hank, you've got to tell me what you and Michael discussed."

"He's trying to help you."

"Help me what?"

"Find the witch."

Okay. *He could have just gone home and painted a picture of whatever the hell is going on.* "And how is he going to do that?"

"I told him about Stanley Broken River."

Oh, that rings a bell. "Stan Rivers?"

"That's what he calls himself."

"Used to live in the trailer park?"

"Don't know where he used to live," Hank says, shifting in his chair and turning toward me. "Spends time in the mountains, though. Goes up there to work magic. He's a skinwalker."

Christ! "Do you know where exactly?"

"No." He turns his gaze back to the fire. "Michael said he felt something, though."

"What?"

"He had a dream about a dog. The dog was sad because he used to be alive. He turned into a Spirit Dog and told Michael what to do."

I want to stand up and shake Hank about as hard as I can and scream at him *Will you please cut this crap and tell me something I can use to find Michael.*

Instead I just sigh and watch Hank raise his hand and rub his cheek. "And that's all you talked about?"

"We talked about the bones too. Don't know if they're old or new, but...."

"What?"

"We both touched the dust. We spoke without words." He moves his hand to his other cheek and rubs it. "It was for a curse. Somebody was gonna die."

"Why does it matter if the bones were new or old?"

He looks at me. "If they were new, then somebody died for them. If they were old...."

"Okay. Haven't heard of any murders up here lately."

"Me neither. Doesn't mean it didn't happen."

We both look toward the wall the stove sits in front of when a gust of wind shakes the whole house, and a puff of smoke comes out of the front of the stove.

"Storm coming," Hank says.

"Yeah. I know it." I stand up and look at Hank for a moment. He's folded his hands in his lap, and he stares at the fire. If I were to describe the meaning of the word serenity, Hank would be it right now. A thought crosses my mind, and I ask the question it has proposed. "You and Michael.... When you speak without words?"

He glances up at me. "Yes," he says.

"Is there any, oh, distance restriction on that?"

He nods. "I'll try to talk to him, Sheriff."

"Okay. You got enough wood and food for a couple of days? We're supposed to get a shitload of snow."

"Yes. Me and Charlie will be okay."

"All right." I start to walk toward the door, then stop. "Tell Michael to come home."

"If he's listening," Hank says.

As I walk toward Brunhilda, I glance back at Hank's shed. The door is still slightly open and bangs against the frame as another gust of wind whooshes from the northwest. Not that I think the freak bear is going to reanimate itself and walk out of there, nor that the little wood plug Hank uses to keep the door closed would be any impediment if it did want to do that, but I think the door ought to be closed and locked. I walk to the shed, look around for the wood plug, and see it on the ground. Another gust swoops from the hillside as I bend down to pick up the plug, and the door opens a little more. Maybe I'm just curious, or maybe something else prods me to go in there, and I do. I see the little fire pit Hank made and then look at the body now covered with a blanket. I lower to my haunches and pull the blanket off what I know is underneath. But what I see is the freak bear now on its stomach, the back of its skull missing.

"I think a skinwalker got to it." The voice coming from behind me is the last thing I need right now. I roll to my side, right onto the little fire pit, and grab for my weapon.

"Jesus Christ!" I stand up and brush myself off. "Why didn't you tell me?"

"Nothing you can do about it, Sheriff."

"Yeah. But…. You piss me off sometimes, Hank. You really do."

"Better to be pissed off than pissed on."

I don't know whether to laugh at the straight face he's showing me right now or continue my little tirade. "C'mon. Let's get out of here."

I close the door, engage the latch, and stick the plug in the loop. Hank is walking back to his cabin, and I yell over the sound of the wind tearing through the treetops, "You think what was in that bag was from the bear?"

He stops and turns toward me. "Maybe," he yells, his white hair whipping in the breeze. He then turns and steps onto his porch.

CHAPTER EIGHTEEN

WHEN MICHAEL and I went up to our property to see how the work was going, we were both surprised by what we saw. The ramshackle cabin had been restored. New logs had been worked into the existing structure, windows had been refitted, and Mr. Bellomo's crew had replaced the roof. A new wellhead sat about fifty feet from the cabin, surrounded by a temporary wire fence, and off to the side of the cabin, two round metal disks poked slightly above the ground, evidence of where they'd put the septic. The equipment that surely must have been used to accomplish all this was gone, and there was a business card taped to the front door.

"Vince does good work," Michael said, pulling the card off the door.

"Vince?"

"My dad's guy. He runs the residential crew."

"We're paying your dad back for all this stuff."

"Already did." He opened the front door, and I followed him in.

They'd converted what had been two distinct rooms into a large parlor and had put in a river-rock fireplace over much of one wall. They'd also put in a little kitchenette, and beyond that they'd added a small bathroom. The floor had been replaced with weathered oak.

"It's even got a shower," Michael said after he peeked into the bathroom.

"Well," I said, taking it all in as Michael looked in the midsize stainless steel refrigerator, "I've got to say they did a very nice job. Can't believe they did it so quickly."

"We'll put our bed in here," Michael said, turning a full circle in the room.

"I don't know where else we'd put it. But yeah, we'll sleep in here."

Michael held out the card he'd taken off the front door. "Vince wrote on the back."

I took the card and read it. *When you're ready for add-ons, call me.* "Good. Where do you want to put the bedroom?"

"God, I don't know," Michael said. "And we'll have to enlarge the kitchen, and maybe have a little dining room. We'll need a laundry room too. And…." He sighed and put his hands in his pockets. "I love it." He bobbed up and down twice on his tiptoes.

There are times when you can't help but be reminded why you fell in love with someone. It usually happens when you least expect it, some momentary thing that takes you back to the precious things in your past—an instantaneous kaleidoscopic journey where all is right with the world. When I looked at Michael standing there, his hands in his pockets, his brown eyes alive with happiness and possibilities, I wanted time to stop right there. There was no need to go any further.

I stepped to him and put my hands on either side of his face. "I love you more than you know," I said, kissing his lips, brushing my hands through his hair, and as always—I cannot help it—I cupped his ass in my palms.

He managed to get his hand in the front of my jeans. "I do know how much you love me," he said, "and I love you more."

We got our pants down to our ankles. Michael eased down to his knees and….

That was the first time we made love in our cabin. Michael braced himself before the window, and spread his legs. I entered him, both of us looking out onto the meadow, the tree line rising in the distance, the blue sky spread as a gracious sacrament interrupted only by the ridgeline of mountains to the west.

WE COULDN'T bring any of Michael's furniture with us when we moved into the one-room cabin, except for his bed, a love seat, and a small coffee table, and we bought a very small round dining table and two chairs that we put to the side of the fireplace. Before the summer was done, we had Vince's crew come up and dig the foundation and construct the frame for two bedrooms, an enlarged kitchen, dining area, and a small room for a washer and dryer. We also had them do the prep work for a mudroom at the front of the cabin where the door was.

When the imminence of fall began to whisper across the meadow, Michael and I, with the help of a couple of local carpenters, enclosed the entire new construction and had a roofing company come up and top it off.

It was that first fall in the mountains when I began to notice Michael's darker side with more frequency. It was subtle at first and not something I worried about but just accepted as something two people who love each other should be prepared for—the inevitable epiphanies that eventually arise in every relationship.

CHAPTER NINETEEN

WHY EVERY front that comes our way has to begin with a half day or more of wind is a question I always ask, even though I know the answer. I don't mind the cold or snow, but the goddamned wind is a major pain in the ass. Even Brunhilda is shaking as I turn from Hank's drive and head for Cathy's house. I've got to talk to Missie whether she wants to or not. And right now as another gust of wind hits Brunhilda right in the face, sounding and feeling like the locomotive from hell, I'm in no mood for whatever emotional crisis Missie might be going through. She knows what's in that bag and why it's there. And she's going to tell me all about that or.... Well, I don't know right now what the consequences will be if she clams up, but I'm sure I'll think of something.

After three miles on the county road, I turn onto Cathy's drive. It's another half mile, and Brunhilda manages the trek much better than Michael's truck did last night. I'm amazed that Michael's truck made it at all, as I see the depth of the snow I had to drive through the last time I was here. And yeah, drifts are beginning to build as the wind continues to blow like the son of a bitch it is.

Before I get out of Brunhilda, I take my Resistol off and flip my jacket's hood over my head. Since deciding one of those floppy-eared hats wasn't my style, and realizing my Resistol wasn't adequate in this kind of weather, I'd grabbed my hooded coat this morning before I left the cabin.

Cathy's house is almost lost in the whiteout in front of me. I step out and immediately lean into the wind, holding my hood down with my hand and planting each foot securely before I take another step. When I reach the porch, the wind becomes more of a vicious noise than a physical force. I flip my hood off and knock on the door. After about thirty seconds, I knock again. Another thirty or so seconds pass. I'm about to knock again but don't when I hear the lock disengage and see the door open a crack.

"Missie, it's Sam." I see one eye and a bit of her blue hair. "I need to talk to you." She opens the door a little farther. I step into the house, close the door behind me, and pull off my hood. She's walking down the hallway to the parlor. As I follow her, the wind outside becomes a dull rumble. It's a sound that makes me uncomfortable for good reason. The possibility of fifty- or sixty-foot-tall Douglas firs losing their grip on the ground and falling onto the house is not out of the realm of possibility.

"It's cold in here," Missie says as she opens up the woodstove's door and throws in two logs. She shuts the door, hugs herself, and turns around to face me. "I'm sorry about last night," she says, her voice on the edge of breaking.

I sit down on the love seat and open up my coat. "That's what I need to talk to you about. Why don't you sit down."

She grabs an Indian blanket that's draped over the other love seat, unfolds it, and wraps it around her shoulders. She sits and pulls the blanket tighter around herself. "I just got up, so I'm still a little...." She doesn't finish her thought and bows her head slightly.

"I found the black bag you kept your antique watch in. It was behind the café. You know how it got there?"

She raises her head. "I... I thought I'd lost it."

"Do you know what was in that bag?"

She pulls her legs up under her and again tightens the blanket. "It was something that.... Stan said it would protect me."

"Would that be Stan Rivers?"

"Yes."

"So, Stan Rivers made whatever was in that bag?"

"Yes."

Okay. This is going better than I'd thought it would. "How do you know Stan?"

She again lowers her head.

"Missie."

"He...."

She looks at me. I don't think she's going to cry, but her face looks about as sad as a kid whose balloon has just burst.

"When I first came up here? You know about that?"

"When Cathy found you on the café's porch?"

She nods. "Yes. But.... Stan put me on the porch. He told me that somebody would be there soon and...."

"And what?"

"Stan found me in the woods. I'd been…. The two guys I'd gotten a ride from in Denver—they'd said they were going to Vegas too—left me in the woods." And now she does begin to cry, pulling the ends of the blanket up to her face.

I get up and walk over to the other love seat, sit, and put my arm around her shoulders. Her whole body is shuddering as she sobs, a moan tinged with sorrow coming from inside her.

"They… raped me."

I look on the coffee table and don't see any tissues, but I do see a couple of linen doilies or napkins or whatever you call them, and I pick one up. I give it to her, and she blows her nose on it.

"They weren't going to Vegas at all," she says, and then she erupts into another full-body sob.

After first hearing about Missie's arrival on Cathy's porch, I've always wondered what the real story was. And as far as I know, I'm the first one she's ever shared this with. Yes, maybe by now she's told Cathy. But that's not why I'm here. The vision I've got in my mind of Michael out there somewhere trying to, as Hank said, help me find a goddamned witch is why I'm here.

"Missie, can you tell me what you know about Stan?"

"He's an Indian," she says.

"I know that. But what else?"

"He's…. He knows the magic they use to…. He was friends with John Spotted Elk."

Okay. All kinds of things come to my mind right now, not the least of which is the freak bear in Hank's shed who is now missing a large chunk of his skull. "Hank told me that John Spotted Elk was a skinwalker."

"Yes."

"And Stan knew that?"

"Yes."

Yeah, I've got to ask the next question. "Is Stan Rivers a skinwalker?"

"He knows the magic," she says, wiping her eyes and looking at me. She's stopped sobbing and appears to be ready to discuss this damned thing with more than one-word answers. But she didn't really answer my question.

"Did he—"

"When he found me in the woods... I couldn't really tell if he was... a man. All I remembered was this dark hulk picking me up. And the... odor. He smelled like... damp earth or something. I didn't know it was him until he showed up at the café when I was leaving to go home about a month after that. He asked me if I was okay."

"Then what?"

"Oh." She wipes her eyes again. "He was nice, Sheriff. He lived in the trailer park."

She looks at me, and I believe her. But whether he was nice or not doesn't matter right now. My mind is taking me to some conclusions that need confirmation. "I'm going to cut to the chase here," I say, knowing that what I'm thinking is batshit crazy. But I say it. "Did Stan give you what was in that bag? A potion or something that maybe.... You said he said it would protect you. Was it... poison?"

"Maybe. I don't know. The two guys that... did what they did to me, came up here a couple weeks after Stan found me. They just sat in their car outside the café. Every time I'd look out the window, there they were looking at me, smiling. One of them even waved at me. I noticed too that there was some guy I'd never seen hanging around across the street. He just stood there, leaning against the side of Glen's store, looking at those two guys in the car. I was scared, Sheriff. I really was."

"And the other guy was Stan?"

"Yes. He finally introduced himself. He told me he was the one who found me that night and put me on the porch. He said he'd seen those two guys drive away from where they left me. He told me where he lived and if I wanted to talk about anything to come and see him."

"And you did?"

"Yeah. I couldn't tell Cathy what had happened. But Stan was... I felt I could trust him."

"And you told him what the two guys did to you?"

"Yes."

I feel like we've circled the wagons on this thing for about as long as I can take it, and I ask her *the* question. "So, he tells you he can give you something that'll protect you from those guys. Maybe he says all you have to do is get some of what he's going to give you on their skin or somehow get them to ingest it and...."

"He said it has to touch your blood or get inside of you. Those guys kept coming up here, Sam. Finally, a couple weeks ago I told Stan that I needed whatever he had to give me. For protection, as he said. I gave him my watch in exchange for it. He didn't want anything, but I insisted. We arranged to meet in back of the café the night before last so he could give me what he'd made. He put it in the watch bag. But I dropped it. We heard you inside and…. We both ran, and I dropped it."

We're getting somewhere. "What about afterward? I came back a second time, and somebody had been in the café. All the stuff from your shelf was on the floor. Somebody had unlocked the front door, and it looked like they'd left just before I got there."

"That was me. I'd left my tote bag in there. My car keys were in it. I had to go back and get it. You'd locked the back door, so I had to take the key from under the rock. I didn't turn on any lights and just knocked everything off the shelf when I grabbed my tote bag. I looked for the bag out back, but it wasn't there."

"Where was your car? I don't remember seeing it when I went there the first time."

"I'd moved it from in front of the café. I knew I was meeting Stan later, and I just didn't want… I didn't want anybody to know what we were doing back there."

"Why hadn't you agreed to make the exchange at his trailer?"

"He didn't want to. I only found out he didn't live there anymore when I went there that night."

"Do you know where he is now?"

"No," she says. "I only went to the trailer a couple of times. He wasn't a talker, Sheriff. He was very shy, and… I got the feeling there was a lot about him that I couldn't see. That he wasn't sharing."

"But why did you go there last night?"

"I thought he might have found the bag."

"Okay. I guess that's—" My cell starts to beep. I reach into my coat pocket and pull it out. It's Mary. "This is Sam."

She tells me that Don just radioed in to report that he saw a vehicle heading up an old logging road about four miles west of Joe Parsons's place.

"Was it Michael's?"

"It was the right color, but he wasn't sure."

"Is he following it?"

"Don't know where you are, Sam, but can you see how much it's snowing right now?"

I look out the tall windows beyond the stove, and yeah, the storm is here. "I see it. Tell him to just hang tight where he is. Is Digger back yet?"

"He's on his way."

"Don't we have two more pairs of snowshoes in storage?"

"We had four pairs before you and Digger lost two of them."

She's protective of every piece of equipment we've got. She even calls us to task when she thinks we're using too many staples. "In the line of duty, Mary."

"You're not going up there, are you?"

"Probably."

There's silence on the line for a moment, then, "I'll dig them out and have them ready when you get back."

"Thank you. I'm heading back now." I end the call and put the phone back in my pocket.

"I've got to go, Missie. I appreciate all you've told me." I stand up, and she looks up at me.

"This is all pretty weird, Sheriff."

I nod. "Yeah. Tell me about it. One last thing."

"Yes."

"Did you believe that what Stan gave you was, oh, a magic potion or something?"

She looks at me for a moment and then shakes her head. "I don't know. All I knew is that I believed him when he said it would protect me. They raped me, Sheriff."

"Why didn't you come to me about this?"

She waits for a second before answering. "I've got a history with cops. Drugs mostly."

"Okay. What kind of car do these guys drive? You know their names? Descriptions?"

"It's a green Toyota. Older model. They said their names were Mike and John, but I don't think that's their real names. They were... I try not to remember what they looked like, Sheriff."

"I understand. We ought to talk some more about them, though. If you see them again, you know what to do."

"Yes, I do."

"You take care, Missie. We'll sort this out one way or another."

THE TRACKS in the snow that Brunhilda made when I'd driven up to the cabin are now completely gone, and I bet there's already two inches of new snow on the ground. The wind has stopped, though, and I'm thankful for that. I raise my index finger and take a look at the paper cut I'd inflicted on myself a couple of days ago. I can barely see it. And as I remember what Missie told me about the poison or curse or whatever it is in that black bag, I hope Cathy and Michael had no open scratches or abrasions on their fingers when they touched that shit. It's got to touch your blood is what Missie said. Or get inside of you. Or, I'm thinking right now as I turn onto the county road toward town, maybe it's harmless unless you're the intended recipient. Tell you what. If I'd known Pine County was a hotbed of witches or skinwalkers, I'd have suggested Michael and I live somewhere else. Not that I believe in all that crap, and not that I don't. So, too, if I'd known about Michael's sensitivity to just about everything, it might have caused me to think twice about.... No. Hell, I wouldn't have thought twice about that.

"Nope. Not for an instant," I say as Brunhilda shudders with a gust of wind I'd thought had evaporated once the front had reached us. The road ahead disappears momentarily, and I take my foot off the gas. Brunhilda and I are both idle for a moment, waiting for the road to reappear.

CHAPTER TWENTY

THE FIRST fall we lived in the cabin was memorable in many ways, not the least of which was seeing Michael's gradual journey into what I suppose you could call his extra senses. Shortly after we first met, I'd realized he was a complicated man—artistic, intelligent, and something of a mystery.

Yeah, I was good-looking, and I won't deny I'd been desired by more than a few good men before I'd gone off to the Middle East, and I'd not let my assets, so to speak, go to waste while I was in college. After I'd come back, though, the war had skewed my view of life to such an extent that what I'd felt about it before I'd gone now seemed surreal, unauthentic. Life had become only a façade that lacked, oh, I guess passion would be the right word. And it wasn't the passion of the moment I'd felt with any of the men I'd slept with before I'd gone to the Middle East. No, I came back with a new realization that just waking up in the morning was an answered prayer, and that the simple things in life necessarily evoked wonder, and wonder evoked passion. I could no longer interact with another man without assessing the wonder of their eyes, their voice, the smell of their skin and hair, the way they cocked their head (or didn't) at something I had said. The few encounters I'd had since I'd come back from the war had been unfulfilling. The passion of the bedroom could no longer trump the wonder I'd not seen in their eyes or heard in their voice. And then Michael appeared. And wonder was restored to my life.

MICHAEL HAD always craved his quiet time, and I gave it to him. I'd yet to even think about running for sheriff, and it would be another year before that idea crossed my mind. I spent most of my time finishing what was left to do on the cabin, leaving Michael to work on his art, something he appeared to have become obsessed with. And as the days became shorter and the breezes became colder, we settled into routines that fit both our priorities—mine to get things done for winter, his to explore whatever it was the mountains had inspired him to create. Oh, he'd help me when I needed it. And at least once a week, we'd hike into the hills and see what we could see. But as I look back on it now, that first fall was when I began to notice that there was something else going on in Michael's fine mind—something dark and foreboding.

We hiked west one morning, toward one of the fourteeners that rose in the distance. We weren't going to try to climb it, but the base was our destination. It was cold that day, and we'd dressed accordingly, both of us wearing long pants and layers. We stopped for lunch—Michael had made tuna sandwiches and had packed some fruit and wine—in a pretty little meadow that caught the full force of noontime sun.

We sat on the wild grasses, and as Michael started to unpack our lunch, he stopped what he was doing and turned his head to the right. "Did you hear that?" he said.

I looked to where he was looking. "No. What was it?"

He stood and began walking toward the tree line about forty yards to our north. "I didn't so much hear it as…."

"What?" I said, following him.

He stopped walking and stared into the tree line. "It spoke to me, and I answered."

I sidled up to him, saw the intensity of concentration on his face, and then again looked to where he was staring. I will admit that the hairs on my neck felt as if they were poking straight out, my hackles, as it were, responding primordially to whatever threat or eerie presence was just beyond the tree line. I wanted to ask Michael the four questions I'd learned to ask myself before I entered a potential combat area: What do I see? What do I hear? What do I smell? What do I feel? Most of the time I'd skip to that last one—What do I feel?—because I'd learned the answer to that question was the most reliable. It had kept me and my unit from harm a number of times. The gut knows, man, and you'd better listen to it.

I waited until he appeared to have lost interest in his imaginary friend, then grabbed his hand as we walked back to our little picnic.

"That was odd," he said as we both sat.

"What'd it say?" I worked the corkscrew into the bottle, knowing my question was certainly strange, but not as strange as what he'd said—he'd talked to it, for Christ's sake.

He shook his head. "Something like, 'I'm here.'"

"And you said?"

He held out his plastic cup, and I tipped the end of the bottle over it. "I said, 'I know.'"

"And did you?"

He took a sip and handed me a sandwich. "Sam, just forget it. It didn't mean anything. I've been hearing... things my whole life."

"And talking back to those things?"

"Eat your tuna fish. I told you about this stuff in Taos."

I unwrapped my sandwich and took a bite. I watched him take a bite of his and then subtly turn his head a little to look back at the tree line.

There were quite a few incidents like this, but I decided the less I said about them, the better. I was in a learning mode and figured in time I'd come to understand the nuances of this beautiful man whose smile could touch my soul. That was something I didn't want to jeopardize—imaginary friends or not.

AFTER THE first snowfall in mid-October, Michael and I hunkered down to the inevitability of what we knew was coming. We'd lived in Denver all our lives, had both skied the Rockies since we were kids, and we knew what was ahead. We'd cut about two cords of wood, all of it from the dead trees that were plentiful on our property. We knew they would burn, unlike the cord we'd taken from trees that were still alive. We stacked the green wood separately from the other and had built a wood bin just off the back porch where we'd stack logs taken from the bigger pile whenever we needed to. We kept busy finishing the interior of the cabin, and every few days Michael would tell me he wanted to take a day off to paint. We'd set up his studio in the second bedroom. The light was good in that room, and he'd spend hours at a time in there, coming out only to eat and at bedtime. He never said it, but I got the feeling he'd prefer I stay out of that room. And I did.

Near mid-November, Michael and I were sitting in the parlor, a nice fire in the rock fireplace, red wine on the coffee table, candles on the windowsill throwing off a dim glow, their flicker reflected by the glass. We were both tired, having worked all day to finish painting the kitchen and the little laundry room.

"We need to buy some furniture," Michael said.

We'd put some of our furniture in storage in Denver, having decided that we'd wait to actually furnish the cabin until we were done with everything we needed to do. We were getting close to being finished with all the projects, and I agreed with Michael.

"Yes, we do. What about the stuff in storage?"

"Nah. Let's get new things. The stuff in storage is too… citified. It wouldn't look right up here."

"Okay."

We listened to the utter silence of the night, something that had taken a while to get used to. Then a pocket of sap hissed from the fireplace, sending some sparks up and out, and we both looked that way, toward the fire.

"What have you been working on?" I asked. Like I said, I didn't go into his studio, and I was curious.

"The painting?"

"Yes."

"Would you like to see it?"

"Of course."

He slid off the love seat and walked into the second bedroom. He came out with what looked like an 18x24 canvas, the back facing me. He turned on the lamp we kept on the coffee table.

"Remember our picnic when I thought I heard something from the trees?"

"Sure. We had tuna fish."

"That's the one." He smiled. "I painted that scene."

He turned the canvas around, and yes, he'd painted the scene exactly as I remembered it. His perspective, though, was from the south, looking toward us sitting in the grasses, with the tree line behind us.

"Wow. That's really nice, Michael. Acrylic?"

"Yes."

He propped the canvas against the coffee table where we could both look at it. And the more I looked, the more I knew he'd put something in there that I hadn't at first seen. I leaned down and picked up the canvas.

"In the trees, there's something…. Is it an animal? It looks almost human, but…. What is it?"

"It's what was there that day. It spoke to me."

I sat the canvas back on the floor and looked at Michael. I couldn't read his expression. It was as if he'd left his body, and his body was simply waiting patiently for him to return.

Our first Christmas up here was eventful in the sense that Michael cleaned out the little general store's supply of string lights and hung them up outside on the blue spruce and the two Douglas fir trees in front of our cabin. He made a hot toddy concoction, took the legs off the barbecue's bowl, sat the bowl outside in the snow, and then carried our two pine chairs from the porch and sat them in front of the barbecue. We started a fire in the metal bowl at about nine o'clock, put the grate on top, and then Michael sat the pot full of toddy on top of that. He told me to have a seat, and we both sat, wearing our parkas and stocking caps. The sky was dressed with the hundreds of thousands of stars, more likely millions or billions, that you can see up here, and we both just looked at the spectacle of it for a while as we waited for the toddy to warm up. When it did warm up, Michael grabbed two cups he'd brought with him from the cabin, handed me one, and then grabbed the pot and poured the steaming concoction into my cup and then his.

"Don't drink it yet," he said. He leaned over and plugged the string lights in to the extension cord he'd earlier strung out there. The colored lights seemed to ooze on, and we both said *Ahhh* in unison. "Okay. Now you can drink it."

We sat there for a moment, and then I asked Michael if he believed in the Nativity.

"It's a nice story," he said. "The no-room-at-the-inn thing. Swaddling clothes."

"But do you think it actually happened?"

"I think it's a nice story."

"Was there actually a Jesus Christ? A Savior?"

Michael took a moment to refill our cups and then said, "I think it doesn't matter. The animals in the manger mattered. They knew more about the earth, the mysteries of the earth and the sky…." He looked up then and smiled. "There was never any more inception than there is now, nor any more youth or age than there is now, and will never be any more perfection than there is now, nor any more heaven or hell than there is now."

"I've heard that before. Who—"

"Walt Whitman. That's what the animals knew, Sam. That and so much more."

"And you memorized that?"

"Yes. A long time ago." He turned to me, reached over with his free hand, and grabbed my hand. "Merry Christmas," he said.

"Merry Christmas."

He then held his cup up, and I clicked mine against his.

We didn't trade gifts that Christmas, and that was fine by me. What he gave me, though, was some more insight into who he was. And if I could love him any more than I did, it was that night, that Christmas night when I realized that he and I had about the same perception of why it was we were breathing—the perfection of each moment after another. As we sat there holding hands, I looked up at the stars and imagined what I'd see if I was looking down on us from miles above. And as the image of Michael and me holding hands, the three trees all lit up, the small fire before us, formed, I thought that too was a nice story worthy of remembrance.

CHAPTER TWENTY-ONE

I STOP Brunhilda outside the office, and there are two pairs of snowshoes and four ski poles leaning against the wall by the door. I get out and take a look at the shoes. They're older than the ones Digger and I lost in the bowl, and some of the rawhide lacings are unraveling. They're still intact, though, and will get the job done if we have to use them. And that's not a big if. There's got to be almost seven inches of snow already and certainly more in the drifts the farther west you go, and if I wait any longer to go inside, I might have to strap them on just to get to the door. I'm glad Mary thought to bring out the poles too.

"Digger will be here in a few minutes," Mary says when I walk into the office.

"Good." Jim Harris isn't at his desk, and I notice that his personal items are gone. "Jim moved out already?"

"Yes. And we're having his retirement party next Friday."

"Okay. You got the recruitment notice in the paper?"

"Yes." She gives me one of her *I already did that* looks.

"Nothing from Don or Michael?"

"Don's still out there waiting for you. And Michael hasn't called."

"Prob'ly doesn't have a signal." I notice the Cherokee pull up next to Brunhilda outside the window behind Mary. "Digger's back."

We listen to him stomp his feet outside before opening the door. "What a storm!" he says as he comes inside. He shuts the door, doesn't look at us, and immediately heads for the coffeepot.

Mary and I watch him fix his coffee, turn around, and as he brings the cup to his lips, he says, "Oh. Sorry, Sheriff, I didn't see you standing there."

"What are you sorry about?"

He looks a little confused, glances at Mary, and then says, "I guess I'm not sorry about anything."

"Good," I say. "Was the CBI able to take a look at what's in the bag while you were there?"

"Just a best guess kind of thing," he says. "The lab technician had about ten things to do before getting to the bag, but she did spread a little out and said it looked like bone."

"You told her how important it is?"

"Oh sure. But she said that's what everybody says, and…. They're really busy, Sheriff."

"Yeah, well…. Mary will fill you in on what's going on. You stay here and take any calls that come in."

"What's going on?" Digger says, his blue eyes wide with anticipation of an adventure.

"I've got to go," I say, taking a step toward the door. "You did hear what I said, Digger?"

"Yes. Mary will fill me in, and stay here for calls."

"Good. Mary, can you give me a handheld?"

She turns and grabs one of the handheld radios on the credenza behind her and holds it out to me. "I wouldn't have let you leave without one, you know?"

"I do know that. And thank you." I take the radio and walk to the door. "You know where we'll be. Right?"

"You and Don will be somewhere in the mountains trying to find Michael."

I think a moment about a more definitive location and decide Mary has probably hit the nail. "Yeah, we'll be out there somewhere." I start to leave and then remember what I'd wanted to do as I'd driven back here from Cathy's. "Digger, get Missie on the phone—she's at the cabin—and get a full description of Stan Rivers aka Stanley Broken River. Write it up and get a bulletin out. Just note that he's wanted for questioning about…." About what? Witchcraft? "Just say he's wanted for questioning."

"Yes, sir," Digger says as he sets his coffee on his desk and takes his coat off.

I walk out of the office, hook the handheld on my belt, grab the two pairs of snowshoes and the four poles, and smile at Brunhilda. She always waits patiently there—wherever—for me, eager to serve with only the barest hint of reluctance, especially when the wind chill is somewhere around twenty below. Other than that she's ready to go. Hell, I think as another gust blows the snow sideways for a moment, the wind chill is only about—fifteen right now.

"Good to go," I say, opening the hatch and tossing the snowshoes in. I get behind the wheel and start her up. God, but I do love to hear her purring without burps.

As I head west out of the Junction, I realize I'm not as concerned about Michael as I should be. Knowing he may be traipsing around in the hills somewhere with only his light jacket on and those soft leather boots he wears is a worry, but not that much of one. Why? Something keeps telling me he's okay. What that something is, I have no idea. But it's there at the back of my mind as a comfort I can't shake. I suppose that after being together for almost five years, I'm tuned in to him, and what's at the back of my mind is just his psychic whisper. Old winds? No, that's not what I hear. Thank God I'm not tuned in to those.

When I see one of our two county snowplows coming up from behind me, I'm not so much surprised as relieved. It usually takes them a while to figure out the good sense of plowing before we get a foot or two of snow, but not today. My side mirror reveals that it's Glen Hague, the owner of the general store across the street from Cathy's Café, who has obviously rotated into the duty schedule today, and I pull over a bit and let him pass. He honks his horn and waves, easily swerving the big C8500 Chevy truck around me. He's creating a nice single lane right down to the hardened snow that's remained on the road for over a month. The spreader doodad on the back of the dump body is throwing off a dusting of a mixture of sand, pebbles, and ground-up asphalt. I just hope he's planning to go at least as far as where Don has parked his Cherokee.

I get another message from somewhere, maybe from my gut or from those old winds, that Michael is all right, and I believe that, but I still need affirmation. If I didn't believe it, I don't know what I'd do, except what I'm doing right now. I need to see him, though. I follow about four car lengths behind Glen, staying out of the swirl of snow and sand that comes off the back of the truck. He's driving at a good clip, and I wonder if he's left the store in the hands of his wife, Doreen, who's always reminded me of Shirley Temple. She's a petite woman who wears her hair in long curly loops, always with a few tiny bows tied here and there. Glen is a big man, maybe two fifty or more, and sometimes I can't help but wonder how they manage themselves in bed. The sex part, that is. The image is not something that crosses my mind that often, but I am curious. They've got two kids—Glen Jr. and Russell—both of whom grew up here and have since gone off to find their fortunes—Glen Jr. to Denver and Russell to San Francisco. The times I've seen Russell, he's impressed me as probably being gay, not in appearance or affectations but just because those of us who are, know with about a 90 percent certainty who else is. Something in the eyes, of course. And yes, Russell used to take obvious pleasure in decorating the little store for holidays, particularly Halloween. And he always seemed to be more attentive to Michael's needs than he was to anyone else's.

The image I see right now is Michael, smiling as he does, his hair brushed across his forehead, his eyes deep enough to swim in. I'm glad I see him smiling. I hope he still is.

I pass Joe Parsons's place and give a thought to Apollo and wonder where Joe buried him. If Don was right about where he's waiting, I've got another four miles to go before I get there. Glen is still chugging along in front of me, and I hope he doesn't decide to turn around until he gets to the fork in the road, which is about another eight miles ahead. All I can see of him and his truck are the orange lights flashing on the four corners of the dump body and the dense cloud of snow following behind him. Right now, though, the distance between us is shortening, and his brake lights pop on and stay on. He's come to a dead stop.

I pull up behind him, take my hat off, and tug my hood over my head. I get out of Brunhilda, and there's Glen with his door open, standing on the step below the door and looking in front of him.

"What's up?" I say when I reach him and look to where his attention is focused.

"Saw somethin'," he says, turning toward me, and then he immediately turns back.

"What?" I step in front of the big cab and look west. The snowfall is now almost a whiteout, the flakes thick, and right now they're coming straight down.

Glen climbs off the truck and stands next to me. "It was over there," he says, pointing slightly to the right of the road.

"What was it?"

"That last gust of wind kind of cleared my sightline for a minute, and I thought…. Shit, I don't know what I saw, Sheriff."

I ask him again, "What was it?"

"Some critter. Brown or black. It was… standing on two legs. Appeared to be looking right at me, then it dropped down to all fours and took off."

"Right over there?"

"Yeah. Optical illusion, I guess."

"You going as far as the fork?"

"That's where we always turn around."

"Okay. I'll stay behind you."

"Did you see it?"

"No," I say, remembering what I'd seen when I walked back from Skip's after leaving Brunhilda there for her spa treatment. What he's describing sounds familiar. "Let's get going."

"Yeah," he says. "Let's…."

We both get back into our vehicles. I wait for him to get a head start and then give Brunhilda some gas for her to work with. She slips a little on the hard packed snow but gets a grip, and we're off.

Yeah, that walk back to the office from Skip's is running through my mind much like one of those recurring dreams that never reveal an ending. I saw what I saw, and the similarity with what Glen described is disturbing. Michael is up there somewhere, and wherever that is might be the freak thing's destination. I try to beckon the image of Michael that I'd had just a few minutes earlier, and it doesn't return. All I see is a critter standing on its hind legs knowing more than I do about all this crap that's been going on. But does it know more than Michael? I don't know the answer to that question, but I do know Glen should give that big Chevy some goddamned juice and get his ass up the hill. My earlier comfort level with Michael being somewhere up the mountain is gone.

CHAPTER TWENTY-TWO

OUR FIRST winter in the cabin was cozy and quiet, both of us acclimating ourselves to the absence of traffic noise, neighbors, the once-a-week shrieks of garbage collection trucks in the alley, night skies where only the brightest stars were visible, brick-and-mortar structures spanning window views, sirens, the heavy boom of car amps broadcasting rap or hip-hop punctuated with the words muthafucka and ho that so elevate the genre. Michael spent a lot of time in the second bedroom working on his art, and I finished up all the inside work on the cabin.

We'd gone down the mountain to Denver to buy furniture before winter set in with the vengeance we'd been told by the locals it would. And it did, but we were sublimely comfortable, happy, and grateful that we'd made the perfect home for ourselves.

By the end of that first winter, I was getting bored. When spring started to emerge—if you've never seen springtime in the Rockies, I suggest you put that on your bucket list—my boredom turned to antsiness, and my antsiness turned to an idea.

Michael and I started mingling more with the locals. We shopped at Glen's Groceries and paid without comment the outrageous markup he put on everything. We ate at Cathy's Café, where the first time I met Cathy our back-and-forth banter revealed we were kindred spirits, trading barbs with a glint of a smile we both understood. Michael seemed to attract the attentions of the female locals—I think it was kind of the mothering thing women exert toward good-looking young men—while I found it easy to talk to the male locals who, once they found out what my background was, couldn't help themselves from affirming their support for God, country, and the flag. I wasn't comfortable sharing what I'd done and seen in Iraq and Afghanistan, but the little I did relate brought out their stories—bullshit, lies, and yes, truths that were hard to tell—from those who'd also served in the military. The older men who'd served in Nam were, like me, reluctant to share details beyond the basics. A person doesn't understand war unless they've been face-to-face with the very real and immediate prospect of killing before you're killed.

When I met Howard Slaughter, who was then the sheriff up here and had been for the last twenty-seven years, I was impressed with his hard-case mien but immediately saw his vulnerabilities. His kind, for better or worse, had vanished from the west a long time ago. He was a cowboy with a six-shooter and a badge, and he believed the law was what he said it was. And I was going to change that.

When I told Michael what my plans were, he looked at me as if I'd lost my mind.

"No," he said as we sat in Cathy's Café, a plate of purple and green weeds before him, a bottle of water half raised to his lips. He sat the bottle back on the table and said it again, "No. You're not."

"Oh, yes I am." I grabbed a french fry and dipped the end of it in the pool of ketchup on my plate.

"You'd carry a gun and wear a badge?"

"Yes. I'd have to get elected first, though."

"And how are you going to do that?"

"Get people to vote for me."

"Sam, the people up here are... conservative. They're gun people. They all have... flags in front of their houses."

"Yes, they do. But—"

"And you're gay," he said, leaning across the table and lowering his voice.

I leaned over the table too. "Have you taken a good look at Cathy? And we met Denice and Audra. You can't tell me they don't go to our church. And just yesterday, we met James and Carl, who were shopping for flower seeds and macramé at Glen's."

He sat back and smiled. "Wow. You've got five votes already."

"It's a start. My degree in criminal justice and my Army experience.... We'll knock on every door in the county."

"We?"

I hadn't expected that he would question the *we* part of my plan. "I just thought.... Well, you know."

He nodded. "Just kidding, my dear. If this is what you want to do, then *we'll* do it."

"Oh. Look," I said, nodding toward the window behind him. A small box-shaped truck had just pulled up outside the little knickknack store across the street. "I think they're moving out."

Michael turned and looked out the window. "Oh, that would be perfect for me," he said when he turned back. "We've got to check that out. I wonder who owns the building?"

"The one across the street?" Cathy said as she stopped at our table.

"Yes," Michael said.

"That building, along with Glen's store and every other building on that side of the street, belongs to Elenore Emerson."

"Don't think we've met her yet," I said.

"And you won't. She stays up at her place and only comes out when she has to."

"When does she have to?" Michael said.

"When she feels like it. You need anything else here?"

We both told Cathy we were fine for now, and then I asked her where the Emerson lady lived.

"She's got about 900 acres at the edge of the county. The western edge."

"How can we find out if the space across the street is available?" Michael said.

"You could call her, I guess. Or talk to the guy who takes care of her properties."

"Who would that be?" I said.

"He's standing right there." She pointed out the window, and we both looked across the street. There, a huge man, more broad than tall, stood in a black suit with a fedora on his head, appearing as though he was supervising the move.

"That's Tony Fuschi. Be careful with him, though."

"Why's that?" I said.

"He's...." Cathy began and paused a moment. "Stories about the Emersons, especially after the husband died, have circulated up here for a long time. Something to do with the mob in Denver and Pueblo. And Tony is always at the center of it. It's all speculation and probably bullshit. But if it isn't, just be careful. Okay?"

"That's Anthony," Michael said. "I know him."

Cathy and I both looked at the back of Michael's head as he continued to stare out the window. I looked at Cathy, and she rolled her eyes.

"Of course he does," she said as she turned and walked back to the kitchen.

Michael pushed his chair back and stood. "Wait for me," he said. He quickly walked across the dining room and out the front door.

I watched Michael approach the guy, say something to him, and then the guy took off his hat, bowed slightly, and grabbed Michael's hand. He then embraced Michael in a bear hug. I thought a moment about the implications of this. I'd married a mob kid. Though Michael had promised that his father's business was now legitimate and legal, I still couldn't shake the conclusion that our cabin had been reconstructed by the mob. And now Michael was across the street commiserating with what I'd concluded was a mob goon who apparently represented the interests of the mysterious Elenore Emerson. Not that my life wasn't enriched by all the surprises Michael had brought to it, but it was just I wasn't sure what some of those surprises might bode for our future.

As we drove back to the cabin that day, Michael told me that Anthony said the now-vacant space was already spoken for by one of Mrs. Emerson's Denver friends, who was going to sell cookies and fudge out of the storefront.

"Anthony said he doesn't think the fudge shop will last the summer. And he said if it does, he'll make sure it doesn't last another summer. He said if I want the space, he'll make sure I get it."

"Oh, Michael. You mean he's going to…. What does that mean?"

"He'll just convince her to leave."

I glanced at him sitting on the passenger seat. "So he'll off her if she doesn't leave?"

"No. Nothing that drastic," he said.

He said this with a straight face and a serious tone. I looked over at him again and wondered about all the surprises he'd given me. Yeah, I guess I concluded that day that once a mob kid always a mob kid. Maybe a little of what his father had spent his life doing had rubbed off on Michael. As kind and gentle as I had found him to be, I realized there was yet another component to him that begged credulity. My lover, my husband, was becoming an enigma. I loved him with my whole heart and soul, but did I really know him? Would I ever really know him? And that day, as we drove home amid the magnificent surge of springtime in the Rockies, I didn't think it would ever really matter. The mystique surrounding Michael was fascinating. Well, except for the scary parts. But even those were fascinating to a point.

As we lay in bed that night, I asked Michael to clarify what the mob guy might do to the lady who wanted to sell fudge in the Junction.

"He's not a mob guy, Sam. He's just…. He and my dad were tight in the old days. He worked for my dad, as a matter of fact. He dealt with the real estate stuff, just like he's doing now."

Okay, I thought. He's avoiding my question. "Michael, you said he'd make sure you got the space. How's he going to do that?"

He grabbed the book I was reading—*Gallatin Canyon* by Thomas McGuane, a favorite for sure—and laid it on the bed and scooted next to me. "First off, do you really believe a fudge and cookie store can make any money up here? Sure, for three months in the summer it will, but after the summer is over? No way. And I have no idea what he'd do to make sure I get the space. Maybe he'd buy out her lease. Maybe he'd find her a better spot in Evergreen or somewhere."

I considered what he'd said and was comfortable with that. What I'd earlier thought about the whole thing was probably just overreacting.

"Of course, if all else fails," Michael said, "he might garrote her with a piano wire."

"Okay." I inched a little closer to him, wrapped my arms around him, and moved my hands down to cup his naked ass. "If I'm sheriff then," I said, squeezing those luscious orbs, "I'll get you as an accessory, handcuffs and all."

"Promises, promises," he said as he slid under the covers and placed his mouth on my dick, concentrating on the head, then enveloping the shaft.

I will admit that in spite of the pleasure he was giving me, the image of Anthony "Tony" Fuschi strangling some old woman with a piano wire crossed my mind as more of a probability than a possibility. The image didn't lead to deflation, though, and I gently held Michael's head as he worked his magic, stroking himself and releasing the moment I did.

We cleaned up and then settled back in bed. I asked Michael how he thought his friend Tony had found himself in Pine County taking care of some woman's real estate holdings.

"I mean…. Why here?"

"To protect Mrs. Emerson," he said. And in his voice, I heard the dreamy quality that it took on when he spoke of things I didn't understand, the things carried on winds I couldn't hear.

CHAPTER TWENTY-THREE

GLEN SWERVES to the left, and there's Don's Cherokee on the side of the road to the right. I pull Brunhilda over behind the Cherokee, and Don opens his door and steps out. He walks back to Brunhilda and gets in the passenger side.

"Goddamned wind is a motherfucker," he says as he takes off his gloves and brushes his hands against the heater outlet.

"Sorry you had to wait so long. Had to get Missie's statement before I came up here. Where's Michael's truck?"

"You see that ridge up there?" He points to the mountainside in front and to the right. "It's parked on the road about a mile up the side. I figure he couldn't go any farther, got out, and started hiking to wherever the hell he's going."

I can't see Michael's truck because of the snowfall and the intermittent gusts of wind that obliterate everything. "You up for a little snowshoeing with me?"

"The last time you put snowshoes on didn't turn out so well."

"No, it didn't. But I don't think we'll have to deal with the same conditions—the bowl and all. We can follow the road. What's up there?"

"The last time I was up there was elk season. The miners used the road, and there was some logging there too. A few shacks up there. It was originally a game trail."

"Indians used to live up there?"

"Sure they did. Hell, there are places up there I've heard about, but have never seen. Hank once told me some Indians *still* live up there."

And yes, I do remember Hank telling me that the freak bear was actually John Spotted Elk, a skinwalker, who lived, as he said, over the mountain. Over Hank's mountain would be the area that now spread out before Don and me.

"Well. Let's do this thing." I got on the radio and told Mary where Don and I were going.

"Snowshoes?" she said.

"Yes."

"We'll be praying for you."

"Roger that. Instead of prayers, though, if you don't hear from me in a couple of hours, I'd prefer you advise search and rescue where we are."

"The real one or the local one?"

She, of course, has a point. The local search and rescue team consisted of Skip, Glen, and a couple other guys who are also volunteer firemen. Not that they're inept when it comes to search and rescue, just that the professionals in the county are, yeah, professional.

"Both of them," I said, hedging my bets.

"That's a ten-four."

I hang the mike back on the dashboard and look at Don. "You ready?"

"Yup."

We get out of Brunhilda, walk behind her, and I open the hatch. I give Don one pair of shoes, and I also pull out the ski poles. In the few seconds we've been outside Brunhilda, we're already covered with snow.

"I'll lead," Don says, resting the shoes and one pole on his shoulder. He carries the other pole with his free hand and starts walking up the road.

As I follow him, I start to ask him why we aren't driving up the mountain as far as we can and immediately understand why. We could try it, but given the immensity of the storm, we'd never get back down.

We hike only about fifty yards, and Don stops and faces me. "Gotta put on the shoes," he says. "Drifts are getting deeper."

"Yup," I say, and we tie on our shoes, our hands now free to use the ski poles.

When we reach Michael's truck, we stop and look inside. There's nothing in here, and we close the doors.

"I figure he kept going up the road," Don says. "It was probably still visible when he came up here."

I again agree and follow Don as he heads farther up the incline where he knows the road is but is now just a bare outline of itself. The snowfall is over a foot deep, and though the snowshoes help, we still sink in about six inches with every step we take. Thank God we're on the lee side of the wind. The gusts are still rampaging through the tops of the trees, and each time they do, swirls of snow envelop both of us. I don't know how Michael could have made it very far in these conditions and shake my head almost in anger. *Why the fuck did you come up here?*

Don stops again and waits for me to catch up with him. "I think there's a shack up ahead," he says, motioning with his ski pole. "It's about fifty yards off the road. You want to check it out?"

"Yeah," I say, nodding. "He had to have had a destination in mind."

"Okay. It'll be rough going."

"Gotta do it."

Don turns and recommences the climb. We plod on for another hundred yards, and then Don stops, again motions with his ski pole, and then starts to climb up the side of the mountain. I don't see the shack he said was there, but I trust him. He's hunted in this area, and I haven't. I've never hunted, and I've never seen the sport in such a thing. But I do know from the stories I've heard from hunters that they remember their kills and where they happened, usually with great specificity. They'll recite the time of day, the distance from the creek or the river, or from somebody's fenceline, or from the boulder that looks like a jaguar's head. And I'm confident that if Don says there's a shack where we're now heading, there'll be one.

Another gust of wind hits the tops of the trees, and we are both enveloped in the rush of snow that appears to come at us from all sides. When it clears, I see Don waiting for me about thirty yards ahead.

"You see it?" he says when I catch up with him.

I look up the slope, and yes, there it is. You don't see straight lines in nature very often, and up ahead there's the distinct shape of human construction buried in snow. "Yeah, I do."

We trudge up to the structure, which is a low to the ground one-room shack, and there's no sign of any kind of activity. We walk around it and see nothing that would indicate anyone or anything has been here.

"There's a window," Don says as we both stop in front of it again. He brushes off the snow that has accumulated on the window, leans forward, and peers inside. "Nothing," he says.

I scan the rise of the mountainside behind the shack. "Anything else up there?"

"Yeah," he says. "There's another one up a ways on the summit. This is Emerson land."

"I've heard about her."

"Yeah. Just the old woman now, but the property spreads all over this area. When we hunt up here, we have to get permission."

"Don't tell me. Tony Fuschi?"

"Yeah. You met him?"

"No, but Michael has. Michael knows him, in fact."

"Bad business there," he says as another gust of wind whirls up a whiteout.

I want to ask him about what he'd just said, but he's already heading up the mountainside. I follow behind, using my poles as anchors. The accumulated snow from this storm and the ones that have preceded it is probably two feet deep or more.

Bad business, he said.

The climb is steep, and both Don and I struggle with it. It seems like an eternity has passed when up ahead I see another structure on a small patch of flat land much like the one we left behind—a small shack built close to the ground, and there's a stream of smoke coming from the metal stack on the roof. We shoe the additional fifty yards or so to get there, and just as Don is about to put his hand on the front door, we are startled by an ungodly wail that comes from our right. We both look, and there, not twenty yards to our right, is what appears to be a huge black wolf standing on its hind legs, its head raised, its front legs clawing at the air. It lowers to all fours, begins a deep-throated dangerous rumble, and starts to slowly approach Don.

No wolves in Colorado! Before I can give it a second thought, I've got my .45 in hand, and I yell, "Stanley Broken River, you are a skinwalker!"

The wolf appears as if it's been stunned by an electric shock. It stops dead in its tracks and, without another sound, falls down into the snow. I stare at the thing, and as I turn my head to look at Don, who is just now raising his weapon, I see that the shack's door is open, and Michael is standing under the frame, his eyes frozen on the creature that is now becoming overlaid by the snowfall from above.

Chapter Twenty-Four

MICHAEL AND I spent a lot of time during our second year up here getting to know the locals. And of course, there was a method to that. Given the longevity of Howard Slaughter's incumbency as sheriff, I knew if I were to take his office away from him, I'd need all the votes I could get. There weren't that many people who lived in Pine County, but they were spread far and wide, and I told Michael the sooner we got started befriending people the better.

Michael was better at this than I was. I've never been fond of small talk, but Michael was a pro at it. Especially with the women. He knew the right thing to say at the right time, and the ladies just seemed to adore him as he commented on whatever they had on their mind when we'd interact with them. Michael was also tuned in to the things I could not see when we'd visit with folks just on Main Street, in the café, or inside people's houses.

When I finally signed all the rigamarole to get my name on the ballot and it was generally known in the county that I was running, Michael and I started knocking on doors, traveling the county from one end to the other.

One day we stopped at the Hargrove property. Karen was the court clerk for the county judge, and her husband, Ned, pursued endeavors not well defined. It was about six o'clock in the evening when Michael stopped the truck he'd just bought from Denice and Audra. (We'd been using Michael's BMW all-wheel-drive to get around, but he'd already sold it to some guy in Denver whom he'd known in college and was just waiting for the guy to pick it up. It was a sudden decision. He told me one day that the car just didn't fit our lifestyle anymore.)

Karen greeted us at the door with a smile and invited us into her home. It was a cozy little place about two miles from the Junction. Her husband had yet to come home from work—whatever it was he did—

and she invited us to sit down in her parlor where a nice fire was burning in the woodstove.

"As you probably know," I told her, "I'm running for sheriff and just wanted to tell you a little bit about myself."

Michael reached into the tote he carried with him and pulled out a slick-papered campaign document he'd created, noting my credentials. "He's really qualified for the position," Michael told her as he handed the document to her. I noticed that he made an effort to touch her hand.

Just then the front door opened, and Ned walked in and slammed the door behind him. "Son of a bitch" were the first words out of his mouth. "Who's parked in the drive?"

Michael and I both stood and watched Ned come into the parlor. He looked like he hadn't shaved in three days and appeared as though he'd just woken up.

"This is Sam Daly," Karen said as she also stood. "He's running for sheriff. And this is his... friend, Michael. Sam, Michael, this is my husband, Ned."

I held my hand out, and Ned and I shook.

"I guess that's your truck blocking my garage, then?" he said as he shook my hand.

"That would be my truck," Michael said, holding his hand out. "I'm Michael."

When Ned grasped Michael's hand, I saw Michael's smile evaporate. He stared at Ned's eyes as if he were reading a very interesting book. When he realized he wasn't releasing Ned's hand, he did that and took a step back.

"I'm sorry... I'll move my truck."

"No. Hell, I can wait," Ned said.

We all sat as Ned stepped into the kitchen and came back with a beer. He didn't offer us one, and Karen didn't either. In fact, Karen just clammed up and sat there like the proverbial bump. It didn't take me long to give my spiel to them. I knew Michael was probably as uncomfortable as I was, and we left shortly after that.

As we drove to the next property on our list, Michael was quiet and once again inside himself. I didn't want to say anything because I'd read his mood. Pretty soon, though, he shook his head.

"He's not a nice person," he said. "He beats her. He beats her bad."

I looked at him then, his eyes on the road ahead and his expression one of immense sadness. "You felt that?"

"I saw it and felt it. It was in his eyes. His soul."

I remembered Sister Mary Jo Hartig then, who'd taught summertime catechism in southwest Denver when I was a kid. She told us once that God knew what was in our souls, and when we died he'd take a close look at what he saw inside of us, our souls. She told us that all our sins and our atonements would be in there for divine inspection, and what was found would determine which way we went from there—only two choices, up or down. By that time, I was sure my unclean thoughts about other boys had surely filled my soul nearly to the brim, and atonement through confession and penance would be my redemption. But as that summer wore on, baseball, swimming, and bicycles gradually took precedence over the taint of my soul, and I never did admit to Father Schmidt my impure indiscretions.

And as I looked at Michael that day after we'd met with Karen and Ned Hargrove, and he'd shared what he'd seen in Ned's soul, I wondered how he managed to cope with those kinds of things. How did he protect himself from the heartbreak?

When we sat before the fire that night in our cabin, I asked him if he was okay.

"Yes," he said. "Are you?"

"Oh, I'm fine. But I'm not the one who felt... I guess you felt evil when you touched Ned?"

"Yes." He nodded. "But she's going to leave him."

"How do you know that?"

"I touched her too."

"Oh," I said as if that was a logical answer. And maybe for him it was. I wanted to talk some more about this new revelation that he could read.... Souls? But.... What the hell. I didn't want to admit that this was becoming the norm for us, but there it was. Michael was who he was. And I was becoming more fascinated and frightened by it with each passing day.

CHAPTER TWENTY-FIVE

MICHAEL STEPS from under the doorframe and plods through the deep snow to where the black wolf lies. He kneels down next to it as Don holsters his weapon and walks the few paces to join Michael. And I... I just stand here, realizing that I'd just killed a creature I didn't believe existed until just a few moments ago. Skinwalkers? Well, yeah. Okay. And the freak bear in Hank's shed? I guess I get it now. I don't fully believe it, but.... But what? Hell, I don't know. I join Michael and Don, all three of us now on bended knee, looking down at this thing that defies my understanding of reality.

"He's dead," Michael says. He brushes his hand against the thick black fur on the thing's back, and he looks at me and says it again. "He's dead."

"Yeah," I say, noticing that just like the bear, the hair on this one's face is sparser than it should be if it were a wolf.

"Goddamn," Don says. "What is this thing?"

"Skinwalker," Michael says.

"Stanley Broken River," I say.

Don looks at me. "Skinwalker? What the fuck!"

"I'll explain later. What's going on, Michael?"

Michael continues to stare at the thing, still moving his hands against its body. "Hank said I needed to come here. He said I needed to go where the Spirit Dog wanted me to," he says. "He told me...."

We both stand up at the same time, I grab his arm, and we move several yards away from Don.

"What'd he tell you?" I say, leaning into him.

I see the pain in his eyes. He hugs himself as another rush of wind stirs up the snow. I pull him into my embrace. He's shivering like a Chihuahua puppy.

"He said I'd find the answer to what's in the black bag."

"What should we do with the carcass?" Don yells over the rush of the wind.

He's come up next to Michael and me, and I turn my head toward him. "We can put it in the shack. I want to look around in there anyway."

Don walks back to the carcass, and I tell Michael that we'll talk about this later. I don't want Don to hear what Michael has to say. Yes, I'll admit it: seeing for me is believing. But I doubt that Don is at that point in his understanding of what just happened, and I'd just like to have some time to sort this all out. Without Don's *WTF* stare and incredulity.

"Let's take a look inside first," I yell at Don as he once again goes to a knee to look at the carcass. He stands up, and we all approach the shack. Don and I take off our snowshoes as Michael goes inside.

It's a one-room affair with an old iron woodstove right in the middle. Laid across the floor along one wall is an elk hide, and atop the hide are white, gray, and black chunks of something. I look closer, and yes, there's what looks like part of a skull. There's also a couple more hides bundled up in the corner.

"Look at this," Don says from the other side of the room.

I walk over to where Don is standing. He's looking down at a large flat rock on the floor, and next to it is a steel-headed mallet. There's white dust on the rock, and the wall above it is nearly covered with what I believe are wampum, lengths of beaded hide that may tell the story of what's gone on here.

"This is where it came from," Michael says, standing near the woodstove.

"Where what came from?" Don says.

"The—"

"Let's get that thing in here, Don," I interrupt Michael, giving him a quick glance. "Michael, you stay here. Get warm." I definitely want this revelatory conversation to be between Michael and me. I'll deal with Don later.

As Don and I walk outside, he stops me just past the doorway. "What's all this about, Sheriff? What the fuck is going on?"

"It's a long story, Don. I'll tell you everything once we get back to town."

He looks at me, probably attempting to gauge the extent of my mendacity, and nods. "Okay, I'll hold you to it."

"Sure," I say, leaving my snowshoes where they are, and walk toward the carcass. We've pounded down enough of the snow that we don't need them right now, and I look back, and Don is still standing there looking at me. "C'mon." I gesture with my arm. He walks over to me, and we both once again stand over the thing now almost completely covered with snow.

"You get the rear end, and I'll get the head."

Dead weight would be an understatement. It's got to be a hundred and twenty or thirty pounds, and we both ease ourselves more toward the middle of the body and manage to get it inside the shack. We lay it down next to the wall farthest from the door.

"Heavy son of a bitch," Don says. He lowers to his haunches and reaches for one of the legs. "Look at those feet. They're enormous. The claws too."

Michael and I take a look, and everything Don has observed is true. I look at the head and again notice, just like Hank's bear, there's something odd about the distribution of hair on the face and along the snout.

"We'll have to come back up here with Rick Williams," I say.

"Yeah. The forest service needs to take a look at this," Don says.

Don and I stand up, but Michael remains on his haunches, his hand resting upon the thing's head.

"Once that fire is out, it'll freeze," Don says, both of us looking at Michael.

"And," I say, turning to look at the mallet, then looking at what's on the elk hide at the other side of the room, "we ought to treat this like a crime scene. I'd bet that's part of a skull."

Don steps over to the elk hide and gets on his knees. He studies what looks like the rounded portion of a skull. "Yup," he says. "That's bone for sure. Probably skull."

I turn my head when Michael stands up. He looks at me with that sorrowful face. I nod and motion for him to come away from the body. I'm hoping he knows that what he has to say can wait until we're alone. I step over to the corner and pick up one of the bundled hides. It's still got fur on one side, and I hand it to Michael. "Okay. Put this over yourself. Let's get the hell down the mountain."

Don gets up, and all three of us walk outside, where it seems the storm is abating. Don pulls the door closed, and then he and I put on our snowshoes.

"Michael," I say, "you walk behind Don. I'll walk behind you. You still cold?"

"No, I'm fine. What about my truck?"

"I think it's probably snowed in. We'll come back for it when this storm clears."

"I could get it out," Michael says.

"Maybe you could. But please, just come down the mountain with us."

"All right," he says. "First opportunity, though."

"Yes. I promise. We'll come back and get it."

As we begin our little parade, I keep waiting for another gust of the goddamned wind to shower us with snow, but it doesn't happen. I look up at the tops of the trees and see that the sky appears to be turning brightly white in places, a sure sign that the clouds are breaking up, and we might just see some blue sky by the time we get off this mountain. And once Michael and I are alone, I have no doubt that he will tell me what he has seen today—things that neither Don or I are capable of seeing, nor would probably want to.

BOTH THE Cherokee and Brunhilda start up on the first try, and Michael and I watch Don make a U-turn and head back to town. I make a U-turn too and follow behind Don.

I grab the mike from the dash. "Mary, you there?"

"I'm here," she says.

"We've got Michael. Don will be there in a few minutes. I'm taking Michael home."

"Thank God," she says.

"Roger that. Any word from the CBI about that bag?"

"Not yet."

"Okay. I'll be at the cabin."

I hang the mike back on the dashboard and look at Michael, who's still got the hide wrapped around his shoulders and is leaning forward, holding his hands over the heat outlet at the top of the console.

"You want to tell my why you went up there?" I say.

"Because of what Hank and the Spirit Dog told me."

Okay, I think, knowing that what Hank told me about what was in the black bag didn't include whatever it was that put a hair up Michael's ass to climb that mountain. He must have told Michael about the shack and what he'd find when he got up there, or maybe the Spirit Dog told him that.

"Hank tell you about that shack?"

"Sort of," Michael says, pulling the hide off his shoulders and throwing it in the backseat.

"Can you explain that?"

Michael turned toward me. "Is this an interrogation?"

"Yes. That's what I do."

"I couldn't tell you, Sam, where I was going. There was too much.... You probably wouldn't have believed it."

"I can tell you that after what I saw up there, I absolutely believe in skinwalkers, and I absolutely believe in you. It's still some fucking weird shit, Michael, but.... Well, I saw it, and now I believe it."

He reaches his hand out and grabs my arm. I take my hand off the steering wheel and clutch his hand in my own.

"Stanley Broken River shouldn't have been killed, Sam. I could have convinced him to stop what he was doing."

I quickly take my attention off the road ahead and look at him, his eyes. He's crying. I grab his shoulder and pull him closer to me.

"He was going to attack us, Michael."

"Maybe," he says, resting his head on my shoulder. "But he still didn't have to be killed."

CHAPTER TWENTY-SIX

OUR THIRD spring in Pine County, I was elected sheriff by seventeen votes. The election was in May, and by mid-June, I'd pinned on the badge and holstered my .45 on my hip. Howard Slaughter, the man who'd been sheriff for twenty-seven years, packed up his things, went home to his wife, and in less than a month had packed his earthly belongings and took off for someplace outside of Tucson. My only conclusion about that was if he'd wanted warmer climes anyway, he should have left a long time ago.

I inherited Slaughter's staff and soon found them to be good people who were dedicated to what they were doing. I also inherited Brunhilda and began the love affair with her that continues to this day.

Michael's favorite uncle died not long after I became sheriff, and we both went down to Denver for the rosary and the funeral. I had left the Catholic Church a long time ago, but as some say, the Church never leaves you, and as the prayers were muttered during the rosary, I found myself joining in. Michael too remembered the words we'd both been taught as children, and I can say it was a good experience as he and I joined the whispered chorus from those still practicing their faith. The occasion was solemn, though, and when Michael and I walked up to view the body just this side of the altar, Michael grabbed my hand and told me that his uncle Frank was the kindest man he'd ever known. I'd met Uncle Frank a year before and had no illusions why he was a kind man, especially to Michael. Uncle Frank was an old queen without the bitchiness. He adored Michael, and Michael adored him.

The church was packed that day, and I'd never before seen so many Italian people together in one place. And I have to say that Michael's father was treated with deference by all of them. It was as if he was, yes I'll say it, the Godfather incarnate. When he was surrounded by what I would characterize as his *made men* during the reception, I once again felt that tinge of danger and horniness knowing that I'd be sleeping with Michael that night. More than sleeping, of course, but you understand.

We'd decided to get a room at the Westin Hotel in downtown Denver for one night rather than staying with Michael's parents. We both acknowledged we didn't want a repeat of the angst that apparently occurred every time Michael and his mother found themselves together in the same room at the same time. So we stayed just a few minutes at the reception. Michael said hello to family members and friends he hadn't seen in a while but stayed clear of where his mother and father had roosted. I told him I'd just wait for him, rather than mingle. I'm lousy at small talk with strangers, and he said that was okay.

I found myself an unoccupied corner of the room and watched Michael greet folks, his smile genuine and unaffected. From the crowd, though, a short white-haired priest appeared, and he headed right for me. He was wearing a cassock black as shadows with the white tab at his neck. The garment reached down to just above his shoes, and as he approached, I noticed all those buttons on the front of the thing and remembered something I hadn't thought about since my childhood catechism classes—thirty-three buttons, one for each year Jesus Christ was supposed to have lived on the earth. For some reason, at that moment, I thought that was amusing. Why buttons to commemorate the supposed longevity of Christ's time on earth? So as he approached me, I was smiling like a fucking Cheshire cat, but he wasn't.

"I'm Monsignor Tumino," he said, holding his hand out.

The Monsignor. I grabbed his hand, noticed the dark rings around his eyes and his stare that appeared, if not angry, surely intense. "Sam Daly," I said.

"You're Michael's friend," he said, and it wasn't a question.

"We're more than friends, Monsignor."

He continued to stare, and I was feeling a little uncomfortable.

"Michael is special," he said.

"Yes, he is."

"He was given a divine gift at birth. Something that sets him apart from most of humanity."

"So I've been told."

"The dark veil. A curse if it's not used properly."

I looked at this little man, his white hair, the dandruff on his shoulders, his black crow-like eyes, his odor that I'd just identified as something between mothballs and death, and I smiled again.

"Michael is my husband. I love him more than I've ever loved anything or anybody in my entire life. If he is cursed, then he's cursed with everything that's bright and beautiful in this world, the dark veil, as you say, notwithstanding. Tell you what. You and Michael's mother need to loosen up, maybe step out of the church every once in a while and smell the fucking roses, the trees, take a look at the sky, and see the beauty of the world rather than the dark mysteries that apparently you're both so fascinated with. Whaddaya think? That sound like a plan?"

He smiled. And if I'd had Michael's talent, I would have captured that smile in my mind and painted a picture of it—Beelzebub himself.

"What matter the world, when eternity is the goal? You are a sinner, Mister Daly. And you are ill-equipped to deal with Michael's curse."

I can't say I really disagreed with him on that last part, though I hadn't exactly characterized Michael's weirdness as a curse. It was just who Michael was, and I was trying to deal with that. Long ago, though, I realized it's practically impossible to talk reason or logic to anyone who believes the sum total of reason and logic is contained within the pages of a single book written by men at a time when the world was still flat.

"Tell me something, Monsignor, do you really drink your own piss?"

Before he could answer, Michael said, "You ready to go?" as he approached us with a big smile.

"Yes, I am."

Michael didn't even acknowledge the monsignor's presence and grabbed my arm, and we left the reception holding hands.

"I heard what you asked him," Michael said as we drove to the Westin.

"Good. I would have liked to have heard his answer, though."

"You suppose he undoes all those buttons before he pisses or just the ones in the middle?"

"Depends on if he squats or not."

"Hah." Michael laughed and scooted a little closer to me. "I love you."

"Oh," I said, putting my arm around his shoulder. "You have no idea how much I love you."

And yes, disparaging someone for their religious beliefs is wrong. Even something as silly as the symbolism of buttons on a cassock shouldn't be the subject of derision just because I think it's silly. People can believe what they want to believe. Just don't think it's all right to impose those beliefs on others. The Mormons did that to the Utes. So did the itinerant Methodist preachers who skulked the Rocky Mountains and the plains to the east with the intent of making Christ-loving farmers out of Native peoples who'd come to their own terms with Mother Earth and Father Sky a thousand or more years before. And now that I think about it, some men in black cassocks buttoned down the front have their own sins to answer for. Why is it in the very nature of organized religions to strive to subjugate others to their beliefs? The monsignor's buttons should be the least of my focus on what's worthy of disparagement.

MOLLY'S FUDGE and Cookie shop lasted for two seasons, one season longer than Michael and Tony Fuschi thought it would. When she moved out, Michael was ready to move in, having already worked a deal with Fuschi to buy the space rather than just lease it. Fuschi arrived at the closing with Elenore Emerson's power of attorney in hand, and Michael signed the papers after handing over the check representing just some of the funds his uncle had left him in his will.

It didn't bother me that much when Michael named his shop Needful Things. I did give a few thoughts to the creepy things Stephen King had written about in the story of the same name. And I did wonder about all the creepiness the so-called dark veil had already and might in the future visit upon Michael and me. But when I saw Michael's happiness, his utter joy with having something he'd dreamed about for so long, I concluded that whatever the future held for us would be tempered by the gift of what we had so far made of our lives together. No, I didn't think that love could conquer all, but I did believe it could make a pretty good dent in it.

CHAPTER TWENTY-SEVEN

WHEN WE get back to the cabin, I put the Indian blanket we keep draped on the back of the couch over Michael's shoulders and then start a fire. Michael curls up on the couch and pulls the blanket tightly across his chest and even drapes the end over his head. I remember Missie doing the same thing when I spoke to her, and I want to tell Michael what I found out during that conversation.

"You warm now?" I say, looking at the little tent he's made of himself, only his face visible. It occurs to me that I once observed that Michael was cold-blooded. But not now. Not after coming off the mountain.

"Getting there," he says.

I step into the kitchen and grab the bottle of Grand Marnier and two glasses from the cupboard and go back into the parlor. "I spoke to Missie about what was in that bag," I say, filling both of the glasses halfway. He pokes his hand out from the blanket, takes the glass, and I sit down beside him.

"I'm sorry I just left."

"We're beyond that now, Michael. Drink some of that."

He does take a sip, and I do the same.

"What'd Missie say?"

"She said that Stan, Stanley Broken River, gave it to her as protection."

"Protection from what?"

"There were two guys—stalkers, I guess is the right word. They'd raped her, and Stan put her on Cathy's porch when she first showed up here in the Junction. She said Stan told her the powder had to be ingested, or it had to touch the blood of those men to be effective."

"Raped her? Jesus. And stalking her? Who are these guys?"

"I don't know. We'll have to watch out for them if they ever come back. But the powder? Is that how it works?"

"Yeah, that's how it works."

"And she said that Stan was the one who found her back in the trees and put her on that porch."

"You shouldn't have killed him."

He said that on the mountain. "Why is that?"

"He was...." Michael pauses. He leans over and puts his glass on the coffee table. "I might have been able to talk to him. To make him see that what he was doing was wrong."

I'm wondering how to say this in a way that I understand it as well as Michael might. "So some skinwalkers are not all bad? And I do believe in them now. I saw it with my own eyes."

"Stanley Broken River was a shaman. A medicine man. Whatever you want to call it. He was also a skinwalker. I think he was able to.... Oh, maybe merge the two. He'd gone too far, though. He was trying to become more... powerful. I could have reasoned with him."

Michael turns to look at me. I have never learned how to deal with Michael's sadness. My first impulse has always been to hold him, just hold him with the hope that whatever he's feeling, whatever it is that's inside of him, which I cannot see or understand, can in some small way be assuaged by my touch. And I do that now after setting my drink down next to his.

I embrace him. I kiss him. And I say, "Oh, baby. I'm so sorry. So sorry."

"You said those words, and he died," he says, beginning to sob.

"I know. I'm sorry. It was just instinct. It.... He was moving toward us, and I remembered what Hank had told me, and I just said it. I just...."

I don't cry often, and when I do, it's always in response to something that has just taken a piece of my heart away or just added a piece to it. The death of a brother in battle, Michael's grief, or the magnificent simplicity of a sunset, or the first sight of deer's white-spotted fawns in the springtime. Tears seem to span the gamut of emotions. But right now I'm thinking of what otherwise is the absurdity of this moment. I killed a skinwalker using the words Hank had said would do just that. And I'm comforting Michael, who has just told me that skinwalkers can be reasoned with. And yes, if I could paint this picture it would be a study in the absurd. What the fuck should I do?

Michael's sobbing eases, and he wipes his eyes with a corner of the blanket. "I know you didn't know," he says. "I'm sorry."

I release my embrace on him. I want to know what he and Hank talked about that had caused Michael to head up that mountain. "Tell me something."

He reaches for his glass and takes a sip. "Why'd I go up there?"

"Yes. What did Hank tell you?"

Michael cups the glass in his palms. "Mostly we spoke without speaking. I know. I know," he says. "Just bear with me." He takes another sip and begins again. "He told me there was a place where the magic was made. He didn't need to give me directions. I could see it. The Spirit Dog showed me the way. In my mind. He said that Stanley Broken River was a shaman and a skinwalker. He said there are others too. Not shamans but skinwalkers. Just like John Spotted Elk. Your freak bear?" He glances at me.

"Yes."

"He said I had to go up there. That my... magic was greater than his. That I had to tell Stanley he couldn't do what he's been doing anymore. Like the powder in the bag. It's from parts of bodies. It's.... Even Apollo's. The Parsons's dog."

I nod. How in hell will I tell Joe Parsons no, it wasn't a Satanist cult from Denver who killed your dog but a shaman skinwalker named Stanley?

"Stanley killed the dog, Sam."

"Why a dog?"

"I don't know. If I could have talked to him.... That's why I went up there. Hank said Stanley would be afraid of me. That he'd have to talk to me and that he'd have to listen to what I told him. Hank said Stanley would know that I am... special."

Right now I think that Hank owes me an explanation. He knew where Michael was going and why. And now that I think about it, Hank has probably not shared half the secrets he and Charlie keep up there in their little cabin strung with juniper berries. And as much as I feel an urge to head up there right now, I've got to stay with Michael. Michael's magic may well be stronger than Hank's or any shaman or skinwalker who may or may not prowl this part of Colorado, but—and maybe I'm the only one who knows this—Michael is fragile. He's... human, for Christ's sake.

"I'm really tired, Sam."

"You think you can sleep?"

He finishes his cognac and stands up. "Yes. I think I can."

I walk him to the bedroom. He hands me the Indian blanket and pulls back the covers on the bed.

"Can you stay here? In the house?" he says.

"Yes. I'll be here when you wake up." I give him a hug, and we kiss.

He strips to nakedness. I try to remember the last time he wore underwear, and I can't recall a single time. He once told me that wearing underwear was unnatural. As he slips under the covers, I lean down and give him another kiss.

"You're safe here, Michael."

"I know I am. I love you."

"I love you too," I say. I step out of the bedroom and close the door behind me.

I go back into the parlor, refill my glass, sit down on the couch, and stare at the fire. What a helluva day. I take a sip, and what the hell, I down the rest of it. The fire cracks a bit and sputters, and I see within the flames horses leaping, their forelegs raised high. An impossible thing, but so are skinwalkers and shamans crunching bones into curses. And then there's Michael. As impossible as it has been to actually know this man with whom I've shared so much, whom I've loved unconditionally and whom I believe loves me in the same way, I cannot see the absurdity of what I've come to know about him. The other stuff? That which is outside Michael, that which has come to affect us both since we moved up here over three years ago is beyond belief, but yet believed because I've seen it. It's like the war I knew so intimately where absurdities, one right after another, transformed what I knew of my life in the world to that point of it into a dismally bizarre reality that defied logic or even common sense. And right now I see that the horses within the fire have been replaced with creatures too terrible to imagine—forms with eyes shimmering a blackness from the deepest pit of hell. I lean my head on the back of the couch and close my eyes against the images of....

"There," Joe Hill says. "Look there!"

And I do look at what he's pointing at, and I see him, a man walking with a cloth bag hitched over his shoulder, holding a wire in his hand that's attached to the bag. And the woman who's approaching him with her child hears Joe's voice, and she too looks at the man. She stops, picks up her child, who is only four or five, drapes her abaya around the child, steps to the wall of the building to her left, then kneels down, her face to the wall, her back to the man who still walks down the middle of the street.

I tell Joe to get down, and he does, both of us with our faces to the ground. I tell him there is no time. "Do it now!" I say. And I reach into my pocket and feel the PFC insignia that I want to give him tonight when we're back in the compound with beers in our hands. I want to surprise him with the promotion that came through the channels only this morning. But now—oh, right now—the explosion is immense. Rocks, dirt, metal fragments hiss their passage right above our heads. I cannot hear. I touch my ear and feel wetness. Joe and I raise our heads. I see through the still-rising dust that the cowering woman and her child she'd earlier draped her black abaya over are not there anymore, and the man is gone too, but.... No. This is not possible. This is....

Hundreds of owls rise from the dust where the man had stood. Oh, I know what this is. Joe had told me before, there, when we'd seen through our NODs the shadow of a man take form after an owl had appeared from the night, settling next to the mud house. The owls hover above us, their wings frantically flapping. They surround us, alighting now on the ground, taking shape as men, all in black dishdashas, their eyes red, their smiles.... God! They're smiling!

Joe slaps me on the shoulder. I look at him. I cannot hear what he's saying, but he's screaming something and pointing behind us. I look and.... Michael? Oh. No! Michael, you can't be here. And Michael too is smiling. He's standing there naked. So beautiful. So.... He crouches and appears to fold in on himself, and now he is lost in a fog of sand that's now turning to snow? And from the fog, a creature rises, a black-haired creature, the hair shimmering, so... black. A leopard. Standing on its back legs, it's seven, eight feet tall, and it's speaking, and I can hear it. The voice is calm, loving, comforting. "It's all right," it says. "You'll be fine," it says. "I'm..."

"... here."

I jerk awake, and Michael is kneeling in front of me. He's again wrapped the Indian blanket around himself, and he extends his arms out to me, his hands now on either side of my face.

"You had a nightmare," he says. "I'm here. You're all right. You said I couldn't be here."

"Oh, man," I say, leaning forward, grabbing my head with my hands. "Yeah. Yeah, it was a nightmare."

"Were you back in the war?"

He puts his palms on my thighs, and once I raise my head, he stares into my eyes, and I stare into his. My body gives up just a shiver, and yes, it's the *trembling pain* of loving someone so much that it hurts.

"What did you see?" he says.

"I saw.... You."

His expression changes from one of concern to one of confusion.

"Was I that scary?"

"Not to me, you weren't. Come up here," I say, pulling him up onto the couch with me. I don't want to tell him the details of the dream or nightmare. We've already had enough of that today.

He snuggles next to me and leans his head on my shoulder. I look at the fire and see nothing but a fire that's petering out. The day is leaving us too. I wonder if it's too late to call Rick Williams, the forest service guy, and tell him he needs to get up to the shack on the Emerson property to take a look at what we found there. I decide I won't do that. It's been one helluva day. I kiss the top of Michael's head.

"Thank you," I say.

He raises his head and kisses my cheek. "You're welcome."

CHAPTER TWENTY-EIGHT

IT'S A beautiful morning—blue sky and sunshine. Michael is already up and sequestered in the spare bedroom. "You want some breakfast?" I say, knocking on the door.

"I'm fine. Just working on something," he says from behind the door.

His voice is upbeat, and that's a good thing after what happened yesterday. "Okay. I'm going to shower and then head to the office."

"Have a nice day," he says.

I stand outside his door a few seconds, wondering if I should pursue what he's just said. Neither of us have ever been *have a nice day* kind of people, and since he's said that, I can't help but wonder what's going on with him.

Instead I just say, "Okay. I'll try." I listen for anything else he might have to say, and when nothing more comes, I head for the bathroom.

I think a lot of people have their most incisive moments while showering. I know I do, and as I let the water cascade down my back, I consider the pros and cons of telling Rick Williams that he needs to go up and take a look at what reposes on the floor of that shack. So far it's only Don, Michael, and me, and of course Hank, who know about all the goddamned magic that's going on here. And I guess magic might be the wrong word. Weirdness? Bizarreness? And what does Don really know? Hell, all he saw was an enormous wolf that shouldn't have been there about to take a piece out of him. He did see what else was in the shack, but is he really that... open-minded? But maybe that too is the wrong word. Maybe inquisitive is the right word. Don's a good cop, but everything I know about him goes back to that observation—he's a good cop. And good cops are inquisitive. I turn around and let the water hit me in the face. I grab the edge of the towel hanging on the shower door, wipe my eyes, and turn back around. What in hell good can come from this thing becoming general knowledge, with every goddamned idiot on the planet heading up here to see the spectacle which, yeah, would be characterized as a hotbed of freaks? Skinwalkers? I turn off the faucets and grab the towel. I have no idea how I'm going to finesse this thing. Or will I finesse it at all? I rub my hair dry with the towel and again see the specter of that big black wolf drop dead before me because I'd said the words that killed him. Skinwalkers? Yup. They're real. They're as real as war—phenomena that have their own particular reserved seats in the grotesque section of the arena.

I STOP at Cathy's, telling myself I'm hungry for breakfast but knowing I'm just putting off the inevitable. What the hell am I going to do when I step into the office?

"Last time I saw a face as long as that," Cathy says, coming from the kitchen, "was the last time I saw you. What's chewing on your ass this morning? As if I didn't know." She ushers me to a table near the windows.

"Missie come in today?"

"Yeah. She's staying in the back, though. She doesn't want to deal with customers."

"She tell you anything else?"

"No," she says, sitting across from me. "She's been really quiet. You going to tell me what she told you?"

"She tell you she'd been raped?"

Cathy sighs and reaches across the table for a menu. "Yes, she did. Right after I found her outside on the porch. I agreed I'd never say anything about it to anyone."

"She tell you that the boys who did that to her were stalking her up here?"

"No."

"She tell you about Stanley Rivers?"

"No."

"She tell you—"

"Sam. Stop it. She's told me nothing. Except about the rape." She fiddles with the menu, turning it over and opening it, then closing it. "I don't even want to know about the powder in the bag. And the more you dig into this, the more chance there is for everybody up here to know what Missie has gone through. You can't do that to her, Sam. You can't."

I hadn't thought about that part of the story. Yeah, Missie's past would necessarily have to be revealed. When I write the report about all this—*if* I write a report—it will all be there in black and white. I nod. "Okay. How about eggs well, some bacon, toast, and coffee?"

She puts her elbows on the table and rests her head on the fists she's made of her hands. "You said 'okay.' You mean that?"

"Right now I do. If I don't get my breakfast soon, I might change my mind."

She looks at me as if she doesn't believe a damned word I've said. "I'll get your breakfast. If you expose Missie, though, I'll hunt you down, and the next meal I serve you will be your balls."

I imagine the unpleasant image of my balls on a plate, Cathy setting it down in front of me with a smile. "Gonna have to change the menu for that: Sam's Balls a la King. Prob'ly put it right next to the Rocky Mountain oysters."

"You know what I mean."

"I do." I look at what now is a plea in her expression, and I nod. "I do."

"SHERIFF," DIGGER says, popping up from his desk as I walk in the door. "The CBI said that stuff is definitely bone, but since it's in a powder form, they'll have to do some tests to see if it's human or animal. And they're going to call me in a day or two. And Merle Stacey—the trailer park manager?—wants to know if he can help us with the guy who used to live in that trailer, and—"

"Digger," I say, holding up my hand. "It'll be just a minute. Let me sit down and we can talk about everything. And no, Merle Stacey can't help with anything." I glance at Mary and nod for her to follow me. I walk past Digger, step into my office, and take off my coat and hat.

"Where's Don?" I say as Mary comes in and sits down in the chair in front of my desk.

"His boy, Nathan, the skinny one with glasses?"

"Yeah."

"Nathan broke his arm sledding yesterday while Don and you were out doing whatever. Don's taking him to the hospital."

"Why didn't his wife take him yesterday?"

"She didn't think it was broken. Swelled up overnight."

"He say anything?"

"Nathan?"

"No. Don. Did he tell you or anybody else about what we found up there?"

"He came in here after coming off the mountain, stayed about ten minutes, and then said he was going home."

"So, he didn't say anything?"

"To tell you the truth, he looked beat to hell, and he kept shaking his head like.... Well, like he couldn't figure something out."

"Okay. What else is going on?"

"I got a bite on the deputy position. It was posted for only about a half hour when I got a response."

"Who from?"

"Well.... It's a woman. She's a Denver cop right now, but she wants to live in the mountains. She e-mailed her resume to me, and it looks good. She's a veteran."

"You tell her what the salary is? Doubt she'll want to leave the DPD."

"I did, and she doesn't have a problem with it."

"And you only got the one bite?"

"That's it."

"Get her scheduled to come in, then."

"Already have. She'll be here tomorrow."

"Anything else?"

"Glen Hague says he saw a huge wolf when he was plowing the county road yesterday. That's the other thing Digger wanted to tell you."

"Christ! Who'd he tell?"

"Everybody."

"Goddammit!"

"Was there?"

"No. There wasn't." I can say this without lying. It wasn't a wolf. "It was probably a dog, or hell, maybe it was a bear that crawled out of its den earlier than it should have."

She looks at me, her head cocked a little. "Why do I get the feeling you're not telling me everything about what happened up there?"

"I don't know why, Mary. Why don't you send Digger in here, and he can tell me everything you've already told me."

She smiles and stands up. "Be nice to him, Sheriff. Ever since you and he.... Ever since the bear incident, he thinks you've been shutting him out. He thinks you don't trust him anymore."

"If you can remember the words to 'Kumbaya,' maybe we could all just have a little moment here in my office. We could all do a group hug. Maybe burn some incense."

"Maybe we could," she says as she steps out of my office and tells Digger that it's his turn.

Before I can take my next breath, Digger's standing in front my desk, his sweet smile just so damned perfect.

"Glen said he saw a wolf," he says.

"Sit down, Digger."

He looks like a ten-year-old boy about to burst with an epiphany, probably about how fast he could run with a new pair of Nikes.

"Glen didn't see a wolf. We don't have wolves in Colorado because they were all killed off a long time ago. And I doubt any have migrated here from Yellowstone or Montana."

"He said it sure looked like—"

"You couldn't see your hand in front of your face out there, Digger. He saw something black. No way could it be a wolf."

He loses his sweet smile and says, "I guess you heard about Don's kid?"

"Yes, I did. And about a potential new deputy. The CBI say anything else about that bag?"

"Just what I told you. They'll let me know when they have any more information. You want me to call them again and see if they can hurry it up?"

"No, that's not necessary." I know what's in that bag and how it got there. "Why don't you go out on patrol. With Don out, we gotta have somebody out there."

"Okay," he says. He stands up and begins to walk out of my office and then stops. "Where'd you find Michael?"

"Oh...." Yeah, this isn't going to be easy. I've yet to formulate the fairy tale I'm going to tell everybody, and I'd better start propagating that lie right now. "He just thought he'd go for a hike and try to get some pictures of the storm."

"That sounds like something he would do," he says. He smiles again; then he walks out of my office.

And yes, that does sound like something Michael would do. Something natural, like not wearing underwear. I've got to go talk to Glen about what he saw yesterday. I really dislike having to douse all these burning bushes before they turn into the conflagration I know they will. And, also, there's something that's been bugging me about Mrs. Emerson, whom I've never met, and the fact that the only shaman or witch I know about in the county was crunching bones on her property. My impression is that Tony Fuschi keeps a pretty close eye on her property and.... Well, I guess the question that's bugging me is who knew what and when? If they did? They? Yeah, I need to meet Mrs. Emerson. And I need to talk to Hank. Why does it always come down to Hank?

There's nothing much on the desk that can't wait until I cover my ass, and Michael's too, with the hopefully believable bullshit I'm trying to concoct about yesterday and every other goddamned thing that's happened since Digger and I fell into the bowl. I stand up, grab my coat and hat, and walk out of my office.

"I'm going over to Glen's, and then I'm heading up to Hank's." I notice that Digger has already left, and Mary's the only one here. I stop in front of her desk and look at her. She's sitting there with a little smirk on her face. "What?"

"When you're done with everything you need to do right now, maybe we, just you and me, could sit down, and you could tell me what's really going on."

"I...." No, I can't bullshit Mary. I found that out a long time ago. "If I said you wouldn't really want to know, would that be enough for you?"

"What do you think?"

We smile at each other, both of us knowing the answer to that question. "Did Slaughter tell you all his secrets?"

"No. But I knew them anyway."

I nod and button my coat. "Maybe this afternoon we can have that sit-down. We'll close the door, maybe order in, maybe.... Hell, maybe we could consult with Uncle Jack as I bare the secrets of my soul."

"That works for me."

"Okay, then. You have a nice day." I can't believe I just said that.

She says, "Ditto," as I open the front door and walk out.

I WALK across the street, and there's Glen outside his store, shoveling snow off the sidewalk in front of it. I notice that the three-foot and higher aprons of snow that line the edges of Main Street on both sides are absent from the front of Glen's store. I suppose since it was Glen who plowed

Main Street, it was left to his discretion whether or not he kept the access to his store clear. Obviously, he took pains to do that.

"Hey, Sheriff," he says as I approach him.

"Glen, I—"

"That wolf show himself when you and Don went up the mountain?"

"No. No, it didn't. In fact, Glen, that's what I wanted to talk to you about."

"That was a huge…. Damn! I bet he weighed a hundred and fifty pounds."

"Glen, it wasn't a wolf."

He looks at me as if I've lost my marbles. "Hah! You shittin' me?"

"I don't know what it was, and you don't either. You can't make assumptions about things that just aren't possible. There aren't any wolves in Colorado."

He considers what I've said for a moment.

"That might be right. Maybe it was…. No, couldn't have been a bear either. Hah! Maybe the creature from the black lagoon."

I have an urge to tell him that he might be on to something and, well…. Sure. Let's lighten it up a bit. "That's gotta be it, Glen."

"Or some damned Abert's squirrel on steroids," he says, raising his head and letting go of a spasm of laughter that nearly knocks him over.

I wave at him, turn, and walk back across the street toward Brunhilda. God knows what else he'd come up with if I hung around a little longer. Glen's a good man with two good-looking boys and a wife, Doreen, who sails in her mind on the Good Ship Lollipop. I don't think he'll stick to the wolf story because, all things being equal, he does have a modicum of common sense, and I hope I pointed out to him that common sense precludes there being any wolves about. Skinwalkers, yes. But, wolves? Nope.

As I sit down behind the wheel, it occurs to me that I probably ought to talk to Don before I head up to Hank's place. I start Brunhilda, and she purrs to life with no hint of reluctance. I pull my phone from my coat pocket and punch Don's number. He answers on the second ring, and we exchange a greeting. He sounds tired, and I can understand why.

"Nathan okay?"

"He's good. I'm out in the hallway at the hospital. They're putting a cast on now, and the wife is in there with him. I'll probably come into the office after a while."

"No, don't do that. Take a day off. You deserve it."

"You know," he says and pauses. "What happened up there has been on my mind. All night, in fact."

"Yeah. Me too. I wanted to ask you to just keep it to yourself, though. We need to go over it. Just us."

"Oh." He manages a laugh. "I'm not telling anybody about anything. My wife would have me committed if I told her what I think I saw. You think that shit was weird?"

"Weird as can be. Yeah. We need to sort it out."

"Michael all right?"

"He's fine."

"Good. I think I will take a day off. I need to get some sleep."

"That's fine. See you tomorrow."

"I'll be there," he says.

I put the phone back in my pocket, look out the windshield, and see the back of Mary's head as she does whatever it is she's doing in there. I do trust her and depend on her more than she knows. Or maybe she does. Can I tell her everything, though? I slip the gearshift to *R* and back out of my spot. Hell, she probably knows everything already. She usually does.

As I start up Hank's drive, I see his vintage—vintage as in a piece of shit—Jeep coming toward me. It's one of those two-seaters with a canvas top that he's patched up in about fifteen places with duct tape. It gets him where he needs to go, and right now I'm curious about that. We stop next to each other, and he opens the canvas door with the plastic window. I lower my window and see that he's got Charlie in there with him, sitting in the passenger seat.

"Where you headed?" I say.

"Going down to the store."

"I need to talk to you."

"About Michael?"

"Yes. That and some other things."

"He okay?"

"He's fine. Stanley Broken River isn't fine, though."

"Yeah," he says, nodding. "I know."

"You want to talk at my office?"

"After I buy groceries."

"Okay. I'll head back down there."

"Maybe an hour. Maybe more."

"That's fine." The few Native Americans I've known have never been very good with time. Time is kind of an abstraction for them, something more attuned to the position of the sun than the hands on a clock. "I'll wait for you there."

He closes his door and heads down the hill.

I drive up his lane, turn around in front of his place, and start to go back down the hill when my curiosity gets the better of me. I back up closer to his cabin, cut the engine, and get out. I want to look in his shed, and as I approach it, I see that the snow at its entrance has been beaten down by some kind of activity, and there are tire tracks, as if Hank had backed up his Jeep to the door. I take the peg out of the hasp and open the door. I can't say I wasn't expecting this, but I'm still a little surprised. There's nothing in here except the junk he keeps on the walls and in the corners. The freak bear, aka John Spotted Elk, is gone. The pine frame Hank had put it in is still here, traces of cedar ash remain, but the body is gone.

I close the door and put the peg back in the hasp. There's no sign that the body was dragged anywhere, only the beaten down snow in front of the shed and the tire tracks. All I can do is smile. The wily son of a bitch is two steps ahead of me. Hell, he's several miles ahead of me, and I don't think he's going to buy groceries.

I get back in Brunhilda and grab the mike. "Digger. You out there?"

Sans static, he answers immediately. "I'm here, Sheriff."

"If you see Hank, I want you to follow him. Try not to let him see you, but keep an eye on him."

"His Jeep?"

"Yes. His Jeep."

"Sheriff." It's Mary's voice with a burst of static.

"Yeah?"

"Hank just drove down Main. He's over at Glen's."

"Okay. I'm coming down there."

"You still want me to follow him?" Digger says, again with no static.

"No, Digger. I'll be down there in a minute."

"Ten-four," Digger says, the transmission as clear as this day.

I hang the mike back on the dash and know with certainty that Digger's got an in with whatever gods control radio waves. I suppose a pure heart is a prerequisite for such a thing.

I get Brunhilda going, head back down Hank's lane, and turn onto the county road, Brunhilda's tires hissing on the water and slush pools that are now beginning to appear.

CHAPTER TWENTY-NINE

I DRIVE directly to Glen's, see Hank's Jeep parked there, and stop Brunhilda right behind it. I get out, peek into the scratched plastic rear window, and there's nothing in there, but I do hear Charlie's guttural menace from the passenger seat, and I back away. What the hell? Maybe he dumped it on the way down here. But I probably would have seen him stopped somewhere off to the side of the road. Yeah, no two ways about it: Hank continues to amaze and confuse. As unassuming as he's always appeared to be, he's much more than that. He exists on more planes than I or anybody else up here does. Except for Michael. Or Stanley Broken River. Or John Spotted Elk. Or maybe more that I don't even know about. *Old winds.*

I turn Brunhilda around and park in front of the office. As I get out, I glance toward the café, and I'll be goddamned if there isn't an old green Toyota sitting right out front. Missie had told me about a Toyota that the two guys who'd attacked her had driven, and yeah, this might be them. I open the office door, and it's still only Mary in here.

"Get on the radio and tell Digger to meet me at Cathy's. Tell him to park his car and walk up here. And tell him not to come in. Just stay outside."

"What's going on?"

"Maybe nothing. Just tell him to get over here."

She presses the button on the mike that sits on her desk. I close the door as I hear her get Digger on the radio.

I don't want the two guys who belong to that car to get spooked, and I don't even look at the Toyota as I pass by it and climb the steps to Cathy's front door. I walk in, and Cathy comes from behind the serving counter to greet me.

"You back again?"

"Apparently." I look at the several customers in the dining room and see two young men seated at a table in the corner, both of them wearing ball caps, and the logo on one of them reads Denver Broncos. One of them looks at me and then quickly turns his head away.

"Can't believe you're hungry already."

"I'm not. Missie still in the back?"

"Yes."

"She hasn't been out here at all?"

"No. Like I told you, she doesn't want to handle customers today."

"You serve those two boys over in the corner?"

She looks over there, and I step between her and her line of sight.

"No. Don't look. Just tell me."

"I'm serving everybody today. Why?"

"Those might be the boys who hurt Missie. I need for you to get her to peek out from the back and take a look at those two. Just nod your head if she's able to identify them."

"I'm not sure I want her to do this."

"You don't want those boys to pay for what they did? If they did it?"

"Of course I do. But I don't want Missie exposed to…. It'll be traumatic, Sam. And she doesn't need to relive what happened to her."

"I'll wait until they go outside to confront them. But I won't know if I should do that unless Missie says it's them."

"I doubt she'll press charges."

"Cathy, will you please do what I ask? If they spook on me, we'll have a goddamned melee in here, and I don't think that will benefit anybody."

She gives me one of her *fuck you* looks, turns, and goes into the kitchen area. I don't want to look at the boys in the corner again, but I can't help it and do. This time, both of them are looking at me, and they quickly avert their gaze. I look back at the corner wall back in the kitchen and worry that Missie will refuse to do what I've asked. But there she is, just a smidgen of her head visible. Cathy steps out from behind the wall as Missie's head disappears behind it. She stares at me a few seconds and then nods her head. I nod back at her, turn around, and go back outside.

Digger's just now jogging up the sidewalk, and I stop him before he gets in front of Cathy's. "Hold up here," I say.

"Got here as quick as I could. What's up?"

"There are two boys in there who I'm pretty sure belong to that green Toyota."

"Really?" Digger says, looking at the Toyota.

Before he can ask what offense the Toyota has committed, I tell him I want to talk to the boys about something, and he needs to help me get them to my office.

"Okay." He nods. "I can do that."

"They can probably see out the window, so you keep low, get on the other side of the café, and we'll just wait for them to come out. And leave your weapon holstered."

"Yes, sir," he says.

He bends down and creeps up to the café, keeping his body unseen below the window, then backs himself up against the stairs and inches to the other side of them. He gives me a thumbs-up when he gets in the position I told him to.

I can barely see into the café and can't see the boys from where I'm at. We wait a few minutes, and here comes Glen from across the street.

"You know, Sheriff, I've been thinking about what I saw yesterday and—"

"Can't talk now, Glen."

He sees Digger, looks at the café, and then he looks back at me. "You got some police business goin' on here?"

"Yes, we do. Why con't you go back across the street and—"

The two boys step out of the café and stand on the porch. They see Digger first, and then one of them nods toward me, and they have a little conversation.

"Morning," I say, walking toward the steps, and Digger takes a few steps toward them as well. "I'm Sheriff Daly, and I'd like to talk to you both. In my office just down the street."

"Why?" the one wearing the Denver Broncos cap says.

"Because," I say, noticing that Digger is near the foot of the stairs. I walk there too and see, if not fright in both of the boys' eyes, at least confusion. Hell, they're only about seventeen or eighteen.

"That Toyota yours?"

The other one whose cap I now see reads Deal With It says, "Oh. Yeah, it's mine. I've got the current sticker for the plates but just haven't got around to sticking it on."

"That would be a good idea, but I want to talk about something else."

"They're expired for sure," Glen says, standing behind the Toyota.

I walk up the steps and motion for Digger to come up as well. "Thanks, Glen. You go on back to the store."

Glen stands there as if waiting for a replay of the shootout at the O.K. Corral.

"Let's take a walk just up the street," I say, grabbing one of the boys' arms. Digger takes the hint and grabs the other boy's arm.

Deal With It boy says, "This is police harassment. We got rights."

"Of course you do," I say, feeling through the kid's light jacket that his arm is about the circumference of a fishing pole. "You can make a complaint as soon as we get to the office."

"This is bullshit," Deal With It boy says. Denver Bronco boy keeps his mouth shut as Digger walks him down the steps.

DIGGER STANDS behind the two chairs in front of my desk where who I now know from their driver's licenses is Shaun and Tim sit, both boys wide-eyed and, I think, a little intimidated by the experience. Shaun, Denver Bronco boy, is seventeen, and he's got a bad case of acne. Tim, the civil rights crusader, is eighteen and is one of those kids who wears their dissatisfaction with the entire fucking universe on their sleeves, their eyes defiant. They both live in Shawnee, just a wide place in the road, the closest town to the Junction in the bordering county.

I pick up my landline and dial Mary's number. "Would you kindly tell Glen to get the hell out of here?" I say when she picks up.

He followed us to the station and stands in the outer office peering through the glass at what's going on in my office.

"Will do," she says.

I see her say something to Glen, and he quickly turns and walks out the front door.

"Okay, then," I say, looking at the boys.

Shaun is staring down at his hands folded in his lap, and Tim's pretty blue eyes are staring a hole through my head.

"I wanted to talk to you about an incident that happened quite some time ago and also about what I've been told are your frequent visits to the Junction."

"Like we can't go where we want to?" Tim says.

"No, you can go wherever you want to as long as your motives are pure."

"What?" Tim says, his face all scrunched up.

"Do you know a young woman named Melissa, or maybe you know her as Missie?"

Shaun raises his head, looks at me, and then glances at Tim.

"No. We don't," Tim says.

"Well, let's just say for argument's sake that you do know her and that you raped her a while back and left her out in the cold. Probably to die."

"No! No!" Shaun says, shaking his head. "That wasn't it at all."

Tim rolls his eyes and raises his head up to look at the ceiling. "So that's what this is about."

"Yes, it is."

"She told you we raped her?" Shaun says.

"For argument's sake, yes, that's what she said."

"She's a lying bitch," Tim says.

"So you do know her? Thought you said you didn't."

"We gave her a ride from Denver," Shaun says, his voice cracking.

"Tell me about that."

"She was—" Shaun tries to continue, but Tim shuts him down.

"We went to Denver," Tim says, "just to hang around. There ain't nothin' in Shawnee to do, and we just went down to Denver for some fun. Saw this girl thumbing a ride on I-70 when we were comin' back, and we stopped and picked her up. She was high as a fuckin' kite, and we'd had some beer and…. We told her we were goin' to Vegas 'cause that's where she wanted to go. We stopped here in the Junction to take a goddamned piss, and the bitch jumped outta the car and ran into the trees."

I don't think Tim is lying. "That what happened, Shaun?"

"Yes," he says, his eyes filling up. He wipes his sleeve across his eyes and says, "We didn't do anything to her. Every time we come through the Junction, we stop for a while just to see if we can see if she's all right."

"Okay. Why didn't you follow her into the trees? She coulda froze to death."

They look at each other, and finally Tim speaks up. "We saw somethin' in the trees. Big and black. Couldn't have been a bear, but that fucker was huge. And besides it wasn't that cold out. I stopped Shaun from goin' in there after her. We waited by the car awhile and didn't hear nothin', so we just left. Whenever we come through here, we stop for a little while to see if we can see her because Shaun is worried about her. I keep tellin' him that she's prob'ly in Vegas for all we know, but he still makes me stop. He thinks she's here in the Junction."

I don't know Missie that well. Hell, nobody really knows Missie except Cathy, and Cathy's not sharing much, and Missie probably lied to me when I talked to her. Yeah, I know. Too many times women's accounts of these kinds of things are devalued simply because they're women. But I think these boys are telling the truth.

"Digger, get out your lie detector machine and we'll hook these boys up. See if they're truthful."

Digger looks at me and doesn't say anything. We don't have a polygraph machine, and before he spills those beans, I say, "It's out in the storage shed."

"I didn't know—"

"Just go get it, Digger." I wink at him and hope he understands.

"Sure, Sheriff. I'll be right back."

"I ain't takin' no lie detector test," Tim says. "I've got my rights."

"My deputy has a tendency to get violent with cases like these. I don't know if I could control him if you boys are lying."

"We're telling the truth," Shaun says, now with snot coming out of his nose.

"You telling the truth, Tim?"

"Yeah, I am," he says. "And I can handle myself with your deputy. Just so you know."

I stare at the boys for a minute and then dial Mary on the landline. "Tell Digger we won't need the machine," I tell her.

"What machine?"

"Just tell him he can resume his patrol."

"Oh, Sam. You're playing him again. Shame on you."

"Right. You know how out of control he gets. It's safer for these boys if he goes back on patrol."

"Jesus," she says and disconnects.

"You said Melissa was high as a kite," I say, putting the receiver back on the phone's base. "Do you know what she was high on? And better yet, how did you know she was high?"

"Hah!" Tim laughs. "You kiddin' me? She was flyin' on the thermals of her own little trip. She was trippin', man."

Flyin' on the thermals. Kid's got a knack for words. Or hell, maybe that's the way kids describe it these days. "What was she doing?"

"I felt sorry for her," Shaun says. "She'd be crying one minute then laughing the next. She kept saying something about... I don't know. It was crazy talk."

"Shaun and me don't use," Tim said. "We smoke sometimes, but that's fuckin' legal now. Right? She was on pills or somethin' else. She wasn't mellow crazy. She was batshit crazy."

"When we got here, to the Junction," Shaun says, "we thought she was asleep. We both had to piss, so we stopped by the side of the road, and she grabbed her backpack, opened the door, and just started running for the trees. We hollered at her, but she just kept running."

"Then we saw that fuckin'... whatever it was," Tim says. "Shaun wanted to run after her, but I stopped him. That thing wasn't somethin' we needed to mess with."

"Why didn't you dial 9-1-1?"

"Oh sure," Tim says, once again rolling his eyes. "Open containers. We'd both had a couple beers. A crazy chick runnin' around in the woods. A fuckin' abominable black snowman.... Nah. No way I was gonna call the cops."

Yeah, there's truth here. I watch Shaun once again pull his sleeve across his eyes and then his nose. Tim isn't boring a hole in my head with his pretty eyes anymore, but they're still defiant, and I suspect he'll project that mien for the rest of his life. But why'd Missie lie to me? And maybe Cathy too?

"Okay. I've got your names and addresses. And I won't hesitate to come looking for you if I find out your story doesn't hold water. I might even call your parents and have a little talk with them about this."

Shaun shakes his head, and his eyes fill up again. Tim just continues to stare at me.

I reach over the desk and put their driver's licenses within their reach. "You can go. Get your current sticker on your plates, Tim. And don't antagonize my deputy if you see him on the road. He's a mean son of a bitch, and I don't want to even think about what he'd do if you give him the finger or speed or even look at him cross-eyed. Got it?"

They both stand up, grab their licenses, and walk toward the door.

"Like I said," Tim says, stopping before he goes into the outer office. "I can handle your deputy."

I wave at him and smile. "Sure you can."

He looks like he wants to say something else, but Shaun grabs his coat sleeve and tugs on it.

"C'mon, Tim. Let's go."

I TAKE a few minutes to go over what the boys told me, and that doesn't last very long because Hank walks in the front door and greets Mary with a single rose. She stands up, takes the rose, and Hank turns and nods at me. He's got his hair braided down to just below his right shoulder, and he's wearing his vest with beadwork on the front of it. I motion for him to come into my office.

"I don't get a rose?" I say as he walks across the threshold.

"Glen had one nice one. The rest were dying." He sits down where Tim just was, places his hands on the chair's arms, and smiles. "Had a strong spirit here." He lightly taps the arms with his hands.

No, I'm not even going to go there. "I looked in your shed a while ago."

"Thought you would. John Spotted Elk left."

"Yeah. Don't know if he left of his own accord, but he's not there anymore. From the tire tracks, it looked like you wanted to take him somewhere yourself."

"Was going to take him up the mountain. Snow is starting to melt, and I wanted to get him up there. His spirit was too large for the shed."

He's been here less than five minutes, and he's mentioned that word, spirit, twice already. "The man's spirit or the skinwalker's spirit?"

"All the same."

"Okay. Wanted to ask you why you didn't tell me where exactly Michael was going yesterday. You had talked to him before I got up there, but all you told me was that he was going up the mountain. You knew exactly where he was going, didn't you?"

"Couldn't tell you. He had to go alone. He was trying to help you. He saw the Spirit Dog."

"Listen, Hank." I'm feeling the usual frustration I feel whenever I have a conversation with this man. If cryptic is a personality type, then Hank would fit the bill. "Hank, I know about the bones. I know what they were used for. In fact—and you probably already know this—I killed Stanley Broken River with the words you taught me."

"I saw it."

He *saw* it. "Well, that makes perfect sense. Did you and Michael talk without talking after I left yesterday?"

"Tried to."

"But it didn't work?"

"No. Sometimes it doesn't. I think he already found the place. Too much magic up there."

"Hard to get through with all that psychic energy, huh?"

He just sits there and doesn't answer.

"Tell me about Mrs. Emerson. She owns all that land on the mountain. Does she know about what goes on up there? About Stanley Broken River's little pharmacy?"

"You talk like you don't believe what you saw, Chief. Making fun of it is prob'ly dangerous."

"For who?"

"For you. For the people up here. Can't make fun of it. Michael knows that too."

He's right, of course. Why I've taken this tack with him, though, reflects on my frustration with him. I guess I want to get some kind of rise out of him, and that's not who Hank is. "I'm sorry. You're right. And I do take it seriously. But tell me about the Emerson lady."

"Emersons have been up here for a long time. The man died a lot of years ago. The woman stayed on."

"That all you know?"

"No, I know some more, but I got Charlie in the car. He needs to go home."

I try very hard not to grit my teeth and slam my fist on the desk and probably yell something like *Goddammit, Hank!* "Can you just tell me if the Emersons knew about the shacks up there on the mountain? That Stanley Rivers was using one of them?"

"Prob'ly so. The man who works for the lady knows all about the mountain. Maybe he told her."

"Tony Fuschi?"

"Yes. He sometimes comes up to my place, looks around without getting out of his car. We talk sometimes."

As always, I get the feeling Hank knows quite a bit more than he's telling me. He always has a reason for doing that, and knowing I can't beat it out of him, I suspect he'll eventually tell me. What I worry about, though, is that some goddamned weird event will have to happen before he does open up. But I do have Michael. Of course. I'll just ask him.

"If you have anything else to tell me, please don't hesitate to do that."

"Sure," Hank says. He stands up and hesitates a moment as if he wants to tell me something else, but he doesn't. He walks out of my office, says something to Mary, and then walks out the front door.

CHAPTER THIRTY

MICHAEL SAW the Spirit Dog. That's what Hank said, and I remember Michael telling me about a vision he'd had of an old dog sitting in the middle of a rock circle, glowing with heat and looking up at a circle of faces. He'd said the faces were Native American. The Spirit Dog? Maybe.

I stop at Mary's desk, smell the rose Hank had given her, and tell her I'm going home for lunch and to check on Michael.

She has a serious look on her face. "You suppose Digger beat those two boys senseless out on the road somewhere?"

"Probably did. You know Digger. He's got that mean streak when it comes to law enforcement."

"You've got to stop doing that."

"I know." I open the door. "We'll have that little conversation we discussed when I get back."

"Can't wait," she says.

I nod at her and walk outside. Of course she can't wait for it. As I get in Brunhilda, I wonder about how much I'm willing to share with her. Probably everything. And I realize she's probably got some things to share with me. The Emersons? Hell, she's been up here forever, and she should have been the first person I asked about the Emersons.

I PUNCH in Michael's number on my cell, he answers, sounds fine, and I tell him I'm coming home for lunch.

"Good. I've got something to show you."

"What?"

"You'll just have to come home and see for yourself."

"On my way. We could probably go get your truck before we eat."

"Already got it."

"How'd you do that?"

"I started walking up there, and two young guys stopped and gave me a ride."

"Green Toyota?"

"Yes. They were going to Shawnee."

Of course they did. "Started okay?"

"Yes."

"You didn't go up to the shack, did you?"

"No. Tried to, but the snow is too deep. I don't think Stanley is there anymore."

I don't ask him how he knows this. *Old winds. Speaking without speaking.* I get it. "Okay. I'll be home in a bit."

I PUT the phone back in my pocket, and there's Digger in the Cherokee coming toward me. I ease to a stop, and he stops too. We both roll our windows down.

"Everything okay?" I ask.

"Yes. Fine," he says. "Those two boys passed me in the Toyota, and the driver gave me the finger. They had somebody in the backseat with them. Kind of looked like Michael."

"What'd you do?"

"Gave it back to him."

I can't help but smile. "Not very professional, Digger."

"I know. But sometimes you just have to do what's right."

"Well, yeah. Sometimes you do. You going to lunch?"

"Cathy's got a special today—meatloaf and mashed potatoes."

"Sounds good. I'll be back shortly."

"Okay," he says, and I do love his smile.

SURE ENOUGH, Michael's truck is outside when I get to the cabin. I walk in, and he's in the parlor. He's set out lunch on the coffee table. I take off my coat and hat in the mudroom and hang them on the hooks. "What'd you make?"

"Just PB&Js and tomato soup. Didn't have time for anything else." He steps from behind the couch, and we give each other a hug and a kiss. "How's your day?" he says.

"Fine. Tying up some loose ends, and that's always a good thing."

I sit on the couch as he goes into the kitchen for our drinks. He's leaned a large canvas against one of the windowsills with the business side of it turned toward the wall.

"You finished a painting?"

He comes into the parlor, sets two glasses of what I expect is iced tea on the coffee table, and sits down next to me. "I've been working on it for a while. Wanted to finish it this morning, and I did."

I pick up half of my sandwich and take a bite. The last time he kept the subject matter of a new painting turned away from me was when he'd painted Digger's and my adventure in the bowl before it had even happened. "Can I see it?"

"You remember when I told you I had a vision of a dog talking to a circle of men's faces?"

"Yes. I was reminded of that just a little while ago."

"That's what it depicts."

"Okay. Any reason why you've got it turned around?"

"First," he says, breaking up some saltines in his soup with a spoon, "tell me why you were reminded of that."

I think a week ago I might have hesitated to even bring this up. Now.... Something's changed. With everything that's happened lately and what we've discussed about his—okay, I'll think of it as *his gift*—I no longer have that nagging feeling that he'll retreat inside himself if I mention another spasm of weirdness that's occurred. "Hank told me today that you'd seen the Spirit Dog. You'd told me about that some time ago, and Hank mentioned it in connection with your jaunt up the mountain."

He's silent for a minute as he spoons some soup to his mouth. "That's right," he says, placing his spoon on the napkin next to his soup. He stands up, walks to the picture leaning against the wall, and turns it around.

"Wow," I say. It's a very striking picture of the vision he'd told me about. He's done it in reds, grays, and blacks, and it shows the dog with its head upturned toward a circle of old Native American men whose faces show stripes of paint, and they wear bands across their brows, and some have feather headdresses. "It's beautiful, Michael."

"It's the Parsons's dog, Sam. I at first thought it was Charlie, Hank's dog. But when I started painting I knew it wasn't because... I just couldn't paint it that way. It's Apollo. Joe Parsons's dog. It showed me where the... magic was."

"The shack? Stanley Broken River?"

"Yes."

"What about the Indians? Are they and the dog...?"

"Speaking without speaking? Yes, they are. Apollo was lured out of the run by.... Someone. Maybe Stanley. With magic."

Yeah, here's another spasm of weirdness. "Apollo is telling the men that...."

"He didn't want to die. His spirit is angry. It's very sad. I just can't believe it was Stanley Broken River who did it."

"But why did the Spirit Dog take you up there?"

"The magic is very strong there. I felt it. Killing Apollo was... evil. His spirit doesn't understand. Apollo's spirit led me there because it wanted me to know."

"And maybe do something about it?"

"Yes."

I look at our lunch—my one bite out of the sandwich and Michael's one spoonful of soup. I then look at Michael. He's staring at the picture. God, let him not be retreating into that dark place. "You all right?"

He turns to me and smiles. "Yes, I am. But we've got to do what Apollo is asking."

"Yeah, I guess. But what would that be?" I'm loving the *we* in his conclusion. "Sorry, but I'm not really that hungry anymore."

"Me either," he says. "We need to find out why Apollo was killed."

We turn and face each other, our eyes meeting. I grab his hands. "Please don't do anything without me."

"I know. If you had been with me on the mountain, Stanley wouldn't be dead. I would have stopped you."

"I'm sorry."

"So am I."

I pull him into me, our arms clutching each other as if that alone is all we need for the rest of our lives, to be melded like this to the exclusion of the rest of the world outside us. "I've got to take care of some things at the office," I say, loosening my hold of him, again looking into his eyes. "When I get home, we'll try to figure this out. Okay?"

"Okay," he says.

I stand up and walk toward the mudroom. Halfway there I stop and turn back to him with a question that's just occurred to me from, yes, another spasm of weirdness. "You think this might be...? Did Stanley Broken River go rogue or something?"

"I think....," he says, and he stands up and walks from behind the couch. "I think we are going to find out."

His tone is definitely determined, and I see no hint of his mind slinking back into some cavern of darkness.

I nod, turn, and grab my hat and coat from the mudroom. "It's a beautiful day," I say as I button my coat. "You ought to open up your shop. Stay busy until we can sit down again and talk about this."

He walks to the edge of the mudroom and smiles. "You afraid I'll go up there again?"

"No. I think you ought to get out of the house for a while. Come into town. Dust off your dream catchers and the other shit in there. Make sure Digger and I aren't.... Well, you know."

He crosses his arms. "But you don't want me going up the mountain again."

I turn and open the door. "That's right. I don't," I say over my shoulder and close the door behind me.

As I drive back to the Junction, I wonder if there's a handbook for skinwalkers. You know. Something that provides the parameters within which they're supposed to operate. Yeah, I know. But still. There's got to be some mystical understanding about the dos and don'ts of skinwalking written for skinwalkers or those thinking about taking up the craft. Silly questions maybe, but where else can my mind take me after talking to Michael? And evil skinwalkers? Doesn't the very idea of skinwalkers suggest some kind of evil intent? Even Stanley Broken River, who, Michael told me, was not evil and that he didn't deserve to die, and now he, Michael, isn't so sure about that.

Then there's Apollo. If the magic potions or curses were created from bones—and I think that's exactly what they were created from—wouldn't the standard practice be to take them from human remains or even from some human being you'd just killed? Why a dog? Why Apollo? To my knowledge—and I would know—there hasn't been a murder up here in a long time.

When I get back to the office, Mary's smile is too big to ignore. "Let's do this," I say, walking into my office.

"Will Michael be around this weekend?" Mary says as she sits down in front of my desk.

"I believe so. Unless he's got a hair up to climb some more mountains. Why?"

"Phillip, my grandson, is going to come up for a visit. And I don't think he's coming up here to see me. You know how he and Michael are when they're together."

"Yeah. They're *artistes*. Sure, Michael would love to see him. It would be good for Michael too." I pull open my bottom drawer, grab the bottle of Uncle Jack I keep there, and set it on my desk. "Guess you ought to get your coffee cup."

"Oh, we are going to have that conversation." She stands up, walks back to her desk, and snatches her cup.

When she sits back down, I pour a couple fingers into her cup and then do the same with mine. "To truth," I say, holding my cup out to her.

"Exactly!" she says, clicking her cup against mine.

"Here's the deal," I say, leaning back in my chair. And I take about forty-five minutes telling her everything that's happened since Joe Parsons's dog was found dead. I even back up a bit and tell her that I've evolved somewhat since the freak bear—now admittedly a skinwalker—fell on top of Digger and me. "And just now, when I was at the cabin, Michael told me that Apollo's spirit called him up there to the mountain."

"Interesting," she says, and I'm impressed that she hasn't laughed or even smiled through the whole narrative. "I think I need a little more of that." She holds her cup across the desk.

I give her another couple of fingers and replenish my own supply of mind-numbing comfort. "That's the story. The facts and nothing but the facts. Whaddaya think?"

"I think," she says, pauses a moment, and then begins again. "I've been working here for almost thirteen years. I've lived up here ever since Dan, my husband, decided our first child, Dan Junior—turned out to be our only child—would be born and live in a place where our well-being didn't depend on home security systems and chlorine in the water. I've never regretted our decision, Sam. And through all those years, especially when I worked for Sheriff Slaughter, I learned about as much as there is to know about Pine County and Gunderson Junction—the people, the places, and yes, the secrets. But I figured out a long time ago that what I know about the secrets of this place is something that...." She cocks her head a bit and sighs. "I keep things to myself, Sam. I always have. But now.... Ever since you and Michael moved up here, there's been a... tension in the air. It's like you can almost touch it. And I don't think it has anything to do with you. It's Michael. Whatever it is about him.... He's—oh, I don't know—encouraged the things we don't understand to come out. To... feel their oats, I guess would be the best way to say it."

We both turn our heads when Digger comes into the station. He waves at us and walks over to my office and stands in the doorway.

"Hi," he says. "All's quiet on the western front. And Cathy's meatloaf is the best."

"Good," I say.

He glances back at the table where we keep the coffee. "You want me to make some more coffee? Looks like you're enjoying it."

"It's not coffee, Digger," Mary says.

I put my finger on the top of the whiskey bottle. "We're getting drunk in here. Why don't you close the door when you leave."

"Oh," he says. "Yeah. Okay."

As he reaches for the doorknob, I say, "Just kidding, Digger. Why don't you get back out there? Go serve and protect for another hour or so."

"Sure, Sheriff. I can do that."

Mary and I watch him walk back to the outer office and then out the door.

"You really need to treat him like a... grown-up person," Mary says.

"I know I do. But.... Sometimes I just can't help myself."

She sets her cup on my desk and folds her hands in her lap. "What you told me about Missie and those two boys you brought in?"

"Yes."

"You and Cathy have a... thing. You understand each other. If Missie was involved with drugs or has some mental condition, don't you think Cathy would discuss it with you?"

"Obviously she hasn't. You do know that Cathy and Missie are.... Well...."

"Yes, I know. I think everybody knows."

"Maybe Cathy is working with her on her issues. But Missie lied to me. Why? What's she hiding about Stanley Broken River?"

"And what is Cathy hiding?"

"Yeah, that too. Tell me something. You said things we don't understand got all stirred up when Michael and I moved up here. What'd you mean? What are those things?"

"The secrets."

"Okay. What are the secrets?"

"Bears that aren't bears. Wolves that aren't wolves. Birds that disappear into shadows of people."

I see Joe Hill from what seems like a thousand years ago giving me my first lesson on skinwalkers. "Skinwalkers," I say.

She nods and wrings her hands a bit in her lap. "Over the years, it rarely happened. When it did, when somebody like Glen would see something, we'd all wonder what it was, but we'd usually just let it go. Like it was Glen's imagination going off on a tangent. Sheriff Slaughter would always discount anything anybody saw that was unusual. When I started working for him, though, we'd have little talks, just like we're doing now, and.... As much of a tough, macho kind of guy that he was, Slaughter believed there were things going on here that defied logic. He called them the mysteries of Pine County. He was so intrigued by sightings of unexplainable things—the bears and wolves—that.... A couple times he followed up on something somebody had seen. He'd sit right where you are now and tell me that he followed bear tracks into the woods that became human tracks leading him nowhere through the forest. He didn't understand it."

"Did he talk to Hank about any of this?"

She smiles and grabs her cup. "He didn't like Hank. He didn't like any Native Americans. He called them savages."

"Of course he did. What about the Emersons? I've got a gut feeling that something about them isn't right. And Tony Fuschi? What about him?"

She takes a sip and again sets her cup on my desk. "Here's what I know about the Emersons."

CHAPTER THIRTY-ONE

THE FIRST Emerson to set foot in Pine County was Martin Emerson, an itinerant Methodist preacher who showed up sometime around the mid-1870s, twenty years after his predecessor Hiram Gunderson had tried to bring the red-skinned savages up here into his fold, an endeavor that at first proved a failure but would eventually become an inevitability. The difference between Gunderson and Emerson was that Emerson detested the savages and traveled all over this area spreading the Methodist word of God to all white men who would listen, emphasizing that the only good Indian was a dead one. And when the Ute people in northwestern Colorado had had enough of the white man's imposition on their way of life—Nathan C. Meeker, the Indian Agent for the area had insisted savagery could be eradicated if only the Ute people started farming and worshiping a Christian God—the Utes revolted in what is known as the Meeker Massacre. The massacre gave Hiram Emerson the perfect opportunity to enlarge and rally his white flock with the fear and loathing that had careened from northwestern Colorado—the savages had to be eradicated in the name of the Good Lord. Martin Emerson became a hero of sorts to the white locals up here and soon established himself on the western edge of Pine County, where he built a house on the 900 acres he and his followers had staked out for him. Besides that, Emerson found silver on his land and operated two mines that by 1893 had made him a wealthy man.

Succeeding generations of Emersons bought up a lot of the land and water rights around Gunderson Junction and became the driving force in county politics. But after WWII, sometime in the early 1970s, something happened to the Emerson family when the heir, Malcolm, married a woman named Elenore. It was apparently a mystery where he'd met her, but Malcolm set her up in the big house on those 900 acres. It was only the long-time locals who'd ever seen her, describing her as a black-haired woman with high cheekbones. After Malcom died, the

Emerson property became something of a fortress, metal fencing and gates were constructed, and anyone approaching the front gates found themselves menaced by burly men who denied them entrance. Old friends of Malcolm who wanted to pay their respects were turned away at the front gate.

When Malcolm died—the death generally known only because the county coroner (a position not requiring a medical license, just the ability to shake hands during an election cycle) was called to the Emerson fortress late one Friday night—only the residents of Pine County knew who he was or had been. He was quietly buried on the property, leaving Elenore alone, except for the mystery men who still lurked around the property, including Anthony Fuschi, who became the public face of the Emerson holdings.

Mary paused a moment before she told me the next part. When she began to speak again, she prefaced her words with, "Some of the oldest locals, who were here years before Don and I moved up here, insisted that Elenore had Indian blood in her or was full-blooded and had somehow tricked Malcolm into marrying her. They said she was...." And then Mary paused again, taking a moment to swirl the last of the whiskey in her cup and then drink it down. "They said she was a witch, Sam. And these were older white-haired staunch Republicans who believed in God, guns, and apple pie. They weren't the kind of people you'd expect to believe in the... black arts."

MICHAEL LISTENS to me recite what Mary told me without asking any questions at all. We sat on the couch after we'd finished dinner, red wine on the coffee table, a fire going, the vista beyond the windows now covered by night.

"And besides what Mary told me, Cathy told me that there's some connection with the Emerson woman, Tony Fuschi, and mob stuff that used to go on in Denver and Pueblo. And I'm curious about the fudge lady. You told me she was a friend of Elenore Emerson, and that's why she got the storefront. As far as everything I know about Mrs. Emerson, she doesn't seem to be the kind to befriend ladies who make fudge for a living."

He keeps eye contact with me and nods. "Yeah," he says, "you're probably right. But Tony.... It'd been a long time since I'd seen him. I used to call him Uncle Tony when I was a kid, Sam. He was a nice guy. Always bringing me things—toys, candy. The Denver and Pueblo mob stuff? That was before I was born."

"What about the Emerson lady? Did your dad have dealings with her? Is that why Tony hooked up with her?"

He shakes his head and picks up his glass from the coffee table. "Not that I know of." He takes a sip.

I wait a minute for him to do what I'd expected him to do—bring up the suggestion or rumor or fantasy that Elenore Emerson is both Native American and a witch. It's a curiosity for me that he hasn't done that yet. "What do you think," I say, "about what Mary said about Mrs. Emerson?"

"When I was up on the mountain waiting for Stanley to appear, I looked at all the stuff that was there—the wampum on the walls, the hides in the corners, the... bones. I kept thinking, this is only the workshop. This isn't where the magic begins. Apollo's spirit showed me the way, but...."

He closes his eyes for a moment, and I imagine him taking another look at what he'd found up there and what he'd perceived of the place. He opens his eyes and gives me a slight smile.

"Apollo's spirit was just sad, Sam. He doesn't understand. And I don't think there's any way any of this can be explained unless we go to the center of the magic. Where it resides. Where it's always resided."

"The Emerson place?"

He nods. "Ever since we moved up here, I've always found myself drawn to the west. Not just the mountains but something else. It's also a feeling that... I'm drawn to it and repelled by it at the same time. Do you know what I mean?"

"I think most soldiers and Marines who've seen combat would know what you mean. Do you think you could get Fuschi to get us in there?"

"Don't know. I do know that I need to talk to him, though. I've got a lot of questions for him."

"You want me to be there?"

"No. That wouldn't.... I want to ask him about my father too. About the old days."

Whether Michael has ever really been interested in his father's history, the old days, as he says, is something we've discussed or, to be more precise, is something he's told me very little about. Whenever I've tried to pin down just exactly what it is his father does for a living, Michael has always deflected the answer toward a pleasing picture of a family business that's thriving and legitimate. The first time I'd asked him what that family business was or is, he'd told me that I didn't want to know. If he doesn't know many of the details—I think he knows more than he's told me, though—maybe now with the odd appearance of Tony Fuschi in Pine County and Fuschi's association with the mysterious and maybe magical Elenore Emerson, I suspect he's feeling a new curiosity about his father's dealings, both current and past. He did admit to me when we'd gone to visit with his parents for the first time that, yes, there'd been some hanky-panky that his father had had a hand in a long time ago, but it'd all been in the past.

As Michael readies himself for bed, I break up what's left of the fire and then place the screen flush against the firebox. I blow out the candles Michael always lights on the sills of the four windows in the parlor. As I lower my head to blow the last one out I see the unmistakable reflection of the dim light from eyes set close together right outside the window. I jerk my head away from the glass and see a shadow blacker than the moonless night that surrounds it disappear into the distance. As I turn from the windows, I see Michael standing just at the edge of the parlor.

"It found us," he says, his voice matter-of-fact.

"I won't ask what *it* is. I guess I already know."

"Yes," he says, "you do."

I follow him into the bedroom wondering if those dried up and dead juniper berries on all those bushes that spot our property would work as well as the spring-fresh ones. They probably would, but right now I've got little interest in picking them and hanging them around the cabin. I do conclude that if some stranger knocks on the door, I won't let him in unless he gives me his name. The fact that I now know how to kill them is a comfort. No problem. No problem at all.

We slip into bed, his back to me and my arms wrapped around his chest. We say nothing, listening to the yips of coyotes not far away, probably the family that dens up just at the edge of our property.

CHAPTER THIRTY-TWO

THERE'S NOT much privilege that goes with being the sheriff, but there is a parking place for me just outside the office. There's a little metal sign that reads Sheriff, and you can't miss it when you're pulling into the spot. Digger and Don have both parked their Cherokees this morning in the spots reserved for Deputy Sheriff, but my spot has been taken by a 1970 glossy black Ford Mustang with an engine scoop centered on the hood. It's got shiny chrome exhaust pipes and slightly tinted windows. I'm not much into cars, but this one is a beauty, and though I don't forgive whoever the asshole is who took my spot, I'm more curious than pissed. I pull into the spot reserved for a county commissioner—their offices are next door along with the county judge—knowing that they only show up here when they've got a meeting. Brunhilda gives a shudder when I turn her off, and I suspect she's a little miffed about the situation.

I peek in the front window and see the back of Mary's head, and sitting across from her is someone I don't know—an African American woman whose hair is cornrowed.

I walk in the door, and there's Digger sitting at his desk, and Don is at his, and they're both staring at this unknown person sitting in front of Mary's desk. Everyone in the room takes a second to realize I'm standing here, and now all eyes are on me.

"Good morning," Mary says, a big smile on her face, something I don't see that often.

"Morning," I say, closing the door behind me. "Who's parked in my spot?"

"That would be me."

The unknown stands up and thrusts her hand out to me. She's got to be no more than five foot six, her teeth are as white as Digger's, and her smile is reflective of his too. She's a little broad from her neck to her thighs, and I wonder if it's all muscle.

"Nice car," I say, wondering—because it dawns on me who this is—if the DPD has height requirements for their personnel.

"Nineteen seventy. Mach 1. Four-barrel V-8," she says.

Her handshake is determined if nothing else, and I think she's just getting the answers about her vehicle out there before I ask them. "Okay. You're the applicant for the deputy position?"

She lets go of my hand and nods. "Yes, sir. That again would be me. I'm Brianna Lincoln."

"I'm Sam Daly."

"You're the sheriff, then?"

"Believe I still am. You want to go have a seat in my office?" I say, nodding toward it.

"Sure," she says.

As she walks across the room, I turn to Mary, who is holding a manila folder out to me.

"Her application?"

"Yes," Mary says, and she gives me a wink.

I don't know what the hell that is about, and as I turn to follow this woman into my office, Digger and Don are sitting there with little smiles on their faces. "Shouldn't one of you be on patrol right now?"

"That would be me," Don mimics what the little lady has just said. He stands up and grabs his coat off the back of his chair.

"We'll talk about what we discussed after lunch," I say. "What happened on the mountain?"

"Yeah," Don says. "We've got to do that."

I look at Digger, who is just sitting there. "I don't see that you've got your thumb up your ass, so I guess you're about to get busy too?"

"Oh," he says, losing his smile. "I'm just getting ready to head out to Skip's. I'm due for an oil change."

"The Cherokee might need one too." I step into my office and close the door behind me.

"So," I say, taking off my coat and hanging it up, "you think you might like to be a deputy here?"

"Yes, I would."

"And why is that?" I sit behind my desk and open the folder Mary handed to me.

"It's always been my dream to live and work in the mountains, and besides that, I'm tired of dealing with the fucking assholes who live in big cities."

And you're the asshole who parked in my spot. "Okay. We've got some assholes up here too."

"Nothing like what's in Denver."

I take a second to look at her application. "Degree in English lit. Military police. Afghanistan. DPD for four years." Something doesn't ring true here. A degree in English lit, for Christ's sake. I look at her, and she's just sitting there staring at me with an expression that reeks of knowing what my next question will be.

"You see combat?" I ask, hoping I've taken her a little off her game.

"Can't spend very much time in hell and not see it, but being a woman, I didn't get that close to it. Fourth ID Infantry Brigade Combat Team. Arghandab River Valley, Kandahar City, Kunar Province, and other points east and west."

"I saw it up close," I say and leave it at that. And yes, she's on her game like a rank bull the moment the gate is flung open. "I would always rather be happy than dignified," I say, quoting the only thing I remember from *Jane Eyre*, written by one of the Bronte sisters, Charlotte, who I discovered in one semester of English lit. I don't know if I'm trying to find a crack in her story or just trying to outwit her.

"'It is vain to say human beings ought to be satisfied with tranquility; they must have action; and they will make it if they cannot find it.' That's my favorite quote from *Jane Eyre*."

Okay. She trumped me. "You know anything about skinwalkers?" It's out on the table before I can even think about not saying it.

"Native American lore that's probably bullshit, but I keep an open mind."

"And you'll keep that open mind if I introduce you to my husband?"

"If you've got no qualms about a little black lady dating a tall white woman."

We stare at each other for a moment. Then I read the three recommendation letters that are in the folder. One is from her supervisor, a sergeant, and she's got one from a lieutenant, and another from a captain. They're all good and portray Brianna Lincoln as the epitome of the word exemplary. I don't like the word exemplary. I think anyone who's ever supervised a human being has at one time or another used that word because they couldn't think of some other word that means the same thing. Be that as it may, they are good letters, and I tell her so.

"Nice letters," I say. "Why do you think they're so nice? They want to get rid of you?"

"They want me to do what I love."

"You've told them about this dream of yours to be in the wide-open spaces? Fighting crime in a place where there isn't very much of it?"

"Yes, I have."

Again we stare at each other as if we've got a Mexican standoff going on, both of us waiting for the other to blink.

"You have any questions for me?" I say.

"Are you skeptical about hiring a woman? A black woman?"

"Hasn't crossed my mind."

"I could start tomorrow. I'm on vacation right now. I'll put in my notice today."

I grab my landline's receiver and call Mary. "We get any more bites on the position?" I say when she picks up. She tells me no, and I hang up the phone.

"You have any experience with young women on drugs or emotional conditions?"

"More than I can tell you."

"C'mon," I say, standing up and grabbing my coat. "Let's take a walk."

When we get outside, I point out to her that she parked in my spot. "Probably ought not to do that from here on out."

"Sorry," she says. "Won't happen again."

"THIS IS Brianna Lincoln." I introduce Brianna to Cathy, who greets us as we walk in the café's front door. "She's applied for the deputy position." I read Cathy's shirt—*You Want Your Balls Handed to You?*—and remember our last conversation about that subject. I'm sure she's worn it for my benefit.

"Very nice to meet you," Cathy says, shaking Brianna's hand.

"Is Missie here?"

"No," Cathy says. "She wanted to stay home today. Said she wasn't feeling that well. What'd you find out about the two creeps from yesterday?"

"I don't think they're creeps. Just two boys who've yet to become men. But I'm convinced they didn't do what Missie said they did."

I'm waiting for her to get her butch on and tear into me with a defense of Missie, but she doesn't do that.

"So you want to talk to her?"

"Yes. Thought I'd bring Brianna along. Just having a woman there might, oh, ease the tension a little."

"She's at home," Cathy says.

She turns from us and walks into the kitchen. As well as I know her, I'm not sure how to interpret her demeanor. Either she's had a heart-to-heart with Missie about what I've determined was a fabrication of the worst sort or she's on something that's zapped her usual feistiness. I suspect the former.

BRIANNA AND I walk back toward the office and get in Brunhilda, who still sits in the county commissioner's space. Not that I expected her to be somewhere else, but you never know. She's sensitive and prone to sulking.

I back Brunhilda out of the space and head down Main Street. I pull out my cell and call Michael. "You at home?" I say when he answers.

He tells me that he is still at home, but he's going to take my suggestion and come into the Junction in a while to check on his shop.

"You going to try to find Tony?"

"Probably," he says. "I should meet with him alone. He.... Well, that kind of guy doesn't really like to get that close to cops."

"You tell him I'm just a teddy bear in a uniform? I would like to talk to him. And I'm not sure you should be meeting with him alone."

"We already discussed this. I'll be fine. I'll be safe. Remember, he used to work for my father."

"I know. Maybe that's what I'm concerned about."

"Sam," he says, his tone a little hard, and I get the point.

"All right. I know. You can take care of yourself. I'm going up to Cathy's house to see Missie. Maybe I'll see you at your shop later."

"If I'm not there, call me."

"Will do."

As I put my cell back in my pocket, I tell Brianna who I was talking to.

"So you're legally married? Good for you."

"Thank you. You and the tall white woman? She a steady or just a…?" I'm thinking fuck buddy but don't know the appropriate word as it relates to lesbians.

"We've been seeing each other for almost six months," she says. "She might move up here with me."

"Good. There are several same-sex couples up here. And I guess you might have got a vibe from Cathy?"

"Yes, I did. Even read it on her T-shirt."

"Lesbians don't like balls, huh?"

"Not when they're rubbed in our faces, if you know what I mean."

Yeah, I know what she means. "Brianna Lincoln. They call you Abe down in Denver?"

"No, they don't. A few have tried, but that didn't work out very well for them. Bri works, though."

"Okay, then. Bri it is. By the way, this big gal we're riding in is Brunhilda. We don't have a dog yet, and she's the closest thing I've found to one."

"I named mine Sly."

"Your car or your dog?"

"Don't have a dog. Sly is my car."

"Reflective of its personality, then?"

"More reflective of mine. I do have a cat, though. I named her Necro."

"Don't tell me. Short for necromancer?"

"Of course," she says with a wink.

Yeah, the last thing I need in my life right now is more magic. "This young woman we're going to see came up with some cock-and-bull story about two boys raping her some time ago. Talked to the boys yesterday, and there's no way Missie's story is true. There's a very long story behind that, but I don't have time to tell you. She also might have been a substance abuser or might still be one. As *sly* as you are—" I glance at her and smile. "—I'd like you to just listen to what she has to say and try not to spook her any more than she already is."

"I can do that."

I turn onto Cathy's drive, and after about a quarter mile, I don't see the red Subaru outside the cabin. "Well, her car isn't here."

"She knows you talked to her alleged assailants?"

"Yes. She identified them yesterday."

"Then I'd bet she's gone. Nothing like the truth to light a fire under a skirt."

I'm not sure I understand her allusion but let it go as I stop Brunhilda in front of the cabin. "Let's go see if she's home."

We walk onto the porch, and then I ring the bell and knock on the door. "Missie, it's the sheriff," I holler. There's complete silence from inside, and I knock again. "Missie!"

Bri tries the doorknob. It turns, and she opens the door.

"Is that unusual?" she says.

"No. *Locked* doors are unusual."

We walk into the cabin. "You check out upstairs. I'll look around down here."

My walk-through reveals nothing out of the ordinary except Missie's absence. She is supposed to be here, but it's clear that she isn't. Bri affirms my conclusion when she comes back downstairs.

"Some of the drawers are open in the bedroom," Bri says. "Looks like clothes are missing from the closet, and some hangers were left on the bed."

I pull my cell out and dial Cathy's number.

"Cathy, she's not here."

Cathy sighs. "I was afraid of that. We had a… discussion last night, and she didn't exactly change her story but admitted that parts of it weren't true."

"Any idea where she might go?"

"No, but…. Ever since she came to live with me, she's…. She goes somewhere in the evenings. Two or three times a week, she takes off and just tells me that she needs her own space. She's got issues. I should have told you about this before, Sam. But I thought she and I could work it out. No, I don't know where she could be."

"You knew she was seeing Stanley Broken River when he lived in the trailer park?"

"No, I didn't. Why didn't you tell me that?"

"I guess for the same reason you didn't tell me about her nighttime travels. She's an adult, and you're not her mother. I figured there was no reason to complicate things."

"Yeah, well, maybe you should have."

"Hindsight, Cathy. Hindsight. I've got to go. I'll let you know if we find her."

I put my phone away and turn to Bri. "I don't think it'd be of any use to start looking for her. Either she'll show up or she won't."

Bri nods her assent, and we walk out of the cabin and get back into Brunhilda.

"Tell you what," I say as I back up Brunhilda and then head down Cathy's lane. "If you want to commute up here during your vacation and work with us, that's fine. I can't promise you'll get paid for it for because I'll have to get the paperwork in and deal with the county commissioners. I'll want to bring you in at a higher salary than a starting deputy, and that will require the commissioners to allocate a little more to my budget. Might take a few weeks. But if you want to work for us, I'd like to have you."

"I've got some savings," Bri says. "Yeah, that would work."

I glance at her once I'm back on the county road. "You don't want to take a vacation on the South Seas with that tall white woman before you start a new job?"

"No, I don't. Vacations have always turned out bad for me anyway. Have a problem doing nothing. Besides, that tall white woman burns easily in the sun."

"Okay."

"Thanks, Sheriff."

"Thank you," I say, knowing I've made a good decision. I expect she'll be a major pain in the ass as time goes by, but well, sometimes that all works out for the best.

CHAPTER THIRTY-THREE

I WAIT for Bri to pull Sly out of my spot and then ease Brunhilda into it. I get out and look across the street, and there's Michael's truck outside his shop. I walk into the office and tell Mary to let Don and Digger know that Missie is gone again.

"You want her brought in if they find her?"

I wonder what pretense we could bring her in on, and there isn't any. "No. Just.... Hell, I don't know. If they see her, tell them to let me know."

As Mary leans her head down to talk into the mike on her desk, I go back outside and walk across the street. Michael is in his shop, his back turned to the window, and I just watch him for a minute. It looks like he's rearranging things on shelves and maybe dusting a little. It's always a pleasure to watch him when he doesn't know I'm looking at him. It's as if I've got this insatiable desire to know him even in his solitary moments when he's completely absorbed in himself and I'm temporarily out of the picture. And for the thousandth time, I ask myself if anyone can really know anyone else. I don't know the answer to that, but when he finally sees me standing out here, he smiles and waves for me to come in.

"Voyeur," he says when I walk into his shop.

"Probably. I was just thinking how much that doggie in the window might be."

"This doggie," he says, walking behind the counter, "is very, very high maintenance. You might think twice about lusting after it."

"Yeah." I stand across from him, the counter between us, and lean into him. "I just need a little taste, though."

He gives me the kiss I've asked for.

"I called Tony," he says.

"And?"

"He said he'd meet me here this afternoon."

"What time?"

"About two or three."

"You tell him what you wanted to talk about?"

"I told him that I really want to find a place where I can paint, a studio where I won't be distracted by anything. I mentioned that I'd been told there were a couple shacks or cabins on the Emerson property, up the mountain, that might be the perfect spot for me."

"Oh man...."

"Yeah. He asked me where I'd heard about the shacks, and I told him I couldn't remember exactly, but it was somebody who'd hunted up there."

"Okay. So when he comes in here and you play twenty questions with him about the Emerson lady and not specifically about this studio you want to make of one of those shacks? How's that going to work out? Oh, and the questions you've got for him about your father?"

"I'll handle it fine," he says.

"Just remember I'll be right across the street. Probably watching. With binoculars."

"Voyeur," he says again.

"No. Just serving and protecting. That's my job. By the way.... You mentioned yesterday that you don't think Stanley is still up there in the shack. I wasn't going to ask you how you know this, but it's working on me."

"I didn't feel the presence," he says. "I'd hiked up to my truck and thought about going farther, but... I just didn't feel that he was still there. Besides, the snow was still too deep on the road. I didn't think I could get up the mountain."

"But you would have gone up there again if the snow hadn't been too deep?"

He gives me a weak smile. "Don't know. I promised you I wouldn't. And I didn't."

I suppose that's good enough for now. And as much as I want to trust him not to do something stupid, I can't help but worry. I lightly slap the top of the counter. "Okay. Just remember, I'll be watching."

We lean into each other again and kiss.

DON PULLS up outside the office as I cross the street, and I remember I'd promised him we'd talk about what had happened up the mountain. I hate loose ends, and this is one of them.

"Why don't we go to lunch?" I say once he gets out of the Cherokee.

"Sure," he says.

We walk up to Cathy's, and I hold the door for him. Cathy greets us with a snarl and shows us to a table without saying anything other than, "You find Missie?"

"No," I say as I sit down.

"No special today," she says. "What'll you have to drink?"

We both order Cokes, and she heads back into the kitchen.

"What's her deal?" Don says.

"She's having a bad day. You know Missie left, and she and I had a conversation about that, and it didn't go very well."

"Yeah," Don says. "I thought when she took Missie in that it was a bad idea. Missie seems like a good kid, but to just take her into her home after finding her passed out on her porch. I guess they've got a… special relationship going on."

"Suspect they do," I say. "Don, what we saw on the mountain yesterday was—"

"Sam," he says, shaking his head. "I've thought about that a lot. I overreacted to it, and I'm sorry about that. Things happen up here that aren't easy to explain. Even when Slaughter was the sheriff we saw some odd shit like that. But not up close like I did on the mountain. As my wife says, you embrace it and find Jesus. It's not easy embracing it because there's no rhyme or reason to it. But if you don't embrace it, you go batshit crazy thinking about it. And finding Jesus is just a way of putting it into the *great mystery* category of things that can never be explained logically. It might be hard to embrace it, but what else can you do? You know what I mean?"

"Yes, I do. I think the worst thing that can happen is for folks to speculate on it. Like Glen, who was telling everybody who'd listen that he saw a wolf up there while he was plowing the road."

"Well, that's what it looked like—a fucking big wolf." Don lifts the Coke that Cathy has just put on the table to his lips.

"What'll you have?" Cathy says.

We order cheeseburgers.

"Thing is," Don continues after Cathy steps away from the table, "you and I both know that wasn't a goddamned wolf. I'll embrace that conclusion. I don't know what the hell it was, but it wasn't a wolf. What

I don't understand is what Michael was doing up there. Why was he there, Sam?"

Don deserves an explanation just like Mary did. "I spent some time with Mary yesterday talking about a lot of things. She told me that, as you say, odd things have been going on up here for a long time. She also told me that these... oddities seem to have accelerated since Michael and I moved here. Have you noticed that too?"

He cocks his head a little and nods. "Now that you mention it, yeah. Like I said, I embrace this stuff because that's about all I can do. But yeah, since you and Michael came up here, the odd shit is happening more often."

"Michael is...." Telling Mary about this was one thing. But Don? "Michael has some, oh, I guess you could call it psychic ability. I won't go into the details, but he feels things, Don, that aren't... normal. I mean for you and me and pretty much everybody else it isn't normal. Michael was up on that mountain because he had a notion about what or who had killed Joe Parsons's dog, and also because of an incident that happened with Missie."

"The powder in the black sack that Digger told me about?"

"Yes."

"Crushed up bones?"

The curiosity of cops. "Yes, it was."

"And what we saw in that shack was where it was made?"

I nod. "Yup."

Cathy brings out our cheeseburgers, sets them down on the table, and stands there looking at me.

"Looks good," I say.

"You should have told me about her spending time with that Indian," she says.

"Well, I didn't."

"I know," she says, turning when a couple customers walk in the front door. She gives me one last surly look and goes off to take care of the newcomers.

Don and I prep our cheeseburgers for eating. He's ketchup; I'm mustard. I wonder if he knows anything about the Emersons or Tony Fuschi.

"You ever hear any stories about the Emersons?"

"Sure," he says, cutting his cheeseburger in half. "She's a witch, and she killed her husband. Sucked out all the blood from the dead body and then ate the entrails."

I set aside my curiosity about him cutting his cheeseburger in half. I've never seen a grown man do that instead of just enjoying the unwieldiness of the thing. As he picks up one half of it and takes a bite, I say, "That's actually what people believe?"

He chews a bit and holds the half in front of his face. "That's the story teenagers tell when they're around a campfire. As long as I've been up here, I've never met the lady. After the old man had died years ago, she hired her goons, and Fuschi is one of them. Actually, he's the only one who shows himself in town."

I take my first bite as Don takes his second. "You ever talk to him?"

"A couple times. He only shows up when something is going on with the old woman's properties."

"What's he like?"

Don wipes his mouth with a napkin. "Nice enough guy. All business."

"You know, I've never seen the Emerson house. Where is it?"

"There's a turnoff from the county road as you go west, then another mile on the access road. It's unmarked, and there's no reason to think anything is up there. I'll take you up that way. About time you found out where it is."

"Yeah, let's do that. Fuschi is supposed to meet with Michael about two or three, and I want to be around when that happens. But as soon as we're done here, let's take a drive up that way."

"Sure. With all this sunshine, the snow is melting pretty quickly. The road oughta be clear. Or clear enough."

We continue eating for a few minutes, and then it dawns on me I haven't told anyone about my decision to hire Brianna. I should have told Mary first, but hell, as usual, I suspect she already knows.

"I hired that young woman who was in the office this morning."

Don nods. "Yeah. I thought you would. Before you came in, she and Mary were talking, and she seemed like a crackerjack—you know, a tough cop who you'd be fine with watching your back."

I'm surprised with Don's response. He's never impressed me as being very open and accepting of…. Well, a black female cop who kind of exudes testosterone is not something I'd think Don would be all that enthusiastic about. And a lesbian? But then he's never seemed to be uncomfortable with Michael and me. Maybe I'm too quick to judge.

"I think she'll work out just fine," I say.

"Digger still going into Denver for that forensics class?" Don says.

"Yeah. He'll be gone next week. Brianna said she'd commute up here starting tomorrow. She's on vacation with the DPD, so we'll be covered while Digger's gone."

"Good. She's a lesbian. Right?"

"Yes, she is." Okay. I never knew Don was that insightful. When he continues to eat without saying anything else, I do the same.

We finish our meal. Then I step to the counter to sign the check. Cathy sees me from the kitchen and comes out, takes the check, and says, "On the county?"

"Yes," I say. "It might help if we talked about this."

"Not ready for that," she says, punching numbers into the cash register. "And I'm sorry for…. You were right, Sam. I'm not her mother. But I thought she and I were okay together. I thought she trusted me. I thought she'd tell me what was on her mind." She hands me the tab, and I sign it.

"You've got to tell me what else was going on with her."

"I will," she says. "Just not now." She closes the register. "I'll call you tonight."

"That works."

She smiles and walks back into the kitchen. I walk across the dining room and see that Don is waiting for me outside on the porch.

"Let's take that ride up to the Emerson place," he says when I step outside.

"Sure." I look at my watch. "We got about an hour before Fuschi is supposed to show up."

We walk back to the office, where I open the door and tell Mary where Don and I are going. "We'll be back before two."

"You hired her, didn't you?" she says before I close the door.

"Yeah, I did."

"Good choice," she says.

"Appeared to be the only choice."

"Oh," she says, "I had a couple more bites I didn't tell you about."

About all I can do is shake my head, take one last look at the big smile on her face, and then close the door and walk over to Brunhilda.

CHAPTER THIRTY-FOUR

"THAT'S IT," Don says, pointing to an unmarked access road about five miles west of the Junction.

I turn onto it, and after only about a hundred yards, I see off to the side a metal post that appears to be a sensor of some sort. "Apparently they want to know who's coming up their way," I say, pointing to post.

"Yeah. I'm sure they do. They'll probably send somebody out to meet us before we get too close. They usually do."

I realize we've used the amorphous *they* a couple times. "Do you know anybody connected with the place except for Fuschi?"

"Nope. He's the only one who shows himself in town. The others? Hell, I don't even know how many others there are."

"You said the house is about a mile in?"

"About a mile. Maybe a little more."

Off in the distance there's a small rise with a large house on it. It's surrounded on three sides by tall evergreens. "I assume that's it?"

"It is. And sure as shit, here they come."

Emerging from what is now clearly a gate about a hundred yards in front of the house is what appears to be one of those small Hummers, a boxy black vehicle that looks military.

"They usually stop and just wait for you to come to them," Don says.

And after whoever is driving the Hummer puts about fifty yards between them and the gate, it does stop.

"What's their usual MO when you get this close?" I say, slowing Brunhilda slightly.

"The private property spiel."

"And you've come up here in the marked Cherokee?"

"Yeah. They know I'm a deputy. 'Course I didn't have any compelling reason for insisting they let me go up to the house."

"Okay. Let's just see what happens."

I keep Brunhilda moving until we get to about twenty yards from the Hummer. Then two men get out of it and walk to the front of the vehicle.

"Big guys," I say, noticing that they're both tall and wide. I stop Brunhilda, and Don and I get out. I wave at the men as we walk toward them.

"This is private property," one of the men says. He's got short black hair and appears to be Native American.

"And I'm Sheriff Daly," I say, stepping closer to them.

"What's your business here?" the same big guy says.

I think the other guy, the silent one, is Native American too.

"Just on patrol," I say. "I've never met Mrs. Emerson, and I'd like to do that."

"She's not available," the talker says.

"Why don't you check on that."

"Don't have to. She's not available."

Don takes a few steps off to my side, and the guys appear to brace themselves slightly as if they're prepared for a fight.

"All right," I say. "You give Mrs. Emerson my regards. We'll come back when she is available." I turn and begin to walk back to Brunhilda when I notice that Don is still facing these guys off. "Don. You coming?"

"Sure," he says, slowly backing up but keeping his eyes on the two guys. He now unzips his coat and pulls back the bottom of it, exposing his holstered Glock 22.

I look at the guys again and see that the talker has his hand under the bottom hem of his coat. Whether he's got a weapon under there, I'm not sure, but Don has obviously made his own conclusion.

I rest my hand on the butt of my .45. "C'mon, Don. You, gentlemen, take care."

Don and I walk backward to Brunhilda, keeping our eyes on the two men, who've not moved. The talker eases his hand from under his coat, and I get in Brunhilda. Don sits down too, and we each stare at the men, who are now getting back into the Hummer.

"I guess we overstayed our welcome," I say, starting the engine.

We close our doors, and Don says, "That was interesting."

"Yeah," I say as I back up a bit and maneuver Brunhilda around so she's pointing in the opposite direction. "The same thing happen when you came up here by yourself?"

"They always meet me, but not like this. Those boys appeared to be tense about something."

"They certainly did." I give Brunhilda some gas. She spins her wheels a little, then grabs hold, and we're off down the road. I wonder if the untimely death of a skinwalker cum shaman up on Mrs. Emerson's mountain might have something to do with the tenseness Don and I saw in those two men.

We take a slight curve, and there's a small rise to our left. I ease Brunhilda to a stop. "Think we can see anything from over there?" I say, motioning toward the rise.

"Don't know," Don says.

We get out and then plod through the snow and up the little hill. The area in front of the big house is visible, and we see the Hummer pulling through the iron gate, and then it heads to the right.

"There're a couple more vehicles over there," Don says.

"Yeah, there are." I see the distinct shape of an old two-seater Jeep, and there's a little red car parked next to it.

"That's not Hank's Jeep, is it?" Don says.

"Believe it is. And I'd bet that's Cathy's old Subaru sitting next to it. There's a second Hummer there too."

"What the hell?" Don says.

"Yeah. What the hell?"

WHEN WE get back to the Junction, Don gets in the Cherokee and starts his afternoon patrol. Before I go into the office, I pause a moment on the porch and look over at Michael's store. I can see him in there, still fooling around, still dusting or rearranging the items on the shelves. My impulse is to go over there, give him a hug, and then hide in the little back room and wait for Fuschi to arrive. I don't do that because I know Michael wouldn't let me. As much as he's lately exposed more of that part of his life that I'm not fully comfortable with, he still maintains a stubbornness when it comes to his ability to take care of himself. I respect that. I don't like it. But I respect it.

"SIGN THIS," Mary says, holding up a piece of paper as I walk in front of her desk. "It's the deputy position voucher."

I take a look at the voucher and note that Mary's already figured out we can't hire Brianna at the starting salary. She's put in a midrange number. "Looks good," I say, taking the pen she holds out for me. I sign the thing and scoot it over to her. "You ask Brianna if that's okay?"

"I did. She's okay with it."

"Just okay?"

"She was making almost twice that in Denver."

"I know it. It was her choice to make the move."

"Let me put it another way," Mary says, standing up, holding the voucher. "Brianna is delighted to be a deputy in the Pine County Sheriff's Department. I'm going to walk this next door and get the wheels turning."

"Oughta grease those wheels with some donuts or chocolate cake. Commissioners are meeting this afternoon. Right?"

"Yes, they are. I told them you'd be available if need be. And I've already taken over a plate of cupcakes that I made last night." She grabs her coat from the tree next to the door and then walks outside.

Yes, Mary's got her finger on the pulse of Pine County. Nothing gets done up here unless the county fathers—there aren't any county mothers yet, though Cathy's been hinting she might run next spring—are pacified with sweets. And speaking of sweets, as I pass by Digger's desk, I notice he's got a screensaver on his computer showing a white kitten with great big eyes sitting on the back of a huge dour-faced mastiff. I can't help but smile. If he were here, I'd give him a hug, pat his ass and.... Well, no, I wouldn't. I'd probably just ask him if he thought his screensaver was appropriate for a law enforcement setting. He'd probably squirm a bit, and I'd get whatever pleasure it is I find in seeing him do that. I know. I've got to stop it.

I walk into my office and immediately step to the window. I look across the street and see only Michael's truck outside his shop. I can't see him inside from here, and I grab my binoculars from the top of the file cabinet and take another look. And there he is, standing in front of the display counter looking out the window, probably anxious for Fuschi to show up now that it's past two o'clock. Digger pulls up in the Cherokee, and I lower the binoculars.

I sit down at my desk as the words "curiouser and curiouser" occur to me. Mrs. Emerson wasn't accepting guests from the Pine County Sheriff's Department, but an old Indian and a young woman with issues were apparently on whatever guest list was posted for today. I should have pinned Hank down yesterday about the Emersons. He'd sat right in front of me, told me what I already knew about them, and then said he knew some more, but he had to get Charlie home. Dammit! That old man has a knack for skirting the periphery of things. And I consistently let him do it.

I watch Digger sit down at his desk, check something on his computer. Then he pops up and stands in my doorway.

"I got an update from the CBI," he says.

"What'd they say?"

"Human and animal bones mixed up together."

"Okay. That all they're going to give us?"

"Yes, unless we want to know what kind of animal it was."

"I think we already know."

"We do?"

"Circumstantial, Digger. But something killed Joe Parsons's dog and took some bone matter from it."

"Oh. Yeah," he says, nodding. He then looks out my window. "Looks like Michael has a customer."

I turn around, and sure enough, there's Fuschi getting out of a black Hummer. I stand up and grab the binoculars. "Why don't you hang around here for a while," I say as I hold the binoculars up to my eyes and focus on Fuschi.

"Yes, sir," Digger says. "Right here. Or should I go back to my desk?"

Lord. "You can go back to your desk. I'll let you know if I need you."

"Sure thing," he says.

Fuschi walks in the door, and he and Michael shake hands. They talk, and then Fuschi appears to be looking at the tourist crap Michael keeps on the shelves. He picks up a small dream catcher, puts the looped hanger around his finger, and holds it up. They look at the thing as if waiting for a dream to catch in it, and then he puts the thing back on the shelf. They talk some more, and then Michael walks off to the side and returns holding his jean jacket. He puts it on, and then Fuschi opens the front door and Michael follows him outside. *No, don't do it, Michael.* They get in the Hummer. *Goddammit!*

I grab my coat and hat. As I walk out of my office, Mary comes in the front door. "Michael just got in that car with the Emerson guy," she says.

"I know. Digger, you come with me. Mary, get on the radio and tell Don to watch for a black Hummer that might be headed for the Emerson property. Tell him Digger and I will be following it."

"You want him to stop it if he sees it?"

Two things necessarily pass through my mind—Michael will be upset, maybe even furious if we stop Fuschi, and if we don't stop him, the last place on earth I want Michael to be is inside the Emerson house without me. "Tell him…. Tell him to just hold back. I'll let him know. C'mon, Digger."

I crack the front door open and wait until Fuschi backs out and heads west on Main Street. "Let's go," I tell Digger when the Hummer gets about a quarter mile down the road.

"What's going on?" Digger says as we both go outside.

"Just get in." I open Brunhilda's door. Digger gets in, and I start her up. As I back out of my spot and accelerate down Main, I say, "That wasn't a customer at Michael's store. It was Anthony Fuschi, who works for Mrs. Emerson, and he and Michael are in that Hummer ahead of us."

"Mrs. Emerson? The witch?"

I glance at him. He's got his hand braced on the dashboard, and his glare is on the road in front of us. "Yup. The witch," I say, wondering how long he's known the lore about the Emerson woman.

"Sheriff," Don's voice crackles over the radio. "You there?"

I grab the mike. "Right here."

"I'm back at the Emerson's road. You want me to hang out here? See if they come this way?"

"Yes. Just park on the side so Fuschi will know you're there. Let me know if he turns onto the road."

"Will do."

I put the mike back on the hook and ease up on the gas pedal. I want to stay as far in back of Fuschi as I can without losing sight of him.

I wonder if I should just call Michael. Of course I should. I pull out my phone, hold it in front of me, and scroll down to his number. I press the Call button.

"Hi, Sam," Michael says after I wait for what seems like forever.

"Michael. How are you?"

"I'm fine. We're wondering why you're following us."

"I'm not." I take my foot off the gas. "I'm not following you. Is there any reason why I should be? Where's he taking you?"

"Tony thought we ought to talk at his place. He's got an office at Mrs. Emerson's house, and he thinks he's got some old pictures of him and my dad there."

"He can't hear us. Right?"

"Right."

"Don and I were up there earlier. I think I saw Hank's and Cathy's cars parked at the house. Missie's been using that car, and she, oh, I guess she ran away from Cathy's. I don't know what's going on up there, Michael. I don't want you going in there alone."

"Yeah, I'm excited to see what Tony has. Maybe I'll even get to meet Mrs. Emerson."

Okay. I understand his agenda. "I don't like this, Michael."

"Yeah. It'll be fun."

"You keep your phone handy. Keep my number up, and press the Call button. We'll come in there if you need us."

"Okay," he says. "I'll see you for dinner. Bye."

I steer Brunhilda to the side of the road and let her coast to a stop.

"What'd he say?" Digger asks.

"Not much. Get that shotgun out of the rack." I give Brunhilda some gas and get her back on the road.

"You have the key?"

"Digger, the locks are all keyed the same. You bring your keys with you?"

"Oh," he says, reaching into his pocket. He pulls out his keys and finds the one that opens the weapon rack. "Here it is." He turns in his seat and unlocks the bracket that holds the shotgun secure at the top of the backrest.

"Load it," I say.

He pulls the FN P-12 shotgun from the rack, points the barrel down at the floor in front of him, and then turns again and opens the small box affixed to the rack. He fishes out five twelve gauge shells and loads them into the weapon.

The Hummer is now about a mile in front of us. I again grab the mike from the dashboard. "Don, they're coming your way. Just sit tight. And load your long rifle."

"Will do," Don says. "Yeah, I can just barely see them now."

"Hang tight," I say and then stick the mike under my thigh. I glance at Digger, and he's still tensed, his focus ahead with the shotgun's butt between his knees.

"Why don't you want Michael going in the Emerson house?" Digger says.

"You said it yourself, Digger—she's a witch. Right?"

"Yeah. But... I mean, that's just what people say. I don't think she's really a witch."

"What if she is?"

"Sheriff, I don't...."

We look at each other at the same time. "You don't what?"

"Never mind," he says.

Up ahead, I see the Hummer take the turn onto the Emerson property, and there's Don's Cherokee just past the turn, on the side of the road. I grab the mike from under my thigh. "Don, follow the Hummer for about fifty yards, then stop. I just want them to know we're here."

"Roger that," Don says.

We're about a half mile from the turnoff, and I see Don's Cherokee move from the side of the road and enter the Emerson access road. It only takes another few minutes and I do the same, and reaching Don's Cherokee, I stop Brunhilda behind it. Digger and I get out and walk up to Don, who's already standing outside his vehicle.

"Michael called me a few minutes ago," I say. "He said Fuschi wanted to take him to his office in the house."

"Michael sound okay?" Don says.

"Yeah. He wanted to get in there anyway. I told him to keep his phone handy."

"A phone isn't going to protect him," Don says.

"I know. But if he can just—"

All three of us jerk a bit when my cell rings. I pull it from my pocket. It's Michael.

"Michael," I say. "You okay?"

"Yes, I am. Tony said to tell you that he's going to ask Mrs. Emerson if you can come down here too."

"Okay."

"He doesn't know why you guys are following us."

"Where are you?"

"I'm in the foyer, just inside the front door. This is a beautiful place, Sam."

"He left you there alone?"

"Sort of. There's a guy standing across the room from me."

"He Native American?"

"Looks like it. Tony's coming back. Wait a second...."

I wait, and then Michael comes back on and tells me that I can come down to the house but not Don or Digger.

"All right. But they're going to park just outside the gate."

I hear Michael tell Fuschi what I just said.

"He says that's fine," Michael says.

"Okay. We're on our way."

CHAPTER THIRTY-FIVE

THE BIG Native American guy, the talker from earlier, escorts me from Brunhilda and into the house after I'd been allowed to pass the iron gate. I am surprised he doesn't ask me to hand over my weapon before going inside. Digger and Don are in the Cherokee outside the gate.

"You okay?" I say to Michael for about the fourth time in the last ten minutes as soon as the door is closed behind me. We're in the foyer he told me about.

"Yes," he says. "I'm fine." And then he leans in a little and whispers, "Lots of magic in here."

"We finally meet," Tony Fuschi says, coming from a hallway off to our right.

He's wearing a very nice dark blue suit, a silk blend probably, and his tie reminds me of vomit composed of beer and half-eaten pizza.

I shake his hand. "What's all the security about?"

"Oh," he says, smiling one of those smiles that you know right off the bat is hiding truths. "Mrs. Emerson likes her privacy. Please follow me." He walks toward the closed double doors directly in front of us and across the foyer. He opens one of the doors and stands back, holds his arm out in invitation, and Michael and I walk into the room. I glance behind me, and the Native American guy has taken a post outside the door.

The room is very large, with a curved wall at its back. The wall is made of floor-to-ceiling windows, all draped in what looks like red velvet. The bottoms of the drapes are tied up, giving the light from the windows an upside-down V pattern. Outside the windows, I can see the mountain where I killed Stanley Broken River. Centering the room is a cluster of furniture that I'd call antique, but a more practiced eye might call American Victorian, French Provincial, or something or other. There're two couches facing each other, four side chairs, a nice long coffee table in the middle, and there are side tables by each chair and at the ends of the couches. The furniture sits on a square rug woven in a Native American design—reds, blues, yellows, and browns are woven into a pattern that I can't see the entirety of.

Tony tells us we can have a seat and that Mrs. Emerson will join us shortly. He goes out the door we came in, and Michael and I sit down on the couch facing the windows.

"I'm impressed," I say.

"Yeah," Michael says. "So am I."

His tone of voice tells me he's headed for that faraway place I've seen him go to before. I look at him, and yes, he's on the verge of tripping into whatever whispers he's hearing.

I grab his hand. "You're feeling the magic in here, then?"

"Yes. It's very strong."

"You and Tony get a chance to talk much on the way up here?"

"No. Not much. He was more interested in you following us than anything else. When he saw Don parked off to the side of the road, he told me that it's probably time for you and me to meet Mrs. Emerson. He said we'd talk about my father later."

We both look behind us when the door opens again. A Native American woman maybe sixty or more years old comes in carrying a silver tray with a silver teapot and five white cups on it. She says not a word as she places the tray on the coffee table. I try to catch her eye, but she's intent on doing just what she's doing.

"Thank you," Michael says, and the woman nods, looks at him intently for just a second before going back the way she came in. The door closes behind her.

"I guess it's tea or something," I say, leaning over and looking at the pot and the fine porcelain cups. There are silver spoons there too, and I pick one up. "Heavy little thing."

Again the door opens, and we turn our heads to see who's there. A slight woman comes in first, dressed in a blue gown that touches the tops of her feet. She's obviously older, maybe seventy or seventy-five, and her black hair is braided, a single thick braid hanging over her right shoulder all the way to her waist. Three or four multicolored necklaces of beads hang down her front. Behind her is Hank, and next to him is Missie. Michael and I stand up.

"I regret it's taken so long for us to meet," the woman says as she walks to the other side of the coffee table. "I'm Elenore Emerson."

She holds out her hand across the coffee table, extending it to Michael. Hank stands before one of the side chairs at the end of the coffee table, and Missie stands before the one at the other side.

"I'm Michael Bellomo," Michael says, grabbing Mrs. Emerson's hand.

I glance at Hank and then Missie, and they both appear to be enraptured by the scene of Michael and Mrs. Emerson holding hands. Michael and Mrs. Emerson look into each other's eyes, still holding hands, and I know without a doubt that they're speaking without speaking.

Mrs. Emerson smiles, and she releases her grip on Michael. "And you're Sheriff Daly," she says, turning toward me with her hand extended.

"Yes," I say, shaking her hand. "Very nice to meet you."

"You know Henry and Melissa," Mrs. Emerson says as she sits down.

I nod at Missie as we all take a seat, and Mrs. Emerson reaches for the teapot.

"Let's have some tea." She nearly fills each of the five cups with a dark brown liquid. "Please," she says, setting the teapot down. "It's a Native American mixture. We make it here."

We all do as we're told. I hold the cup and wait for somebody else to take the first sip. Not that I believe Mrs. Emerson would want to poison us all upon first meeting, but there's no need for me to be the one to affirm that. When Mrs. Emerson takes a sip, I do the same. It's bitter but surprisingly good. Kind of warms me up as it goes down.

"Melissa wishes to tell you something," Mrs. Emerson says, placing her cup on the coffee table.

All heads turn to Melissa. She looks tired, exhausted really, and closes her eyes for a moment. When she opens them, she too sets her cup on the table.

"I'm sorry," she says, her eyes filling up, her voice tiny.

"It's all right, Melissa," Mrs. Emerson says. "Remember what we talked about."

"Yes," she says, pulling a tissue from the pocket of her jeans. She wipes her eyes and blows her nose into the tissue. "Sheriff." She looks at me. "I wasn't raped. But you know that. I.... Stanley Broken River and I were friends. Good friends. He found me that night in the woods. He was walking. Skinwalking. He was Wolf. I didn't know it, but he was. I was out of it, but I remember the hair, the odor. After that, after Cathy took me in, I'd go see Stan at his trailer. He taught me things. He told me about who he was and what he could do. He told me...." She stops a moment, closes her eyes again, and then opens them, looks up at the ceiling as if seeking some solace there. She then looks down at her hands, which she's folded in her lap. "Stan told me," she says, "that an evil presence had come to the land. He said that he needed to destroy it before it destroyed him and all the other walkers who are up here." She starts to tear up again and holds her tissue to her eyes.

"Go on," Mrs. Emerson says after we all wait a moment for her to continue.

Missie looks at me and then at Michael. "He said it was you, Michael. He said you were the evil presence."

Of course. The magic or curse in the black bag wasn't meant for those two boys at all.

"So that night at the café?" I begin to ask the question that's just occurred to me.

"Please," Mrs. Emerson says. "Let Melissa finish."

"Since I worked in the café, it wouldn't be that hard to put some of the… curse into whatever Michael ordered. After Stan told me what I needed to do, he said we shouldn't be seen together. He told me not to even go to his trailer anymore. So I met him behind the café that night, Sheriff. And when I dropped the bag, I panicked. I had to see him and tell him what had happened. That's when I found out he'd moved. I'm so sorry, Michael. So sorry." She raises the tissue to her eyes again and begins to sob.

The door opens behind us, and the woman who had brought in the tea comes into the room and walks to Missie.

"It's all right, Melissa," Mrs. Emerson says. "Rachel will help you back to your room."

Rachel places her hands on Missie's arm, and Missie stands up. "I'm so sorry," she says again as Rachel escorts her out of the room.

When the door is closed, Mrs. Emerson looks at Michael. I look at him too, and he's sitting there with his head bent, his cup cradled in his palms. He raises his head and looks at Mrs. Emerson. I can't help but think he's responding to whatever words she's just projected to him.

"Yes." He nods, smiling at Mrs. Emerson. "I would have known before I ate it. I was wrong about Stanley Broken River, though. I thought I could have talked to him."

"Henry," Mrs. Emerson says. "Can you speak about this now?"

Hank waits a moment before answering. "The Spirit Dog told Michael where to go. I knew that Stanley Broken River was gonna do what he did. He was afraid of Michael because Michael's magic was much stronger than his. The Spirit Dog wanted revenge. I didn't tell you, Sheriff, 'cause I knew Michael was gonna be okay. It was something only he could do."

I suppose there is a certain irony in that it was I who killed Stanley. I was the doubter, Michael had the magic, but it was I who'd remembered Hank's lesson on how to kill a skinwalker.

"But I killed him, Hank," I say.

Hank smiles. "Yeah. Helluva thing, Sheriff."

We sit a minute without speaking. Mrs. Emerson takes another sip of her tea and refills her cup.

"Gotta get home," Hank says. "Charlie is by himself."

"Thank you, Henry," Mrs. Emerson says.

Hank stands up and puts his cup on the coffee table. He turns to walk toward the door and then stops. "The shack collapsed," he says, turning back to us. "Too much snow on the roof. Don't think anything is left in there anyway." He then walks to the doors, opens one, and walks out.

I look at Michael. He's staring at Mrs. Emerson, and she's staring at him. I don't know if I should interrupt whatever conversation they're having, which I can't hear. And now that I think about it, why have I assumed Mrs. Emerson is capable of speaking without speaking?

"I guess," I say, "there's only one more story to tell."

Mrs. Emerson slowly fixes her gaze on me and nods. "Yes," she says. "There is."

MRS. EMERSON'S voice is that of a woman half her age. As she speaks, I wonder about the blackness of her hair—not a single strand of gray in it. She's a slight woman, but I get the impression she'd give anybody a run for their money.

She tells us that she met her husband, Malcolm, when he showed up at that part of the Navajo reservation in Southeastern Utah where she lived with her family. He was with a group of white men who'd arrived in fancy vehicles and were given a tour of the area by an Indian Agent, who she'd seen pocket a chunk of cash from one of the men as they'd huddled near their vehicles. She says she was only sixteen on that day when the white men arrived. And one of the white men caught her eye because she had caught his.

"Malcolm was a man who knew what he wanted and always got it," she says. "He wanted me, and he got me."

She doesn't go into the details of how Malcolm *got* her, but it must not have been a pretty scene. What I remember from Joe Hill's stories about his childhood, the Navajo people are centered on their families, and the separation of a sixteen-year-old girl from her family had to have been a traumatic event.

She pauses a moment and scans the room. Her expression is one of sadness or regret. Then she smiles and says, "Malcolm detested Native people, but he had a desire to sleep with one. And I was that one. I wouldn't share his bed until he married me. I would not be his concubine. And I had the... means to convince him that we must marry. It was then that I took the name Elenore. My given name is Adeezbaa, which means in my native language, woman who leads the fight. And I did. I do. That's what I do here."

"The fight?" I say.

"Yes. The fight."

Michael nods as if he knows this already. Maybe he does. Maybe their discourse, which I cannot hear, has already touched on this.

"My husband did not know that I knew the magic of my people," Mrs. Emerson says. "He also didn't know that from the moment he took me from my family, I vowed to kill him."

I see that Rachel has come into the room. I didn't hear the door open, but there she is, standing at the edge of the coffee table.

"You can take the tea setting," Mrs. Emerson says. "Please bring in the spirits."

Rachel places all the cups back on the silver tray, picks it up, and carries it out of the room. I smile at my vision of Rachel walking back in the room followed by an assortment of amorphous forms hovering about our heads and whispering in our ears.

"Malcolm brought in a tutor for me. He wanted me to be a respectable woman—his words—worthy of his family's name. And early on, I learned what my husband's business was," Mrs. Emerson says. "He and your father, Michael, were very close, very attuned to making money any way that they could. Behind your father's back,

Malcolm called him a greasy wop, a dirty dago, but he understood his own fortunes were tied to your father's. And over time, they became good friends. But that was a long time ago. I met your father several times, Michael. Did you know that?"

Michael shakes his head. "No," he says. "I didn't know that."

Christ on a cracker!

"Your mother too. But she didn't like me. I think she thought I was evil."

When she says that word, evil, my skin crawls a little, and then I jerk slightly when this time I do hear Rachel come into the room. She carries another silver tray, this one with wooden handles on it. There are three brandy glasses and a bottle of Louis Royer cognac on it. She sets the tray on the coffee table, then silently walks back across the room.

"Would you pour, Sam?" Mrs. Emerson says.

"Of course," I say, leaning into the table and filling the glasses half-full.

I take mine and settle back against the couch. Michael and Mrs. Emerson take theirs.

"To our friendship," Mrs. Emerson says, holding her glass out.

We click our glasses together, and then we each take a sip. This is damned good stuff.

"When I discovered," Mrs. Emerson says, setting her glass on the table, "that there were Native people living up here, even on my mountain, I was delighted. My husband was oblivious to what was going on on his land. He spent most of his time in Denver and Pueblo. But almost every day I explored on horseback. I heard and felt the magic that was carried on the winds. I had learned as a child to know its presence. And I was not so delighted when I understood what the magic was telling me—there were skinwalkers here who had lost their way."

She picks up her glass and again sips. "One day I was riding and came upon a man picking juniper berries. It was Henry Tall Horse. His dog, Charlie, came from the tree line, his barks frantic, his teeth bared. He was such a strong, vibrant animal then. My horse spooked a bit, but I calmed him as Henry called to Charlie. When Henry faced me, I knew he was Native, probably Ute. And we spoke without speaking. I learned that he wasn't picking berries to make his own wine. It was for protection.

"Henry invited me to his cabin, where we sat for hours that first day. I went back a second and a third day, and he told me about the magic up here. I was like Coyote, who is never sated. He said the magic had been here for many generations. He told me about the skinwalkers."

Okay. Hank and I have a pretty good relationship. He's told me a lot of things, albeit in that habit of his to tell me half of anything he knows, leaving me to figure out the other half on my own. Right now I'm trying to figure out how old Charlie must be in dog years, and conclude what I've come up with is impossible. Wishing I could have been there when he and Mrs. Emerson had had their tête-à-têtes, I look at Michael and see that he and Mrs. Emerson are nodding at each other.

"I have a feeling," I say, "that you and Michael are having a conversation that I can't hear. I think I know why Michael can do that, but why can you? You learned that when you were a kid?"

"The Dinè, the Navajo, believe there are Earth people, who are mortal, and Holy people. The Holy people are entities who can help or hurt mortals. Sometimes, with some Earth people, there is a connection with the spirits. I don't know why it is that only certain mortals have this connection, and I never questioned it when I discovered it in my own life. Those who have that connection can speak without speaking to each other. Michael has explained this to you? Yes?"

"Yes, he's explained it. But he's not certainly not Navajo and—"

"Of course he's not," she says. "Michael is Italian. Maybe the magic that has come to him is as old as mine, or probably older. Do you remember John Spotted Elk?"

"How could I forget. He probably unwittingly saved my life."

"John was Lakota. He knew the magic. But he used it to hurt mortals. Henry knew that as well as I did. That's why he called him out and killed him."

Yeah, and I called out Stanley Broken River for no other reason than I knew how to do it, and yes, I guess there had been the possibility he would have torn Don's throat out up on the mountain. I'm getting the feeling that Mrs. Emerson, like Hank, is talking around things. She's garnered my interest but hasn't given me chapter and verse yet.

"Mrs. Emerson, you and Michael know a hell of a lot more than I do about what's going on up here, but I know a whole lot more than most people. And what I don't understand right now is why you seem to be at the center of all this... stuff that's been going on lately. You probably know that the locals call you a witch. Why is that?"

"Because I am," she says. "The Ways of my people, Sam, don't make a very clear distinction between witchery and spirituality. It's the witch who channels that spirituality or directs that spirituality one way or the other. I'm, as you say, at the center of this because I put myself there a long time ago.

"When my husband finally became aware there were savages, as he called them, living all around here, even on his land, he set out to remove them. He'd determined that if they wouldn't leave, he'd make them leave. I think he'd inherited much of what his father and grandfather and many others called Manifest Destiny—a term that was code for the belief that the only good Indian was a dead one. And of course, the belief that the white man's destiny came from a Christian God, who had somehow ascribed that the precious metals in the earth, the trees, the water, the very air we breathe were his to do with what he wanted. And what he wanted was to make a buck.

"I found out what my husband's plan was when Anthony, Mr. Fuschi, told me about it. Over the years Anthony and I had established a kind of understanding between us. We liked each other. And I think Anthony gradually became weary of what my husband and your father, Michael, were doing in Denver, Pueblo, and elsewhere. So when he told me what my husband was going to do, I turned to magic. My magic was strong and focused. And much like the curse Stanley had prepared for you, Michael, I prepared one for my husband."

"You killed him?" I say.

She lifts her glass from the table and sips. "I did."

Yes, there's no statute of limitations on murder, I'm the sheriff, and she's just confessed to killing her husband. As we sit here in the momentary silence, I envision sitting down with the county attorney. Yes, sir, she crunched up some human bones, probably from somebody's skull, made a powder of it, put a death curse on it, and sprinkled it on his scrambled eggs. Or maybe she just shoved a shard of bone into his neck and watched him die.

"And then," she says, "I visited with all the Native people I could find. The ones who were attuned to magic, who had not lost their grasp of the spirituality of their people, understood that my magic was powerful. The ones who I knew—and they knew I knew—were skinwalkers took my warning to heart. I told them that their magic was no match for mine and that if they used their magic for ill, I would respond."

"What about my father?" Michael says.

She looks at Michael. "Your father found out what I did to Malcolm. I suppose one of his associates who spent time up here overheard something or just put two and two together. Anthony warned me about it. Your father sought revenge. I had taken from him someone who not only was important to his business but someone whom he had come to like. I believe he still seeks revenge."

"And that's why you have all the security around this place?" I say.

"Yes. That and the... stirrings that were caused when you and Michael moved here."

"Skinwalker stirrings?" I say.

She nods. "Anthony moved in shortly after my husband died. At that time, it was the fear that Mr. Bellomo would seek revenge. Later on, when, as I said, you two moved here, there was also the concern about the... activity of those whose magic seemed to be revitalized by Michael's presence. Anthony hired Native men to work for him. Some of them already lived here. A few are Lakota Sioux from up north. For a long time, though, Anthony continued to work with your father. I asked him to do it even though he didn't want to. I thought it was best that he keep an eye on things from inside your father's operation."

Yeah. It was Lakota Sioux who showed George Armstrong Custer a thing or two at the Little Bighorn.

"But my father was so supportive of Sam and I moving to Pine County," Michael says. "He never said anything about you."

"Three times over the years I've been shot at, Michael. Twice, wildfires have been started near this house. Three of my dogs have been poisoned. The last time I was shot at was about three months before you and Sam moved here. And then it all quieted down. I don't think that was a coincidence."

Yeah, but it's all circumstantial. Sure, Point A usually leads to Point B. "So," I say, "you think Mr. Bellomo, Michael's father, had some, I don't know, *Italian* thing going on—an eye for an eye kind of thing? And that he thinks Michael might be able to use his... magic to fulfill that blood urge? Or just get close enough to you to do some serious harm?"

She smiles. "I guess the only way we'll ever know that is if Michael's father asks Michael to do something. He hasn't yet, has he?"

"No," Michael says. "I don't talk to him that often, but.... He and I have never had much of a relationship. And I don't think he knows about my abilities."

I think about all the years Mrs. Emerson has lived here, behind these walls and surrounded by her protectors. What has she done with her life? What has she found fulfilling up here that's kept her determined to stay? "What keeps you busy?" I say. "This is a nice house, but I can't imagine you just sit around all day and.... Whatever."

"My horses," she says. "My dogs. I believe I've mapped in my mind every inch of the property here. I know the flowers, the birds, the critters who share my land. And I paint."

Michael perks up. "You paint? So do I. Can I see your work?"

"Of course you can," she says. "Let's finish our drinks and I'll show you."

"Before we go," I say, "can you tell me why Missie is here? And what's going to happen to her?"

She does finish her drink and sets the glass back on the table. "When I discovered that Melissa was seeing Stanley Broken River," she says, "I had Anthony bring her up here one night. I tried to warn her that she shouldn't be keeping company with him, but she wouldn't listen. I guess he'd captured her imagination, and he'd been kind to her. I got the feeling that no one had ever really been very kind to her, except Cathy, who.... Cathy wanted something from Melissa that Melissa still isn't sure she can give. Melissa was confused and afraid. She came to me, Sam, when she was sure you'd discovered her lie. As I said, she was.... Well, she *is* confused and afraid. She can stay here as long as she wants. She'll be protected."

"I'll have to tell Cathy about all this."

"I know," she says. "I know." She stands up. "Let me show you my paintings. I'm sure they're not as good as yours, Michael. But they do reflect what I see around me and what I perceive within me."

As Michael and I follow her toward the double doors, I wonder if everything she's told us is everything there is to tell about who she is and what's happened up here for all the years she's quietly tarried at the foot of these mountains. Like with Hank, I get the feeling there's more to her story than what she's shared. But hell, I know more than what I did when I first sat down with her, here in this—I want to say lair, but that wouldn't aptly describe this place. And I've finally met the witch of Pine

County. For now, that's enough. When Michael and I get back home, I suspect he'll have more of the story for me, the one I couldn't hear but which I'm sure he's cogitating on right now as Mrs. Emerson opens one of the double doors. We follow her across the lofty foyer and then up the staircase to the second floor.

CHAPTER THIRTY-SIX

IT'S ALREADY dark, and a breeze is coming off the mountains that usually signals another storm building to the west. When we get back to the cabin, I get busy starting a fire, and Michael turns on the kitchen light and then sits down at the dining table to go through the mail that was in the box at the entrance to our road.

We'd not said much to each other as we drove back from the Emerson house with Don and Digger following behind us. Michael seemed to be lost in his thoughts, as was I. I did take a minute to call Cathy and tell her that Missie was okay, that she was at Mrs. Emerson's house. She didn't have much of a response but thanked me for calling. As we turned onto our road, Don honked the Cherokee's horn as they went on to the Junction.

After I get the fire going, I walk into the kitchen and sit down with Michael.

"Anything interesting?" I say.

"Just bills and junk," he says. "Like we always get."

I wait a minute before asking what he thought of our visit with Mrs. Emerson. And in that minute, I wonder if I should let all my observations, thoughts, and questions about that visit just ride for a while. Maybe I ought to wait until he brings it up. I have lived with him long enough to know that it's best to let him and those whispers he hears simmer for a bit before digging into what's on both our minds. I am surprised, though, that he hasn't yet said a word about it.

"You want a sandwich or something?" I say.

"Yes." He smiles and tosses the junk mail into the trash can we keep near the table. "I am hungry. And I want a sandwich. Salad won't do it for me right now."

"Okay." I stand up and walk to the refrigerator, thankful that I got a smile out of him. "By the way," I say as I grab a bag of turkey breast and a head of lettuce from the fridge, "Mary said Phillip is coming up for a visit tomorrow."

"Excellent," he says, stepping to the counter and taking the plastic thingamajig off the end of the bread sack. He opens a cupboard, places two plates on the counter, and then pulls four slices of bread from the sack and puts them on the plates. "He can help me in the shop for a while. Why doesn't he stay with us? I could show him what I'm working on."

"That's fine by me," I say, leaning back into the fridge to grab a tomato and the mayonnaise. "I'm probably going to work tomorrow anyway. Got a new deputy starting and…. Yeah. You and Phillip can do your thing, and I'll do mine."

Michael leans against the counter watching me slice the tomato. "You didn't tell me that you hired somebody. This new guy have as nice an ass as Digger?"

"I didn't hire Digger for his ass. And this new guy isn't a guy. It's a woman. A black, lesbian, DPD cop who's got a 1970 primo Mustang that she named Sly."

"Wow," Michael says. He opens the sack of turkey and puts a couple slices on the bread. "I assume she knows about us?"

"Yes, she does. She's got a girlfriend who burns easily."

"What?"

"I told her she and her girlfriend ought to take a cruise to some beach before she starts working up here, and she said she couldn't because her girlfriend sunburns easily."

"So she's qualified? Did you interview anybody else?"

"Yes, she is. And she's the only one I interviewed. Or," I say, putting tomato slices on the bread and then tearing some lettuce from the head, which I put on top of the tomatoes, "she was the only candidate Mary let me interview. Mary liked her, and I guess that's all that matters. You want some mayonnaise?"

"Just a little," he says.

As we sit back down at the table to eat, I'm still hoping that he'll start the conversation I've been wanting to have since we left Mrs. Emerson's house. I take a sip of the beer he sat out for me, and for right now I'm just happy that he's happy, eating a sandwich instead of picking at a plate full of multicolored leaves. I am surprised, though, that what we learned about his father hasn't come up yet. I'd thought that knowledge would surely put him in a weeklong funk, but that hasn't happened. *Thank you, Jesus.*

"You think I ought to call my father?" he says.

Okay. I was just thinking about this. If he's now able to read my mind, I'm in trouble. "If it's about what Mrs. Emerson said about him, I don't know how you'd approach that in a conversation. Hey, Dad, are you trying to kill the witch of Pine County?"

"No. I wouldn't do it exactly like that. I think I'll just tell him that we met this nice old lady who said she'd met him. See what he says."

I watch him pull the brown crust off his bread, then eat the crust. "That might work," I say. "Why do you do that?" I've never asked him about this bread thing before, but now I'm curious.

"What?"

"Pull your crust off and then eat it."

"Just something I do," he says, taking a sip of beer.

"You have any comments about our visit with that nice old lady?"

"I wonder where she's buried all the skinwalkers she's killed?"

No, I wasn't expecting that. But it is a good question. "Good question," I say.

"She's killed a lot of them over the years."

"That something you two talked about?"

"She told me that. Yes, we talked about it."

"So was she also the one who removed John Spotted Elk from Hank's shed? And if Stanley Broken River's body isn't on the mountain anymore, I'd guess she was also responsible for that removal?"

"Yes." He nods, takes another bite of his sandwich, stands up, and grabs the potato chips from the top of the refrigerator.

When he sits back down, I watch him dig into the bag and put some chips on his plate. As much as I'm pleased that he hasn't slipped into some quasi coma after our trip to the Emerson house, I'm a little concerned that he seems too, oh, unaffected by it.

"You're okay? Right?"

"Yes," he says, giving me a smile.

He eats a couple chips and washes them down with a swig of his beer.

I wait a minute before I ask him what the hell is going on. He never eats potato chips, and I could count on one hand the times he's scarfed down a sandwich with animal meat in it. And a beer instead of wine? I never thought I'd be concerned with him acting like a normal human being.

"I've got to say that you're taking all this a little too in stride. We just met with who I suppose you could call the Grand Empress of the Netherworld and…. You sure you're okay?"

He brushes his hands against each other over his plate and, once again, flashes that smile. "Sam, I'm processing. Maybe tomorrow morning we can get into the nitty-gritty of everything. But I've got to tell you that I understand a lot more after meeting with Mrs. Emerson than I did before. It's like… I don't know. It's like all these loose ends are coming together for me. I almost get it now. You know what I mean?"

"Okay." I'm not sure that I do know what he means, but what the hell…. "We'll meet here again in the morning while we're having a nice breakfast."

"Maybe. Remember I've got a date with Phillip."

"Yeah, I remember. But Michael, you've got to tell me what you learned from Mrs. Emerson. The things you two talked about that I couldn't hear."

"For now," he says, "just know that I'm okay. It's kind of like when you're a kid and figure out that Santa Claus is really your dad and mom. All kinds of questions are answered without having to ask them."

Though it's now well past Christmas, I can't help but envision him as a young boy sitting on a mall Santa's lap.

"Well, that's a good way to put it, I guess. But I've still got a lot of questions to ask. Remember, the only conversation I had with Mrs. Emerson was the one I could hear. And it just dawned on me. Rather than talking to your dad, why don't you have the conversation with Fuschi that you never got around to? Since he apparently had some issues with your father a long time ago, maybe he can fill in the blanks. Bet he'd tell you the truth."

"Yup," he says, standing up and clearing the table. "Already thought of that. But I do still want to talk to my father. You done with this?" He's got his hand on the edge of my plate.

I grab his wrist, tug him over to me, and pull him down onto my lap. "So, young man, what do you want for Christmas?"

He looks at me for a second as if I've lost my mind, and then he smiles. He then touches his lip with his index finger and says, "Well,

Santa, let me see." He taps his finger against his lip and then nods. "I want a life-size blowup doll dressed as a cowboy sheriff, and I want it anatomically correct. You know, holes where holes should be, and the part that inflates and deflates on the front has to be capable of at least eight or nine inches of very solid growth, and…."

Yeah, that did it. "Let's just leave the dishes," I say as we both stand up. I clutch his hand and lead him into the bedroom. "Let's see what's under all that wrapping." I face him, pull his shirt over his head, and unbutton his Levi's.

As he begins to unbutton my shirt, he says, "Yeah, I never did like that don't-open-'til-Christmas rule."

WE HAVEN'T yet crawled out of bed when someone knocks on the front door. Michael quickly pulls the covers off, steps on the floor, and puts on his Levi's. "I'll get it," he says. "It's probably Phillip."

I look out the bedroom window. It's lightly snowing, but the morning outside is bright, and the snowflakes are coming straight down. Good. No wind. I sit up and put my feet on the floor. From the mudroom, I hear the voices of two young men who'll probably keep talking nonstop for the next eight hours or however long they're together.

"Phillip's here," Michael says, walking into the bedroom and grabbing his shirt. He puts it on and then sits down to put on his socks and shoes.

"I guess we're not going to have that talk we were going to have over breakfast."

"Can't," he says, standing up. He steps into the closet and comes out pulling a sweatshirt over his head. "I promise we will, though. We're taking his car into the Junction. We'll be at my shop." He walks back out of the bedroom.

I grab my jeans from the floor where I left them last night and pull them up my calves. I stand up and finish the job, buckling my belt and then sitting down again to put on my socks and boots. Michael could have waited to leave until I had a chance to say hello to Phillip. But when they get together, they become like teenage girls who've saved their secrets only for each other's ears. That's fine. I'm happy he's got a friend he can share things with—things, of course, that don't involve witches, shifters, curses, or messages from Spirit Dogs carried on old winds. I'm glad he's able to compartmentalize those things. I, on the other hand, find it hard to do that. And the irony of it all brings a smile to my face. I can't hear those old winds, but I'm the one that can't stop thinking about them. Well, that and the feisty young woman who's probably waiting for me right now to show up at the office.

I SEE Bri's Mustang parked in one of the county commissioners' spaces and shake my head. I pull into my spot, noting that Brunhilda gives me a satisfied shudder when I turn her off. Bri gets out of her baby, Sly, and I give Brunhilda's dashboard a little loving pat as I get out.

"Why didn't you go in?" I ask her as she steps onto the porch outside the office.

"I saw two young punks go into that shop across the street," she says, nodding toward Michael's store. "Didn't look kosher to me. Thought I'd just sit here and see if they were up to something."

I glance across the street and see what is probably Phillip's car outside the shop and lights from inside. "One of those punks is my husband. He owns the place," I say, hoping the slight edge to my voice will communicate she's stepped over a line. I open the door and wait for her to step in.

"Can't be too careful," she says as we walk into the office.

Digger has the duty today, and he's sitting at his desk looking at us, smiling as always.

"Morning," he says.

"I think you've met Brianna Lincoln," I say. Bri and I stop at his desk before going into my office. "She's going to fill Jim's slot."

"Not officially," he says, standing up. "But I was here when she came in yesterday."

They shake hands, and then Digger motions toward the little table where we keep the coffeepot.

"Hot coffee if you want some."

"Sure," Bri says. She walks over there and pours a cup. "You want one, Sheriff?"

"Yes. Black."

"Anything going on?" I ask Digger.

"Nothing. How'd it go at Mrs. Emerson's?"

"Went fine."

"So she's not a witch?"

"Depends on how you define that word."

"What word?" Bri says as she walks toward us holding out a cup for me.

"The sheriff and I were…," Digger says. "There's this woman who lives at the base of the mountain, and the sheriff and I were, well…."

"Witch," I say, taking the coffee from Bri. "I asked Digger how he defined that word."

"Carly Fiorina," Bri says, handing me my coffee.

I smile, and Digger looks like he's considering Bri's comments to see if the shoe fits.

"Yeah," he says. "She is a scary lady."

"C'mon, Bri," I say, lightly touching her shoulder. "Let's sit awhile and talk. Digger, since you're holding the fort together today, pretend I'm not here."

"Yes, sir," he says.

Bri and I go into my office, and I close the door behind us. "Have a seat," I say, placing my cup on the desk. I take off my coat, then hang it up. "Can I take your coat?"

She puts her coffee on the desk next to mine, takes off her coat, and hands it to me. After I hang it over my coat, she sits down and grabs her cup.

"Your husband looked really young."

"He is. I'm a few years older."

"And he owns the place?"

"Yes, he does."

"What's up with the other kid?"

"Don't know what you mean."

"They have a… thing going on?"

"No. That's his friend Phillip. Mary's grandson. And this sounds like an interrogation."

"Old habits," she says, then takes a sip of her coffee.

I'm beginning to doubt that I made the right decision in hiring her. Yeah, I knew she was probably a hardcase law-and-order type of gal, but this is a little extreme. At least she seemed to have a sense of humor, albeit a dry one, the last time I saw her.

"It's probably not necessary to delve into every little thing that might seem odd or out of sync with your notions of how things ought to be. You do that up here and…. Well, half the folks who live in this county are demonstrably odd and—"

"Sheriff," she says, holding her hand up palm facing outward. "I was playing you. Sorry, but I was. I know. It's a bad habit I've got. When we were driving up to Cathy's house yesterday to look for that young woman, you spoke with your husband on the phone. You told him you might see him at the shop later. When I parked here earlier, I saw those two young men park across the street. I saw they'd parked in front of that tourist trap junk shop, and I said to myself, aha! One of those young men is the sheriff's husband. They were gabbing away at each other as they got out of the truck, one of them gesticulating as if he had a soap bubble wand in his hand. I figure the dark-haired one is your husband. The hot one who glanced back at me with a look that, honest to God, made me feel like he knew more about me than I did about him. Am I right?"

Yeah, she's a cop all right—the inquisitiveness of the gut hunch. "Yes, you are. And I'm impressed. What other perceptions did you get of this mountain paradise yesterday?"

"Oh, not a whole lot. Lots of obvious drama. This young woman we were looking for yesterday is a problem child who Cathy, the café lady, loves, but I get the feeling she's not really loved in return. You mentioned the name Tony when you spoke to your husband on the phone, and I think Tony is someone you're a little concerned about, especially because he and your husband have some kind of relationship that you're not a part of. And yeah, the skinwalker thing. I guess," she says, putting her coffee back on the desk, "that you wouldn't have mentioned that unless you were serious about it. You are—and excuse me if I'm out of line—a bit of a smartass, Sheriff, but you're also pretty much all business. I think you wouldn't have asked me about skinwalkers unless you had a good reason to. Oh, and you treat your deputy, Digger, like a moron."

Yeah, I've got to smile, and I do. This one's a catch if there ever was one. "Good. Excellent. And no, I don't treat Digger like a moron. I'm sending him to forensics school and trying to enlarge his police experience. He'll be heading to Denver on Monday."

"That's a good thing. He does have a nice ass."

"Yes, he does."

"So, tell me about this skinwalker thing," she says. "Why'd you bring it up the last time I was here?"

I'm wondering if I should pull her into the loop. But if I don't tell her, sooner or later she'll find out about it on her own. And how do I explain it all to her—she, with the degree in English literature, for Christ's sake!—without sounding like a fucking nutcase?

"I'm going to tell you a story," I say, "that might stretch your credulity a bit. You did say you're open-minded, but this stuff is.... Well, it's weird shit that took me a long time to get a handle on."

"Try me," she says, snuggling herself into the chair as if preparing for a long journey.

"Okay. It all began with a freak bear in a snowstorm." I lean back in my chair, and I too prepare for the journey I'm about to take her on.

I eat up an hour and a half taking her through the delightful recent history of Pine County, ending the story with Michael's and my sit-down with Mrs. Emerson. She's not asked one question during the telling of this saga, and her expression has remained intent, her eyes never leaving mine.

"So that's it," I say.

She nods and says, "Okay. Got it."

I wait for her to say something else. "Questions?"

"No. I will say, though, that I don't think Mrs. Emerson has told you everything about what's going on. And Hank? Henry Tall Horse? He's holding back too."

"That would be my conclusion."

"And Michael," she says. "I don't think he's suddenly turned into some happy-go-lucky guy who's content to spend time with his playmate—what's his name? Phillip?—just because he says he's figured this whole thing out. From what you've told me, Sheriff, your husband's got some irons in the fire that maybe he's not telling you about."

What she's just said is, of course, something that's crossed my mind about a hundred times since Michael and I sat down to have dinner last night. He's acting normal. That's not Michael. And yes, I know normal is one of those words that begs a subjective viewpoint. And that's exactly how I'm looking at it.

"You've read my mind," I say. "In fact, you've read my psychic e-mails, the ones I send out into the ether about every three seconds hoping for answers from somebody."

"I guess the question you're asking yourself is what the hell are we going to do about it?"

"I really don't have a fucking clue right now. How about you?"

"I think," she says, "that we serve and protect. We're cops. That's what we do. And this crazy shit? This—" She raises her right hand and sweeps it from left to right. "—Pine County haven for skinwalking Native Americans, and the queen of the skinwalkers holding court at the foot of the mountain where all the dead freakish critters reside, and apparently where the live ones bow down in supplication... I think we just tend to do what we know best. We serve and protect. We leave that crazy shit alone unless it crosses over into our jurisdiction of the quasinormal, sometimes law-abiding, sometimes innocent realm of relatively *normal* human beings."

She's raised her voice through this soliloquy, and I'm wondering if her childhood was schooled by the raucous tendencies of black Baptist preachers, whose singsong sermons surely raised the specter of salvation through shouts of amen and a few robust hymns. I glance into the outer office and catch Digger turned in his chair, staring at the back of Brianna Lincoln's head.

"Praise Jesus," I say.

"Sorry. I got carried away."

"But that's what you think we ought to do?"

"Yes, it is. As a matter of fact, I think the only normal"—she embraces that word with finger quotes—"crime you've had up here lately is somebody or something killed a dog, and maybe we could get Melissa for giving a false statement to a police officer. Those are the *normal* crimes I think you've had here lately."

"Well, not *that* normal. And Michael? What about him?"

"Oh, that's something else altogether. You and he are gonna have to work that out by yourselves."

I'm envisioning right now the nuns in *The Sound of Music*, singing that song about Maria. How do I solve a problem like Michael? But he's not a problem. He's my husband.

"Glad we had this chat," I say, standing up and stretching. "One question, though. All this crazy shit, as you say? Do you believe it? Do you believe me?"

She stands up too and bends her torso from side to side. "If I didn't I'd be walking out that door, Sheriff. Won't work with a psychopath who has visions, though I had to work with a couple on the DPD before I passed probation. Hah!" She shakes her head. "Love to get those two up here and see what they think of all this."

I look at my watch and see it's only a little past eight. "How about a late breakfast?"

"Sure," she says. "I'll buy."

"We've got a tab at Cathy's that the county pays."

"Wonderful. I was waiting for you to tell me about the perks. Is that the only one?"

"Glen Hague will give a 5 percent discount on nonedibles over at the store."

"So, laundry detergent and such?"

"Yeah. That and toilet paper. Probably feminine products as well. 'Course he hikes everything up about 300 percent anyway. So...." I step from behind my desk, hand her her coat, and pull mine from the tree.

"I think I'm going to like it just fine up here," she says, stepping to the door and opening it.

Walking out of my office, I stop at Digger's desk as Bri reaches the front door. "We'll be back in an hour."

He nods, stands up, and leans his head close to mine. "Did I hear her say something about the queen of the skinwalkers?"

"You did, Digger. That's what she said."

"What does that mean?"

"I don't know. Maybe she'll explain it to us once we get to know her."

"Oh. Okay," he says. "See you in an hour."

I wish I had just a mere thimbleful of Digger's sweet innocence. The world would appear so much nicer and uncomplicated.

Chapter Thirty-Seven

CATHY ALL but ignores us as we take our seats in the café. She listens to our orders, nods, and gives us a curt, "It'll be just a few minutes," before she goes back to the kitchen.

"She's usually more talkative," I say.

"That's okay. She's probably hurting a little."

"Yeah, I suspect she is. If Missie doesn't return.... Hell, she'll get over it. She's a strong woman."

"We all break just like little girls sometimes."

"A Dylan fan?"

"Of course," she says, opening her napkin. "And I don't like anybody who isn't."

As we talk over our meal, I can't shake what she told me in my office. I've been so consumed with figuring out what the hell is going on up here that I now realize I've kind of lost track of what I've been charged by the good people of Pine County to do. I'm a law enforcement officer—an elected one at that—and there's nothing in the manual relating to manifestations of black or white magic, skinwalkers, windborne voices, Spirit Dogs, or anything else that's lately captured my time and imagination.

"You know," I say, interrupting her narrative about the interesting characters she'd worked with on the Denver Police Force, "you've caused me to take a look at the other side of the coin."

"What coin is that?"

"The side that is grounded in reality. Or reality as it is for most folks."

"Ah," she says, laying her napkin on the table. "You mean the kind of reality that for all intents and purposes is what keeps us centered, keeps us doing our jobs as police officers and not going off on unproductive tangents that we don't understand and never will?"

"Yeah, that's the one."

"Listen, Sheriff." She leans toward me as if she's got a secret. "When you first asked me about skinwalkers, I told you that I thought such a thing was bullshit embraced by Indian lore."

"Yes, you did."

"Did you believe I meant that?"

"Sure. I think you say what you mean or think."

She leans back and smiles. "You remember what I named my cat?"

"Yes. Necro."

"Short for necromancer."

"Okay. Believe we discussed that."

"That suggest anything to you?" she says, raising an eyebrow.

"Your cat's a sorceress?"

She smiles and gives me a wink. "What else?"

I'm not sure what she's trying to get at, and this circling of the subject matter is something I don't like to do. It's hard enough trying to get something out of Hank. Now she's doing it.

"I don't know what else, Bri. You tell me."

She folds her hands on the table. "There's a murder cop with the DPD. He's got about a 90 percent solve rate. Remarkable stats given that the national average is about 60 percent. You know how he does that? How he solves his cases?"

"Don't tell me. Magic?"

"He talks to the dead bodies. He leans in and whispers in their ears, and the dead tell him about the whys and wherefores of their murders, things that aren't observable and usually can't be determined by forensic investigation. All the other murder cops can't figure it out. How does he do it? He shared his secret with me because… I knew what he was doing, and I told him I knew. We got pretty close. I was temporarily assigned to him for a while. The dead speak to him, Sheriff. How and why is a mystery. He calls what he does necromancy."

"Oh, that's magical. No doubt about it." I'm not sure I believe what she's just told me, but stranger things have happened.

"You don't believe me?"

"I guess. With everything that's been going on here, I don't doubt there's a shitload of weirdness in the big city."

"Not my point," she says, shaking her head. "My point is that there are things we don't understand but know in our guts that trying to understand them will prove futile. That murder cop on the DPD didn't understand it himself. And neither did I. But we both knew that trying to dissect why he could do it was a useless cause that would lead to a blank wall."

If I'm reading her right, I think she's adding more fuel to the *embrace it and find Jesus* conclusion that Don has borrowed from his wife in order to remain somewhat sane in the face of the happy-crappy goings-on up here. She'd begun this argument in my office, and now here in the café. And I don't disagree with her.

"I do get your point, Bri. I—"

Cathy places the check on the table without a word and then heads back to the kitchen. I pull out my pen and sign it.

"You think she'll ever talk to you again?" Bri says.

"Sure. She just needs some time. She's not mad at me. Life just shit on her over the last couple of days, and she's got to take it out on somebody. Let's get out of here."

WHEN WE get back to the office, I tell Digger to take Bri on patrol with him. The usual routine on weekends is for the duty deputy to remain in the office, answering the phone when it rings, if it does at all, and staying near the radio if any fire district calls go out. Digger's not one to embrace a change of routine easily, but I tell him I'll be around the office for a while, and Bri needs to get a sense of what it is we do here. Besides that, I want Digger and Bri to have a little bonding time.

After they leave, I walk across the street to Needful Things and find Michael and Phillip inside, where they're moving display cases around.

"Hi, Sam," Phillip says.

"How are you, Phillip?" He's a handsome man and, like Digger, is either not aware of it or is not affected by it.

"I'm fine. Michael said you hired a new deputy."

"I did. Actually, your grandmother hired her. I just signed the paperwork she handed to me."

"She's a black lesbian," Michael says as if such a thing were exotic, exciting even. "She's special too."

Special. I know him well enough to wonder if he means magical. "She's also a helluva cop. Well, as far as I can tell. You're rearranging the shop."

"Yeah," Michael says. "Phillip had some good ideas about what should go where. You know? Merchandising? And he's going to consign some of his work to me to sell."

"Just some oils I've done," Phillip says. "It'll be fun to see if anyone's interested in them."

"Good," I say, thinking that they ought to advertise in the gay rag published in Denver. I see a full-page spread with them standing side by side, their smiles an allurement sure to bring the Denver boys up the mountain.

"I called Tony when we got here," Michael says. "I'm going to take your advice and speak to him before I call my father."

"He going to meet you here?"

"Yes. He should be here by now."

All three of us look out the window.

"Well, better here than Mrs. Emerson's house," I say.

I look at Michael with what I hope he sees as a *You know what I mean?* expression. He just smiles back at me with his *Get over it, Sam* expression.

"All right, then," I say. "I'm going back to the office."

"No binoculars this time," Michael says. "I think he's on our side."

I stop with my hand on the door handle. What *side* are we on? Truth, justice, and the American way? Better yet, what are the sides? "I think he's on Mrs. Emerson's side, Michael. I don't know if that's our side or not."

"She's okay, Sam. Trust me."

"Okay. If you say so." I step out and recross the street. All I can do is take some comfort in knowing that Michael is more attuned to the unknowable than I am. And with each passing day, it appears he's becoming more comfortable with it. I don't think I'll ever get to that point. *Embrace it and find Jesus.*

I DON'T go into the office but head for Brunhilda instead. I want to talk to Hank, and as I back out of my spot, I grab the mike and tell Digger what I'm doing.

"Roger, Sheriff. Okay if I show Deputy Lincoln some properties for sale?"

"Sure, Digger. You can call her Brianna."

"Roger that. Just using radio protocol."

Sweet Digger. I put the mike back on the dash and wonder if Bri is smiling right now. Not that Digger is wrong, just that he's so… Digger-like all the time.

The light snowfall has stopped, and as I drive up Hank's road, small pockets of blue sky have appeared above the tree line. Hank is bundled up, sitting on a kitchen chair he's put on his porch, and Charlie is lying there beside him. I ease Brunhilda to a stop and get out. Hank gives me a wave.

"Morning," I say, stopping about ten feet from the porch. "Nice day."

Charlie raises his head and dares me to step up there with them. I stay where I'm at.

"Yes, it is." Hank reaches down and lightly pats Charlie's head.

"So…. The last time we talked about Mrs. Emerson, you didn't have much to say. I guess, though, you've known her for a while."

"Ever since Mr. Emerson brought her to his house. She's got strong magic. I felt it before I met her."

"She told us she was more or less kidnapped from her family in Utah, from the Navajo Reservation up there?"

"She was taken from her family."

He doesn't shed any more light on that event and just stares off into the distance. I look behind me and don't see anything of interest except more blue sky appearing through the thin layer of clouds.

"Hank, how long has there been skinwalker activity up here? Mary said there were odd things going on when Slaughter was the sheriff, and even when she and her husband first moved here. She didn't call it skinwalker activity, but I think that's what it was."

"Never talked to Slaughter. Sometimes he spit in the street when he passed me in town. Mary is a good woman. I think she knows a lot about things."

"But how long has it been going on? And why here?"

"A long time," he says. A momentary breeze sweeps off the mountain, rustling his hair that he's left unbraided. "Before Slaughter. A long time before you and Michael. The magic has been here maybe from the beginning of time. I don't know. But it calls to witches and others who hear the old winds." He raises his right arm and sweeps it from left to right. "Maybe the Earth Mother had to have somewhere to put them. Maybe Father Sky agreed."

I realize that ever since I first approached Hank about the weird goings-on up here, I expected, or at least hoped, for some detailed explication of the whole business, something I now realize he's incapable or unwilling to provide. And even if he did provide it, what would that matter? *From the beginning of time.* Christ, leave it up to me to dig into matters that apparently had no beginning and probably will have no end. *Embrace it and find Jesus.*

"Okay." I nod. "And I guess you were up at Mrs. Emerson's house yesterday because…. She's a strong witch, isn't she Hank?"

"Before Michael, she was."

I don't like that answer, and it gets me to thinking. Does she see Michael as a threat? "You think she'll try to harm Michael? Get rid of him?"

Hank stands up, and Charlie rouses himself too. "Nah," he says. "She likes him being here. She's getting old. I think she's happy for somebody to help her out."

"In what way?"

"To keep the skinwalkers in line. You want some elk meat?"

"No thanks. Hank—"

"Getting cold, Sheriff, and Charlie's hungry."

"But…."

He opens the door for Charlie, and the old dog walks into the cabin. "Saw the woman with your helluva deputy a little while ago. They stopped to say hi. I think she'll help Michael. She's got some strong magic too."

He goes into the cabin and shuts the door, leaving me standing here wondering what the fuck that was about. *Strong magic*? Brianna? Nah, she's…. Hell, she's a tough cop with a degree in English literature who's memorized bits of Bronte, a quick mind, and she's as much of a smartass as I am.

I get back into Brunhilda, start her up, and turn her around. I drive down Hank's road, and for what it's worth, recall what Bri named her car—Sly. And she named her cat Necro. I put them together, and yes, it comes out Sly Necromancer. Nope. Hank's just playing with me. He's done that ever since I first met him. Wily old lovable son of a bitch that he is, I can't give credence to what he'd just told me. Brianna? No. Not.... Possible? He said *strong magic*, though. And as many times as he's used that term, I do know what *that* means. Still....

CHAPTER THIRTY-EIGHT

DIGGER AND Bri aren't back at the office yet, and Phillip's car isn't outside Michael's shop. Where the hell did they go? I've got my cell and listen to Michael's phone ring too many times. When his message comes on, I end the call. I take off my coat, sit, and put my feet up on the desk.

I remember something from Thomas McGuane, an author I enjoy and have probably read to excess: "Giving freaks a pass is the oldest tradition in Montana." No, this isn't Montana, but we do have our freaks in Pine County, most of whom I've come to understand are skinwalkers. Well, no, that's not completely true. Most of our freaks are otherwise quiet and seldom seen human beings who've somehow become attuned to witchery and sometimes take the form of a critter with fangs and a lust for blood, or maybe they just like the feel and freedom of becoming feral. Even I have wondered through this whole strange business what it would feel like to race across fields and mountainsides after taking the shape of a wolf or a mountain lion, or to soar above it all as an owl or a raven. This is the stuff of fantasy. At least for me it is.

"Michael," I say, answering my cell on the first ring.

"Sorry I didn't pick up when you called," Michael says. "We're at the cabin with Tony."

"You and Phillip?"

"Yes. We're having that conversation we talked about."

"How's it going?"

"Good."

I hear Michael tell someone who I presume is Phillip that the corkscrew is in the cupboard.

"You're having some wine?"

"Yeah. The red you like," Michael says. "Hope you don't mind. It's the last bottle."

"No. That's fine."

"Just wanted to tell you where we are."

"I was wondering about that. Tony's... okay?"

"Yes. Of course. I'll tell you everything when you get home."

"Be careful."

"Always am. Bye."

I don't know how Phillip will take a discussion about the nefarious nature of Mr. Bellomo's past, but I suspect the wine will help. And Michael? What state of mind am I going to find him in when I get home? I glance over my shoulder to see who is coming into the outer office. It's Digger and Bri, back from whatever adventure they've shared. Digger's smiling, and so is Bri.

"How'd it go?" I say as Bri steps into my office.

"Well," she says as she sits in front of my desk, "looks like I may be living in a trailer for a while."

I scoot my feet off the desk. "Nothing wrong with that. Digger lives there."

"He showed me. He's got a nice little place. Even showed me the picture Michael gave him for Christmas."

"The naked boy riding a horse."

"Yes. Riding bareback. Michael is very talented."

"He is. At a lot of things. You know when you saw him from your car earlier?"

"Yes."

"He saw you too. He said you were special."

"He's very perceptive."

"Yeah," I say. "Went to see Hank this morning. He saw you with Digger before I got there. Know what he said?"

"Can't imagine."

"He said you've got strong magic."

"Hah! Most men think black women have some secret juju up their sleeves. You know, kind of like everybody thinks black men have huge dicks. Most of them do, but their allure is a mystery to me."

I rest my forearms on the desk and lean toward her. "I don't think Michael is interested in your sexual juju, or Hank either. Thing is, when Michael called you special I think he meant something else. And Hank's comment? Strong magic? That means a whole lot to me because I know what Hank meant by it."

She bows her head slightly, then raises it, a soft smile on her face. She stands, takes off her coat, hangs it up, then steps to the door and closes it. When she sits again, her face is serious. "I'm no stranger to Pine County, Sheriff," she says, her voice soft, intimate. "I've known Tony Fuschi for a long time, even before I went to work for the DPD. And I know Mrs. Emerson, though I call her Adeezbaa—she who leads the fight. I've never sat down with Hank, but, well…. You know all about speaking without speaking."

She pauses to gather her thoughts, and I fist-bump myself in my mind, knowing that my hunch was right. Or rather that what I surmised from what I and others had observed about her was right on. I do feel, though, a little tingling along the hairs of my neck.

"You're one of them?" I say.

"I didn't think we'd have this conversation so soon," she says.

"Yeah, and I didn't think my encounter with a freak bear would turn out to be just the tip of the iceberg."

"For you, I guess it was. Adeezbaa called me up here, Sheriff. It was after you and Michael moved in. Things were getting a little hairy for her, and…. She's managed to keep things on an even keel, to use a metaphor that seems pretty apt right now. How deeply do you want to me to go into this? The whole nine yards, or just the surface stuff?"

"Metaphors aside, just tell me how Michael fits into all this. I know the… demons were roused when we moved here, but…. What is he? A conduit for…. Jesus, I don't even know the right question to ask."

"Those attuned to magic are attracted by, oh, instances of a more potent source of it. Michael is—and take my word for it—a potent source, Sheriff. So potent that some are intimidated by it to the extent they are compelled to destroy it. Case in point, Stanley Broken River. He was…. He was working his way to the top, so to speak. He couldn't get to Adeezbaa with all the protection she's got, but… I'm told you know how he attempted to get to Michael?"

"Yes, I do. Missie told us when we were at Mrs. Emerson's."

"Stanley knew I was onto him," she says. "He moved out of his trailer after I'd paid him a little visit one night. But apparently I hadn't instilled the fear of…. No, I can't say God in that context. He apparently didn't get my message and just hid out on the mountain."

"So you were called up here by Mrs. Emerson specifically to protect Michael?"

"Would have been up here full time if you had posted that deputy position sooner."

I guess Mrs. Emerson is okay, as Michael had told me. But there's something that doesn't ring true about all this.

"Having trouble, Bri," I say, "believing you'd give up your DPD career just to come up here to protect Michael."

"Oh," she says, "everything I told you about wanting to live in the wide open spaces was true. I've had it with the city."

"Something else crosses my mind too."

"What's that?"

"You told me about that homicide dick who speaks to the dead?"

"Yes?"

"You made it sound like he taught you to do that?"

She nods.

"I think it was the other way around."

"Not really. I'd sensed he was a little special himself, that he had the ability to enhance his gut hunches with the spiritualism that just oozed from him every time I was near him. When I finally asked him about it, he said his car had broken down years before on a trip to Steamboat Springs. A Native American woman, a Ute, and her daughter approached him. That woman too must have sensed his magic. When he told her he was a cop who worked on homicides, she taught him to use his magic to speak to the dead and to hear their responses."

Gut hunches. Yeah, I get them too, but I've yet to speak to the dead. Right now I'm feeling a little inadequate. What a helluva cop I'd be if I had the magic she's got.

I start to tap my fingers on the desk, wondering where this all goes from here. "I guess I need to thank you for...." What? Protecting Michael? Helping out with what is apparently Mrs. Emerson's almost lifelong task of keeping skinwalkers in line?

"You don't have to say it, Sheriff. I know what you're thinking."

"Literally?"

"Don't worry. I can't read your thoughts."

I'm not so sure about that, but I'll take her at her word. For now. The next time I admire Digger's ass from afar, I'll see if what she claims holds true.

"Did Digger give you a good overview of what we do here?"

"He was charming. He really respects you. Did you know that?"

"I suppose that I do."

"You ought to show him the same thing."

"Just because I—"

"No, Sheriff," she says a little too seriously. "You really need to stop belittling him. I've decided I'm going to put him under my wing, so to speak. He's a good man, and he's got a lot of potential."

"I told you I'm sending him to school next week."

"I know. And I know you know he's got potential. Just tell him that every once in a while."

So we've come from a discussion about her probably being a witch to acknowledging the fact that sweet Digger has potential. I think both are true, and as I look at her expression, that's saying something like *Get over yourself!* I have to smile.

"Okay," I say. "I'll do that. I think I've had enough of truth-telling for one day. And God knows I've had enough of the… underworld chronicles to last a lifetime. I am curious, though, about how many creatures from the black lagoon you think we might have in Pine County."

"Quite a few," she says. "Adeezbaa has a better handle on that than I do. But we'll be okay. Not something you really have to worry about now that I'm here."

"Great. I'll just hand over all the weird calls to you. I asked Hank this question, but I'm curious what your answer is. Why are they here in Pine County?"

"What'd Hank say?"

"Something about maybe Mother Earth thought this was the best place for them. Oh, and that Father Sky probably seconded that conclusion."

"Good answer."

"That's all you can say?"

"Yes."

"Okay. Guess you ought to head over and see Merle Stacy. He's the trailer park manager. Don't tell him you're a lesbian, though."

"Should I tell him I'm black?"

"Sure, if he doesn't notice. Tell him I'm your reference if he asks for one. And if he steps out on his porch with a great big silver .44 Magnum when you drive in there, don't panic. He does that with everybody."

"All right," she says as she stands and grabs her coat. "If he shoots me, it better not be with a silver bullet, though." She pulls her coat on and then stands by the door.

"Not fond of silver bullets, then?"

"No, it's just that if he does, then it might mean he's identified another problem area in the county."

"Werewolves?"

"Maybe. May. Be," she says. She opens the door and stops at Digger's desk, where she leans in and whispers something in his ear. Digger turns and looks at me with a great big smile.

I stand and grab my coat too. It's been a long day, though it's not yet half over. I walk out of my office, and I also stop at Digger's desk. I give him a pat on his back. "You're doing a good job for us, Digger. Keep up the good work."

"Yes, sir," he says.

I glance back at him as I walk across the room, and he's still beaming that shit-eater.

I think a moment about what's going to change with Digger after Bri spreads her wing over him for a while. He'll change for sure. Maybe he'll lose some of his naivety. The sooner the better, I suppose. What a shame. What a fucking shame.

CHAPTER THIRTY-NINE

As I drive to the cabin, I remember the Christmas that Michael showed me what he'd made for the children at that high-end shopping mall: Santa's workshop with all the fixings. Talk about a loss of innocence. Pairing that with his trek up the mountain to meet his likely assassin—a skinwalker who saw him as a deadly threat—turns my mind to questions that I've put off for too long. Does living here put Michael in danger? Of course it does. It has, actually. And if I'd suggest that we ought to move away, back to Denver possibly or to some other place where all this... stuff that's going on doesn't exist, what would his response be? Yes, I don't have to think about that very much. He'd tell me he's fine, and no, he won't leave because he loves it here, and that will be that. Thinking about it, though, maybe he'd be right. Things happen in cities that are at least as weird, even more horrid than the specter of skinwalkers creeping around. And then there's Bri's entrance into the mix. Hell, with her and me hovering around him... I just don't know.

I HEAR Michael and Phillip's chatter from the guest bedroom as soon as I step into the mudroom. As I walk into the kitchen, I notice three wineglasses on the coffee table in the parlor.

"You're home," Michael says.

I pull a beer from the refrigerator and shut the door. I face him, put the bottle on the counter, and hug him as tight as I think I ever have. "I love you, Michael."

"I love you too, Sam," he says, hugging me back. "I heard you come in. I asked Phillip if he'd mind if we had some time alone."

We break our embrace. I look into his eyes and hear Phillip's vehicle starting up outside.

"We do need to talk."

"Yes, we do," he says. He grabs my beer from the counter and then clutches my hand. "Let's sit down."

We sit at the kitchen table, and I feel the warmth of the sunshine coming through the windows at our side. Michael folds his hands on the table.

"So," he says, "I had a nice conversation with Tony. It was short but nice."

"Phillip was there too?"

"Oh, yeah."

"And he wasn't put off by your conversation?"

"No, he wasn't. In fact, he knows about what goes on up here. Did you know Phillip was with his grandfather when he died?"

"Yes, I've heard that story. Phillip was helping the old guy pull an elk kill up the mountain. His grandfather had a heart attack."

Michael smiles and closes his eyes for a moment. "There's more to the story than that, Sam. He was only thirteen, and there was no way he could deal with what happened. His grandfather collapsed, and he couldn't pull him up the mountain. He was afraid to run for help. He said his grandfather was moaning in pain, and all he could do was try to comfort him. He said he was scared to death. Then he saw an owl, a beautiful white owl sitting up the mountain a ways looking at him. When he started to cry, he said the owl blurred into a shape that he at first couldn't make out. He wiped his eyes, and when he looked at the owl again, it had become a woman. A dark-haired woman. He said she was an Indian, who came down the mountain and cradled him in her arms. She told him it would be okay, that his grandfather was now with the stars. She told him help was on the way."

"Mrs. Emerson?"

"I don't know who else it might have been. She stayed with him for hours. Kept him warm. When some men finally showed up—Phillip called them Indians—the woman kissed his forehead, and then she blurred out again. He watched the white owl fly away."

"And he never told anyone about this?"

"No. He thought no one would believe him, that maybe he had just imagined it."

"Why did this come up? Thought you were going to talk to Tony about your father?"

"Yes, we did. But the story Tony told couldn't help but touch on magic, on skinwalkers. Phillip finally realized that what he had seen was not just his imagination. It had been real."

"Damn. And he believed it all? Skinwalkers?"

"Yes. I'd already told him some things while we were at the shop. What Tony told us only made it more real for him."

I sip my beer, set it back down, and nod. "Okay. And what did Tony tell you?"

"Well," he says, "not a whole lot, but enough."

"And?"

"About my father. He inherited his business from his father, who made most of his money during Prohibition. He didn't produce booze but was the middleman—the guy between the manufacturer and the sellers. There was also gambling. Tony called it the *numbers racket* and said it involved everything from horse and dog races to bets on professional sports."

"I remember this, Michael. It's general knowledge that the Bellomos were Denver's version of the Chicago mob. We talked about this."

"I know. But Tony gave me more details. He said my father was brought into the family business when he was eighteen or nineteen. When Prohibition ended, the gambling stuff continued, and there was some drug stuff too. Tony said my father didn't like the drug trade or prostitution or some of the seedier things that were going on. But Tony said my father had no problem with the enforcement end of the business. My father never had any qualms about, as Tony said, teaching people lessons they'd never forget. Nobody ever messed with my father, Sam, because if they did they didn't live long enough to talk about it."

Michael crosses his arms. He looks sad as he stares out the side windows. I don't know how I can ease whatever pain he's feeling right now. I take another sip of my beer and wait for him to continue.

"Tony also said that my father was smart," Michael begins again after turning his head back to me. "He realized that the violence, the old ways of doing things just wouldn't work anymore. When my grandfather died, my father slowly started getting into legitimate business—a restaurant, some Laundromats, a construction company. And it was at about that time that he met Malcolm Emerson. Emerson had run his own crime—oh, I guess syndicate would be the best word—on the Western Slope for decades. He'd made a lot of money over the years. Tony had met him a couple times after my father sent him up here to see if there were any opportunities for expansion of his businesses—both legitimate and not. That's when Tony met Adeezbaa, or Elenore Emerson as you know her."

"No, Mrs. Emerson told us what her Navajo name is. I know that name well after the conversation I had with Bri today. I'll tell you about that after you're done."

"Your new deputy? You know about her?" he says, the tone of his voice rising a bit.

"Yes, I do."

"Good," he says. "Very good. Anyway.... Tony worked for my dad for a long time before Mr. Emerson came into the picture. He never liked how my father dealt with people who disagreed with him or didn't do what he had told them to. He was always looking for a way to get away from my father, to get out from under his thumb. And when he and Adeezbaa met, I guess they... connected. They understood each other. Tony saw in Malcolm the same violent tendencies he'd seen in my father. He saw the way he treated Adeezbaa."

"You said they understood each other. Did Mrs. Emerson tell him about... the magic? What she had found up here?"

"Oh yeah." He nods. "She did. Tony said he didn't believe it at first, but.... You know how hard it was for you to accept it?"

"Yes."

"Tony said it took him a long time to believe what she told him. Then he saw it for himself. She changed for him, Sam—the white owl Phillip had seen."

"What about Mrs. Emerson telling us about what Malcolm called your father? The greasy wop thing?"

"That bothered Tony too. What bothered him more, though, was that Malcolm and my dad started to pool their resources to get back into the criminal stuff. They doped dogs and horses so they'd win races, betting on professional and college sports, and they even started getting in on the drug trade. Tony said it was then that Malcolm and my father seemed to get closer. They became the best of friends."

"And Mrs. Emerson saw all this too."

"Yes. Of course. And Malcolm was still treating her like shit. Tony started spending more time at the Emerson property. He became the liaison between Mr. Emerson and my father. He'd bring cash up here or take it back to Denver. He relayed messages that couldn't go over the telephone. It got really bad. And Tony and Adeezbaa became…. They were lovers, Sam. They *are* lovers."

"So Tony and Mrs. Emerson decided Malcolm had to be killed?"

"Adeezbaa had decided that when Malcolm took her from her family."

"Yeah, I remember now. Wow. All for love."

"That," he says, once again folding his hands on the table, "and their mutual belief that the things Malcolm and my father were doing were… evil."

"Mrs. Emerson killed her husband, Tony defected from your father's operation, and thus the fortress was built at the base of the mountain?"

"Pretty much. Besides Adeezbaa finding Native Americans that shared her… spiritualism."

"Her magic, you mean?"

"Tony said the guys Adeezbaa recruited believed in the old medicine, the old ways of their tribes. Lakota Sioux, Navajo, and a couple Ute. You can't see it from the road, but Adeezbaa built houses for these guys. Some of them even have families."

"We never see them in town."

"That's the way Adeezbaa wants it. Out of sight."

"Out of mind. And there's no, um, tribal rivalry going on?"

"Tony didn't say there is, or ever was. I think Adeezbaa wouldn't allow it. Or if it happened she'd…. She's too strong, Sam. They all know that."

I'm reluctant to ask him this, but I've got to do it. "Where does this leave you with your father? Are you going to confront him?"

"I'm going to…." He stands up and stretches, raising his arms over his head. He's smiling. "I'm going to put my mother and father in a place that won't harm me. Or you." He walks to the edge of the kitchen and turns before he steps into the living room. "They have no power over me now, Sam. I'll leave them in my past where they belong. But now I'm going back to the shop. That's where Phillip went. We're going to clear a space for his work."

"Will you be home for supper?"

"Of course. Will you?"

"Oh, I'm going to take the rest of day off. Maybe take a nap. Will Phillip be joining us later?"

"No. He's going to stay with his grandmother tonight. So you and I can get loud if we want to. Or not."

I stand up and walk over to him. "Yes, I want that. I want to get very loud tonight." I embrace him again as I did when I first came home. "Thank you," I say.

He wraps his arms around my back. "For what?"

"For you," I say.

As we kiss, I inch my hands down to his ass and squeeze. "Yeah. Tonight."

I walk him to the front porch, where I watch him get into his truck and then head down our road.

CHAPTER FORTY

SPRING IS a tentative affair in the Rockies. Once you think it's finally here, you wake up to two feet of snow and temperatures that defy the calendar month. But from mid-May to the first part of June, the signs of spring are everywhere. The Pasque wildflowers are usually the first to push themselves up from the ground, their lavender-and-white petals appearing tulip-like at first. Then soon they open up, signaling the commencement of another season of new growth. Soon to follow are the yellow mustard flowers and orange paintbrushes. The chipmunks reappear after their winter of quasi hibernation. Mama mule deer start to show up with their white-spotted fawns and cow elk with their calves, both the fawns and calves uncertain of where their spindly too-tall legs are taking them. Gray foxes come back from wherever they went after the first snows of late fall. Coyotes, already shedding their thick hair, look disheveled, skinny, and frantic for their next meal. Black bear sows will soon meander from the hills, their four- or five-month-old cubs trailing behind. And the birds you haven't seen for months will revisit the buffet you've kept waiting for them—the Clark's nutcrackers, tanagers, crossbills, and so much more, including the hummingbirds who stop at the red nectar feeder you'd just hung up minutes ago.

It's been three months since Michael and I sat down with Mrs. Emerson in her great room. Everything I learned from that visit and everything that happened before and after it has now become a memory worthy of Michael's paintings. And he has painted many of those scenes, though if you didn't know what they represent you'd just think they were pretty or gruesome or the output of an artist with an overactive imagination.

We had Tony Fuschi over for dinner last week, and I've got to admit, I like him. He's got a good sense of humor, and he's obviously protective of Michael. That's a good thing. With me, Bri, and Tony watching out for Michael, I think he'll be okay. No, I know he will. Besides, if all the magic up here is centered around Michael and Mrs. Emerson and not allowed to get out of hand, then things should stay pretty calm. Or at least that's my hope and prayer.

Michael didn't tell me the whole truth about how he was going to handle the revelations about his father. Though he'd told me he was going to just shove both his mother and father to a place in his past that has no power over his future, he did drive down to Denver one day a month ago. He met his father for lunch at the Northside Italian restaurant that had been in their family for decades. There was still that little issue of his father wanting revenge on Mrs. Emerson for dispatching Malcolm to probably a pile of dust interred among the many remains of rogue skinwalkers on her property. He didn't tell me he was going to do that because he knew I wouldn't have liked it. When he got home that night, though, he told me what he'd done.

"I was very calm," he said as we sat in the parlor sipping wine.

"Was he?"

"Yes, for most of it. I told him I'd met a wonderful older woman who said she'd met him a couple times. He asked me what her name was, and I told him. His face got red, and he started a rant about *that bitch*, saying that she needed to be taken care of and Tony too, and that he wanted to talk to me about that."

"You're kidding."

"No. He actually said that. But before he could say anything else, I told him that if he ever tried to harm her or any of her people, including Tony, that I'd have you get with your buddies at the Colorado Bureau of Investigation. I told him there's no statute of limitations on murder."

"But you don't know if he ever killed anybody with his own hands."

"His reaction said it all, Sam. He got real quiet and wouldn't even look me in the eye."

"So he got the message?"

"Yes. I told him I'd never speak to him or my mother again if he ever sent any of his goons up here to harm anybody, including Adeezbaa's dogs."

"He knew who Adeezbaa was?"

"Yes. And I told him she's someone he really doesn't want to piss off."

I was proud of Michael for doing what he had done. Although I suspected that Tony had probably suggested to Michael how he should handle his father, I didn't mention it. Tony and he had become close in the past few months, not confidants exactly, but more like Michael saw Tony as a grandfather figure. And Mrs. Emerson had become like a grandmother.

Digger did go down to Denver for the forensics school. I'd taken courses in forensics in college, and I knew what he'd be studying. When he came back, though, from that week in Denver, he seemed to have lost some of his innocence. Oh, he was still as sweet as he'd always been. But there was just something about him that had changed. I guess there was a seriousness to him that he hadn't had before he left. I can only speculate that that portion of the class dealing with the dismal reality of murder investigations had struck a tight chord with him. Maybe something about man's inhumanity to man.

Bri moved her girlfriend up here. Her name is Sharon, and she's one of those tall, beautiful women who the moment you meet them you know has balls bigger than yours. She's an editor for a New York book publisher, and it appears as though half the space in the trailer they live in is devoted to her work.

Bri and Sharon have put a bid in on the house that Karen Hargrove moved out of this past winter, that left her husband, Ned, there by himself. Bri, Sharon, and Karen became good friends, being that they lived about fifty feet from one another in the trailer park. And when it appeared as though Ned had vanished off the face of the earth, leaving the house empty and Karen greatly relieved, Karen decided to sell the house. It was in her name, and she'd told Bri and Sharon she never wanted to enter it again.

We, of course, investigated Ned's disappearance and came up with absolutely nothing. Bri and I had a conversation about that shortly after we closed the file. I asked her what she thought had happened to Ned, and she told me that wife-beating sonsabitches don't deserve to live.

"So," I asked her, "you think he's dead? Somebody got rid of him?"

"I think," she said, her smile hinting that she knew more about this than she was willing to share, "he got what he deserved."

I didn't pursue this with her because I probably didn't want to know the truth. By that time I'd learned that, after all that had happened up here, sometimes sleeping dogs are best left to lie undisturbed.

Bri has met all my expectations and more. She's a good cop who gets along with Don, Digger, and Mary. We've had a couple of conversations since she came on the job about the lack of the excitement she'd experienced on the DPD. She agreed that it was a big change for her but one that boded well for the future. She said Sharon and Necro are happy too. I haven't asked her if she's walked lately in some critter's skin since she moved here, but then I don't yet know if she does that or not. And again, maybe I don't even want to know.

I went into Glen Hague's store the other day, and he and his wife, Doreen, caught me first thing and told me they needed my and Michael's help. Seems their son, Russell, who had moved to San Francisco several years before, had come out to them over the telephone, and Glen and Doreen were beside themselves with concern. In fact, Doreen's Shirley Temple curls appeared to unravel before my eyes as she explained they didn't know what to do with this new information from their son. Michael and I had known about Russell the first time we'd met him. But Glen and Doreen were apparently in the dark about it. They asked me if Michael and I could show Russell the ropes about being gay.

"You know," Glen said, "just teach him the ins and outs of it."

I didn't respond with my first thought: Well, yeah, that's about it—in and out. But I did tell him Michael and I would be happy to talk to Russell. "Though," I added, "I do think if he's lived in San Francisco for all this time, he probably knows what being gay entails."

"Oh, I don't think so," Doreen said. "He's coming for a visit in July. Please, please, couldn't you and Michael tell him what he needs to know as he starts this journey?"

I told her we would, and they both smiled with relief. Glen even gave me a 10 percent discount on the candy bar I'd come in to buy.

Missie never returned to Cathy. Tony told us that Missie stayed with Mrs. Emerson for about a week and then left for points unknown. I suspect she's probably where she wanted to go in the first place—Las Vegas. Though when I think about her, I remember what someone once told me: A change in geography rarely results in a change of person. If you're an asshole in Peoria, you'll probably be an asshole in Des Moines. Not that Missie was an asshole, but she was disturbed, and I can't help but worry about her.

Cathy and I have resumed our faux dislike for each other, which means that if we both weren't homosexual, we'd probably be lovers. No, I take that back. It means we've once again connected on that unique plane where insults are a sign of love and respect. I could never be her lover because that would take Michael out of my life. And if I weren't queer there'd be no Michael.

I went up to Joe Parsons's place not long ago and told him that we'd been unable to determine what or who had killed his dog, Apollo. And I guess I still don't know if it was Stanley Broken River who did it. It probably was, but I couldn't tell Joe that. Joe took me out to the meadow where he'd buried Apollo. And once again it was affirmed that most dog lovers grieve more deeply for the loss of their dog than they do for the loss of another human being. Joe's sobs were witness to that. I put my hand on his shoulder and told him I was sorry for his loss. Of course my words couldn't ease his pain, but what else could I do?

Michael and I went down to Golden, Colorado, last week and took a look at some rescued Alaskan malamutes. As irascible as Charlie is, we've always agreed that if we ever got a dog, it would be a malamute. One of the rescues named Al, simply Al, was a five-year-old beauty that took to Michael like an old friend he'd been looking for his entire life. Al's history was that he'd allegedly killed two chickens and one cat at his previous home, and the people he'd lived with just couldn't have that kind of behavior amongst them. My thought was that if Al had actually done what his prior family had alleged, and if they took offense at that, then that family was ignorant of what an Alaskan malamute is—the first cousin to Wolf. (Naming a malamute Al is, I suppose, further evidence that they hadn't given much thought to having a northern breed dog in the first place.) We signed the papers, paid the fee, and Al rode home with us, his head out the window, tasting the air as if it were ice cream. We haven't changed his name because he seems to be comfortable with it. Al is our first child, and Michael and I have discussed the prospect of having another.

RIGHT NOW I'm heading toward Hank's place with Brunhilda's windows open, her engine contentedly purring. I haven't seen him for a while, and though I've checked on him through the winter, I worry about him and Charlie, especially since Michael showed me a painting he'd completed of them just yesterday. They're both old and getting a little decrepit. And if Michael thinks of Tony as a surrogate grandfather, Hank would be mine.

As I drive up his road, there he is on his porch, and Charlie is lying beside him, his stare directed at Brunhilda and me.

"Hey, Hank," I say after closing the door and taking a few steps toward him. Hank's hair is braided, the two braids hanging down to the top of his chest. He's wearing the vest with the intricate beadwork on the front of it. I'm still wary of Charlie and stand at the bottom of the porch.

"Sheriff," Hank says. He looks at me and puts his hand on Charlie's back. "Sit down with us."

"Okay. Charlie won't mind?"

"No. Charlie might die today. I think he's ready."

This hits me like a punch in the gut. Until today, I haven't noticed that Charlie was failing, other than that he's always been half crippled. He's never liked me, but as I sit down on the porch, the old boy strains to sniff my leg. "Sorry to hear that, Hank. He sick?"

"His legs have gone out. He thinks it might be time. He hung around 'til the whispers faded."

I reach my hand out and scratch Charlie's head. He reacts only with a little sigh, then lowers his head to the ground. "You doing okay?"

"Sure. It's a nice day."

I glance behind me and see that he's not yet started his annual restringing of juniper berries around the doors and windows.

"You going to put up your junipers again this year?"

"Don't think so," he says. "Ever since you killed Stanley Broken River, the whispers have settled down. Prob'ly not a good idea to get on a ladder. My legs are going too."

I try not to linger on what I'm thinking: If Charlie dies, so does Hank. And same as I observed of Charlie, today is the first time that Hank appears feeble. "We, Michael and I, can help you with whatever you've got to do here. We'll even string berries if that's what you want."

He shakes his head. "Not anymore. Might not ever need them again."

"Wish you had a phone, Hank. If something happened up here, I don't know how anybody would know."

"Michael will. Adeezbaa will know too."

Of course they will. "Wish I understood better about how all this stuff works."

"The magic?"

"Yes."

"It's not for you to know, Sheriff. Don't worry about it."

Embrace it and find Jesus. "Okay, I won't."

He holds his arm out to me. "Help me up," he says.

I do that, and then Hank looks down at Charlie, who has raised his head to look at him.

"Can you get Charlie up?"

I stand up and then bend down and put my arms under Charlie's chest and hind end. He whines as I lift him to his feet. Hank walks down the two steps, and Charlie follows, but his legs won't hold him up, and he falls.

Hank turns. "We need to get out there," he says, pointing to the grasses twenty yards from his cabin. "Can you carry him?"

I lean down and gently brace my arms under Charlie. This time his whine is pathetic as I pick him up. I carry him out to the grasses, where Hank has stopped and eased himself down to the ground. He sits cross-legged and motions for me to place Charlie at his side.

"Thank you," Hank says when I put Charlie down.

Again, I'm concerned that they've become so old in such a short period of time. "Hank, I'm worried about Charlie. And you too."

Hank puts his hand on Charlie's head and then raises his own head toward the sun. He closes his eyes and begins a chant, a whisper of words I don't understand. He reaches under his vest and pulls out an eagle feather. He raises it and draws it back and forth in front of him and Charlie. I'm immediately brought back to the painting Michael showed me yesterday. It is this scene, the one I'm watching right now—Hank and Charlie in the patch of new spring grasses, Hank's head is raised, an eagle feather in his hand. I should stop this because I think I know how it will end.

"Hank."

My voice is constricted, and I feel a knot forming in my throat. Hank continues his chant, and Charlie has closed his eyes. Someone is turning into Hank's road. I look down that way, and it's Michael's truck. He stops halfway up the road, gets out, and runs toward me. He grabs my hand and says nothing as Hank lies back, one hand still on Charlie, the other resting on his chest with the feather still in his hand. A white owl alights on the porch rail.

CHAPTER FORTY-ONE

MICHAEL SPREADS the blanket he's pulled from his backpack onto one of the few portions of the huge bowl that are level. When we were last here, Digger and I were buried under snow with a dead skinwalker in the shape of a freak bear on top of us. Now the bowl's entire expanse is thick with wildflowers, and at the bottom of the depression is a small lake that reflects the blue sky and the puffy white clouds that are above us.

It was Michael's idea to come up here, and I didn't object. We'd had a hard week.

After I had the county coroner come up to do what legally needed to be done when Hank died, I followed through with county regulations and had a permit issued to allow Mrs. Emerson to take the body and inter it on her property. And according to Ute custom, she and her people washed the body, wrapped it, and took it up to the mountain for burial. Charlie was placed on top of Hank's body, and the grave was covered with rocks that we all—Michael and I, Mary, Glen and Doreen, Bri and Sharon, Don and Digger, Mrs. Emerson and Tony, and a few others—carried from the mountainside and gently placed atop it. The grave is in a clearing, surrounded by aspen trees, with an upward sightline of the sky. There was no cross or other marking placed there, and the only words spoken were the thoughts each of us passed through our own minds. Mrs. Emerson then asked those of us who weren't Native Americans to allow those who were to be alone with the grave for a while, and we did that. As we hiked down the mountain, we heard the chants and some wailing from up above. It's a beautiful place, where the seasons will come and go and where Hank and Charlie will repose in peace.

Today we left Michael's truck at Hank's cabin and hiked up to the bowl. We did spend a few minutes inside the cabin, though, both of us noting how few possessions Hank had had and how neat he'd kept the place. I've yet to locate any of Hank's relatives, if he had any left at all.

Michael and I have talked about what's going to happen to his property, because there would be something wrong with letting it fall into disrepair and eventually be taken back by nature, which is something nature has a habit of doing. After we walked through the cabin and then took a look at the shack, we decided we'd box up his personal stuff and store it at our place just in case a relative pops up. But I doubt that will happen.

I sit down on the blanket and watch Michael pull the makings of our picnic from the backpack I carried out here—wine, cheese, salami, crackers. He didn't bring his camera this time. I had reminded him before we left our cabin, but he said he didn't want it, adding that the camera only captured what used to be. I thought about that for a minute and guessed he was right—the pictures from cameras only tell a story about the past. It's odd that he left his camera at home, though. Although he hasn't slipped into a mood for quite a while, after Hank and Charlie died he's been kind of quiet, as if he's busy with his own thoughts.

"You could have gotten some nice pictures," I say as he kneels on the blanket and opens the wine bottle.

"It would have been a distraction, Sam." He pulls the cork out, unscrews it from the tip of the opener, and puts it aside. Finding the plastic cups in my backpack, he hands me one and then tips the bottle over it. He pours some into his own cup, sets the bottle down, and then holds it out to me. "To us," he says.

"To us."

We lightly touch our cups together, and then we both take a sip.

"If you'd brought your camera we could have captured this moment," I say.

"Pictures only evoke memories or awe about things that have already happened in time—that moment when they were taken."

"Yeah. And when I've lost my mind, I can pull out the pictures and remind myself of the special moments we've had together."

"Sometimes your memory is better than any picture, Sam. Sometimes it's just worth it to let your mind go and see those things as if it were for the first time. I want it to be just us today. Just you and me. No distractions."

"But if I've lost my mind—"

"Shut up. If that happens, I'll find it for you. I've got magic powers, you know?"

Yes, you do. "That's a deal."

"You remember," he says, sitting down, "how I used to be afraid that what I painted might actually come true? It was after you and Digger had the... accident?"

"Yes. I remember."

"And I painted Hank and Charlie outside on the grass before they died."

"Yes."

He looks away from me, taking in the full spread of the bowl, dressed so beautifully in reds, yellows, blues, greens, and the lake down below.

"I think," he says, turning his gaze back to me, "that I was supposed to paint those things. There was something that required I do it. And whatever that something was didn't mean for it to be a warning. It meant for it to be just a... whisper. Just something that is or will be that I'm not supposed to fully understand."

"Okay." *Old winds.* I don't know if I understand what he's just said, but if he's come to terms with what used to frighten the bejesus out of him, then it is okay. "Something like fate, then?"

"Maybe," he says, looking down for a moment, then looking back at me. "Maybe it's that I now know I'm not responsible for what happens if I see it before it does."

"Of course you're not responsible. To be responsible, Michael, would mean that you are like—" I don't say God, which is what I was thinking.

He smiles. "I know what you were going to say. And no, that's never crossed my mind. What has crossed my mind is that what I see, what I feel and hear is something that can't be explained. It's too large, too... unknowable. The concept of God, anyone's God, is too immense to.... Well, it's something that can't simply be represented in words printed in a book. I think Native American beliefs are closer to the truth—Mother Earth, Father Sky. They don't, oh, care how many angels are on the head of a pin. They just embrace what they see, what they have."

Embrace it and find Jesus. "Hank once told me that you're an old soul caught in the whispers of old winds. He told me that after I'd asked him how to protect you from demons. I didn't tell him that I believed those demons were both inside and outside of you. Do you know what his answer was?"

"What?"

"He said the only way to do that is to love you."

He sets his cup down, then scoots behind me and wraps his arms around my chest, leaning his head on my shoulder. "Hank was right," he says, kissing my cheek. "Thank you for telling me."

"You're welcome." I turn around and face him.

We look into each other's eyes, and I feel like he's peering into my soul. I know I see his. And it's a good place to be.

GEORGE SEATON lives and writes in the Colorado mountains. He shares his life with his husband, David, and their Alaskan malamute, Kuma ("Bear" in Japanese). His lifelong love of Colorado—both the magnificent land and the critters that inhabit it—is the subject matter of most of his writing. He is an Army veteran, and that experience also carries over into his storytelling.

George was first published in 2009, and his novels, novellas, and short stories have all centered on the interactions of people intent on finding the best path through life, where love is usually the healing salve that makes the journey worthwhile. His stories reflect the conflicts in life that we all must overcome in our search for that place where our hearts tell us peace resides.

George says he writes because he breathes.

Facebook: www.facebook.com/george.seaton
Website: www.georgeseatonauthor.com
Twitter: @GeorgeSeaton
E-mail: seatongm@gmail.com

SHANE THORPE KNEW JESUS AND RODE BULLS

STATES OF LOVE

GEORGE SEATON

Eighteen-year-old Joe Vasquez leaves Denver for Texas with Harley Bray, the cow kid who never fit in at their high school. In spite of discovering there's another side to Harley's nature—occasional "withdrawals" from roadside convenience stores, a nefarious skill he teaches Joe—Joe shares Harley's dream of riding bulls and a life together on the Texas plains outside of Abilene. A life that will hopefully see the fulfillment of another of Joe's dreams—to become a veterinarian.

When a rank bull kills Harley in a rodeo in Longview, Texas, Joe accepts an offer from another bull rider, Shane Thorpe, to partner up and ride the circuit together. The problem is that the blond-haired, blue-eyed Shane found Jesus a long time ago, and he's torn between his faith and his attraction to Joe. As they make their way across Texas, Oklahoma, New Mexico, and Arizona to their final stop on the circuit at the National Western Rodeo in Denver, Joe bides his time for what he hopes will be a relationship with Shane as fulfilling as the one he'd had with Harley. His hopes for the future, however, are challenged along the way when he discovers that his "withdrawals" have captured the attention of a dedicated Texas Ranger.

States of Love: Stories of romance that span every corner of the United States.

www.dreamspinnerpress.com

CPSIA information can be obtained
at www.ICGtesting.com
Printed in the USA
FSOW02n0404291216
28916FS